IN L💗VE
AND WAR I

W0006306

# NORTH
## OF THE
# STARS

International Bestselling Author
# MONICA JAMES

Cover Design: Perfect Pear Creative Covers
Photographer: Michelle Lancaster
Cover Model: Christopher Jensen
Editing: Editing 4 Indies
Formatting: E.M. Tippetts Book Designs

Follow me on:
authormonicajames.com

# OTHER BOOKS BY
# MONICA JAMES

# AUTHOR'S NOTE

Although this story is loosely based on history, this is a work of fiction. Some places, people, and events are based on fact, therefore, it may resemble other works you've read or watched before. But if you are looking for a history lesson, this book is not for you.

However, if you like alpha Vikings, a fiery Princess, and dark, angsty love stories, then North of the Stars will devour your devilish soul.

Happy reading…

Victory or Valhalla!

# DEDICATION

*Michelle, we are magic. The universe told me so.*

# THE GODLESS
## Chris Jensen

For the air is thick with the stench of fear as they cower to breathe life to my name.

Fields will burn as my Danes lay wasted to your God, your lands.

Fueled by my lust for revenge.

Destined to fill the void.

For I am no stranger.

The timeless halls of Valhalla must wait.

My blood-lust.

Hungers to rip flesh from bone.

For I am the Godless.

For I am their end.

And I will burn this kingdom down.

Odin, hear me.

# ONE

### The Kingdom of Northumbria 9ᵗʰ Century AD

*Princess Emeline*

And alas, his skills are once again absent. Shall I intercede, mayhap?"

"Hold your tongue, child, before your father, the Lord King, hears such blasphemy." Sister Ethelyn softly shushes me, but she knows I won't be silenced.

"And if he does? He'll be able to see that his son, Aethelred, is nothing but a horse's arse."

The arse in question proves my point when Lord Robert, my father, King Eanred's most trusted knight, knocks Aethelred to the ground. Just like they do every day, Lord Robert attempts to better my brother's swordsmanship, and just like every other day, Aethelred embarrasses the family with his gaucherie.

"I cry your mercy!" Sister Ethelyn exclaims, crossing herself while I giggle. "You will ask for God's forgiveness in prayer this afternoon for speaking that way."

Ever since I can remember, Sister Ethelyn has tried to curb my rebellious ways, but her horror only encourages me further. I may only be twelve years old, but I understand the reason I'm to sit silent and act proper is because I'm a girl.

It matters not that I'm far smarter and far braver than my brother. He is the firstborn son of King Eanred, and once my father dies, my brother will be crowned king. The duty of a princess is to remain virtuous while her father negotiates with the highest bidder and then sells her off like livestock.

It matters not whether the princess agrees to this transaction or, in fact, if she even likes her suitor. It's her duty to obey.

I, however, will not obey any man just because of the prick they wield between their legs.

"I want to practice with real swords," Aethelred whines, picking up his wooden one with a twisted scowl. "I want to feel the weight in my hand. Such imitation is what hinders me."

Snorting under my breath, Sister Ethelyn gently nudges me to remain quiet, but Aethelred's furious gaze lands my way.

"Don't you have needlework to do?" he says with bite, reminding me that regardless of his inadequacy, I could never pick up a sword and engage in battle.

"What would you like me to stitch, dear brother, your failed attempts at being a warrior?"

He storms forward, teeth bared like a rat, but Lord Robert grasps his arm to stop him. I don't cower. I simply sit on the bench seat in the gardens, daring him to advance.

"I cannot learn with her here. We will resume tomorrow," he orders, shrugging from Lord Robert's grip and tossing his sword to the ground.

He storms off in a huff while I can't hide my smile.

Lord Robert looks at me, attempting to conceal his own amusement, but I see the humor hidden beneath his armor. He is one of the only men in my father's service who doesn't treat me as some inept little girl.

The rustling of fine silk can be heard, which can only mean one thing—Queen Eleanor, my mother.

Jumping up from the bench seat, I turn and run toward her. "Good morrow, Mother," I happily say, giving her a tight hug.

Her three ladies stand behind her, ready and waiting for her every command. But my mother is kind. She doesn't rule with terror like my father. She is respected for her compassion and clemency.

"How fare ye, my sweeting?" she says, kissing the top of my head. "I just saw your brother in a rage. I don't suppose you had anything to do with that?"

Pulling out of her embrace, I smile sweetly. "Me? I wouldn't do anything of the sort."

She arches a dark brow, smirking. "You were the best of friends when you were smaller. I wonder what happened."

"He grew up to be a giant ars—"

Mother clears her throat, indicating a princess isn't to speak that way—no matter the truth. No husband wants a wife with the tongue of the devil.

"You are full of spirit, Emeline. Be careful who sees it," Mother warns as she cups my cheek tenderly. "We have a duty to uphold. Never forget who your father is and the power he holds."

Nodding, I remain silent because I know she means well. She was forced to marry my father when she was twelve. She has often told me the story of how she grew to love my father over time, but from the many mistresses he has, I don't think the feeling is reciprocated.

My mother has only been able to produce two living heirs, which angers my father. He calls her incompetent with a barren womb. It matters not that six out of their eight children that she birthed are buried in the royal cemetery.

It was her fault they died. Apparently, she is cursed. This excuses my father's philandering.

I don't know why he'd stray. My mother is the comeliest woman in all of the kingdom. With long brown hair that is softer than silk and large green eyes, she is the envy of many—men and women. Her porcelain white skin is flawless, and one cannot help but covet her full ruby lips and scarlet cheeks.

She looks and acts how a queen should—regal, elegant, and refined. She is never without a veil or her decorative gold crucifix.

Many have said I am the spitting image of her, but I don't see it. I could never be as sophisticated as she. Besides, I have many freckles across my nose and cheeks, something which Aethelred teases me about daily. He says I'll never be a queen because, who would want an imperfect wife?

Aethelred is five years older than me, and he ensures I know it, which is why occasions like today give me great pleasure. He belittles me daily and expects me to say nothing all because I am younger. And of course, because I'm a girl.

The church bell sounds, alerting the kingdom that my father is home, interrupting my thoughts.

Mother clutches at the large gold crucifix around her throat. "I thank thee, God."

We are of a strong Christian faith. God has aided my father in battle many times, he's said. God is good, Sister Ethelyn says often. So, I pray to Him every day in hopes that my future will change and Father will change his mind to whom I'm betrothed to.

Before I was born, I was promised to Prince Aethelwulf, the son of King Egbert of Wessex. It didn't matter that he was already a young man. My father has made clear that the moment I become a woman, I will be wed.

This is why I pray every day. I pray that I won't be sold to a man when I'm only a girl.

Deep down in my heart of hearts, I know that no matter

how hard I pray, it won't make a difference because the palace is rife with rumors. This union between Aethelwulf and me is to strengthen ties between Northumbria and Wessex because my father's kingdom is losing power.

He needs this union to safeguard the future of Northumbria. He needs this union to ensure he remains king. Therefore, I know, regardless of how hard I pray, I will be Aethelwulf's wife.

"Come hither, let us greet your father. Beatrice, fetch Aethelred."

"Yes, Your Grace." Beatrice curtseys before quickly going in search of my brother.

The two remaining ladies scurry behind Mother as she takes my arm and leads the way. She's always in a hurry when my father is involved.

The lavish hallways are a flurry of excitement as the king and his finest knights have arrived home from battle. Stonehill Castle is my home, the kingdom my father rules. I've often heard my father boast that our home is impenetrable because being on top of a vast volcanic crag overlooking the North Sea gives us an advantage.

However, if that were true, then why has Father left Lord Robert here with us instead of taking him into battle? I know it's because he fears *them*.

The attack on the Lindisfarne Monastery changed my father. The stories I overheard him sharing about what *they* did to the monks gave me nightmares for a week. For this reason, my father, the king, has made it his mission to fight the unholy heathens.

The Northmen. Or, as some call them, Vikings.

He wants to protect his kingdom against the ruthless men and women who have continued to raid England, looting for treasure and other goods, as well as capturing good Saxon people as slaves. They care not for our religion as monasteries have been destroyed. They seek precious silver and gold relics, disrespecting our God, as they don't believe in one Holy Father.

They believe there are *gods*.

Odin and Thor are names I've heard men speak of in secret. I do not know who they are…but I want to know. Those who are feared by all; I want to know why. I want to know them because I do not fear them.

I know I should. I know they are pagans who some claim have no soul, but I want to know if they feel, bleed, and love like we do. I've only ever heard of their ruthless acts because I've never seen one before, but if God has created all, then what purpose do the Northmen serve?

People fear what they don't understand, but I will not allow that fear to control me. Fear makes us blind to the truth, and I refuse to cower.

We rush down the stairs and into the bailey, where our sturdy horses await us. Once we're ready, we ride into the village, where everyone has gathered to greet Father and his men. Guards escort us, and when they deem it's safe, we dismount our horses.

The crowd bow and is in awe of our presence, but they know better than to approach us. Commoners don't interact with royalty—a fact which seems rather unfair.

Mother waits by the stairs of the church while I climb up onto the fountain to get a better view, and the moment I see my father proudly leading his knights, I realize why he went into battle.

A long line of prisoners follows him, shackled and stumbling on their feet. My father has paraded them like his latest hunt. The sight turns my stomach, and I look away.

However, when I hear the stunned gasps of bystanders, my disgust turns to interest.

Returning my attention to the display, I wonder why an echo of whispers begins to pass between the crowd.

"That's him. I swear it," a villager in front of me murmurs behind her hand to a woman close by. "Look at the marking on the side of his head."

"Who? Who is he?" the woman replies, standing taller to get a better view.

"It's Skarth Gundersen…son of Gunder Bloodaxe."

"What say you?"

"*That's* the Viking, Skarth the Godless. It's been heard his father raided Lindisfarne Monastery with Ragnar of Lodbrok."

"Marie, I shall pray for your soul for listening to such gossip."

But Marie's friend needs to pray for both their souls because, with mouths agape, they fixate on the tall, muscled prisoner who is last in line. It seems no one else can take their eyes off the man who, unlike his fellow prisoners, doesn't stumble or cower. He stands proud.

I've never seen someone so big before. Nor have I ever seen such an interesting marking printed on the side of one's head. I wonder what the pattern of lines and half circles means.

His dirty blond hair is as long as mine but is cut at the sides. He wears it tied back, which allows us to examine his mud-smeared face. Underneath the filth, piercing blue eyes dare anyone brave enough to meet his stare.

No one dares to.

In fact, the moment he walks past them, they instantly avert their gazes, too afraid of the repercussions they would face.

He is bare-chested, which is sacrilegious for exposing so much flesh, but it allows one to see the scars on his body as well as the many colorful images on his skin. I also see a silver relic tied with black leather around his neck. I wonder what it means.

My father comes to a halt in front of my mother, where she curtseys. "Lord King. I see you were most successful on the battlefield."

My father removes his silver helmet, revealing a bloody, sullied face. I wonder how many men were slain.

The king is a short, plump man with nothing unique about

him. He makes up for his dullness by inciting fear from those around him. "Of course we were. My men don't fail!"

The crowd erupts into a frenzy, cheering and clapping wildly at their king's words.

"Where is my son? Does he not greet his father?"

Mother peers around nervously, straightening her red gown. "He comes, Lord King. Your daughter awaits you, however."

My father scans the crowd, and when he sees me, he nods, clearly annoyed I'm not Aethelred.

I jump down from the fountain and make my way through the crowd to greet my father. I curtsey and bow. "How fare ye?"

"Do you like what your king has delivered?" he asks, gesturing toward the prisoners.

The men groan and smell hideous, but I nod. "Yes, Lord King. I do. You are fearless and so brave."

My response is dripping with mockery, but it appeases him, and he smirks. "As are you, sweet child, and because of that, I give you this opportunity to pick one prisoner."

I tongue my cheek, unsure what he means.

"One prisoner to save," he clarifies while a horrified gasp leaves my mother.

"Lord King, the princess is expected at church with Sister Ethelyn."

But my father has spoken, and his word goes.

His chest heaves as he waits for me to reply. He hates

waiting, so I do as he says. I commence walking down the line of prisoners, wondering what their fate holds. I wonder what they did to end up here.

"Please, Princess, I just wanted to feed my family," one man begs, interlacing his shackled hands.

One of my father's knights strikes him in the back of the head for speaking out of turn.

My heart beats wildly, but I don't let it show. If I want Father to respect me, then I have to control my fear. No one else speaks, as they don't desire the same punishment as their friend. Everyone simply watches me as I slowly take my time examining each man, obeying the king's wishes.

The closer I get to him, the faster my heart beats. The villager said he is Skarth the Godless. I wonder why he chose that name. To be without God is a dire circumstance, which is why I stop when I reach his side.

He is taller than I thought. Much taller than anyone I have ever met before. He is also a lot younger than the men he is shackled with. No older than eighteen, I'd guess, but his persona is developed. He seems…worldly.

He has another marking in ink on his left shoulder that appears to be a raven. And a twisted silver bracelet on his right wrist that seems to hold some importance. He also has two small hoops pierced in his nostril, something I've not seen before.

He intrigues me, and when his blue eyes lock on mine, that

intrigue feeds the interest in me, and I point my finger. "This man."

Horrified gasps fill the courtyard as the bystanders cross themselves, fearful my choice will pollute their faith.

Skarth the Godless cocks his head to the side, observing me closely. He watches for any signs of deceit, but there are none.

"A mistake is made," my father says, eyeing the man I chose with malice. "Choose again."

But I will not. I won't allow him to ridicule me in front of the kingdom. I won't allow him to treat me as if I'm some stupid little girl.

"No, Lord King, I make no mistake. I choose this man to be saved."

I never break eye contact with Skarth the Godless. Nor does he with me.

"Princess Emeline," Lord Edward says in his nasal voice. "Your eyes must deceive you. That is a Northman you choose to spare."

Lord Edward is my father's adviser, an ealdorman. I'd like to blame him for the cruel decisions my father has made, but sadly, my father doesn't need any encouragement. He was born cruel, and that's proven when he jumps down from his horse and marches to where I stand.

The crowd steps back, bowing to their king, but he doesn't appreciate their admiration as I've dishonored him in front of his people. I don't cower, though. I made a choice, and I refuse to take it back, just how he refuses to rescind my marriage to Aethelwulf.

"I know who he is, Lord Edward. My eyesight is quite fine. I fear yours may be failing you, however. Mayhap you should step away from my father's shadow once in a while to gain some light."

More gasps and Lord's Prayers are recited as I've just told Edward in a nice way to get his head out of my father's arse, but when what looks like a twitch touches Skarth the Godless's lips, I revel in the disorder.

I know what this means, but I dare my father to punish me in front of his legion of adoring fans. He won't, though. He won't want them to see him for the monster he truly is.

"Emeline, is this the man you choose?" he questions, curling his lip in disgust as he looks at Skarth the Godless.

The Northman merely smirks in response.

My mother shakes her head, begging I don't defy him. But I am not her. I never will be.

"Yes, I choose this man. The Northman."

The veins in my father's neck pop as he attempts to control his temper. Once composed, he gestures with his head toward Skarth the Godless. One of my father's men unshackles him, and as I sigh in relief, the guard uses the blunt end of his sword to wind him as he drives it into his belly.

Skarth the Godless flinches but does not fall.

"No!" I cry, tears filling my eyes. "You cannot do that. You cannot go back on your word."

When the guard punches Skarth the Godless in the face, I attempt to help him, but my father grips my chin between his fingers, squeezing hard.

"I am the king. Therefore, I can do what I please. Guards, taketh him to the dungeons."

"No! You cannot!" I continue to fight until my father slaps my cheek so hard my teeth rattle in my mouth.

The bloodshed should disgust these vultures, but it only excites them further.

"Let this be a lesson to you all," my father exclaims. "No mercy toward any Northman, and that includes my daughter, who will be locked away until she can obey orders."

This was his plan all along.

My father knows me too well. He knew my thirst for knowledge would have me choosing the Northman. Therefore, he could make an example out of me. If he can treat his own daughter this way, then let this be a warning to anyone who would dare sympathize with a heathen.

Two of my father's guards take hold of me, but I fight wildly against their restraints. "Let me go! A plague upon thee!"

They pay no heed to my outburst, and I lock eyes with Skarth the Godless for one last time. "I'm sorry," I cry, insulting my father further by apologizing to a pagan.

Skarth the Godless opens his mouth, and when he speaks with an accent I've not heard before, a calm overcomes me. "It's all right, *hugrekki.*"

Gripping the small gold crucifix around my neck, I pray that he is right. But deep down inside, I know that life as I know it has changed forevermore.

# TWO

*Princess Emeline*

Literature is usually my favorite subject, but I can't concentrate. Being locked away in my chambers for a week is the cause. I know it.

"Princess, do you wish to break?" asks Hilda, my tutor.

Sighing, I continue to peer out the window, looking out into a world I cannot be a part of because I don't belong.

My brother is in the gardens, once again failing terribly at his swordsmanship. My father needs to realize that no matter who trains my brother, he will never be the warrior my father wants him to be.

"Princess?"

"What will happen to the Northman who Father captured?"

I ask Hilda, turning over my shoulder to look at her.

I haven't been able to stop thinking about our encounter. What was the name he called me in an accent that intrigued me as much as the foreign language he spoke?

"I do not know, Princess, but I assume he'll be sold into slavery or executed," Hilda replies softly as she doesn't want the guards to overhear. "Because he is a pagan, it's likely he'll be executed. If he hasn't been already."

"That doesn't seem fair. Why must Father base the actions of Skarth the Godless's people on how he treats the Northman? If I was to be judged by my father's actions, then Lord have mercy on my soul."

Hilda stands up quickly, nervously straightening out her skirts. "You will not speak that way," she frantically whispers. "To speak that way about the Lord King is treason. Do you want to end up in the dungeons alongside the Northman?"

I don't reply because at least I'd have someone to talk to.

I'm just as much a prisoner as he is. However, our conditions cannot be compared, as I doubt the Northman would be given food or any warmth from the cold.

I'm ashamed I would even compare our situations.

"Princess, your food is prepared," my personal attendant, Lella, says, knocking on the door.

"I'm not hungry," I call out, not that it makes a difference. If the king wants me to eat, then eat I shall.

"Time has escaped me. I'll return later," Hilda says with a

smile.

Gathering her things, she knocks on the door, alerting the guard she's ready to leave. He opens the door and grants her permission, snickering when I sit taller from the window ledge, hoping he'll grant me the same luxury.

He doesn't.

Once Lella places my meal on the table, the guard slams my door shut. I can see his loathsome head through the bars of the small window on my door. The guards may change, but one always stands outside my door, ensuring I'm behaving, but more importantly, ensuring I'm obeying the king.

Jumping down from the ledge, I see food is once again a watery vegetable broth. Our food is scarce because the Northmen have pillaged the lands, and the other kingdoms won't help us. This is why my union with Aethelwulf is so important to my father. It will not only save his reputation but it will also save the good people of Northumbria.

My appetite is also prisoner, so I walk to the end of my bed, where I drop to my knees, interlace my hands, and look at the wooden crucifix nailed above my bed.

"Please Lord, give me a sign to guide me on my quest. I know it's my duty to serve my king, but how can I marry a man I've never met? I know nothing of being a wife."

I've been briefed on what's expected, but the concept is so foreign to me that, regardless of my being schooled on it, it'll always be a topic I will fail.

Interlocking my hands tighter, I beg He shows mercy. I beg He shows me the light because I'm drowning in the darkness.

If only I could get out of this room…

The guard—who has relieved the other—outside my door coughs hoarsely, and just like that, an idea strikes. Looking at the crucifix, I don't know if this is a sign from the Lord, but I don't question it as I slowly rise to my feet and tiptoe toward my lunch.

Gripping the bowl, I draw it to my nose and don't need to pretend that it makes me nauseous because the smell turns my stomach. With bile in my throat, I retch loudly and toss the contents of the bowl onto the floor.

"Princess?" the guard asks through the bars on my door. "Are you all right?"

I don't reply and instead pretend to heave, coughing loudly. "Help me, Lord."

Once the key turns in the door, I smile, unbelieving this has actually worked. "Princess, what's the matter?"

Hunched over the spilled soup, I peer over my shoulder at the young guard, dribble spilling from my mouth. "I'm unwell. Perhaps it may be…the sickness?"

Instantly, he takes a step back, crossing himself as he turns a ghastly shade of white when he mistakes the spilled broth for vomit.

"Prithee, fetch my lady. I must see a doctor. You must be discreet, however. We do not want to alert the palace."

When he hesitates, I place a hand to my brow and fake fainting. "Oh, woe me."

He catches me, just as I knew he would, which allows me to undertake my plans. He doesn't question me because he would rather be anywhere else. The sickness is known to infect those by breathing in the same air as the diseased.

He quickly places me onto the bed, then runs out the door like the devil himself is at his heels. The moment the lock clicks into place and I hear his frantic footsteps echo down the hall, I open an eye to ensure I'm alone.

I am, which means it's time to leave this prison once and for all.

With the key I stole from the oblivious guard in hand, I push a chair against the door and stand on it. I peer out the barred window with caution and almost cry out in relief when I see no guard outside.

Jumping off the chair, I push it aside and pocket a piece of bread in case I get hungry during the night, then I place the key into the lock. As it clicks over, I look at the crucifix above my bed and make the sign of the cross. "Thank you, Lord."

Carefully opening the door, I make certain the hall is empty, and when I see that it is, I quietly close the door and lock it. I place my cloak over my head to shield my appearance and take off down the dark hallway like a thief in the night.

With adrenaline coursing through me, I head for the kitchen as no one would dare tell the king they saw his daughter escaping out the back door. As I turn the corner, I see two guards outside the chapel where my mother says her daily prayers.

They're too busy chatting to notice me, so I press my back against the stone wall and keep to the shadows as I overhear them talking.

"The Northman is strong," one of the men says, shaking his head. "He's as tough as an army of men. Selwyn has tortured him day and night, yet he won't speak. He won't reveal where the other Northmen are.

"The king has finally given orders for his execution. He will not die an honorable death as he will be weaponless. No Valhalla for him."

"Valhalla?" the other guard asks, as confused as I am.

"Aye, that's where they believe their dead warriors go."

"Good. Let's send them all to hell."

Such hatred is a sin, but so is believing one isn't to go to heaven or hell once they leave this earth.

The candlelight is dim, so I'm able to slip past the men undetected. As I race for the kitchen, their words play over and over in my mind.

*"No Valhalla for him."*

The thought of him being condemned to an existence of peril has me stopping abruptly. I wouldn't wish that fate on anyone. Clasping the crucifix against my throat, I hope He guides me this one final time as I change course and head for the dungeon.

With my head down, no one seems to notice me creeping through the castle, which is exactly what I hoped for. However, when I reach the dungeon and find it manned by two guards, I wonder if my luck has run out.

But I haven't come this far to give up.

"I'm going to take a piss," one of them says while the other chuckles.

"Be sure not to get lost in Lady Beatrice's chambers on the way."

I cover my mouth, muting my gasp as the lady he speaks of is one of my mother's ladies.

Straining my eyes to see in the candlelight, the guards are men I do not know. There is a chance they don't know me either, and it's a risk I decide to take when one man leaves, leaving only one guard behind. I step out from the shadows and approach him.

He reaches for his sword, but when I remove my cloak, and he sees I'm a girl, he smirks. "You lost, little one?"

Good, he does not know me as he would not dare address a princess in this way.

"I'm here to offer prayer for the prisoners."

He is clearly confused as no one but a priest would usually undertake such a task.

When he continues to stand unmoved, I pull back my shoulders, hinting I'm not going anywhere. "Please open the door."

The bars on the metal door allow me to see inside the dark, dank vault behind the guard. The smell of death is unmistakable. And the anguished groans echoing off the stone walls hint that in a place such as this, death is a mercy.

Being alive down here in these horrific conditions is the worst form of any torture.

"Hurry prithee, it's been rumored the sickness may have slipped past the palace walls. I must do my charitable duty and then return to the nunnery for prayer."

The moment I mention the sickness, the guard blanches and nods quickly. With one hand over his nose and mouth, he unlocks the large metal door with a brass key. It swings open, and he gestures with his head that it's now or never.

Stepping past him, I walk into the dungeon, giving my eyes a moment to adjust to the darkness. The metal door slams shut behind me, frightening me as I am once again a prisoner—but by choice, this time. But as I take a look around, I see that the real horror has only just begun.

Metal cages hang from the ceiling packed full of emaciated men. Most aren't moving. The stench is unbearable, and I reach into my tunic for a cotton handkerchief. Pressing it over my nose, I commence my journey along the uneven stone floor as I search for the Northman.

I'm surrounded by death.

Corpses of men hang limply from the wall where they remained shackled, even in death. Rats feast on their flesh, and they'll be indulging for a long while because I appear to be one of the only living souls down here.

As I continue walking, using the occasional wall sconce for light, I scour the prison cells for the Northman. I know he's down here as the guard said he will be executed soon. I just need to find him.

"Northman?" I whisper, my voice echoing off the walls.

The anguished groans of men echo all the way to my very soul, and I remember the man who begged for clemency as he was captured for merely trying to feed his family. What sort of king is my father for allowing such atrocities to happen within his kingdom walls?

The farther I venture, the colder and darker it becomes. When will this hellish nightmare end?

"Northman?" I announce again.

The men in their cells who are unfortunate enough to still be alive look at me with hollowed eyes. Their spirit has withered and died as they await their painfully slow death.

"I'm here," a man suddenly says.

I freeze, attempting to gauge where the voice is coming from.

"Come to me," the voice sounds again. "Please help me."

It's coming from down the path where the darkness is so thick, it robs me of breath. But I force myself to continue because the Northman won't hurt me. I don't know how I can be so certain of this, but I just know he won't.

As the path becomes a steep incline, I brace the wall for support, which is my error as I've strayed too far off course. I am suddenly knocked to the ground, where a putrid, sweaty mass pins me under him. He has one arm shackled to the wall but has somehow been able to free the other, and he uses that arm to his advantage by crudely attempting to lift my tunic.

"No!" I scream, pummeling his perspiring, bare chest with my tiny fists.

But my cries are in vain.

"Scream, little maiden. I love it when they scream." That voice is the same as the one that called me over. I was stupid to fall for his lies as I should have known the Northman would never beg for mercy.

The way he stood in line amongst the prisoners was a sure sign he didn't believe in clemency. This is my error, and now I will pay.

"Unhand me!" I flail wildly, kicking my legs in hopes of throwing him off balance.

When he attempts to press his mouth over mine, I rear up and bite his nose. A warmth coats me, and when I realize his blood squirts down my throat, I spit it out, gagging uncontrollably. I want no part of him inside me.

But when he rips my undergarments, making it clear I may not have a choice in the matter, I know I'll need a miracle to set myself free.

With all my might, I fight him, but he's so strong, and the

violence fuels the bloodlust. "I'll be gentle with you, *Princess*," he mocks, indicating he will be anything but.

Tears spill from my eyes because I am defeated. He knows I am the king's daughter, but he doesn't care. However, the fact that I *am* the king's daughter has me refusing to surrender. I refuse to prove to my father that I am what he says—a feeble little girl.

Frantically searching my pockets for a weapon, my fingers come in contact with the key I stole from the guard. Without thought, I retrieve it, and just as the man readies himself to take my maidenhood, I ram the key into the side of his throat.

His eyes widen before I am showered with his thick, warm blood. My vision is nothing but red as I shove him off me, desperately scrambling backward. Wildly wiping my eyes, I watch in horror as a pair of hands extend from between the bars and grip the man.

Those hands then slam his head once, twice against the metal bars, splitting open his skull as brain matter spurts from the wound. The man collapses onto the floor but is still strung up to the wall by one arm. He is twitching violently as the hands behind the bars let him go.

Only when the man stops jerking do I realize what I've done.

"Forgive m-me, Lord," I sob, shakily getting onto my knees and interlacing my bloody hands. But the sight contradicts the purpose of praying.

My soul is tarnished. I am a sinner.

"I killed a man," I cry, rocking backward and forward, turning my hands over and over. "Strike me down, Lord, for I deserve your wrath. I am a s-sinner. I must repent."

Hysterically wiping myself clean, more blood takes its place because no matter how hard I scrub, I can never clean my soiled soul.

"I killed a man," I whimper over and over, peering at the now lifeless man feet away. But when I hear a calming voice, I wonder if God himself has pardoned me from my crimes.

"He was no man. He was a *vámr*. You didn't kill anyone. I did. Your conscience is clean. You're still in favor with your God."

"But…but," I fumble over my words, refusing to accept this pardon.

"But nothing. His death is my doing, not yours. It's all right, *hugrekki*."

A calm overcomes me, just as it did when I last saw him. "Skarth the Godless?" I question softly, sniffing back my tears.

When he doesn't answer me, I crawl toward his cell, ensuring I keep my eyes focused on him and not the corpse that lies between us.

He shifts into the light, allowing me to see it's him, and the candlelight illuminates him in a way that presents him as holy. He is my savior because if it wasn't for him, I'd be polluted forevermore.

He is filthy, but the dirt doesn't look out of place on him. It hardens him in a way I don't understand. He doesn't belong in riches or armor. He is a warrior.

He grips the bars, watching me closely, and I instantly avert my eyes, for staring at a strange man is ungodly.

"My name is Skarth," he says, hinting his sobriquet isn't one he cares for.

"I'm Emeline," I reply, still peering at the ground. "Gramercy for your bravery."

"Do not thank me for morality." His comment isn't unkind, but it's blunt, which has me realizing Skarth could have allowed the man to rape and defile me as he owes me nothing, but he didn't.

He acted how any decent person should. He acted how a pagan would not.

"You're to be executed," I state, waiting for the shock to overcome him. It doesn't, however. "But I will not allow it."

"Thank you, my lady, but I fear the decision is already made."

Cocking my head to the side, I take a look at this "heathen" because he certainly doesn't behave how I thought heathens would. They are rumored to be uncivilized, savage, and cruel, but Skarth speaks with grace.

"No, I swear it. I will save thee, just how you saved me."

"I am indebted to no one. No one will ever own me," he snarls. It's clear he'd rather be dead than owned. "I belong to no one."

I feel his admission to my very core.

"You will not be indebted to anyone. Your reputation is infamous, and I plan on using that to save you."

"How?" he asks, watching me closely as I devise a plan which will not fail.

"You are called Skarth the Godless for a reason, and I'm guessing it's because you are an exceptional warrior?"

He doesn't reply.

"Well, my brother, the king's firstborn, is not. But you can change that. Teach him how to fight. How to be the most feared warrior in all of the kingdom, and I swear it, you will live."

"I don't fight *with* Saxons. I fight against them," he spits, gripping the bars on his cell. "They are the reason my kin are dead."

Gasping, I clutch at the crucifix around my throat, sickened to know my people could do that to Skarth's family. "Then don't allow their deaths to be in vain. You have a chance to live, taketh."

His jaw clenches as he clearly doesn't like being given orders. Something we have in common.

"If I can convince the king to spare your life, will you accept?"

His silence encourages me.

"Will you accept?" I press harder, refusing to surrender.

Something passes over him, something I can't place. There

is so much I want to learn from him.

"Yes, Princess. I will accept…only because I plan on taking your father's head, as he did to mine."

My heart threatens to burst free, but I will my nerves to calm. "Then it is settled. There is no time to waste. I will send word soon, Skarth the Godless."

He continues looking at me, an expression of confusion plaguing him. "Why would you help me when you know what I am? I am a Northman. You are a Saxon. We are enemies, and nothing will ever change that."

His words of warning only straighten my spine. "Because there is one thing I want from you."

He licks his bottom lip in contemplation before nodding.

"I want you to teach me how to fight. Not with wooden swords but with real steel."

"Why would a princess need to learn to fight?"

"Because like you…no one will own me. I belong to no one." I don't elaborate further, but if this marriage to Aethelwulf is to occur, then I won't walk into war without being prepared for battle.

Something passes between us, something which will secure Skarth into my life evermore. "All right. I will teach you. But come the time, I promise you, your father's life will be mine."

Extending my hand, I slip it through the bars, meeting Skarth halfway. The choice is now his.

He peers down at it, his astute blue eyes studying me like

I'm a mystery he can't decode. Regardless, on an exhale, he takes my hand in his, and we shake, cementing our destiny in bloodshed.

I've just condemned my father because I know Skarth will be the one who takes his life.

Slipping my hand from his, I reach into my pocket and offer him the bread I stowed away. He doesn't accept, however. Instead, with eyes still locked on mine, he reaches between the bars and rips the key from my attacker's throat.

The noise makes my stomach turn, but I don't let Skarth know how it affects me. If he is to make a warrior out of me, then I need to harden up. He offers me the key—an exchange, as Skarth doesn't want to owe anyone anything. And for that, I respect him.

I accept the key while he accepts the bread.

"Anon."

He nods, tearing into the bread with bloody hands. He is savage, and God strike me down, he intrigues me more than he should.

With the key in hand, I come to a stand and make my way through the dungeon, leaving this hell on earth a changed girl. My cloak conceals the atrocities I committed, and I walk past the guard undetected. The moment I'm free, I break into a dead sprint, a sense of freedom lapping at my heels.

I was almost raped by a monster and then watched that monster be slain by a pagan. The reality of what I witnessed should weigh me down, but it doesn't. I only run faster.

My chamber door is still unmanned. Again, I read this as the Lord intervening. I slip the bloody key into the lock and enter my room with a sigh of relief. Quickly disrobing, I clean myself up and slip into a new tunic.

The clothes I wore are covered in blood, so I toss them into the fire that warms my chambers.

As I sit, watching them burn, the door groans open, and I wonder if the king has changed his mind. When I see Aethelred, I think he must have. Otherwise, why is my brother here?

"I heard you are sick. You look fine to me. I told them you were only doing it to trick them."

Rolling my eyes, I continue staring at the fire as I'd prefer to look at it than my idiotic brother. When he doesn't leave, though, I decide to implement my plan. I'd rather speak to Father first, but he won't listen to me.

Yet he will to Aethelred.

He walks to my window and peers outside. "Do you like watching me?" he asks, back turned.

"Yes, I rather enjoy watching thee be knocked to your arse."

He snickers, and I wonder why he would ask me this. It's not interested him before.

"I heard Father talking," he says while I hold my breath. "He said there's something wrong with you. He said you've not bled yet."

I don't know whether to be relieved or horrified that we're

discussing this instead of where I've been.

"I cry your mercy! That's no business of yours," I snap, reaching for a poke to ensure no scrap of evidence will be left.

"It is my business. You have one job—marry Aethelwulf and bear his sons. If you cannot, then the fate of this kingdom lies solely on me."

"Lord help us then," I mutter under my breath. "The way you fight, Northumbria is condemned."

He storms over, gripping my shoulder and forcing me to look at him. "You will not speak to me that way."

"I will speak to you any way I wish," I argue, ripping from his hold. "Maybe if you were a better fighter, you'd have not only my respect but also the respect of the entire court."

He is seething, his cheeks blistering a bright crimson. "It's not my fault Lord Robert is a useless arse."

This is my opportunity, and I take it. "What about—" I soon stop, however, shaking my head. "Never mind. You won't want to hear it."

"Tell me," he orders, placing his hands on his hips as he attempts to assert his dominance, just how I knew he would.

"What if you had another teacher?"

He arches a dark brow, indicating he's listening.

"Father has captured the most feared warrior in all of England, and he's going to execute him? Seems rather wasteful to me. Why not exploit his knowledge? Unearth their fighting strategies so when another battle arises, Father's men will be able to fight back using the Northmen's own methods to conquer them.

"He would be a hero in all the kingdoms. And so could you."

Aethelred listens closely as he knows what I share makes sense.

"If the Northman taught you to fight, you would be unstoppable. You would go into battle with Saxon *and* Northman training. Not to mention, I am certain the Northman has knowledge that would prove useful to you and Father.

"He knows his people, while we are simply guessing. Father has a subject, one which he can study and use for his gain. But instead, he'd rather kill him because he is afraid. The Northman can be an ally, not a foe."

My chambers suddenly become smaller as Aethelred steps forward. He towers over me as he's had a growth spurt, and the way he looks at me turns my own cheeks scarlet.

"Aethelred—"

But it's too late.

He strikes my cheek with an open palm. "You will not speak of Father this way. He isn't afraid. He is the king! How dare you speak otherwise!"

Stepping back, I cup my cheek, surprised he struck me because he's never done so before.

"Father is right; you do not know your place. Maybe you need reminding. On your knees."

"Wherefore?"

But he doesn't answer my question. Instead, he grips behind my neck and forces me to the floor. I don't have a chance to fight because he's torn the back of my tunic, exposing my flesh.

"Aethelred!" I cry in horror, clutching the front of my garment as I don't wish for my brother to see any more of my flesh.

But my screams are in vain because I hear the slice through the air before I feel a sharp sting across my back. I don't actually believe he's whipped me with his belt until I feel the sting once again. I try to scamper away, but he shoves me onto my stomach, where he presses his boot into the small of my back to keep me pinned down.

He then continues to whip me over and over again.

I count fifteen lashes when my body and soul admit defeat.

By lash twenty-five, Aethelred tires and the belt drops to the floor with a thud. "We are Saxons. We do not make friends with Northmen. Never speak on matters that your tiny brain cannot comprehend."

I don't cry. I simply stare into the fire, wishing I was burning alongside my clothes.

Aethelred crouches beside me and whispers into my ear, "Otherwise, next time, it will be your arse I take…sweet sister."

Shock stuns me into silence, and I remain quieter than a mouse. He has instilled the fear of God into me, and I cannot stop my tremors.

Aethelred snickers as he comes to a stand. I wait for more punishment, but instead, he spits on my back and is out the door.

I lie on the cold floor for what feels like hours as my body has gone numb. I just want to slip into a slumber and never wake because I've never felt so defeated before.

"Princess!" Hilda's voice awakes me from the safe place I transported myself to, the place which helped me cope with what just transpired. "Can you rise?"

The truth is, I don't know.

She gently helps me stand, ensuring my modesty is covered as she retrieves hot water and some herbs. She then cleans my wounds, hissing at the mess my brother left behind while I remain perfectly still.

"Princess, I fear these may leave scars."

A betrayal tear trickles down my cheek, one which I tried so hard to keep at bay. I wipe it away furiously as crying won't solve a thing.

I don't reply because the scars inflicted on my soul are far worse than any physical wounds. Peering at the crucifix on the wall, I wonder if He is forgiving, after all.

# CTHREE

*Princess Emeline*

I wake to find my chamber door unlocked, not that it matters because I barely have the energy to move. But I don't want to arouse suspicion, so once I dress on my own—I sent Lella away, not wanting her to see my wounds—I go about my daily routine like normal.

With my prayer book in my lap, I pray to the Lord, but after yesterday, I can't help but feel betrayed. What did I do to deserve such injustice? Being born a woman is what.

Cutting my prayer short, I decide to sit in the gardens as it's my most favorite place to be.

Like a good princess, I sit quietly, admiring the greenery as I commence embroidering a veil my mother has insisted I wear once I meet Aethelwulf, which is why I refused to do it. But now, however, I wonder if the meeting will ever take place as I am now damaged.

My back aches, but I withstand the pain as it's a reminder of my insolence.

I've tried to be strong, but I'm beaten, and I've accepted defeat. There is no place for women in this world. Those who wish to defy end up beaten, almost raped, and threatened to be sodomized by her own flesh and blood.

Tears threaten to spill, but I sniff them back. I won't allow them to pollute this happy place.

That is soon to change, however, when I hear Aethelred laughing with his childhood friend, Raedwulf. The moment I see them approaching, I spring to my feet—ignoring the pain in my back—not wishing to be anywhere near my brother or my father, who follows closely.

"Good morrow," Raedwulf says with a kind smile. His father is a part of the Witan and a close confidant to the king.

I curtsey and attempt to make a quick escape. "God spede you."

Sadly, the king's presence doesn't allow it.

"Daughter," he says with a broad smile. "How fare thee?"

My eyes snap to Aethelred, who folds his arms across his chest, daring me to divulge to the king how I am. I cannot do that, and he knows it.

"I fare thee well, thank you, Lord King."

"Will you not stay?" he asks me, which stuns me as he's not asked this of me before.

"Of course, Father. If this pleases you, then I shall."

He nods happily and cups my cheek, again confounding me. "You are kind, just like your mother. And Aethelred has the brawn and brains as I."

I wait for him to speak because I have no idea what he's talking about, but my questions are soon answered when I see Lord Robert lead a prisoner into the gardens. However, he is no longer behind bars.

Skarth is dressed in a linen shirt and trousers, his feet bare. A prisoner wouldn't be dressed as my father wouldn't waste garments on someone who is about to be executed, so this means...

"Oh, sweet child. There is no need to be afraid," my father coos, believing my silence is because I am frightened. "The Northman won't hurt you. He's here on the advice of your brother. We will exploit him and his knowledge for our gain.

"He is a Northman. Therefore, he thinks like a Northman. I've promised to spare his life, and in return, he will be my loyal subject to do with what I please. He's now in my service."

I bite the inside of my cheek to stop my mouth from gaping open.

This glorious plan was mine, and yes, this is what I wanted—for Aethelred to relay the proposal to Father. But after he punished me so viciously, all for him to then accept praise, it suddenly feels like being whipped all over again.

"Sit, and let us see what the Northman can do."

The sun catches the gold in Father's crown, illuminating Skarth, who stands behind him, awaiting command. When we lock eyes, I instantly avert mine, afraid he can read what lays hidden beneath my tunic. I've opted for a black robe, as it feels fitting to complement what I'm feeling on the inside.

I do as Father says, flinching when I sit on the stone bench seat. It's the smallest of movements, but it hasn't gone unnoticed by Skarth.

"Continue looking at her, Northman, and I'll have your eyes," Aethelred warns, while Father laughs merrily.

Lord Robert waits for my father's command, and Skarth's shackles are unfastened with a simple nod. He flexes his hands, as this is probably the first time he's been freed. Even shackled, he could kill a man with his bare hands.

Suddenly, the thought of Aethelred facing Skarth seems like a glorious plan.

Lord Robert passes Skarth the wooden sword. He turns his lip up at it but doesn't say a word. Aethelred is unhappy to be fighting without real swords once again, but this is a test to see if Skarth will obey.

"Go on then, Northman. Let's see if you leave these gardens with your life in hand."

Lord Robert steps back, hand on his sword, which is *not* made of wood.

Skarth's long hair is tied back, allowing me to observe the marking on the side of his head. My brother is dressed in his finest red embroidered cloak with the embellishments on display to ensure Skarth appreciates his royal status—like he could forget.

His leggings are white, and I relish the fact that they'll be sullied once Skarth is finished with him.

Skarth begins to circle Aethelred, who matches him move for move. Both are waiting for the other to make the first move, but Aethelred soon grows tired and swings out, attempting to connect with Skarth.

Skarth is on the defense, reading Aethelred perfectly, and blocks the attack. He then advances for Aethelred with a burst of strikes, which Aethelred pathetically wards off. Father grumbles beside me.

They continue to spar, and anyone can see that Skarth is simply playing with Aethelred because Skarth isn't even trying. Each time Aethelred attacks, he blocks him, only to deliver a succession of blows that knock him off balance.

Lord Edward appears, ruining the mood as he walks toward my father. "Forgive me, Lord King, but I must speak with you."

"This cannot wait?" my father says, never taking his eyes off Aethelred. Maybe he believes if he stares hard enough, he shall see the son he'd be proud of.

"No, Lord King, I'm afraid it cannot."

With a heavy sigh, my father stands. "You will not leave

here until the Northman's arse hits the ground, Aethelred."

It's an order, one which has Skarth smirking.

My father and Lord Edward rush off with heads together as Lord Edward details something that turns my father's cheeks white. Whatever they speak of can't be good. I fear for my kingdom as Wessex and Mercia grow stronger every day.

If alliances aren't formed, I don't know if Northumbria will survive.

The moment the king is gone, Aethelred advances for Skarth with a roar. In response, Skarth coolly flips the sword, driving the end into Aethelred's stomach, winding him.

Both Raedwulf and I laugh, which infuriates my brother.

"Fetch me some ale," he orders me. "I'm thirsty."

We have servants for this, but Aethelred has done this to ridicule me. However, I know better than to argue and rise. Ignoring the pain in my back, I hobble toward the kitchen, which isn't too far away. The servants are horrified that I've been sent to fetch ale and insist on taking it to Aethelred themselves.

I notice the produce in the kitchen is quite scarce but don't say a word.

"We're making your favorite," the cook, Merek says, plucking a fowl.

"Sounds wonderful, Merek. I cannot wait."

Once upon a time, we would be feasting on an array of foods, but not lately. I can't help but feel I'm in part to blame for this.

Suddenly feeling unwell, I decide to go to my chambers and lie down as I can't stand another moment being near Aethelred. Just as I step outside, someone grabs my arm and pulls me behind the wall so no one can see.

It's Skarth.

"What's the matter, Princess?" he says, eyeing me closely.

"Nothing, and please don't call me princess," I reply, exhaustion weighing me down.

But he doesn't believe me.

"What did he do to you?"

"Nothing that I didn't deserve," I reply, feeling the weight of the world press down on my shoulders. "I'm pleased you won't be executed, but death may be preferable as being in my father's service means he owns you."

"I told you," he states dangerously low, shaking his head. "No one owns me."

"We are all owned in one way or another." I go to leave, but Skarth grips my arm, stopping me.

No one would dare touch me this way. Well, apart from last night.

"You manhandle the king's daughter?" I half tease. "You really do have a death wish, Northman."

"I thought I wasn't to call you princess?" He smirks while I shake my head.

Things soon turn serious as it was nice to forget for a fraction in time.

"Thank you for doing what you said you would. I won't forget it."

When I lower my eyes, a breath escapes him.

"It was Aethelred?" he asks, his anger rising.

Nodding slowly, I keep my eyes downcast. "I'm just a stupid girl, Skarth. No one would listen to me."

I feel his hesitation, but he gives in, and with strong fingers, he lifts my chin. "You're not stupid. And as for being a girl, the bravest warriors I've fought alongside have been women."

"Maybe in your world, but in this world"—I circle my finger in the air—"all I am good for is bearing the sons of a man I've been betrothed to before I was born."

Skarth frowns, his fingers still gripping my chin. "Who?"

"I am promised to Aethelwulf, the son of King Egbert of Wessex."

Skarth's frown soon transforms into a scowl. Something is wrong.

"You know of him?"

He nods dangerously slow. "Yes, it was during a battle in Wessex that King Egbert took my father's head, blinded my brother, and imprisoned my mother and sister, selling them into slavery."

I blink once, confronted with information that makes my stomach turn. "How did they capture you here in Northumbria then? I do not understand."

"Because I think they are here, in Northumbria. I just don't know where. I was captured because it was the only way."

It takes me a moment, but I soon understand what he means. "You were captured with intent? Your plan was to come to the palace and find out any information you can. That's why you agreed to be in my father's service?"

"Yes. I am certain your father keeps a record of his conquests. I've seen the parchments Saxons keep, but I do not understand them."

He's right. In my father's hall, he has hundreds of scrolls detailing the king's victories. I am certain this would include the battle Skarth speaks of.

I should have known Skarth the Godless would never be captured.

"Your plan was nothing short of foolish. What if you'd died the moment you entered the palace walls?"

"Then I would be feasting in the hall of slain warriors with Odin," he replies without fear.

"Odin is your god?"

"Yes, lady, unlike you, however, it's *gods*."

On instinct, I cross myself because he speaks blasphemy, but where was my God last night? The only savior I saw is the one standing in front of me, which is why I do something which will surely test Him.

"I will help you," I say softly. "You cannot go into my father's hall, but I can. I will see what I can find."

Skarth steps back, appearing to need space between us.

"You'd do that for me? A pagan? Nothing but a heathen who has no respect for your people or your God?"

If this is a test, then Skarth doesn't know me at all. "Yes, I will because regardless of those things, I want to help."

"I will be indebted to you for the rest of my life."

Shaking my head, I want him to know my father may work that way, but I do not. "I thought you didn't want to be indebted to anyone?"

"For this, I will make an exception."

His words touch me in ways I don't understand. "That's not necessary. I do this because I want to. I am sorry for what King Egbert did to your family. My future father-in-law is a monster. I can only hope his son is not.

"Although, his son may seek out another bride after last—" I stop myself, but it's too late.

"What happened last night? After you left me? Tell me."

I am so tired of fighting, so I turn my back and gently pull away the top of my tunic so Skarth can see the top of my back. It's only a sliver of flesh, but it's enough.

"Aethelred did this to you?" he asks hoarsely, barely containing his anger even though he knows the answer. "*Bacraut.*"

Nodding slowly, I allow a tear to fall. "Something ugly transpired last night, and I am afraid his carnal lust will condemn us both to hell."

Skarth hisses, speaking in a language I don't understand.

He's gone before I can stop him, his frantic footsteps slicing through the tall grass.

"Skarth!" I cry out, chasing after him. "Do not do whatever it is you mean to do! They will hang you."

But Skarth doesn't stop. He is a man possessed as he storms toward the gardens. I can barely keep up, and when he comes face-to-face with Aethelred, he picks up the wooden sword and slams it into his chest.

"You want to fight like a warrior?" he demands, his accent more predominant than ever. "Then let me show you how."

Before Aethelred can stop him, Skarth is attacking him with nothing but his fists.

Lord Robert is chatting with one of my mother's ladies, but soon stops when he witnesses Skarth's rage. He attempts to withdraw his sword, but I shake my head subtly, hoping he will read my plea.

He does.

As long as Skarth doesn't kill Aethelred, all will be well. His role is to teach Aethelred how to fight. He is merely doing what the king has asked.

Aethelred tries to stab Skarth, but he ducks and weaves and shoves Aethelred in the back. Something about watching Skarth fight is almost hypnotic. He isn't trained like Saxons are. He fights with heart. Passion.

I am completely under his spell.

Aethelred attempts to knock Skarth's feet out from under

him, but Skarth jumps back and elbows Aethelred in the nose. I hear the crack before I see the blood.

The sight gives me nothing but great pleasure.

With a roar, Aethelred charges for Skarth, but in response, Skarth knocks Aethelred to the ground, winding him. Skarth barely holds back the urge to finish my brother.

The fight is over…for now.

Skarth offers Aethelred his hand in a display of good sportsmanship, but when Aethelred accepts, and Skarth bends low, whispering something into his ear, I realize nothing about this is civilized.

Aethelred glares at me, hinting that whatever Skarth said was a warning. I should feel disgraced a pagan would defend my honor, but I don't.

Aethelred storms away, bloody and beaten, while Skarth turns to look at me and nods. He said he wasn't indebted to anyone, but he lied because this bond between us runs both ways.

Lord Robert speaks to Raedwulf in confidence while I walk toward Skarth, seeing him in a new light. This Northman is vicious and cruel, yet he touches me with nothing but kindness.

"Thank you," I whisper into his ear as I stand on tippy-toes.

"Are you ready?" he asks as I pull away.

"Ready for what?"

"To fight," he clarifies. The defeat that overthrew me earlier is suddenly smashed to pieces. "I promised I would teach you."

I'd forgotten about that promise because when I woke, the fight in me had died. But it's returned, and it's demanding bloodshed.

"Yes."

Skarth looks around to ensure no one is listening as he bends low and says, "Good, because the next time he touches you, you either kill him…or I will."

And just like that…our future is sealed with a bloodstained promise, one which will rule our lives in this lifetime and the next.

# 𝒯OUR

*Princess Emeline*

Two Years Later

The palace is a flurry of excitement as it's Saint Cuthbert's feast day. The king hasn't spared an expense when lavishly decorating the great hall and covering the tables in an assortment of foods. How things have changed in two years, and that change is thanks to Skarth.

Before his arrival, Northumbria was on her knees. But he did what I knew he could—he saved the kingdom from downfall.

My father saw his worth and exploited that for his gain. He learned about the way of the Northmen—their warfare and how they had an array of weapons to fight with, not merely swords. He used this knowledge to overthrow an army of five hundred warriors who attacked Bernicia.

Once word was sent that the Northmen were close, Skarth prepared the Saxons for battle. What they had been taught over the months was going to be tried on the battlefield, and my father didn't realize how valuable Skarth really was until he saw him in battle.

Their shield wall tactic, which was made up of warriors, five ranks deep, was met with confusion from the Northmen as they had never seen Saxons attack this way. They were then quick to ascertain that a traitor was amongst them.

The victory was bloody and brutal, and word spread that Skarth the Godless was now fighting with the enemy. This instilled the fear of God into them, as Skarth's reputation was notorious not only among the Saxons but the Northmen as well.

Since that attack, Wessex and Mercia have asked my father's army to come to battle on many occasions. And each and every time, they've defeated the Northmen. Skarth's bravery is not acknowledged even though everyone knows my father's army is unconquerable because of him.

My father reaps all the glory and has no shame in basking in another man's victories.

The lands now flourish once again, and Wessex and Mercia have resumed trading with Northumbria. They see our power and prefer to be allies and not enemies because the Northmen continue to attack. No matter that they are defeated, more and more come.

Skarth said they'll never stop coming, as it's better to die a warrior than to hide like a coward.

For two years, both Skarth and I kept our promise—he was to train me, and I was to seek out information on his family.

The parchments were most useful, and after relaying what I found, Skarth sought out all possible avenues, but each and every time, he was too late. His reputation has spread—the Northman helping the Saxon king—but some Saxons don't agree with my father's tactics, and Skarth has not always been welcomed with open arms.

This makes finding his family even harder.

Each day, I see his frustrations grow, as I believe he thought he wouldn't be in the king's service for so long. But he won't leave without his family, and keeping ties with the Saxons is the only way to find them.

He needs to side with the enemy, but the truth is, he's now the enemy to both the Saxons and the Northmen.

"Oh, forgive me, my lady," Raedwulf says as he stands on my toes—again.

We are dancing, dressed in our finest garments because Northumbria is favorable once more.

The guards eat wild boar and drink ale. They are in jubilant spirits because peace has settled over the land. We all know it's temporary, but they enjoy it because we don't know what tomorrow holds.

I am now fourteen years old, and although I feel like a

woman, I am not.

I'm still in Northumbria and not in Wessex, married to Aethelwulf, because I still have not had my monthly courses. I wonder if God has answered my prayers, after all—he did send me Skarth. I prayed for a miracle, and in return, Skarth walked into my world.

He is now twenty years old, and although he has many suitors, he remains unattached.

Father refuses to give Skarth land outside of the palace, so his lodgings are in a small cottage in the village. He hates it, as it's a great dishonor that he is still seen as less than a cottar after everything he's done for Northumbria.

But he has nowhere to go.

The truth be told, I'd miss him if he left. I *do* miss him and worry terribly when he's gone. We've shared a connection since the day we met, and that connection just continues to grow; for me, it does more than he.

No matter how many dances I have with Raedwulf, he will never be the man I want to dance with. And soon, I have an engagement with that man in question.

"Are you all right? You're flustered."

Embarrassed, I lower my chin, afraid he'll be able to read the cause of my sudden blush. "Yes, my lord, I am just heated, that is all. I am going to get some fresh air."

Before he can offer to escort me, I make haste and avoid the crowds of rowdy men as they clink their cups together, spilling ale all over themselves and the floor. They are boorish and loud, and I often think they are nothing but hypocrites for calling the Northmen heathens.

Not looking where I'm going is my error as I bump straight into someone I've been avoiding all night—Aethelred.

He clutches onto my arms to stop me from falling, but I'd rather fall than have his hands on me. I don't make a scene as I subtly recoil from his touch. Nothing but condescension is reflected in his eyes as his arrogance only grows.

Like my father, he sees Skarth's victory as his own, and because of this, he believes himself to be untouchable.

He doesn't acknowledge he is the warrior my father is finally proud of because of Skarth's training. He simply basks in the glory, enforcing to the good people of Northumbria that when our father dies, he will be a worthy king.

It sickens me.

"Where are you rushing off to, sweet lambkin?" he whispers, leaning in close.

He is doing this to intimidate me because that's what men like him do—they amass respect through fear, not because they earned it.

"I'm tired," I reply, refusing to show him my fear. "I am going to retire for the evening."

"And miss all the fun?" he mocks, drinking his fine wine from a gold chalice. "Raedwulf is wasting his time on you. I've told him you're cursed."

I clench my fists, focusing on remaining calm in battle, just how Skarth taught me.

"Then best you leave me be. I wouldn't want to sour your luck."

"Luck has nothing to do with it," he snarls, eyes narrowed. "The battles I have won, I've done so with bravery and strength."

If he expects me to bow at his feet, then he'll be waiting a long time.

Aethelred has grown into a man, and his boyish looks are no more. His dark hair is long, which complements the groomed beard he sports. He's tall and has the form of a warrior. Therefore, he's never lacking female company.

Father has hinted he'd like Aethelred to find a bride, but my brother won't settle for one. Why would he when he has the entire kingdom at his beck and call? All but one…

That night, two years ago, when he left permanent scars on my body, has been scorched onto my very soul. Thankfully, he's never visited my chambers since, but I see the way he watches me as he isn't the only one who has grown.

My brown hair is quite long and is left down. It's usually twisted into elaborate plaits on the sides to allow my face to be seen. I prefer less flamboyant garments. The dress I wear this evening is one of my favorites.

Dark burgundy in color, the dress has gold trim on the long hem, and the collar dips tastefully to display my gold crucifix. I like to complement any dress with a bodice.

The one I wear is green, which wraps around my shoulders and ties at the front.

Most women my age wear prettier dresses, but I feel most comfortable in something less ostentatious. I also prefer bare feet to the hideous shoes my father insists I wear. He's often told me that no future queen should be seen barefooted, but I don't think I'll ever feel comfortable sporting shoes or being a queen.

Truth be told, this attire allows me to fight with ease because when Skarth and I meet, it's in secret. No one can know of our meetings. My father would have our heads if he knew what we did late at night.

It's because of Skarth that I can walk alone and not be afraid anymore. I can fight as well as any man—maybe even better because I feel most alive with a sword in hand. However, lately, I'm beginning to wonder if the cause of my vigor is from the training or from being with Skarth.

I am developing feelings for him, ones which I do not fully understand. My heart skips a beat when he is near, and when we part, the longing sets in until I see him again. I dare not tell anyone of my feelings because no matter that he's accepted into our kingdom, he is still a Northman—a Northman which I like more than I should.

The prospect of seeing him soon has the butterflies returning, but I play it coy as Aethelred will have me followed if he suspects anything is skewed.

Thankfully, Bellaflor, the daughter of a wealthy merchant,

hooks her arm through Aethelred's, hinting she wants a moment alone. No doubt he has bedded her, as word across the kingdom is that my brother is quite the philanderer.

He can be charming when he wants to be, but it's all for his personal gain.

I excuse myself with a curtsey and exit the great hall, thankful to be away from court and the prying eyes of those who act as the king's spies. The villagers are drunk on meat and ale, enjoying the king's generosity, so it's easy to slip away.

No one pays any attention to me, as I've learned to blend into the background. Once outside, I quicken my step and make my way toward the stables, where Skarth will be waiting for me. This is where he teaches me. This is our own private rapture.

The shadows allow for men and women to engage in indecent acts, ones which they wouldn't dare commit in the light. The festivities are just an excuse for the people to engage in the depraved—me included because when I approach the stables and see Skarth with a villager I do not know, I do something which I normally would never do.

Instead of announcing my arrival, I hide behind the wall and watch their encounter unfold between the cracks in the wood. The wall sconces allow enough light for me to see.

It's apparent from her body language that she desires Skarth, and a wave of jealousy overcomes me.

I wait for him to push her away, but he doesn't. He simply stands still as she steps forward and runs a finger along the scar under his right eye.

Skarth too has grown since we first met. He was always big, but now, his body is the shape of an unstoppable warrior. His hair is quite long, and I see that he still has the thin plait I knotted in his hair. He told me of his people, of how they prepared for battle. How they paint their faces to intimidate the enemy.

The ink on the side of his head is called an *Aegishjalmr*. It is to protect warriors in battle and ensure victory. Some draw it in blood on their foreheads before battle, but Skarth had it permanently imprinted into his flesh as he said it gives him strength every day.

The Northmen do not use the language we do, but rather, they use runes. They use these runes to change the course of fate. It's nothing but paganism, but I can't deny I find their beliefs utterly fascinating.

During our training, I've done some schooling of my own, educating Skarth in the way of the Christians. He is so curious about everything, which is what makes him a smart warrior. To know your enemy, you must understand them, and I know one day, Skarth will use this knowledge to outsmart the king.

But it appears all smartness is lost when it comes to a pretty girl.

She strokes over the *Aegishjalmr*, taking her time to admire the warrior. I am certain he will push her away at any moment as he doesn't like to be touched, but I am mistaken.

He wraps his hand around her waist and draws her closer as she silently begs he give her what she wants, and when he does, she moans in bliss. It appears he robs her of air as he seals his mouth over hers. But she doesn't mind. She allows him to dominate her in a way I've never seen before.

Fisting her loose hair, he savagely kisses her, allowing no reprieve as he cups her breast in his palm. She rubs her front against his, and when I see her hand slip between them, I use my own hand to cover the gasp which escapes me. I'm not naive to what happens between a man and a woman when they lie together, but this is something I do not know.

Skarth grunts, clearly enjoying her touching him so intimately, and when she drops to her knees in front of him, that enjoyment turns into something more.

She peers up at him as she unfastens his trousers, and when they slip down his legs, time stands still. I've never seen a manhood before, so when Skarth's considerable cock springs free, I lean in, desperate for a closer look.

It is thick, large. It is also very erect. How does he walk with such a weight between his legs? I thought I would be disgusted when I saw my first one, but I am not. Something shifts down low, and I whimper, rubbing my thighs together, hoping to defuse the burn I feel.

I am just as mesmerized as the woman and watch as she grips him, moving her hand up and down, up and down.

My cheeks blister, and I turn away, disgusted in myself for

watching something so wicked, but when I hear a hollowed noise, my curiosity gets the better of me.

Gripping the crucifix around my throat, I turn back around slowly, and what I bear witness to leaves me utterly breathless.

The woman has taken Skarth's cock into her mouth. Her head bobs up and down as he guides her with a hand on the back of her head. She pulls back, gagging, and just when I think she is about to stop, she continues sucking him deeply.

Pure lust is reflected in his eyes as he watches her, and a warmth spreads between my thighs. He is feral and unrestrained, and the sight has every part of me clenching in need. I don't know what that need is, but I like it.

I like it so much that I pretend to be the woman on her knees before Skarth.

I pretend it is I who suckles him deeply, tasting his rich scent that always lingers when he is near me. His fragrance isn't of herbs or perfumes. His scent is that of the earth—a masculine, warm fragrance that makes my mouth water.

Skarth is composed as she pleasures him, taking from her as she increases the tempo of her movements. Whimpers escape her, and when she slips a hand beneath her skirts, my eyes widen as her hands are possessed by that of the devil.

Again, this is foreign to me, as I have no idea what she does to herself. But from the sounds spilling from her, I assume it's not bad. It seems she is enjoying herself.

Skarth wraps her long hair around her fist and pumps his

hips. She grips his thigh to hold on as his actions are not gentle. Her hand between her thighs is working just as desperately as her mouth, and when a cry leaves her, Skarth drives into her mouth once, twice, before a sated groan slips past his parted lips.

He tosses his head back as he pumps his hips, his long hair cascading down his back. The feral sight of him has a wetness pooling between my legs and a heat washing over me. Am I unwell? I don't understand what this feeling is.

Once they're both decent, the woman comes to a stand, wiping her mouth of the liquid trickling from her lips. What is it?

On instinct, I run my pointer finger along my own lip, wishing I was her, wanting to taste what she does.

She bashfully lowers her eyes, but Skarth uses a finger to lift her chin. What happens now?

"Thank you, Cecily," he says hoarsely. "I will see you sometime soon?"

She nods, and her response douses my warmth. Does he plan to court her?

Illogical tears spring to life, ones which I don't understand. But I am caught in a whirlwind because I do not understand anything at the moment.

"Yes, Skarth, I would like that."

Skarth nods with a smile.

As she turns to leave, I duck low, ensuring to remain

hidden. The moment she steps out into the night, the urge to pull out her long blonde hair tackles me, and I chastise myself for thinking such a thought.

When she's gone, I continue watching Skarth as observing him unguarded is a rare sight. He arranges the weapons, clearly waiting for my arrival, which suddenly angers me. How can he behave so aloof when he acted in such a way with a woman I am certain he just met?

Anger courses through me as I come to a stand and enter the stables, pretending I didn't just see him act in such a lewd way. When he hears me, he turns, but soon stops, appearing to examine me from head to foot.

I suddenly feel uncomfortable because something behind his eyes is untamed. It's gone a moment later.

"My lady," he says, smiling as if he's happy to see me.

But I'm not fooled.

Grunting, I walk toward the weapons and peruse over them. I suddenly want to slap his cheek. How dare he taint our place with visions I will never forget?

"Is everything all right, *hugrekki*?"

"Yes," I reply sharply. "Will you finally tell me what that means?"

Although Skarth has been forthcoming with most things, he still won't tell me what that name means. It never bothered me in the past, but now it does.

"No," he counters, and I can feel those blue eyes watching

me. "I don't think all is well."

"I do not care what you think. I'm here to fight," I state, and fight I shall when I reach for the battle-ax.

Skarth has trained me to use many weapons, but the ax is still one I haven't mastered as well as I want. Tonight seems like a perfect time to change that.

Reaching for both axes, I turn and toss one at him, knowing he'll catch it.

He does but arches a dark brow, confused by my behavior. I don't give him time to ponder it because I charge for him, forcing him to defend.

Our blades crash together, but I jump back and try to strike him from the left. He blocks my advances, spinning and attacking from my right. I sidestep his strike and swing hard, hoping to knock him off balance.

He reads my approach, however, and ducks low, driving the ax's handle into my stomach, leaving me winded.

"My lady?" he queries, but I don't give him time to question me as I rush forward, ax raised. We engage in battle, him blocking me as I practice the actions he taught me.

He doesn't allow me to connect, dodging every attack, which merely adds to my irritation. I raise the ax above my head and swing out, but Skarth grips my wrist, forcing me to drop the weapon. He doesn't let go of my wrist, however.

"Fight me!" I order, struggling against him. It's in vain because he only grips me tighter.

"I will not fight you when you're like this. Have you learned nothing?" he angrily snarls, eyeing me furiously. "Leading with your emotions will get you killed. You need to focus. Use the anger to outsmart your enemy, not give them an advantage."

He's right. I know I'm being irrational, but I can't help it. Seeing another woman touch him has roused this demon inside me.

"Again," he demands, and when he releases me, I lunge for the fallen ax, primed on playing dirty.

Skarth is ready for my actions and dives for me, sending us both tumbling to the ground. I attempt to throw him off, but he pins me down, using his body weight to stop me from fleeing. He wrenches my arms above my head, securing them in one wrist as I thrash wildly.

"Let me go!" I cry, wriggling madly.

"I will," he lightly says, tightening his hold on me, "when you calm down."

"I am calm!"

An annoying smirk touches his full lips, and I remember them kissing Cecily passionately. The thought enrages me further.

"You heathen, unhand me!" I can't stop the filth that spills from me.

"Heathen?" He chuckles, using little to no effort to keep me restrained as I fight with all my might. "I've not heard you call me that in a long while. It's music to my ears."

"Fie upon thee!" I curse, which merely humors Skarth further.

I am very aware of his body pressed to mine, and I demand myself not to respond. But without control, my nipples harden, and the warmth I felt earlier returns.

His unique earthy scent is amplified being this close to him. All I want to do is lean up and bury my nose into the crook of his neck. He smells delectable. He feels even better. The candlelight illuminates him in an ungodly way.

God punish me, but I stare at him openly when I should avert my eyes. His thick stubble emphasizes his sharp jaw, and his pink lips only seem fuller. His eyes are akin to the bluest seas, mixed with a storm lingering on the horizon.

His face, though almost always covered with mud, is perfection—it is as sharp and chiseled as is his hard, muscular body.

I know he isn't even trying to keep me detained as I continue to fight him. He yawns, in fact, when I writhe wildly.

Why am I responding this way? I don't understand. Why do I burn for him so?

When memories of his manhood assault me, memories of watching Cecily please him, I can't stop the whimper that escapes me. Skarth hears it, and suddenly, things between us change.

He looks at me with those vivid eyes, attempting to decode what I'm thinking. He examines my flushed cheeks and peers at the way my chest is heaving so. My heart is beating so frantically, I'm certain he can hear it. But when he notices my nipples pressed against the material of my clothing, his confusion turns to dismay.

At this moment, I realize he will never look at me like he did with Cecily. He will never see me as anything but the king's daughter, nothing but a Saxon, while he's a Northman.

Tears spring to life as he crawls off me with haste.

There is an uncomfortable silence between us as I lie on the dirty stable floor, wishing it would swallow me whole.

"Have I hurt you?" he asks with nothing but kindness, mistaking my tears for physical pain. Yes, he has hurt me—he has hurt my heart.

Embarrassed, I sit up quickly, but a pain suddenly stabs me in the stomach. Groaning, I clutch my middle, and then I feel something wet slither down my legs.

He remains kneeled by my feet, waiting for me to speak, waiting for me to tell him it'll be okay. But it never will be okay again.

"Let me help you." He offers me his hand, but I slap it away, not wanting his help.

"Do not touch me," I order cruelly, sounding like my father.

Skarth nods and comes to a stand. He reads this for what it is. Even though we are friends, we are not equals. Here, on Saxon soil, he will always be an outsider.

The moment I get to my feet, the wetness gushes from me,

and I push Skarth, desperate to get inside.

He doesn't stop me, but with my back turned, he whispers, "I'm sorry for whatever it is I did."

I don't reply. I can't because I am the one who should be apologizing, not him.

However, now I must go to my chambers before anyone sees me.

I run from the stables, each step I take confirming my worst fears. When I enter through the back door of the kitchen, I don't explain why I'm here, not that they would ask. They simply go about their chores, ensuring the king's table is never bare.

When I enter the hall, the burning candles illuminate the red droplets trickling onto my shoes. I run past the guards, who don't ask questions, and the moment I enter my chambers, I slam the door shut. Turning my back, I lift my skirt with trembling fingers and what I see has me choking back a sob.

My white undergarments are now stained a bright red. The blood trickles down my thighs, confirming what I knew to be true.

Peering up at the crucifix above my bed, I ask Him if this is my punishment for watching Skarth when I should have averted my eyes. Is this my punishment for…falling in love with a Northman?

Because I am. I do. I love Skarth the Godless. I think I always have.

"My lady, the guards said you—"

With haste, I drop my skirt, but it's too late. My father's personal attendant has seen. She is loyal to the king in every way that there is, which is why she's out the door before I can stop her.

I'm about to give chase, but my mother enters, and when she sees me, I burst into tears.

"Oh, my sweeting," she coos, rushing over to hug me. I allow her to comfort me because once the king hears of this news, my mother's embrace will be a distant memory.

I am now a woman, and it won't be long until I am to perform all roles expected of a woman. "Please, Mother." I sob, holding her tightly. "Please forbid the marriage."

"I cannot, Emeline. You know this." There is nothing but regret in her voice.

"I don't want to marry a man I do not love. A man who is twice my age."

"You will grow to love him," she assures me, but love shouldn't be forced. "It's expected of you. You are the king's daughter."

"I am more than that," I cry, squeezing my eyes shut. "I am my own person."

She doesn't say anything because even though she agrees with me, nothing she can do will change destiny. I am to marry Aethelwulf of Wessex. I've heard rumors that Aethelwulf loves another, but King Egbert sees our union to be far more valuable. I wonder why that may be. What plans does Wessex have for

Northumbria?

Heavy armor can be heard, which alerts us of my father's approach.

My mother quickly pulls me out at arm's length and wipes away my tears. My door opens, and my father, my brother, and Lord Edward appear.

"Lord King." My mother bows in servitude while I simply nod.

"Is it true?" my father says, waltzing into the room. "Is there another cause for celebration this nightfall?"

"Yes, it is true, Lord King," my mother replies, speaking for me as she knows I'm at my breaking point. "Emeline is now a woman."

"Oh, Lord King, this is wonderful news," Lord Edward says, rubbing his portly hands together. "We must send word to Wessex."

His excitement is the last straw, and I snap. "Why are you in here, Lord Edward? In my private chambers? You are the king's adviser, not mine. Do you plan on advising him on a woman's monthly courses? I did not realize you were experienced in such a field."

Lord Edward pales and looks at the king, rendered speechless by my insolence. Aethelred chuckles, but soon mutes his humor when the king exhales angrily.

"I will excuse your impudence just this once, Emeline, for you are overwhelmed. But this marriage *will* take place as it will solidify the union between Northumbria and Wessex.

"King Egbert's defeat of Mercia has made him a very powerful man. With Kent, Surrey, Sussex, and Essex submitting to Wessex, we need this ally. You are doing a great duty to your kingdom."

I am sick to death of hearing this. I am sick to death of being told what to do.

"If you want this marriage so much, marry Aethelwulf yourself. Or better still, maybe Aethelred can. He'd make a pretty bride."

The room falls utterly still as no one, *no one*, has ever spoken to the Lord King this way. I know the consequences as this will not go unpunished.

"Lord King, no, I beseech thee," my mother begs, as she too realizes what this means for me. But no plea is going to save me.

My father stares me dead in the eyes as he commands, "Guards, taketh her to the dungeons."

The men just outside my door jump to command while I smile. Little does he know that place doesn't scare me anymore. I've been inside hell and survived.

My mother drops to her knees in front of my father, interlacing her hands. "Eanred, no, she is just a girl."

"Mother, do not beg for me," I order calmly as the guards flank me on both sides. "And do not drop to your knees for any man…even the king himself."

Lord Edward gasps, crossing himself. "Treason!" he cries, the whites of his eyes showing.

Aethelred's mouth is agape, as he is surprised I would provoke the king further.

"I am your king, child. I demand respect!" he roars, stepping forward and slapping me across the cheek.

My head snaps to the left, and I instantly taste blood. But I don't wipe it away. Turning toward him slowly, I allow him to see what he's done as it trickles down my chin.

"You will never have my respect, *Father*."

"We will see about that," he challenges, refusing to surrender. "A month in the dungeons should change your mind."

"Please, Lord King, no!" my mother cries, tugging at his robes. Seeing her weak and begging for clemency fortifies the fact that I will never bow to any man ever again.

"Make it two," I say, standing tall as the guards seize my arms. "Whether in the dungeons or married to Aethelwulf, I'm a prisoner either way. And given the choice, I choose the dungeons for at least I will die a free woman, not enslaved to some man."

"Lord King, I fear her soul has been taken by the devil. You must call on Father Lucan. We must pray for her soul," Lord Edward says, stepping back, afraid for his soul, it appears.

The king nods in agreement. "Bring her prayer book. That is all."

My mother's sobs follow me as I'm escorted from my chambers, and even though I am being led to my prison cell, I've never felt more free than I do right now.

# FIVE

*Princess Emeline*

"Would you like some bread, Amice?" I ask my friend, Amice the rat. Or maybe it's his brother, Becket. I do not know. All I know is that I've been locked in this cell for what feels like years...and I don't regret a thing.

I understand why men die down here because the darkness, the silence, it drives you mad. My only saving grace has been Amice, whom I've shared my stale bread with since my father locked me up and threw away the key.

As Amice sits on my shoulder, eating the bread I offer him, I wonder if my father intends for me to be locked down here forever. The prospect wouldn't be so bad because then I wouldn't be forced into marriage.

Looking down at the filthy rags I wear, I laugh maniacally because princess or not, I look and smell like a decaying corpse. I'm hardly a prize for any man, and I'm okay with that.

A sadness that I've tried so hard to quash rears its ugly head, reminding me of the one man I thought was different. The man I thought would rescue me as I once did for him when *he* was behind bars.

I don't know where Skarth is.

My well-being has been overruled with thoughts of Skarth. Has something happened to him? Did someone see us?

If my father wanted to imprison him, there is only one place he'd be. But he isn't down here, which has me wondering if maybe my father decided to deliver the fate intended to him all those years ago.

Footsteps echo along the cold, hard ground, and both Amice and I freeze, wondering where those footsteps intend to go. The guards have left me alone, but I don't fear them. Memories of almost being raped assault me, and I wrap my arms around myself, hoping to siphon the chill.

But this cold is one I can never warm myself from. It lingers in my bones and weighs heavily on my soul.

"Emeline?" a voice calls out to me softly. "Princess?"

I strain my hearing, leaning forward apprehensively in case I'm being tricked once again.

"My lady, it's me, Raedwulf."

"Raedwulf?" I say aloud in a voice I no longer recognize as I've hardly spoken since being locked down here.

Candlelight appears, allowing me to see that it is indeed Raedwulf. I hate that he's down here and not Skarth. But I refuse to waste my thoughts on him a second longer. He clearly doesn't care, but Raedwulf does…sweet, kind Raedwulf.

"I'm getting you out of here, my lady," he says, digging into his pocket for the keys. Amice scurries away when the metal door whines open.

I remain on the ground with my knees drawn to my chest. I fear this is a trick, a cruel taste of freedom, only for it to be snatched away from me as a form of torture to break me.

Raedwulf enters the cell, and I scamper backward, frantically peering around the dank cell for a weapon. When my back hits the wall, I whimper, suddenly afraid.

Raedwulf frowns in sadness, then raises his hands in surrender. "I mean you no harm. I promise thee. Take my hand, Emeline."

With great caution, he offers me his hand, ensuring he maintains eye contact. I am torn. If I take his hand, then I will be forced to face the world, and I'm not ready yet. But if I do not, I don't know if I'll ever get a chance like this again.

I won't die in these rags.

Pushing my fear aside, I slowly place my shaking hand in his. The contact with another feels almost foreign. "How long have I been down here for?"

"Two months," he replies sadly while a shiver almost robs me of breath. "Here."

He removes his cloak and gently wraps it around my shoulders.

He helps me stand, encouraging me to lean against him because I am weak on my feet. We then commence a slow walk out of the cell, where I turn over my shoulder and bid farewell to Amice—my only friend.

The candlelight guides us down the uneven path, and when Raedwulf gags, I wonder if maybe he's unwell. But when I notice him staring at a corpse being feasted upon by Amice's family, I realize it's the smell of decay, one which I've become accustomed to, which is the cause of his sickness.

The men down here are either dead or close to death, forgotten by their king because my father is a rotten bastard with no soul.

The cages men are forced into are filled with excrement and piss, but with nothing to eat nor drink, this is their life source. That, and the flesh of other men. One prisoner proves this when he tears away at the flesh of a detached leg.

Blood trickles down his chin as he snarls, warning us that this bone is his. My father has reduced these men to nothing but animals. What sort of king would do that to his people?

Raedwulf pays the guard at the gate with a heavy bag of silver. This was how he could rescue me.

"I'll repay you," I say, allowing him to guide me through the castle as I'm suddenly beyond fatigued.

"I won't hear of it," he whispers, leading me down the dark hallway. "We will ride to my family's estate, where we will then figure out what to do. My father is the Witan. He can talk sense into your father."

My fatigue is suddenly replaced with interest as I dig in my heels. "What do you mean? He still wishes for me to marry?"

"Aye, my lady. That has not changed."

I thought that maybe, just maybe, my insolence would have shown Father that I am not someone he can trade like goods. But all of this was for nothing.

Once we're outside, we make a run for the postern, where a horse awaits. Raedwulf has thought of everything, everything but one vital thing. I know what will happen once we arrive at his estate. His father will call for the king, and both Raedwulf and I will be punished.

I cannot allow that to happen.

Although tall, Raedwulf is slender and not fit for fighting. He is handsome and more suited for privy council than battle, which is why I feel nothing but guilt as I punch him square in the jaw, knocking him out cold.

"Sorry, Raedwulf," I say, shaking out the pain in my fist. Skarth also taught me how to throw a punch without breaking my hand.

The postern is open, so I grip Raedwulf's ankles and drag him out of the castle. I place him out of harm's way and prop him against the outside wall, so if anyone discovers him, they'll assume he had too much ale.

Catching my breath, I don't waste a second longer and mount the horse, clucking my tongue so that she rides like the wind. Her white coat contrasts the darkness of night, and I suddenly feel like I'm gliding on the back of an angel's wings.

The farther away I ride from the castle, the easier it is to breathe. I don't know where I'm going, but anywhere is better than Stonehill. Fatigue is crippling me, but I cannot stop. I need to be as far away from Stonehill as I can be.

We ride for what feels like hours, and as my eyes slip shut, I know I must stop and rest. I'm hidden by coverage of the thick foliage, so I decide to find somewhere dry and rest my eyes for just a few hours. The full moon allows me to see a large hollowed-out tree ahead.

It's perfect.

Directing my horse toward the stream, she takes a long swallow of water while I too do the same. Once we've had our fill, I tie her to a tree and settle into my chambers for the night. The fallen leaves act as the perfect cushion. I'm not used to such luxuries after sleeping on a cold stone floor for two months.

Once nestled amongst the earth, I look up into the sky, and even though He may have given up on me, I haven't given up on Him.

"Lord, show me the way."

For now, however, I will sleep.

I wake, very aware that I'm not alone.

Jerking upright, I scramble to find a weapon, anything that will help protect me. But when I hear the childlike voice of a young boy, I pause.

"What ho! How fare thee?"

Brushing the matted hair from my eyes, I smile when I see the young child. He is no threat. Only curious about the sleeping girl he found. "Good day. What is your name?"

"I'm Cuthbert," he replies, smiling broadly and revealing his missing two front teeth. "Did thou eat?"

My stomach grumbles at the mere mention of food.

"Ma is making pottage. Come then."

Before I can reply, he skips off, branch in hand as he engages in battle with an invisible foe.

Yawning, I peer around at my surroundings as it's now morning. Nothing looks familiar, which is no surprise. The only times I've ventured from the castle walls were with Sister Ethelyn for charity work. Even then, I wasn't allowed to stray far.

Once our duties were complete, we were escorted back to the king's castle, sheltered away from the real world. But now, with no minder on hand, I rise, stretching overhead as I slept like the dead. Untying my horse, I follow Cuthbert.

As I push past the thickets, I see a small village up ahead. Many villagers are working the lands that appear unfertile. The dirt is dry, and nothing grows from it, but nonetheless, the villagers continue to work the land in hopes a miracle will occur.

The villagers look at me with curiosity, wondering who I am. I suddenly feel embarrassed for not knowing them as they are my people—people of Northumbria. I also am horrified they live this way. I never take my wealth for granted, but seeing these people close to starving has me hating my father all the more.

These are his people, and he allows them to suffer this way. Even though they are struggling, I am certain he taxes them vastly. They have nothing, but he doesn't care. He expects everyone to pay, and for what? What do they get in return?

"Princess?" a melodious voice says, and when I look ahead of me, I wonder if I'm still dreaming.

I may not know the villagers, but I know this woman. She is Cecily, the woman I caught Skarth with.

She is even prettier up close. My jealousy returns, but I quash it down because it has no right to be here. This is her home, and I will not allow such immoral thoughts to corrupt me when she stands before me, offering a cup of water.

"Gramercy," I say, accepting her offering and swallowing it down. I didn't realize how hungry and thirsty I am. But now presented with both, I am ravenous.

Wiping my lips with the back of my hand, I notice the villagers are bowed in servitude. I appreciate the gesture, but it feels somewhat wrong—them bowing to me when my father has done nothing to better their lives.

"Please, stand," I say with a smile.

They look around, confused by my order, but thankfully, they obey.

"Princess, it's not much, but please, eat," says a woman with kind green eyes. She offers a large bowl of pottage, which smells absolutely delicious.

"Thank you. This looks simply delightful." I accept the bowl and sit at the wooden table she gestures at.

"I'll have your horse fed and watered, Princess," a young man says as he takes my horse.

"Thank you kindly."

Just as I'm about to stuff my belly full, I realize everyone is watching me, and I suddenly feel awful eating while they are close to starving. They are dressed in dirty rags, and their houses I can't imagine are even warm enough to keep out the winter chill.

"Will you eat with me?" I ask the forming crowd.

It's unheard of for a peasant to eat with royalty, but out here, those rules don't apply. This is their home, and I intend to respect them, regardless of their social standing.

The woman who served me the pottage walks over to the large pot on the open fire and commences serving her kin. I notice, however, that their bowls aren't as full as mine.

"Please," I say, coming to a stand. "Ration it out evenly. I won't eat while your family starves."

"But, Princess—" she says, eyes wide.

But I won't hear a word of it.

Placing my serving back into the pot, I gently take the ladle from the woman's hands and commence serving her and her people.

"Thank you, Princess," a young girl, no older than five, says as I pass her a bowl.

"You're most welcome," I reply, and it pains me to see her, along with most others, wear nothing but cloth over their feet to serve as shoes.

Once everyone has their serving, I then fill my own bowl and sit near the woman who made this wonderful meal.

"What is your name?" I ask her, blowing on the pottage to cool it down.

"Osanna," she replies in what appears to be surprise. I understand that it's a foreign concept for the king's daughter to ask a peasant's name.

"Thank you, Osanna, for your kindness. And thank you for this pottage. It is absolutely delicious."

She nods with tears in her eyes, as these people don't often hear compliments. It pains me this is the truth.

We eat in silence, but I sense the villagers watching me, wondering why I'm here, covered in filth and dressed in rags.

"How did you know who I was?" I ask Osanna, but Cecily is the one to reply.

She takes a seat across from us, smiling kindly. I instantly am ashamed I wished any ill thoughts her way. "We saw the royal seal on your horse. What are you doing so far away from the king's castle, Princess?"

She's thoughtful enough not to mention my alarming appearance as they can all guess that I fled under the guise of darkness.

"Cecily," Osanna gently warns, as it's unheard of for a peasant to question royalty.

Which is why I reply, "I'd much rather be here than the castle, Cecily."

She nods, but I can read her disbelief and also her anger as I know she'd trade places any day with me. She thinks I am spoiled and ungrateful. Who wouldn't want to be the king's daughter?

The one thing my father didn't strip me of was the gold crucifix I wear around my neck. Without thought, I remove it and slide it across the table to Cecily.

"It's solid gold," I state. Cecily looks down at it like it's some sort of trick. "You'll be able to fetch a good price for it."

Osanna gasps while Cecily's blue eyes narrow. She doesn't like charity, and I respect her for that. But she swallows her pride and reaches across the table for it. I can see why Skarth likes her. She is spirited and has the soul of a warrior.

"Thank you, Princess."

"Please," I say to her, letting go of any animosity I felt. "Call me Emeline."

The villagers gasp, looking at one another in astonishment. To address the princess without her title is treason, but no one is here to overhear, just me. These people have treated me with nothing but kindness. I refuse to behave like I'm superior all because of who my father is.

"Has the king come here to see your lands?" I ask, genuinely curious.

Cecily snickers, shaking her head. "The king's men only come when they retrieve their taxes. Or if they want to recruit our men."

Cuthbert appears, sitting on Cecily's lap happily. I wonder if they are brother and sister? Or mother and child?

"I am sorry for my father's behavior. He is—"

"Busy?" Cecily cynically says, filling in the blanks.

But I shake my head. "I was going to say self-absorbed. But busy will do."

A smirk touches her full pink lips. I think we've found common ground.

She appears to be a little older than me, and without question, she is one of the most beautiful women I have ever seen. Her hair is a golden color, akin to the sun, and her eyes resemble a soft sapphire. She is petite but rounded as a woman should be.

Even in her rags, she is striking.

"Cecily, I ask this of you in utmost respect, but would you consider being one of my ladies?"

I know what this means—that she and Skarth will be able to see one another more freely. But if I'm to return to court, I want it to be with a lady I can trust. And for some unexplained reason, I trust Cecily as she has the heart of a warrior.

I can see it.

She licks her lips, looking at Osanna for guidance. They understand what this opportunity could mean for them.

"Please, take some time to think on it. May I trouble you for a place to bathe?" I say, not wishing for Cecily to feel pressured to make a decision immediately.

"Of course, Princess." Osanna quickly stands and disappears into one of the cottages.

While I wait, Cecily watches me closely, attempting to decipher what I want from her. Out of all the women I could choose in the kingdom to be my lady, why did I ask her?

I don't know the reason, so I'm thankful she doesn't ask me. But I know she will accept. Even if she doesn't wish to be my lady, she will do it for her family as this would mean their fields will no longer be barren.

We all do things we wish not to, and I know once clean, I will have to decide what to do. Do I continue on my way, or do I return to my father and accept my fate?

Tears sting my eyes because it seems Cecily and I have a lot more in common than I initially thought.

Osanna appears with clothes in her hands. "Come, Princess. I will take you."

Nodding toward Cecily, I stand and playfully ruffle Cuthbert's brown hair. "Thank you for finding me, brave boy."

I curtsey in gratitude while Cecily smiles. She is fond of Cuthbert. I hope she can see I mean them no harm.

I follow Osanna, taking in the rich sights of my land. The forest is thick with greenery, and the trees reach up into the clouds. Though the terrain is lined with rocks, the soil is soft. I begin to wonder if Wessex will look the same.

I know so little about my future home. But I suppose that also applies to the man I'm supposed to wed. All I know is that Prince Aethelwulf is thirty-two in age and supposedly a weak, indolent ruler who wishes to be his father.

"Do you need help, Princess?" Osanna asks, interrupting my thoughts.

Focusing on where we are, I gasp at the magnificent lake ahead. Surrounded by tall water soldiers, the foliage allows enough privacy for one to bathe.

"No, thank you. I will be all right."

Osanna nods, placing the brown tunic she holds on to the bank. "Here are some herbs—mint, chamomile, and lavender—to wash yourself with."

I accept, cupping my hand over hers. "Thank you for your kindness, Osanna."

These villagers have next to nothing, yet they've given me more than they have. The clothes she offers me are lovelier than hers. Her brown tunic is stained and riddled with holes, and her feet are bare, yet she offers me her finest garments instead of wearing them herself.

"I will look after you and your family. By my troth, you will go hungry no more."

Tears fill her eyes as she squeezes my hand. "God bless you, Princess."

Her gratitude touches me, and I realize my decision is made. I will return to Stonehill, where I will agree to marry Prince Aethelwulf. I do this for my people. I do this to ensure Northumbria's future.

But first, I must bathe, as once cleaned, the future Queen of Wessex will emerge.

I spend the day learning how the villagers live. Even though they live a simple life, they are happy. They live for their family. They live for love.

Osanna offered me her bed, but I wished to sleep under the stars one final time as come morrow, I doubt I'll experience such freedom ever again.

I have accepted my decision, but that doesn't make it any

easier to stomach. Will my husband treat me with kindness? Will he even like me? I am certain he's heard of my rebellion. One can only hope that would revoke our marriage, but I know it will not.

A branch snaps, and I turn to the left, straining my eyes to see in the darkness. I subtly reach for the knife Osanna's husband gave me, wondering if this is a friend or a foe.

Clutching the handle, I lift my shoulders from the ground but don't stand. I remain supine. This gives me an advantage as I blend into the shadows. The rustling of fallen leaves hints the intruder is near, but as a warm, earthly scent catches the cool night air, I wonder if maybe I'm lost to a dream.

He cannot be here.

"You will not need that, *hugrekki*."

His hoarse voice cuts through me like a sharpened blade, and I cannot stop the shiver which rocks me from head to toe.

"Skarth?" I question in case my mind is playing tricks on me.

But when he gets closer, and the full moon irradiates his large form, I realize my prayers have been answered.

Slowly sitting upright, I watch with wide eyes as he stands in front of me. I'm so happy to see him, but then the fact I haven't seen him for two months reminds me that he abandoned me when I needed him the most.

"I suppose my father sent you?" I question, not keeping the bite from my tone.

"Yes, he did."

His short reply infuriates me. As does his stoic expression

"How did you find me?"

"I will always find you," he states, confusing me. "Just as you can always find me."

"How?" I'm almost afraid to ask.

He peers into the heavens, focusing on the twinkling stars. "The brightest light in the sky, it's always found north of the stars. The North Star, an anchor to where I will find you."

"You speak of astrology and stars, like a dreamer," I quip but can't deny the star Skarth focuses on is the brightest in the night sky. It can be used as a marker to help guide those who are lost on their journey. It can be used to find me.

The thought warms me in ways I did not expect.

He appears wounded. I tease, "Well, in that case, by this."

I watch as he unfurls his palm, revealing my gold necklace, the one I gave to Cecily, ending the talk of make-believe.

"That was a gift to Cecily," I say, quickly coming to my feet and marching to where he stands.

"Yes, she told me you had given it to her," he states, standing firm while I leave barely any space between us. "She told me you were here."

"My kindness wasn't appreciated, it seems," I state, unable to mask my disappointment.

"I forced her to tell me," he reveals firmly. "She was trying to sell it, and when I saw it, I knew it was yours."

It's a relief to know she didn't betray my trust as I have no doubt she didn't hand that information over easily.

"So now that you're here, what do you propose to do?"

I only reach Skarth's chest as he towers over me. But I won't cower in fear.

He peers down at me, those poignant eyes searching every inch of me. "How do you know Cecily?"

"I *don't* know her. The same cannot be said for you, however," I reply with bite.

It's the first time he lowers his guard, and I can see his annoyance stamped all over his infuriatingly handsome face.

"*That's* the reason you were angry with me?" he asks, but it's more of a statement—one he says aloud like he's only just worked out a puzzle he's been trying to decipher for a long while.

I don't confirm or deny, but my silence is all the answer he needs.

"I thought—"

"You thought what?" My heart begins to gallop.

My big, stubborn Northman clenches his jaw, refusing to allow the words to escape him.

He is dressed in armor, but it's not Saxon. It's Northman. My father has allowed this, but at what cost? The armor is chain mail, weaved onto leather. Underneath, he wears a linen shirt, and his tight trousers expose his powerful legs.

A short blade hangs from his leather belt, and the long

sword sheathed on his back is one he's had crafted for him. That sword has killed many. *He* has killed many.

Yet he didn't bother to seek me out.

"Where were you?" I question, keeping my temper at bay. For now. "You left me to rot."

He hisses, turning his cheek as if he's been struck. "You were angry with me. I didn't understand why. I thought you'd finally had enough of me, so I gave you time."

"Two months?" I ask, incredulous. "That's a lifetime, Skarth."

"I'm sorry, Princess. I didn't know where you were. I promise you. Your mother promised me you were well. If I knew you were in the dungeons, I would have come for you. I owe—"

"You owe me nothing," I interrupt, not wanting to be anyone's obligation. I want Skarth to seek me out because he wants to, not because it's a command—just like now.

"You've always been nothing but stubborn," he says, the moonlight catching his teeth as he smirks.

"And you've always been an arrogant bastard," I counter quickly, which has him laughing huskily.

"I've missed you, *hugrekki.*"

"And I have missed you, heathen."

His laughter continues, and it's a nice sound to hear as he doesn't laugh often. But things soon turn serious because I know it's time.

"I do not wish to marry him," I confess softly, biting my lip.

"We must do things we don't want," he replies, which sparks an idea, one which will change the delicacies between us forever. I know what I want…but I don't know how to ask.

"Prince Aethelwulf is a grown man," I reveal, watching Skarth's chiseled jaw clench. "I know I must do my duty for the people of my kingdom, but I am…afraid."

It's the first time I've ever told him I'm afraid, and his eyes, those expressive eyes, soften. They soften for me.

I am not like Cecily—full and voluptuous—but I am a woman. My breasts have grown, and my hips have rounded. I am no longer the little girl he once knew. Many tell me I am beautiful, but I don't want that beauty to be seen by anyone other than Skarth.

"You? Afraid?" he mocks, reaching out to brush my cheek with two fingers. "You're braver than any man I know."

His compliment touches me so.

"I will go back with you," I start, "but I want something in return."

He arches a dark brow, waiting for me to reveal what that is.

I wet my lips, hoping to find the courage I seek. "I have many thoughts," I share, inhaling deeply. "What if, what if I was soiled, then the marriage surely would not take place?"

Skarth appears confused, so I decide to clarify things for him.

"Prince Aethelwulf is expecting a maiden, but what if I

was…not? If I was no longer pure, he wouldn't want me."

"Princess," Skarth starts, realization hitting him, but he soon stops, stuck for words.

"I know this is selfish of me, but I can't help but think that even if I was impure and he wanted me still, at least I'd know the touch of someone I…care for."

A hiss escapes Skarth as he steps back. But I reach out, gripping his wrist. His leather wrist cuff creaks under the force because I am not letting him go.

"Pray thee…lie with me. I don't know what to do, but if you teach me, I can—"

But he doesn't allow me to continue.

"No," he firmly spits, shaking his head slowly. "I will not ruin your life. *Sorðinn*."

"You refuse me?" I ask, feeling nothing but a fool. "All I ask is for this one simple thing. But if I disgust you that much—"

He steps forward, wrapping his hand around my waist and drawing us front to front. I am certain he can feel my heart exploding in my chest.

"And that is why I refuse," he declares, his touch setting my body alight. "For you to think what you ask is merely a simple thing…I will not take that innocence away from you. I respect you far too much for that."

"Now you insult me, heathen," I snap, attempting to remove his hand from me. "I am not a feeble child with a weak mind. I know what I ask. I thought you were accustomed to such acts.

You had no qualms with Cecily pleasing you with her mouth."

I've spoken out of anger, and now he knows I encroached on a private moment, one which I had no right to spy on.

"All right, Princess," he says dangerously low. "I will fulfill your request."

Before I can ask what he's doing, he forces me onto my knees, gripping my chin and arching my head back at a painful angle. He rubs his thick thumb across my trembling bottom lip.

"Is this how you imagined it?" he taunts, slipping the tip of his thumb in and out of my mouth.

I suddenly don't like this because his actions are cruel.

"Unhand me," I demand, attempting to stand, but he pushes me back onto my knees.

"No, Princess, this is what you asked for," he maliciously states. "You wanted me to defile you, did you not? Take your virginity, here in the dirt, like the true heathen that I am."

"I do not want that," I say, tears welling in my eyes. Why is he being so heartless? "I thought it involved—"

"Involved what?" he snarls, fisting my hair. "Did you think I would lay you on furs and savor every inch of you? Kiss you until you screamed my name?"

"I-I…" I fumble over my words. I'm nervous, angry, but most of all, wounded he would behave this way.

"It will not be tender because I do not know how!" he exclaims, pulling my head back, exposing my neck to him. "I will have you on all fours, where I will mount you from behind and fuck you brutally until your virgin blood stains this wretched ground!"

Tears trickle down my cheeks. I thought he cared, but he does not. He cares for no one other than himself.

"Are you ready, Princess?" he asks, pushing between my shoulder blades so I'm forced to the soil. I'm at his mercy on my hands and knees as he lifts my borrowed tunic, exposing my chemise. "This is what you wanted?"

"I do not w-want this a-anymore!" I cry, sobbing so hard, my chest shudders. "Please! Skarth, I be-beg thee…stop. No m-more."

Just when I think he's lost to me, he takes three steps and screams gutturally into the heavens. I don't know what's wrong, and I am too afraid to turn over my shoulder and look. He yells in a foreign language, and he's done this so I won't understand.

But even if he spoke words I understood, I wouldn't listen because he's broken me—mind, body, and soul.

"I hate you," I spit, crumpling to the earth and curling into a small ball.

"Good. That's all I ask," he replies with little emotion. "Dry your eyes. Your father will not want to see you looking this way."

"I curse him, and I curse y-you…Skarth the Godless."

In response, I'm greeted with silence. And for once, the silence is welcomed, as it's a sound which will accompany me for all my days to come.

# SIX

*Princess Emeline*

"You look beautiful, Princess," says Luceria, one of my ladies-in-waiting. I have three. None of whom is Cecily.

When I returned to Stonehill, I was broken and defeated. I have fought my entire life and have nothing but a shattered spirit to show for it. Alas, I did what I said I never would—I surrendered.

I told my father I would marry Prince Aethelwulf.

He believed it to be a trick, but he soon saw the defeat in me. He saw I was broken beyond repair, and instead of sheltering me from the cold, he threw me to the wolves.

Word was sent, and King Egbert's men arrived at Stonehill to discuss my worth. In the end, my father sold me for five hundred pieces of silver. That's how much I was worth in his eyes.

King Egbert promised my father the alliance of Wessex and every one of his men if another battle was to occur.

All involved were overjoyed with the transaction, all but me and perhaps my future husband, who I am yet to meet.

So, here I stand, on my wedding day, on foreign soil, about to marry a stranger. So, whether what Luceria says is true or not, I do not care.

My gown is simple, which is what I wanted. It's blue in color with white sleeves. The color was chosen to reinforce my purity. I wear a white veil. My long hair is loose, but Luceria has plaited the sides and joined them together so one can see my face. I don't know what they expect to see because I can't smile. Nor scowl.

I am dead inside.

The good inside me died the night Skarth treated me far crueler than my father ever could. I was foolish to believe he actually cared. But that was my error, one which I will never make again.

A knock on my chamber door has my stomach dropping in dread. But I don't allow my emotion to show.

"It's time, Princess," Lord Edward says from outside.

Of course, my father sent this lickarse to accompany me. He's still afraid I will go back on my word.

Luceria places a white flower in my hair and smiles. "There.

Now you look a bride."

With a sigh, I try my best to return her excitement, but a blind man can see I'd rather be anywhere but here. I walk to the door, and when I open it and see Lord Edward grinning happily, I wonder if I could ask my new husband for a wedding gift—Lord Edward's head.

Pushing past him, I make my way down the long hallway of King Egbert's palace—my new home. The castle is utterly enchanting, twice as big as Stonehill with rich tapestries draped along the walls and gold and silver on display to parade the kingdom's wealth.

No one could ever doubt Wessex's affluence, and with King Egbert being the overlord of Kent, Sussex, Surrey, and Essex, that wealth just continues to grow. He is a shrewd, determined ruler, and I have sense that this union between Wessex and Northumbria will only strengthen *his* reign. Not my father's.

The guards stand on command, their silver armor polished until it gleams. They bow when I walk past them, my ladies-in-waiting trailing behind. Once the chapel is steps away, I inhale, refusing to think about *him* because I know he is not thinking of me.

I've not seen Skarth since he returned me to the king. And I'm glad for it.

We rode back to Northumbria in complete silence, and that silence has continued for weeks. I don't know where he is. He hasn't made himself known.

A part of me wishes he was here because he was my only friend. His familiar face would give me the strength to take these final steps.

Lord Edward, however, aids me as he gently prods me, encouraging me to stop dawdling and fortify this union once and for all. The crowd inside peers outward, wishing to have a glance at their future queen. They all appear in awe of me—the princess known for not doing what she's told.

Word spread about my defiance, so I'm surprised Prince Aethelwulf agreed to marry me. I can't help but think there is a reason for this, but that reason will have to wait because when Lord Edward all but shoves me toward the altar, there's no turning back now.

Even the people of Wessex appear far more prosperous than those of Northumbria. Their clothes are that of wealth, made with the finest materials and complemented with the richest jewels. My father and mother stand near the decorated altar, looking nothing but happy at this union.

Both are dressed in fine silk and jewels, ensuring no one in this kingdom would mistake them for anything other than the parents of the bride. My brother stands behind them, appearing nonchalant. This is the only blessing about this union—I'll be away from Aethelred.

King Egbert and his wife, Queen Redburh, stand on the other side of the altar, looking on stoically. Queen Redburh is extremely beautiful, but I don't allow her beauty to fool me because I sense a cruelness underneath her prettiness.

She enjoys the notoriety that comes with being a queen. My mother's yellow gown pales when compared to Queen Redburh's blue and green silk robes and complemented with a golden, jeweled crown.

King Egbert is known for being a philanderer as his good looks, as well as the title of being Lord King, allow him to choose any woman in this entire kingdom to bed.

I wonder who his son resembles more.

My questions are about to be answered because as my soft footsteps announce my arrival, the man standing at the altar turns around. He examines me from head to toe before meeting my eyes. He is nothing exceptional with no distinguishing features that stand out.

As I approach him, I bow.

"My lord."

"My lady," he says, his voice deeper than I thought.

He wears a black velvet tunic lined with gold trim. The long cape he wears matches his ensemble, and it's safe to assume he had this outfit tailored for today. The elaborate gold embroidery on his front is quite detailed. This wasn't made overnight.

My father clearly assured King Egbert that this union was taking place—with or without my consent.

His brown hair is longer than I expected, but it complements his well-groomed beard. Some may find Prince Aethelwulf handsome, but that doesn't make a difference to me because I will never love him.

The priest stands in front of us, waiting for my father. He offers Prince Aethelwulf a dowry of silver to solidify our union. This is supposed to be a sign of respect, but I feel like I've just been sold.

Once the formalities are sorted, everyone takes their places, and my life changes forever.

"Prince Aethelwulf, wilt thou have this woman to be thy wedded wife?"

Prince Aethelwulf looks at me and nods. "I will."

The priest then asks me if I'll take Prince Aethelwulf as my husband.

My lips part, but the words I know I must speak don't come out. I clear my throat, hoping I'll find them lost in the abyss. But I don't.

The hushed murmurs reveal the scandal I've caused by not jumping to command.

Prince Aethelwulf turns to look at his father, whose lips are pulled into a thin line.

Sweat begins to gather along my brow, and I feel faint. Two simple words have never been harder to speak, and that's because I don't want to say them. I'd rather cut out my tongue.

If he was here, I would be able to do this, but I need to remember he abandoned me time and time again. He doesn't care. He never did, for if he did, he would be here.

*"We must do things we don't want to."* His distinct accent

echoes loudly, one that used to provide me with warmth when nothing could chase the chill away.

But now, it leaves me with a gaping hole, right where my heart once beat…for him.

With tears in my eyes, I pull back my shoulders and promise myself this is the last time I think of him. I cannot revive something from the dead.

With a broken heart, I declare, "I will," much to the relief of my father.

We exchange rings, and the simple gold band on my finger feels heavier than the weight of the world. We bow our heads, accepting the blessing offered by the priest. Once he is done, he announces we are man and wife.

The crowd erupts into happy cheers while my husband and I awkwardly join hands. The people wish to see the happy couple, and we give them that, though both of us are equally uncomfortable. I feel absolutely nothing when we touch, unlike when I was with Skarth.

But he can no longer hold my thoughts hostage. I now belong to another.

I notice a woman with long black hair and cold blue eyes staring at us. She doesn't appear to share the assembly of happiness, and when our gazes meet, she makes it very clear I am the enemy. She stands near Queen Redburh, which has me believing she is someone with ranking.

Prince Aethelwulf leads me down the aisle, accepting the

blessings of his people. I remain dutiful, smiling like the well-behaved wife I am to be. Once we exit the church and are away from prying eyes, Prince Aethelwulf releases my hand.

"I shall return."

"You leave so soon, Prince Aethelwulf?" I ask, unsure if this is etiquette or not.

He doesn't mask his annoyance that I have the cheek to question him. "I am your husband, and you will address me as my lord," he instructs firmly.

"Yes, my lord," I reply, unsure why he's suddenly angry with me.

The answer appears in the form of the woman I saw moments ago. "My lord," she says, sarcasm following her.

I don't understand what's going on.

But when a genuine smile overtakes my husband's face, I understand perfectly.

"Lady Osburh," he says, taking her hand in place of mine.

He offers no explanation when they leave me standing in the hallway, alone and confused. I watch as they huddle close, with her whispering into his ear. He laughs cheerfully, soon forgetting the ring he wears on his finger is supposed to be a sign of his devotion to *me*.

Utterly humiliated, I quickly make a dash for my chambers, swallowing down my looming tears. Once inside, I place my back against the door and allow the tears to fall. I wish I could stop, but I am broken, and I don't think I'll ever be whole again.

Sniffing back my tears, I wipe my eyes and decide to take a moment to compose myself. My father won't come looking for me as the marriage is sanctioned. There are no recants in the eyes of the Lord.

The green gardens just outside the window are a lovely distraction as I walk toward the window and admire my new home.

Is Lady Osburh Aethelwulf's mistress? It's not unheard of. My father has many. But it's in poor taste for him to show her off on our wedding day. My stomach roils as this confirms just what sort of person my husband is.

The door opens, and before I have a chance to turn and see who enters my chambers without knocking, he speaks in that voice which, no matter how I hate him so, soothes me in ways it shouldn't.

"My lady," Skarth says, softly closing the door behind him.

I want to pretend that him being here means nothing to me, but it does. However, I wish for him not to know this, so I put on a brave face as I turn to face him.

"I believe you were not invited," I sternly say, folding my arms across my chest.

He nods, his eyes downcast, which is unlike him. "I was not," he replies, slipping his thumbs through his leather belt.

Why is he fidgeting?

"What do you want?" I have no patience for games.

"I came here, my lady, because I—"

Now he is stuck for words? Something is wrong.

I wait for him to continue.

"I wished to see you," he confesses, which has come too little, too late.

"Well, you've seen me. Good day, Skarth." I attempt to turn around, but he reaches for me, gripping my wrist and stopping me.

"Please, Emeline," he says, again a first—Skarth the Godless begging. "I do not want to fight with you. I wanted to make sure you were all right. King Egbert killed my father—"

And suddenly, the truth leaves me breathless. "Is that why you are here? You wanted your revenge?" I accuse, ripping from his hold. "Now that I am Aethelwulf's wife, you believe I can get you closer to the king. Is that why you wanted me to marry him? For your own personal gain?"

I can't believe I actually thought he was here for me.

"*Sorðinn*," he mutters under his breath.

"Stop speaking in a language I do not comprehend!" I order, frustrated I can't understand him. But it's not merely his words. It's his actions as well.

"I fear you wouldn't understand me, regardless of what language I spoke," he confesses with regret. "I came here because I couldn't stomach the thought of you being mad at me."

But I don't believe him.

"It's too late for that. But if you really mean it," I challenge, walking toward him. He doesn't flinch when I stand on tippy-toes and leave mere inches between us. "Then you will take me away from here. We will run away and be free."

I know I speak of fantasy because that cannot happen. But it's nice to dream.

"I made a promise to my family," he says, which is why Skarth remains. He will not abandon them, which I admire. They are lucky to have someone fighting for their freedom.

I only have myself, which is why, without regret, I utter, "You used to be fearless. Skarth the Godless. But now, you are nothing more than Father's puppet. I will not help you in your quest. You are dead to me."

His jaw clenches as he measures his breaths.

"However, I ask that you promise me something."

He inhales sharply, his Adam's apple bobbing.

I commit him to memory—his earthy scent, his stormy blue eyes. I commit to memory how he broke me, for I will never allow another to do so ever again.

"Promise to never speak to me again."

He doesn't respond. He merely stands perfectly still.

"Promise me," I demand, reaching out and gripping his wrist, rubbing my fingers over his arm ring. I cannot have him in my life. It hurts too much, and I am no longer brave.

He turns his cheek, unable to look at me. If I believed in bedtime stories, I dare say he was saddened by my request.

Peering down at our union, I realize I will miss this—

his darkness has always complemented my light. He was the balance I needed to survive, but I could not rely on him any longer.

"You—"

However, words are robbed from me when he steals the breath from my lungs the moment he presses his lips to mine.

He tastes of freedom, and I am addicted to a taste I cannot have.

We fit in every way that there is, and I know he feels it too. His skin prickles, and his warmth unites with mine. The kiss is chaste, as it's merely a touching of lips, and I know that's because Skarth will never see me as anything but a little girl.

"I promise." He severs our kiss, only to press his forehead to mine. The sentiment is heartfelt. Far more tender than a lover's touch.

"I wish I never met you," I whisper, holding back my sorrow.

"I wish that too. *Far vel, hugrekki.*"

He retreats while I wrap my arms around my middle, barely holding back the torrent of tears.

Before he leaves me, he grants me one final gift. With his back turned, he declares, "It means heart of a warrior…as that is what you are."

He closes the door behind him while I crumple to my knees, sobbing uncontrollably.

Everyone is in merry spirits. Drinking and eating the finest Wessex has to offer. I remain quiet, smiling and nodding like the dutiful wife I am supposed to be.

Aethelwulf sits beside me, but he may as well be in another kingdom. He hasn't asked me to dance, and instead, we both sit at the royal table, watching our guests enjoy our day. It doesn't matter, though, because after seeing Skarth, I am not in a celebrating mood.

My father and King Egbert discuss politics, no doubt, as my father is an opportunist and wouldn't allow an occasion like this to pass. My mother sits obediently. As for my brother, I suspect he is up to his philandering ways.

When my three ladies appear, I know it's time.

"Excuse me, my lord," I say, standing gracefully.

He barely looks at me and sends me away with a curt wave of his hand.

Concealing my offense, I walk through the room, thanking the guests for coming. They all look at me with hope in their eyes, as Aethelwulf and I are their future.

When we exit the great hall, Lady Osburh catches my eye. She is speaking with an ealdorman. The moment we pass, both bow in servitude, but as Lady Osburh goes to stand, she trips and falls into me.

I am about to help her, but what she whispers into my ear has me realizing this was no accident. "It's my bed he shall be sleeping in tonight."

Before I can react, she readily composes herself, feigning embarrassment. "Forgive me, my lady. These shoes are two sizes too small."

Hardly believable because she'd have the tailor hung for such an oversight, but I smile nonetheless. "That's quite all right, Lady Osburh. I believe your dress is a little snug as well? Mayhap you should try another tailor?"

I make a point to glance at her low neckline, which has her cheeks turning a bright red. Insulting one's dress when they clearly take pride in their appearance is akin to treason.

One of my ladies snickers behind me.

"My lord, speaking in shadows with an unwed lady may not be wise," I say sarcastically. "We wouldn't want the kingdom rife with rumors."

The ealdorman's cheeks match Lady Osburh's when they blister scarlet. I want them to know I will not be pushed around.

"Fare thee well."

With my head held high, I gracefully tread away, biting back the victorious smirk which refuses to stay hidden. We enter my chambers, where my ladies help me undress. The unspoken lingers because the dreaded wedding night approaches.

My arrogance soon fades when I am standing in my chemise.

There is a knock on the door, and my mother appears. "Excuse us, ladies."

My ladies bow and give my mother and me privacy.

"Are you all right, my sweeting?" she asks softly, brushing my cheek with her fingers.

"I do not need instruction. I know what's involved," I reply, as I've been told what's expected of me. I'm to lie on the bed, where Aethelwulf will have his way with me. The entire ritual makes me unwell.

"That's not what I ask," she amends, catching me off guard. "You are doing your king a great honor."

"I live to serve the king." I can't keep the mockery from my tone.

"But that doesn't make what you're about to do any easier to accept."

I open but soon close my mouth because what she says is treason.

"Emeline, I am sorry you've been forced to wed someone you do not love." She licks her red lips, appearing to weigh over what she wants to say. "But the man in which you do, you cannot have a future with. You are smitten, and that will only lead to heartbreak."

She has stunned me into silence because she knows. She knows Skarth has my heart.

"You share an unbreakable bond. I know he would do anything to protect you."

"He failed," I whisper, the sadness plaguing me once more.

"This is your duty. This will ensure Northumbria's safety." Before I can snap that I've heard it all before, she adds, "But I am so sorry it has fallen to you. It's expected of us to obey, whether we want to or not. I admire your strength, Emeline. For I could never do what you have."

She bends down and lays a single kiss on my forehead.

"Never forget who you are. You are Princess Emeline of Northumbria. You are my daughter. And I am so proud of you."

With her words, she has given me her strength when mine was lacking. I will do this because I am strong. I am *hugrekki*.

With one final hug, she leaves me with the courage I need to survive this.

I stand in the middle of the chambers, awaiting my husband, who finally appears after what feels like hours. The moment he closes the door and sways to the right, I realize he is drunk.

"My lord," I say, bowing.

But he doesn't appreciate the submission and storms over, slapping my cheek. "You will not speak to Lady Osburh ever again. How dare you embarrass her."

I cup my cheek, anger rising. "She embarrasses herself, fawning over a married man!"

He snickers, making clear he too wishes this union never took place.

"I am your wife. And I will not allow you to treat me like some common whore."

I know I need to stop, but I can't.

Something overtakes Aethelwulf, something cruel. Instantly, I step back, but I'm not going anywhere.

"Yes, you are my wife, and you will please me how a wife should. Take off your chemise."

Nerves overcome me, and I swallow deeply. "A little less light, mayhap?"

I attempt to siphon a candle, but he grips my wrist, stopping me.

"You are hurting me, my lord," I say, attempting to break free. But I'm trapped forevermore.

Before I can protest, he tears the thin chemise down the front, exposing my breasts.

With a yelp, I cover my nakedness, for no man has ever seen me bare before. But Aethelwulf angrily removes my hands, where he then tears the rest of my chemise away. The ruined garment pools by my feet.

I stand before him, naked and afraid.

He takes his time examining me. It appears he likes what he sees. "Your breasts are heavy for a young child."

"I am not a child," I retort, angered he sees me this way yet has no qualms about bedding me.

He reaches out to cup my right breast, squeezing it crudely. I feel like a cow at the market. When he runs his hand down my stomach, I lock eyes with him, refusing to cower because that's what he wants. He wants me afraid because that's what makes cowards like Aethelwulf feel superior.

As expected, he stops touching me. "I can't stand you looking at me. You are hideous. Turn around."

When I refuse, he grips my upper arm and violently spins me around, gasping in disgust. "Your back is just as ugly as your front," he maliciously states when he sees my scars—ones which were no fault of my own. "I was not told you were ruined."

But that doesn't seem to matter when I hear him unfasten his buckle with haste.

He forces me onto my stomach, pressing his hand into the small of my back so I cannot move. "Your virgin cunt will be no more, *Princess*," he snarls, "for when I am done with you, you *will be* nothing but a common whore."

Panic suddenly sets in because what does he mean?

I attempt to scramble away, but he merely tightens his hold on me. "You believed this marriage was to benefit your imprudent king? Oh, silly lambkin. This was always about Wessex, and how you were our way in."

"No!" I fight, but when he spits into his hand and crudely forces those fingers into me, I know this fight is won.

I lost.

"We will tear your precious kingdom apart, where not only will you bow to me, but your father will as well."

Tears leak from my eyes because this was a trick. I am a political pawn, used by Aethelwulf and King Egbert to overthrow Northumbria.

"However…now I will settle for tearing *you* apart." My mind detaches from my body when he thrusts into me, breaking my veil of virginity as well as my soul. "Oh, Princess, your cunt is so tight. A virgin no more."

He commences rutting into me while I grip the blankets beneath me, refusing to cry.

"Once I am done, my men will have their fill, for you belong to Wessex now. You belong to me," he pants, shoving his revolting cock into me over and over again.

It hurts, by God does it hurt, but I focus on that pain and store it deep within because one day, one day very soon, I will inflict that same pain on him.

I was tricked, sold to a monster by my father, who will pay dearly for his crimes. A maniacal laugh spills from me, for I know what fate befalls my father. His precious kingdom will be stolen from him…and I will be the cause of it.

"I belong to no one, my lord," I breathe past the pain as he grunts his pleasured moans. "Break my body for it is nothing but a shell. But you'll never break my heart, my spirit, for they belong to me."

He brutalizes me in ways no man ever should, and when he shudders, spilling his seed into me, I am thankful it is done. It was over far sooner than I thought it would be.

But we are not done. Things have just begun.

"We shall see about that." Aethelwulf grips my hair, arching my neck back at a painful angle, and bites my throat. When he lets go, I feel blood trickle from the wound.

I remain perfectly still as I hear him redress, only to open the chamber door.

"She's all yours."

I quash down my fear, for I remember who I am…a princess…I am *hugrekki*.

"Thou dost takest my breath away," King Egbert says, closing the door. "My son was merciless. But I will not be. I will treat you well. Would you like me to, my lady?"

"Yes, King Egbert," I whisper, suddenly realizing that what lies between a woman's legs can be used for her gain, just as a man's can.

"Sweet lambkin. You serve your king well." King Egbert disrobes and carefully mounts me, complimenting my beauty as he softly caresses my back.

The moment he enters me, commending my beautiful cunt, I disengage from reality and merely focus on the one thing which courses through me—revenge. I will take this kingdom…and burn it to the fucking ground.

# SEVEN

"I wish I could stay longer," King Egbert says, rising from my bed to get dressed. "But I cannot. Queen Redburh is always suspicious."

And she has every right to be. Her husband has snuck into his daughter-in-law's chambers more times than she can count.

Pulling the furs over my nakedness, I smile. It's staged. "It's all right, Lord King. There is no need to explain."

Once dressed, he leans forward, pressing his lips to mine. "I wish things were different. But alas, I am doing the best I can. You are safe here in Wessex, as no one dares to touch the king's mistress."

It's supposed to be a compliment. His way of expressing

that he cares. But all it does is cement the fact that I am the king's whore.

"I bid thee farewell. I will come again soon." He looks over his shoulder at me before he parts, appearing to want to look upon me one last time. He is smitten, while I wish for his death.

Once gone, I toss back the furs and place my feet onto the cold floor. It takes a while to stand as my bones need a moment to warm up on chilly evenings such as tonight. That's thanks to my husband, who broke my legs on escape attempt number four.

Standing, I walk over to the bucket of water and lather the soap to rid myself of the stench that stains my skin. No matter how hard I scrub, the disgusting odor always remains.

When I married Aethelwulf, I knew it would be horrible, but I never anticipated it to be the worst decision of my life.

When he revealed I was to be used as a political pawn, he meant it. Six months into our marriage, King Egbert conquered Mercia, thanks to the help of my father and his army. My father, oblivious to Wessex's plans, thought he was reinforcing his place as king, but little did he know he only incited King Egbert's interest in Skarth.

King Egbert wanted Skarth for his own, but my father would not trade. He knew Skarth was the reason for his victories, and if he forfeited that advantage, his army would crumble. This enraged King Egbert because no is a word he does not understand.

Therefore, King Egbert attacked my kingdom, overthrowing my father. I wondered where Skarth was, for he wouldn't allow them to lose. I suspected my father locked him away because he wouldn't let his prized possession fall into the wrong hands.

In the end, it didn't matter.

King Eanred submitted to Wessex rule. This was the plan all along. This is why they sanctioned the marriage—my father never believed King Egbert would attack his kingdom, as his daughter was handed over in a sign of good faith. I was to be the bridge that knitted Wessex and Northumbria together.

But this made my father weak and complacent because King Egbert had his eye on only one thing—becoming Bretwalda. And now he is.

He is the overlord of the Saxon kingdoms, which means most kingdoms bow to him. However, with his current defeat, thanks to King Wiglaf retaking Mercia, he is out for more bloodshed.

I am the cause of Northumbria's downfall when all I wanted to do was save her.

Under Wessex rule, Aethelwulf had our marriage annulled. Grounds were that we are too closely related because of King Egbert's overlordship. All knew it was nonsense because the moment the marriage was void, he married Lady Osburh.

I was married for one year, and during that year, I was tortured in ways I never thought possible. Physically and emotionally, Aethelwulf did everything to break me, but he never could. He took from me physically, using my body in immoral ways. But it's just a husk—one which refused to break.

He then resorted to breaking me—literally. Every chance I got, I tried to escape, but each and every time, I was captured and punished horribly. When Aethelwulf realized his punishments were ineffective, he resorted to keeping me restrained without shackles—he broke my legs to stop me from running.

He much preferred it this way as I was still a warm body for him to use and abuse, but with broken bones, I couldn't fight. I was what he always wanted—submissive.

I believed they would send me back to my family, but to save embarrassment, they've kept me in Wessex as one of Lady Osburh's ladies-in-waiting. I'd rather they kill me, which is why they keep me here, a prisoner, the king's whore.

I keep to myself. I do what I'm told because I know remaining in the king's favor is what will allow me to get my revenge. I allow him to use me and whisper sweet nothings into his ear, for a smart predator waits for the perfect moment to strike.

Now is not that time, but that time will come. I am sure of it.

Once cleaned, I redress into my simple dress. It's to remind me of who I once was but never will be ever again. No one dares refer to me as a princess even though I still am. My father is still the king, but he obeys King Egbert's command as he is the High King of England.

Once I step out into the hall, I lower my chin as I know my place. I should be sleeping with the other servants, but I have my chambers because of the king, which just ostracizes me all the more. The only reason I haven't been passed around from guard to guard is because of the king. But I don't mistake that for safety. I know, given half the chance, these men would gladly defile me in all ways that there is.

Lady Osburh is in prayer, so I do my duty and check on her son, Aethelbald. Merely a baby, I predict great things are fated for him. I may be biased, however, because Aethelbald has helped heal my wounds.

I was with child. Whether he belonged to Aethelwulf or King Egbert, I do not know, but losing my baby before he even had the chance to live was the one thing that *did* break me. I gave birth to a dead child, and I cradled him as if he were alive.

He is buried in the cemetery. A small cross was the only marker to acknowledge that he was there. That he was mine.

King Egbert tried to console me as he believed the child to be his, but nothing could fill the gaping hole in my chest. I thought I was broken, but this shattered me beyond repair.

"Good day, sweet prince," I say, lifting him into my arms and kissing his rosy red cheek. He smells of innocence—how I once smelled. "Did you sleep well?"

He coos in response.

Lady Osburh will not nurse him. I barely see her interact with her child. She did the Kingdom of Wessex a great honor by bearing a son, so her job is done.

The wet nurse, Sigrith, enters, smiling when she sees me. "Good morrow, Lady Emeline. How is sweet Aethelbald?"

"Hungry, I believe," I reply, laughing when a small hiccup escapes him.

She gestures I'm to give him to her, and there's a reason for it. "My lady," she says, lowering her voice. "I overheard the king speak of Northmen."

Sigrith is my only friend. I've confided in her about my past, so she is aware of Skarth—although I've not mentioned his name.

I have a feeling she harbors her own secrets, which is why I know she won't share mine. The palace is aware of my history, however. King Egbert has asked many times about Skarth. And each and every time, I play the fool.

He wants Skarth for his own as he, like my father, sees his worth. But no one owns Skarth. I tried that once upon a time and got my heart broken.

"What did he say?"

She licks her lips, rocking the baby gently to keep him silent. "Northmen have raided close to Carhampton. They are getting closer. King Egbert appears nervous. It's been said over one hundred ships were seen."

This means the Northmen are preparing for battle.

"I think Aethelwulf means to speak with you about the Northman." The moment his father's name is mentioned,

Aethelbald begins to cry.

"Thank you for telling me this," I say, gently caressing Aethelbald's cheek to soothe him.

This new invasion will only intensify King Egbert's interest in Skarth. I can only hope for his sake that he will stay away.

"I will check on Lady Osburh as she may need someone to peel her eggs," I mock, rolling my eyes.

Sigrith laughs quietly. "She is wearing red today, so I fear her monthly courses are due."

It's no secret Aethelwulf wants more sons to carry his legacy, but each time Lady Osburh wears red, we know his wish has not been granted. Therefore, his foul mood passes to her, and we're the ones who must deal with the repercussions.

God strike me down, but it gives me great pleasure knowing both are miserable. I happily suffer her wrath, knowing she is hurting.

Saying goodbye to Sigrith and Aethelbald, I exit his chambers, only to be stopped by a guard. "Lady Osburh asked for you to prepare her horse."

I sigh, my temper rising. "She doesn't have servants for this?"

The guard glares at me, angered I would refuse an order.

"Very well," I amend, biting my tongue.

He snickers, joyed to have given an order I cannot decline. "On your way, whore," he mumbles under his breath. But he wanted me to hear.

Clenching my fists by my sides, I measure my breathing to calm myself down. The guard dares me to act, but I don't.

Turning gracefully, I walk through the castle, reminding myself that revenge looms. If the Northmen are near and they want Wessex, they won't stop attacking. This means Wessex is in danger, and this is my time to strike.

It's a bitterly cold morning as winter has fallen and fallen hard, so I wrap the fur shawl tighter around me. If it was up to Aethelwulf, he'd have me freeze to death. But King Egbert ensures my comfort, believing he is taking care of me.

It only motivates me further that one day, I will take his head.

The snow is thick, blanketing the once fruitful earth. This has been a particularly long winter, and I wonder if this is why the Northmen have attacked. Are they sick of waiting?

Whatever the reason, I can only hope their defeat is bloody and brutal.

I enter the stables, surprised no one is in here. Lady Osburh probably sent them away so I would be forced to do as she commanded.

Her white horse is a thoroughbred. No one could mistake him for anything other than royalty.

"Good morrow," I calmly say, walking over cautiously. "I am a friend."

He whinnies, taking a step back in his enclosure.

"It's okay," I encourage, walking closer. "We are both

prisoners."

With hands raised, I come to a stop in front of the wooden railing, wanting him to trust me. No one can tame a beast, but they can be subdued with respect.

"Shh, it's all right." With one hand, I reach over the railing, wishing for him to smell my hand.

Smell is so important. It can transport you to any place in time. For me, I take comfort in mint and lavender, smells that remind me of home. Freshly baked bread reminds me of being a child. I never realized how much I loved Northumbria until I was forced to flee.

Another scent hits me, one which I haven't basked in, in a very long time. It's my most favorite smell of all. It's rich, earthy, and warm. It smells of home. It still gives me comfort, even when it should not.

Tears well, which is why I don't allow myself to revisit this memory. Showing any weakness here will be my downfall.

The horse nudges my hand, accepting our friendship. He knows I mean no harm. "One day, we will both be free."

As I'm patting him, a sense of calm falls over me. I've not felt it in years. The last time I remember it, it was with Skarth.

My heart, my broken heart, which beat sluggishly for so long, suddenly kick-starts once again. It beats so quickly I fear something is wrong. I was only half living, but now…I am whole once more.

"Good day…Princess."

Closing my eyes, I pray my mind isn't playing a cruel trick. But when I hear his composed footsteps, I know it is not.

Skarth the Godless is really here…and he is really in danger.

Spinning quickly, I don't prepare myself because after three long years, I can finally see in color again. Skarth stands feet away, but he robs me of air.

His wild hair is styled differently. Small braids are threaded through his dark mane, which forms one long plait that runs down his back. Gold beads fasten the smaller plaits, which highlight the sides of his hair. It is cut quite short and allows me to see he has added more artwork to the side of his head.

His beard is long, fuller. It only draws attention to his full pink lips.

He wears a tight black shirt with a leather tunic over the top. It is fitted with metal studs. His trousers are also tight and dark in color. He wears brown leather boots on his feet. His knife hangs from a thick leather belt, and his custom sword is sheathed at his back.

A thick fur drapes his broad shoulders to fend off the cold, but I am suddenly burning up.

He has always been brawny, but now he is beyond muscle. He is hard and strong—the epitome of a warrior. His chiseled face is slathered in dirt, and he dons a black eye.

I thought I looked at Skarth through the eyes of a woman, but I knew nothing. Seeing him now, I yearn for him in a new light. Every part of me clenches, and my mouth salivates to taste his warm, portly lips. I want to feel his naked, hard flesh pressed to mine.

"You have grown," he says in that accent that brings me to my knees.

"So have you," I reply when I can find my voice.

Those blue eyes study me carefully, and I wonder what he sees. What I see is my Northman…who I still love with every fiber of my being. Staying away didn't snuff out my feelings for him. They only lay idle. But now, they are back and almost winding me with their force.

A guard outside the stable, however, has me forgetting my feelings, and I lunge for him. "You cannot be here," I whisper, encouraging him to crouch low as I peek outside to ensure the guard is gone.

Once we're alone, I return my attention to him, swallowing deeply because we are mere inches apart. The heat of his body sets mine alight. Instantly, my cheeks redden.

"Are you still angry with me, Princess?"

"No. I mean yes," I amend quickly, while an amused smirk tugs at his lips. "But I am not the one you should fear."

"You are the *only* one I fear," he confesses, startling me as his mischievous demeanor fades.

"Why are you here?" I whisper, still crouched low, still inches away from him.

"Your brother is getting married, and your mother requested I come escort you back home."

Has his voice always been this smooth? His breath always this sweet?

Shaking my head, I need to concentrate on the fact that if anyone sees Skarth, they will alert the king.

"Did anyone see you enter the palace?"

"I am sure some did," he replies with a casual shrug.

"Skarth," I gripe. He doesn't seem to understand the severity of him being here. "King Egbert is looking for you. You must leave. This instant."

"Not without you," he counters, stunning me once again. "I have missed you, Princess."

"And I you, heathen, but we can speak when your life is not in danger."

"Then I fear we shall never speak for danger seems to follow me." He arches a dark brow and grins.

"Stop this banter," I say with a smile, mischievously hitting his chest. The moment I touch him, however, playtime is a thing of the past.

"I cannot believe how you've grown," he says once again, heating my cheeks yet again as he peruses me deliberately. "Do you not eat? You are too thin."

"I eat," I reply, ignoring his concern. "That's what happens when time passes us by." There is a sadness to my tone because so much has transpired since I saw him last.

My happiness to see him turns to anger and then sorrow because he left me here to rot.

As usual, he reads me clearly and reaches out to brush the apple of my cheek with his thumb. "Forgive me, Princess. I went back on my promise. I tried to stay away, but I could not."

I don't know how to reply. I asked him all those years ago to leave me be, but I was wrong to demand that of him. I spoke in anger, in self-interest because Skarth never abandoned me. He was just as much a prisoner as I was.

"Please, we will speak about this another time. You must leave."

But all plans to flee are suddenly forsaken when King Egbert and three of his guards arrive. When he sees us huddled, his eyebrows knit together in confusion.

Instantly, I stand, knowing better than to disobey as I bow. Skarth, however, doesn't jump to command. Instead, he leaps onto the wooden railing, taking a seat.

"Bow to your king, heathen," a guard spits.

Skarth merely smirks in response. "He is not my king."

The guard advances, primed to rip out Skarth's tongue for speaking such blasphemy. But King Egbert grips his arm to stop him.

"It's all right. He does not know the way of our values. He is pagan. It's nice to meet you, Skarth the Godless. I am King Egbert. Welcome to Wessex."

Skarth appears calm, but I know he is moments away from jumping down from that railing and ripping King Egbert's beating heart from his chest. This is the man who murdered his father and sold his sister and mother into slavery.

"I am here for Princess Emeline," he states very firmly.

King Egbert looks at me, watching for my response. I remain passive.

"What business do you have with Lady Emeline?"

"Aethelred is to be wed. Lady Emeline's family would like her to be there."

King Egbert waits for Skarth to elaborate, but he doesn't. He doesn't have anything further to say. I'm surprised he even shared that morsel of information.

King Egbert doesn't like to be challenged, and if this were anyone else, they'd be thrown into the dungeons. But King Egbert wants something from Skarth, and he won't let him leave until he gets it.

"King Eanred never sent news of this joyous occasion. Of course, he'd want Lady Emeline there. But first, I ask you stay. Have some ale. Some food. You must be hungry after your journey."

This is the one time I wish for Skarth to read my body language because this is a trap. My expression is solemn, hoping he will decline the offer and leave.

However, Skarth never surrenders.

Jumping down from the railing, he stands beside me, ensuring King Egbert knows he is no fool. "I am quite parched. Thank you, Lord."

"Excellent. My lady?" King Egbert calls to me as he senses

he walked into something more than just a friendly reunion. I don't know what because I myself am confused about this moment between Skarth and me.

But without choice, I walk over to King Egbert, where he deliberately wraps his arm around my waist. Humiliation confines me, and I lower my chin, unable to face Skarth for he will see what has become of me.

His *hugrekki* is no more.

King Egbert escorts me from the stables, ensuring he never takes his hand off my waist. The kingdom stops what they're doing as we pass, for a Northman walks amongst them—freely. I want to turn to look at him, but I can't.

Every action is being watched, and if either of us alerts to something being amiss, we will pay with our lives.

When we enter the castle, I believe King Egbert will send me away. But he doesn't. He leads us into the great hall, ordering the servants to prepare food and ale. He sits at the long table, gesturing for me to sit near him.

The only time I've sat at this table was at my wedding. From that day forward, I was forced to eat in my chambers. When I was given food, that is.

Sitting graciously, I fold my hands on my lap to stop from fidgeting.

Skarth sits on the other side of King Egbert, and I admire his self-control. I doubt King Egbert knows he was the one who destroyed Skarth's family because I don't think he'd be so eager to share a meal with the man who is intent on taking his head.

"How is King Eanred? Last I heard, he was injured in battle?"

He was? Why wasn't I told?

"He is well. Nothing but a scratch," Skarth replies, but I begin to wonder if he said this for my benefit.

A servant arrives with a jug of ale, pouring us a cup each.

Skarth reaches for his drink, tossing it back in one long swig. The servant refills his cup nervously.

"King Eanred is rather selfish, keeping you all to himself," King Egbert commences, hinting at the real reason we're here. "I've wanted to speak with you for a very long time."

I remain submissive, but inside, I want to scream.

"Is that so?" Skarth says, amused. "What would the infamous King Egbert want with a heathen like me?"

King Egbert chuckles, but the sound is far from friendly. "I want to know what keeps you loyal to King Eanred. Why do you fight with him against your own people? I do not understand. What has he promised you?"

This is it, the moment when Skarth reveals just who he is and happily accepts the consequences. His revenge will be worth the bloodshed.

My breathing is labored, and my heart is nigh on exploding out of my chest.

"King Eanred captured me," he starts, reaching for his cup of ale. "I had no choice. But as I trained his feeble army and even weaker son, I realized the rewards I reaped were much more than I could ever have by pillaging.

"Fighting the Saxons, I faced uncertain death. But knowing how both armies battle has worked to my advantage. I have land, silver…and a wife. My life is in Northumbria now. We came here to conquer, and I have done that.

"I have what I want. I am not a greedy man."

King Egbert nods, while I can't get the word *wife* out of my head. Does he speak the truth? Or is this another ploy? I do not know.

As the food arrives, the smell makes me sick. It has nothing to do with the cook, but more so, the thought of Skarth with another woman rubs my stomach raw. King Egbert reaches for the knife, indicating he will slice the meat from the wild boar.

A king serving a heathen, this is sacrilegious, but King Egbert has done this as a sign of respect and peace.

Skarth presents his plate, where King Egbert serves him well. When he reaches for my plate, I shake my head.

"You must eat, lambkin. You are nothing but skin and bones."

He's right. I am not of healthy weight. But my stomach has shrunk due to the years of malnutrition.

Skarth's chair creaks, and I risk a glance his way. I see he is gripping his knife, his knuckles turning white with the force. What has caused this response?

King Egbert ignores my request and places a slice of meat

onto my plate.

A low growl escapes Skarth, which, thankfully, is muted when a servant arrives with more food.

"You are wise, Skarth the Godless. May I ask, why do they call you this?"

"I do not know. It's a name you Saxons gave to me. I assume it's because I am without your God?" King Egbert nods but inhales his boar as Skarth then adds, "However, I've heard that it is because when I kill Saxons, a man will beg for mercy, forfeiting his God because he promises he will obey me solely.

"Maybe I like this name, after all."

Skarth has insulted our faith and at King Egbert's table, no less.

"This boar is delicious," he says, tearing into the meat as if he didn't just speak blasphemy to the king.

I bite the inside of my cheek to hide my smile because Skarth obeys no rules. King Egbert's efforts at behaving civilized have failed because Skarth has no interest in pretenses.

"What if I were to offer you double the amount of silver King Eanred does? And any land you wish? A bordar, mayhap? That allows you to farm ten to twenty acres of land," King Egbert says, revealing the real reason he's here.

Skarth chews loudly, indicating he is bored by King Egbert's offer.

"You will be a constable. You will command my army. Whatever you wish, it can be yours."

This offer King Egbert presents is very generous, which reveals his desperation. Skarth could ask for anything, and the king would agree, which is why he leans forward, staring straight at me.

"And what of Lady Emeline?"

King Egbert and I both pale.

"What of her?" he asks sternly, a vein throbbing at the side of his head.

"You said whatever I wish for can be mine. Well, I want her."

The room falls silent, apart from the thrashing of my heart.

King Egbert clears his throat. "Lady Emeline is not for trade."

"Then we have no deal." Skarth goes to stand, but King Egbert quickly recants his words.

"What do you want with her? She is…special to me, and I cannot let her go without something in return."

How dare he speak about me like I'm nothing but chattel. He said I'm special to him, but he lies. He sees me as his possession, one which he can trade.

Skarth mulls over his request, eyes still locked with mine. "What do you want?"

King Egbert smiles. "Your loyalty and service to *me*." He knows this means the demise of Northumbria but does not care.

Skarth takes a moment to process his demands. He is

twenty-three years old, and an offer such as this will make him far wealthier than men twice his age. But it also means he will be leaving one prison cell for another.

If he agrees, King Egbert will own him—whether he likes it or not. Surely, he will decline.

But within the blink of an eye, he changes the course of everything.

"All right, I agree to your terms," he finally says. "But Lady Emeline is mine."

Usually, anyone claiming I belonged to them would be rather insulting, but it's not with Skarth. I like it.

King Egbert is torn, so the question now is, what does he want more? Me? Or his kingdom?

It is no contest.

"Agreed."

Relief lifts from my shoulders, and I suddenly feel as if I can breathe again. That, however, is short-lived when Aethelwulf and Queen Redburh enter the great hall. Their disgust is evident.

"Since when does she eat at the table?" Queen Redburh snarls, eyeing me viciously.

"Since she is the Princess of Northumbria," Skarth utters, rising dangerously slowly. His immense height is imposing, and Queen Redburh gasps, clutching the jeweled crucifix around her neck.

"She may be a princess in Northumbria," Aethelwulf bites back, "but here, she is a lady-in-waiting to my wife, the future

Queen of Wessex."

Skarth is unmoved by Aethelwulf's words. "Thank you for the ale and food, but I seem to have lost my appetite. Princess, will you please take a walk with me?"

I sit with my mouth open, unsure what I'm supposed to do.

King Egbert nods. "Go. I shall speak with you later."

He won't touch me as he knows Queen Redburh is watching closely.

I push back my chair and stand gracefully but halt when Aethelwulf storms forward, hitting the table with his fists.

On instinct, I flinch, fearful he's about to strike me. Skarth immediately steps in front of me, ready to spring into attack.

"A Northman has no right to make demands here in our home! Guards!" Spittle flies from Aethelwulf as he is furious.

But King Egbert kicks back his chair, standing abruptly. "Have you forgotten that I am king? Not you. You will watch the tone you take with me!"

I take a step forward, hitting the safety of Skarth's back, and it's here I will remain.

"You make a deal with a *pagan*?" Aethelwulf asks, aghast.

He isn't foolish. He understands there is a motive to this meeting, one which benefits the king and no one else.

"I made a deal for Wessex," King Egbert corrects, while Queen Redburh crosses herself, asking the Lord for salvation. "I do not expect you to understand. You do not think like a king."

Aethelwulf's fists rest on the table. He focuses his attention my way. "You are nothing but a whore. Get out."

Before I can stop him, Skarth reaches over the table and grips Aethelwulf by the front of his shirt. He presses them nose to nose, smirking. "Say that again, my lord. I beg of you."

I watch with wide eyes, knowing that if Aethelwulf does what Skarth asks, it will be the last words he ever speaks.

Aethelwulf pushes him away, wiping down his clothes as if they are sullied because they were touched by a Northman. His nostrils flare like an angry bull, but he doesn't say a word.

"I didn't think so. Come, Princess."

I don't need to be asked twice.

The moment I stand next to him, he grips the crease of my elbow and all but drags me from the great hall.

He doesn't let me go. We continue marching through the palace while I'm forced to run to keep up with Skarth's frantic steps. He doesn't stop. He doesn't care that he pushes through ealdormen and ladies who shriek at his presence. Nor does he care that he just changed the course of everything by making a deal with the devil.

He storms outside, heading for the small gardens. It offers us some privacy as it's surrounded by brick walls. He only lets me go once we're within those walls.

I rub my arm because his grip was far from gentle and watch him pace like a wild beast. "You belong to him?" he sneers, refusing to look at me.

"I belong to no one," I sneer, not appreciating his condemning tone. "Just because you have returned does not mean all is forgotten or forgiven. I did what I had to, to survive. Just how you have."

"That's different," he reproaches, finally coming to a stop. He turns to look at me. "You are the king's mistress?"

I cast my eyes downward, which is all the answer he needs.

"*Bacraut*!" he exclaims, his jaw clenched tight. "For how long?"

"What difference does it make?"

"How…long?" he repeats low.

"Since my wedding night! Does it please you to know that I've been passed between father and son since I was fourteen years old?" I cry, angry tears threatening to break the floodgates. "That I've been humiliated all in the name of war!

"I never wanted this, but I endured it because what else was I to do? I had no one. No one! You were the only person I trusted. But you discarded me, just how everyone did."

"Discarded?" he questions, appearing wounded at my claims. "And no, it does not please me in the slightest."

"I begged you to help me. In the forest, you were cruel, far crueler than anyone has ever been to me. The others, I do not care about, but you…I did," I confess sadly. "You said awful things. Then on my wedding day, you could have stopped it, but you did not.

"But now you are here, and you expect me to be thankful?

It's too late, Skarth, for the damage has been done!"

He storms forward, gripping my arms and pulling me toward him. I fight, but my efforts are futile. "I said those things because I did not want to ruin your life! What can I offer you? You were always far braver than I.

"You were the one who had to walk away because I could not. If I was to do what you asked, I knew the dire consequences you would face. I was trying to save you!"

"By condemning me to hell?" I cry, tears of anger spilling down my cheeks. "I would rather die than live this way."

"The marriage was going to happen regardless. Your father ensured it. He told me if you refused, he would have you killed. I would not force that life on you. On the run. A fugitive in your own country, because that was the only other option.

"I thought I was protecting you. I did not know of your situation until recently," he shares, which has me stop struggling. "Your mother told me that your marriage had been annulled."

"What did you think would happen when my father submitted to Wessex rule?" I question, the fight in me fading. "I am a stranger in this land, and Aethelwulf has ensured I know it at every opportunity he has."

"I did not know. I do not understand Saxon law. I thought you would be safe and happy. Your mother assured me that you were. I thought I was protecting you. I tried to get word on your safety, but no one would talk, for who would trust a Northman?"

"Protecting me from whom?"

He lowers his eyes, his mouth slack as he lets me go. "From me."

I don't understand what he means. "Why would I need protecting from you?"

"Because you came to me as just a child. I could not pollute that innocence. You showed me kindness when you were taught hate. You risked your life, you defied your God, your king…for me. I owe you my life, and I was not prepared to ruin yours.

"Fourteen years old, you were nothing but a babe. But now, at just eighteen, you are no longer *meyla,* and this is why I've come."

He remembered I just had a birthday. It touches me so.

His words ricochet loudly as I understand the severity of them. "My mother did not send you, did she?"

He shakes his head. "She did not." He confirms what I knew to be true.

"Is Aethelred getting married?"

"I do not bother myself with that *bacraut's* affairs. I came here to do what I should have done three years ago…I've come to take you home."

I never thought I'd hear those words again. And now that they've been spoken, I wish to hear them again—over and over again.

"We ride from here on the proviso that we are to attend Aethelred's wedding? The king won't suspect a thing."

Skarth nods, his astute eyes scanning the grounds to ensure we are still alone. "I am certain he will send his guards to accompany us, but once we're clear from here, they will be dealt with."

I gulp as their fate is destined for bloodshed.

"We then ride as far away from here as we can."

"Where will we go? I cannot go back to Stonehill. King Egbert will come looking for us once word spreads."

"I know, Princess, this is why I did not want this path for you. You will be a fugitive with all of Wessex and Northumbria searching for you. But we will be all right. I have some friends waiting for us just outside the palace walls."

I lick my lips nervously. "I cannot ask them to risk their lives for my freedom."

"They want to help you, Princess," he assures me, cupping my cheek tenderly. "You do not ask anything they do not want to give."

His touch instantly soothes me, and I lean into him. This indiscreet touching is foreign to me, but I do not object. Once, I was a child and Skarth a man, but now, I am a woman, and I want this man.

However, his words haunt me, and I press my trembling hand over his. "You have a wife?"

I wish for it to be fallacious, but when he tongues his bottom lip in contemplation, I know it is true. "Yes. Cecily is my wife."

I nod with a smile although my heart crumbles. "I am

happy for you both."

Gently, I remove his hand from my cheek. He sighs heavily, then his eyes focus overhead before he steps in front of me, shielding me with his back.

"Someone is coming."

We wait and see one of the king's guards enter the gardens. "The king has requested you stay for tonight's proceedings," he informs us.

"What proceedings are these?" Skarth asks, ensuring I remain shielded behind him.

"The Lord King will host a full banquet in your honor. The villagers have been alerted."

My stomach drops.

"Tell the king I accept. But come morrow, we head out at first light."

The guard nods, not masking his disgust that the king would host a festivity for a heathen.

Once he's gone, I whisper with Skarth's back still turned, "This is a trap."

"I know, my lady, which is why we leave. Tonight."

The prospect of freedom is within reach. But what will we lose in return?

# EIGHT

*Skarth the Godless*

I t pains me to leave Emeline unattended, but I cannot linger, for King Egbert will sense something is wrong. And I will not fail her—not again.

She never left my thoughts. She was with me, always. Had I known she was here, suffering at the hands of these *Níðingrs*, I would have come years ago.

She has grown—my fierce, brave *hugrekki*. But she is broken. Wessex has broken her, and for that, I promise, Wessex will pay.

I don't deserve her forgiveness. I was cruel, but my actions were in kindness. I knew she was smitten—a Saxon caring for a Northman—but she was fourteen. She did not know of love, and neither did I. I refused to corrupt her that way. I respected her far too much for that.

But she is no longer a child. Gone is the *meyla*, and in her place is a woman I knew she was destined to become. She was always comely, but now, her beauty is unmatched. I yearn to touch her, to be near her, because when I do, everything quietens, and I can breathe.

When she was younger, I felt this too. But now, it is different. It has grown. I want her in the way I should not.

Cecily is a devoted wife. She is also brave and strong, but what I feel for Emeline is fated in bloodshed. When our paths crossed, I knew we would be connected eternally, which is why when Queen Eleanor informed me of Emeline's situation, I left everything behind to come for her.

Cecily understood, but she does not know the woman Emeline has grown into. She does not know the feelings I harbor for her will condemn us both.

I am Skarth the Godless. I have killed countless men. But with one look, Princess Emeline has the ability to slaughter me where I stand, and for someone who never wished to be owned, she possesses me—mind, body, and—if I believed in it—soul.

And when she steps into the great hall, my obsession with her just grows.

She wears a blue dress that ties at the front, emphasizing her ample breasts. A darker blue shirt is worn underneath, covering her arms and is modest in the collar, exposing the silver cross she wears around her neck. The blue silk belt emphasizes her small waist, and I vow to fatten her up once we leave this vile place.

Even though her God has forsaken her, her faith is still strong.

Her long hair is loose, but when I see a silver bead strung in a thin plait, a sense of pride overcomes me, for she looks like my people. She looks like a Northman.

Her green eyes search the great hall, and when they land on me, she notices me staring, causing her cheeks to blister red. She smiles in response.

We can't let anyone know what we have planned, so I nod discreetly.

King Egbert and his queen are speaking with the ealdormen, but I note the way he looks at Emeline when she enters. He is in love with her. Or whatever he believes love to be.

It takes every ounce of strength I have not to detach his head from his shoulders as he is the reason I am a Saxon slave. I am finished fighting for King Eanred. I haven't been able to find my family. Therefore, I will try another way, and that way is not being enslaved to a Saxon.

My people see me as a traitor, so I know I will have to do this alone. But I promised my sister and mother that I would find them and avenge my father's death, and I won't go back on my word.

I knew what it meant when I left Northumbria. I knew that

I too would be a fugitive. But Emeline is worth it. She risked her life for me, and I shall do the same for her. Tenfold.

King Eanred would know of my disappearance by now. Therefore, he would have sent his finest knights to find me. I have a three-day lead on them, so time is of the essence. We must leave soon.

Aethelwulf is by my side, and from the smell of him, he's had too much ale. He is a pathetic excuse of a man. "Beautiful, is she not?"

He refers to Emeline.

I don't reply because he is baiting me.

"She is quite wild, in more ways than one."

I clench my fists by my sides.

"I may visit her chambers one final time this nightfall. After Father, of course." He laughs loudly, sipping his ale as he examines Emeline indecently.

Emeline subtly shakes her head, begging I don't give in to temptation and gouge out his eyeballs with my blade. But this cannot go unpunished.

"I believe you'd be no use to her, Lord Aethelwulf," I casually state.

He focuses his eyes my way. Much better. "And why's that… *pagan*?" he slurs, sloshing ale down the front of his white shirt.

"Because I believe Lady Osburh is in possession of your *bqllrs*. In fact, I hear them rattling around in her pouch right this moment."

Aethelwulf opens but closes his mouth when he realizes what I just implied. "What did you say to me, Northman?"

"I said—"

I don't get a chance to finish because King Egbert appears. "Aethelwulf, Father Alwin would like to speak with you."

Aethelwulf doesn't break eye contact with me. He's challenging me, and I will accept. If he draws his blade, I will draw mine, but I will not give him the chance to attack, for I will drive my sword straight through his throat.

"Aethelwulf," King Egbert repeats, this time ensuring Aethelwulf listens.

He snickers but eventually leaves. This isn't done.

"He is angry with me," King Egbert explains. "He thinks I should not trust you."

"You shouldn't," I counter, keeping my eyes on Emeline. "That's the first rule of battle—do not trust anyone. Only yourself."

He's silent as he processes what I just shared. "Three of my guards will escort you back to Stonehill," he says, which is no surprise.

"Thank you, Lord." Sadly, those guards will not return.

"You too are in awe of her beauty, it seems?" He speaks of Emeline, and I want to tear out his tongue for it.

"I'm merely following orders, Lord," I reply, turning to look at him.

It sickens me that he knows Emeline in a way he should

not. He is old enough to be her father. He is not worthy of being anywhere near her. No man is. Not even me.

"Then why did you bargain for her?" he asks. I need to be careful how I answer because if he senses a lie, we won't leave this palace alive.

"Curiosity?" I say like I too don't understand it. "The king's mistress must be something special. I want to know what."

King Egbert laughs loudly. "You Northmen are inquisitive creatures. I admire that. Maybe we are not so different, after all."

I try my best to smile because I am nothing like this vile snake.

An ealdorman appears, hinting he requests council with the king.

"Duty calls," he says softly. "And she is something very special. But be careful…that sweet little cunt may be your downfall. I know that it is mine."

He leaves me seething because he knows I won't act. I want to rip out his spleen and feed it to him, which is what he wants. He wants a reaction. I need to be smart, just how I am in battle because this is war.

I search for Emeline, but she isn't where I last saw her, and when I comb the room, I realize she is gone. Aethelwulf is also missing.

I'm aware eyes are on me, so I casually walk through the grand hall and exit coolly, but inside, I am going to explode. I need to find her, but I don't know where to look. The palace is huge. She was in the royal chambers the last time I was here, but that chamber would now be reserved for Aethelwulf and his new wife.

My heart has never beaten this fast before. Even in battle, when faced with death, I don't think I've ever been more afraid than I am right now.

A guard walks by, and I grab him by the throat, pinning him to the wall. "Where are Lady Emeline's chambers?"

He doesn't fight because I am one indignant Northman who will kill anyone who stands in my way. "That way." He points down the hall, sagging to the floor when I release him.

I make haste, and when the hall takes a sharp left, I follow it anxiously. I'm about to bang on every door when I hear a muffled scream. I block everything out and focus on that sound, as I would in battle. When I hear it again, I run toward the last door and kick it open, unsheathing my sword.

Even though I knew I would find them in here, it doesn't prepare me for the reality of seeing Emeline hurt—her face is bloody, her dress torn. She holds the only weapon she can find—her chamber pot. Aethelwulf is a few steps away, leather belt in hand.

He turns over his shoulder, revealing four bloody scratches along his cheek.

Emeline is beyond terrified, her hands quivering as she clutches the chamber pot like it is her lifeline. But she will never be afraid again.

Closing the door, I lean my back against it, daring Aethelwulf to make his move—who does he want more? Me or Emeline? Whoever he chooses, one thing is for certain—he won't leave this room with his head intact.

With a roar, he drops the belt to unsheathe his sword. I anticipate his move and launch for him before he has a chance to advance. I elbow him in the face, where he staggers back, dropping his sword and cupping his broken nose.

Emeline jumps back, chamber pot still in hand as she watches on with wide eyes. Her back is pressed to the wall. Her terror is soon replaced with exhilaration because she knows what fate is destined for Aethelwulf.

"You'll both be hung for this." He spits out a mouthful of blood.

With a smirk, I cock my head to the side. "What makes you think you will leave this room alive?"

Aethelwulf soon realizes this is a fight to the death, a fight he knows he'll lose. And like the coward that he is, he opens his mouth, ready to call out for help, but is stopped the moment I reach for my sword and drive it into his stomach.

He topples forward, clutching his middle as he gasps for breath. But he doesn't deserve a reprieve—not after everything he's done to Emeline. He has hurt and humiliated her. He has stolen the light from her eyes, and for that, I will steal his.

Gripping him by the hair, I yank his head backward. He is at my mercy. He glares at me, daring me to do my best.

"You filthy heathen," he snarls, pathetically struggling against my hold. "God will punish thee."

Lowering my face to his so we are inches apart, I growl, "Your God is not mine. So whatever punishment he wishes to bestow on me, I welcome, for hearing your cries is worth condemning my soul to your hell."

He opens his mouth, but his time for talking is no more.

With utter fury animating me, I jab my thumb into his right eye socket, relishing in the feel of his eyeball disintegrating under my brutal touch. An anguished cry leaves him as he fights with all his might. But it's too late for that.

His demise is mere seconds away.

I continue tunneling into his socket, blood and other matter slathering my flesh. I relish in the feel of it. I want more.

Once his eyeball loosens, I dig my thumb behind it, resulting in it popping free from the socket. Aethelwulf slaps at my hand, but the fight in him has simmered, and I know he's on the cusp of passing out. Using my pointer finger and thumb, I yank out his eyeball, smirking at the sight.

I hold it in front of Aethelwulf for him to see—out of his good eye, that is.

The gaping hole where his eyeball used to be spurs me on further, and I toss the ruined eyeball onto the ground, it squelching under my boot as I stomp on it. With my grip still fastened in Aethelwulf's snarled hair, I arch his neck back farther and lock eyes with Emeline. The chamber pot now limply rests by her side. Her mouth agape.

Only now do I realize what she just witnessed. She's heard stories of me in battle, but this is the first time she's seen the real me—the callous, bloodthirsty Northman who takes great pleasure in all things depraved.

She's only ever looked at me with innocence, but I know that has now changed. I suddenly am ashamed, for this is who Skarth the Godless really is.

"Princess—" I start, but she shakes her head.

Whatever she wishes, I will do, as she holds me captive in more ways than one.

I wait with bated breath, unsure what she's thinking. She examines the scene before her, her intuitive eyes processing what I just did and what I will do.

Does she regret saving my life all those years ago? Will she see me as nothing but an immoral heathen?

She steps forward, her pace measured, her gaze never wavering from mine.

"You are nothing but a heathen whore!" snarls Aethelwulf, squirming as he attempts to break free.

But Emeline doesn't flinch.

She continues walking toward us in an almost daze. I fear I've broken her for good.

When she is mere inches away, she stops and cocks her head, appearing transfixed by a wounded Aethelwulf. My hold on him is tight, so I don't fear for her safety, but when she reaches out with two fingers and circles them in Aethelwulf's blood, I realize there is no need to fear for her well-being.

However, the same thing can't be said about mine. I am completely under her spell.

Emeline is *hugrekki*. She doesn't tremble in fear.

I'm the one who now watches on in awe as Emeline runs her thumb through the blood on her fingers, transfixed by the texture as well as the color, it appears. She brings two fingers to her face, where she runs them across the apple of her cheek, marking her skin in the enemy's blood.

I'm suddenly parched, but no fluid can quench this thirst, for what I desire is far more precious than a simple swallow. Seeing Emeline painted this way does something to me, something I've never felt before—not even with my wife.

I want Emeline in ways I should not.

"I've dreamt of this day," she whispers, looking at Aethelwulf. "For each and every time you forced yourself on me, humiliated me, I wished for your demise. But now that it is within reach, I see that no matter how much you suffer, it will never be enough.

"I could kill you ten thousand times, and I would never tire of feeling the life drain from your body. You are weak. Nothing but a coward walking in his father's shadow. I curse thee, and soon, you'll be nothing but a forgotten memory."

The worst form of punishment to deliver to a dying man as Aethelwulf's fight would have been for nothing.

"Guards!" Aethelwulf screams, twisting violently. He senses his time on this earth is coming to a close.

Emeline laughs, a maniacal cackle that fuses with my perversion.

"It's time you made peace with your God," Emeline says, and with poise, she gently reaches for the blade which hangs from my belt.

"Are you sure?" I ask because killing a man changes you. Some for good, some for the bad. But when I see the twinkle in Emeline's eye, I know this is the moment she was born to live.

This will transform Emeline into the warrior I always knew she was destined to become.

"Yes," she replies, blade in hand. "No one will kill him but me."

I understand her completely because Aethelwulf's life is hers. No one shall end it, for she earned the right to destroy him as he has done to her.

Arching his head back farther, I expose his neck to her, a gruesome offering only someone as macabre as me can appreciate. And Emeline does.

"Oh, Skarth." She sighs breathlessly, her eyes dropping to half-mast. "You offer me such a delightful gift I'll forever be grateful for."

My insides clench, and Odin strike me down, but I want to make Emeline mine. In the blood of our enemy, I want to fuck her.

"Once I am done with you," she says, lowering her lips to Aethelwulf's, "I shall bestow the same fate to your beloved wife. Fare thee well, sweet husband. 'Tis most splendid delight."

She kisses him softly, coating her mouth with his blood. She seals his fate in a blood-soaked kiss.

With her lips still pressed to his, she pushes the tip of the blade into his throat. His eye bulges open as she swallows his screams of pain.

My cock instantly hardens at this morbid sight.

Just as Emeline runs the blade across his throat, the door bursts open, and who I see changes the course of everything forevermore.

"Skarth," Sigrith says, her blue eyes filling with tears. "I knew you'd come."

She closes the door and runs over, hugging me as best she can. I won't let go of Aethelwulf, but my grip on him loosens because my body has gone into shock.

"Sigrith? It's really you?"

"Yes…brother, it is me."

"Brother?" Emeline gasps, the realization of the situation hitting her hard. She yanks her bloody hand away from Aethelwulf, who has passed out. He still breathes, however.

"Yes, Emeline," Sigrith says, smiling broadly. "I knew he would come. When you spoke of your brave Northman, I knew it was my brother. So, I waited. I endured their punishments because I knew he would come for me."

Emeline's fire simmers when she hears Sigrith's words, for she believes her. I do not wish to hurt my sister, whom I've searched years for, but she is not the reason I'm here. Nonetheless, I am so thankful that she is.

Aethelwulf drops to the ground with a thud as I drop him and embrace my sister warmly. I will never let her go. I inhale her deeply—how I've missed her smell.

"Are you all right?"

"Yes, brother, I am now."

Putting her out at arm's length, I take her in. "How you've grown. What are you doing here?"

When she averts her gaze, I realize she, too, has been forced to do things that have changed her forever. "Have you found Mother? And what of our brother, Knud?"

My stomach drops as a small part of me had hoped she would know where Mother is. "No, I have not. But come, we must go now. We will find her. I promise you. We will find them both."

Our brother became a recluse once he lost his vision, which was another reason I proceeded on this quest for justice.

"I know you will. You are Skarth the Godless. You can do anything."

A shadow overtakes Emeline, cloaking her passion and siphoning her vivacity. I don't know why.

When Aethelwulf groans, I realize we must go, and we must go now. But our luck, it appears, has come to an end when the door opens and two of the king's guards appear.

Pushing Sigrith aside, I don't give them a chance to call out for help as I reach for my sword and brutally attack.

Instantly, they fend me off, fighting for their lives, but nothing will stand in my way. It may be two against one, but I won't be defeated. It's a flurry of swords, but these fools have no heart behind their strikes.

They fight with their heads, not their hearts, which makes them easy to read. And when one guard lunges for me, I spin and thrust my sword into his side. He drops to the ground, gasping for air. I don't give him the chance to recover before I drive my sword into the base of his neck.

The other guard realizes he soon will end up like his comrade, and just as he opens his mouth, crying out for help, I slice my sword through the air and take his head clean off. It rolls along the floor.

The clash of swords is soon replaced with an eerie silence, and when I catch my breath, taking in my surroundings, I see why that is.

I've just made a monumental mistake—one which will haunt me for the rest of my days.

"Who will you choose?" Aethelwulf wheezes as he holds both Emeline and Sigrith by the arms. "Whose life means more to you?"

They struggle against him, but both know if one escapes, the other will suffer when he takes her life.

Aethelwulf's blade is within reach, and even though he is wounded, he will ensure he doesn't go down without a fight.

I look at Emeline, who nods.

She can take him on, but when I hear the unmissable pounding footsteps of the approaching army, we both realize it's too late. I can only save one.

She lowers her eyes, the fight in her dying, for she understands the decision I face. Do I save her? Or my sister?

"Skarth, please," Sigrith pleads, confused as to why we're still here. This decision should be an easy one. But it's not.

"Save her," Emeline says, and when she looks at the blade, she makes clear what she intends to do. She'd rather end her own life than remain a prisoner.

But I cannot allow it. Whatever decision I make, I will regret for all of my days.

"I command thee!" Emeline exclaims, eyes wide as she orders me to obey her. "Take your sister and leave this place. It's what you sacrificed your life for."

I did, but everything is different now. When I made that promise, I wasn't besotted with a princess who set my world on fire from the first moment we met. I cannot live with her death on my conscience, for if Emeline dies...I perish as well.

I do not wish to exist in a world where she does not.

The footsteps are right outside the door, so with no other choice, I run for Aethelwulf. He shoves Sigrith toward me, holding Emeline as he desperately reaches for his knife. The moment he presses the tip into her throat, I am possessed by a force I've never experienced before.

She doesn't fight him. She welcomes her fate, eyes locked with mine.

"No!" I scream, pushing Sigrith aside as nothing, *no one*, will stand in my way.

When a trickle of blood stains Emeline's porcelain skin, a rage bursts from me, and I attack Aethelwulf with utter ferocity. I fight with a passion that blinds me as I make a critical error and wound him, not kill him as I stab him in the thigh, missing his stomach.

The blade to Emeline's throat tumbles to the floor, but it doesn't make a difference because when the door bursts open, I know we're outnumbered.

Sigrith's screams will haunt me forever, and when I see her being captured by two guards, I beg for forgiveness. "I'm sorry. I will come back. I promise you."

"Skarth? Skarth, no!" she cries, fighting against her captors. "Please don't leave me here. Please! I'd rather you kill me than leave me here! Kill me. Send me to Valhalla! Please."

But that is something I cannot do.

When a guard charges for Emeline, I elbow him in the nose and seize her by the arm.

"No!" she screams, fighting me ferociously. "You will do what I command! Take Sigrith. You will do what I say!"

This isn't her choice, however. It is mine, one which I will be forced to live with.

"When do I follow orders, Princess?" I state, shoving her toward the window.

The guards tend to Aethelwulf, who is bleeding profusely, but he shrugs them away. "Don't let them leave here alive!"

Meeting his stare, I promise here, now, that his days are numbered. His life is mine.

Sigrith's hollowed cries for help cut me deeply, but when the guards charge for Emeline and me, I have to act—I must stand by my choice and deal with the consequences.

"Forgive me, Sigrith."

She slumps to the ground, defeated, sobbing uncontrollably when she realizes the choice I've made. "I will never forgive you for this."

"Good, as I will never forgive myself either."

The sight of my sister broken is what animates me to tear this kingdom and its people to the ground. However, now I have another battle on my hands.

Emeline shakes her head when I glare at her as I know she won't come willingly.

"Do not fight me," I sternly warn. "Let us go."

But she stubbornly breaks free.

She picks up a fallen sword, prepared to fight her way through the guards, but she will lose. I won't allow this to be in vain.

Punching a guard in the face, I bend low and pick Emeline

up, tossing her over my shoulder. She kicks and screams, flailing madly, her fists pounding my back, but she's not going anywhere.

I mount the window ledge, but a sharp sting suddenly takes my breath away. I ignore it, and without haste, I jump into the gardens below. The drop is steep, but I don't stop to recover. With Emeline still thrown over my shoulder, I run through the grounds, sword in hand.

Guards scurry from every corner of the palace, but nothing will stop me. I fight for my, for *our* lives, fending off every *bacraut* who blocks my path.

It's a flurry of violence, and all I see is red as I annihilate the enemy. I cut off arms, legs, heads. Nothing is off-limits because when the main gate is within sight, victory lingers on my tongue. But that soon sours, and all I taste is defeat when the portcullis drops, sealing us in.

"*Sorðinn!*" I curse, slicing a guard in half as he charges for me.

I suddenly am weak on my feet, but I cannot stop.

"Turn around!" Emeline orders, and for once, I do as I'm told. "Go to the gardens. There is a postern hidden there."

A back door is our savior, and determination drives me as I fight my way through dozens of men. More only seem to take their place, and before long, we are surrounded.

"Put me down! I can fight!" Emeline screams, twisting violently as she attempts to pry a sword from the hand of the man I just killed.

I know she can fight. I taught her. But the thought of any harm coming to her has me resisting.

"Skarth, we will die!" she cries, begging I see reason. "This cannot have been for nothing. I refuse to accept that fate."

"If anything happens to you—" I can't bring myself to finish that sentence. I can't.

"Nothing will happen to me because you taught me how to be a warrior," she says desperately. "You taught me to never surrender. Better to die on my feet fighting than crawling on my belly in fear. Being on your back this way...I am worse than being on my belly.

"Don't take this away from me. Do not treat me like a little girl, for I am not. I am *hugrekki*. Your *hugrekki*."

My head and heart battle for what I know is right and what I want to do, contest in hopes of conquering the other. But she is right.

Being on my back this way is robbing her of a right she earned. This is her fight. These animals deserve to suffer by her hand. And hearing her speak in my tongue...I am helpless to deny her anything.

Lowering her to the ground, I pick up a sword and toss it to her. She catches it with a cunning grin.

"Try to keep up."

She charges for a guard, ducking and weaving how I taught her before driving her sword through his stomach without remorse. He collapses onto the ground face-first.

She doesn't bask in her victory. She simply fights another man who dares to take her on. She offers me her strength, and a new lease on life is breathed into me as I fight alongside my *hugrekki*.

We are unstoppable, fighting anything that moves. We slowly edge toward the gardens, and once behind the walls, I make eye contact with Emeline.

She is slathered in a thick layer of blood, her hair loose. In battle, I've never seen such beauty until this day. She belongs here on the battlefield, for this is her home, and at this moment, I realize I am lost to her.

I once believed I never would belong to anyone, but Emeline has changed that. I am hers…I always have been.

Gesturing with her chin toward the thick shrubbery to indicate the postern is there, she interrupts my thoughts, thoughts I need to mute. They can never come to fruition, for I am a married man.

Focusing on what I know, I attack and kill anyone who stands in my way. The palace is a frenzy, and it pleases me that both Emeline and I are the cause of the mayhem. If I had more time, I'd burn this fucking place to the ground.

But this is just the start of things to come…

Emeline ducks low, stabbing a guard in the back as she runs for the postern. I follow but am once again unsteady on my feet, so much so, I reach out to balance myself against the wall. My vision blurs, and I clutch my side as it suddenly burns.

When I pull my hand away and see it covered in blood, I realize the sharp sting I felt before jumping from the window was a sword piercing my side. I was running on fury, the adrenaline masking the pain, but now that the end is within grasp, I'm running on fumes.

"Skarth!" Emeline cries, fending off attackers as she attempts to slice through the undergrowth with her sword.

A guard takes advantage of my weakened state and charges for me, sword ready for a kill strike.

With the last shred of strength I possess, I elbow him aside and pierce him with my sword. He collapses with a hollowed thud.

The ground is now painted red—a sight that helps me focus.

Blood seeps from me, and I know I'm moments away from passing out. But I persevere because I won't leave her here alone to fend off the wolves.

I kill countless men to get to her, and when I do, I have to touch her to make sure she's all right.

"Let us go. Now!" she shouts, the clashing of swords echoing against the palace walls.

She shoulders open the door as we fight our way through it. Any man who dares follow suffers the same bloody, violent fate. Once we are outside the castle walls, we both push against the door, fighting an influx of guards to keep them from flowing free.

"Skarth? Are you all right?" Emeline looks at me when she notices me struggling to breathe.

"Fine, Princess. However, I will be better when we are free of this place."

She doesn't press because I take her hand when the door slams shut, and we run faster than our feet can keep up.

"Where are we going?"

I've told Emeline that friends await us, but she doesn't know who.

My energy is depleting with each step I take, but I don't let Emeline know that. I lead her through the thick foliage to where our allies wait. The castle bell tolls, alerting villagers to be on the lookout for fugitives.

We need to hurry.

I knew this would happen, but I thought we'd have a head start. Now, we will have everyone looking for us. With limited allies, our chances of staying hidden are slim. I'm angry with myself for failing. I don't fail. I'm Skarth the Godless, but we will pay the price for my impatience.

I just wanted to protect her...

"Lord Robert!" Emeline gasps, alerting me that we've finally found sanctuary.

"Oh, Princess. You are safe."

She rushes toward him, throwing herself in his arms as he embraces her tightly.

"Lord, you are most holy. I thank thee for keeping her safe."

Sister Ethelyn appears, holding a hooded cloak for Emeline as she thanks her God.

Emeline bursts into tears.

"I thought you said to be discreet," Raedwulf says, guiding three horses through the dense landscape.

These allies are ones I trust with my life because we share one common factor—our love for Princess Emeline. She's the only reason we're working together. If this were for anyone but her, they would have me hung for treason.

Although I know Raedwulf harbors romantic feelings for Emeline, I have to put the urge to murder him aside because I know he will do anything to protect her. I need a man like that on my side, regardless of the fact that I want to gouge out his eyeballs for looking at Emeline the way he does.

"Where do you propose we go? Wessex will be swarming with guards and villagers wishing to please the king with our capture."

"There is no need for you to tell me what I already know," I snarl, wavering on my feet.

The action doesn't go unnoticed by Raedwulf. But I don't give him a chance to speak.

"We ride far away from here. We don't stop until it's safe," I instruct, clucking my tongue at the majestic white horse.

He instantly comes at my command.

"That's your plan?" Raedwulf doesn't mask his disgust, and I don't hide my annoyance that he's still speaking.

Mounting the horse, Emeline instantly walks toward me. I don't miss Raedwulf's disappointment that she's opted to ride with me.

Offering her my hand, she accepts, but the moment I help her onto the horse, she notices my blood staining the horse's white coat.

"Skarth!" she cries, attempting to examine my wound.

I don't have the power to fight her. I don't have the strength for anything. That's evident when I finally surrender to the darkness and slip into the shadows for good.

# NINE

*Princess Emeline*

haven't left his side. I cannot.

All I can see is my brave Northman, sliding off the horse and tumbling to the ground with a brutal thud.

I am angry with myself for not seeing the signs. He wasn't himself when we fought for our lives. I believed fatigue was the cause, but I now know it was because he was wounded when trying to save me.

That's all he's ever done.

He came to Wessex, knowing the consequences. He defied my father. He left his wife. He did all this to rescue me. Usually, I would not appreciate such a gesture as I don't need any man to come to my aid. But with Skarth, it's different.

And that's because I've saved him too.

We are equal, something I've never been. That was evident when we fought alongside one another. Skarth and I trusted each other, and we got out of the palace—together.

But I failed him.

For he has remained unconscious for three days—the longest three days of my life.

"Why won't you wake?" I whisper, dabbing his sweaty brow with a damp piece of cloth.

His body is burning up, and I fear infection has set in. I clean his wound with herbs I picked in the herbarium, but nothing seems to help. His condition only worsens.

We rode as far away from Wessex as we could, but with Skarth wounded, we needed to find sanctuary somewhere. And when we came upon a small monastery, we had no other choice but to ask for refuge.

The monks didn't want any trouble, especially when they saw we rode with a Northman, but Sister Ethelyn promised we wouldn't cause them any harm. It helped we rode with a servant of the Lord, but I know they watch us closely.

Even though our quarters are underground in the cold, dark cellarium, I'm thankful we have a place to stay. A fire keeps us warm, but Skarth still shivers, even though he has a fever.

"It's not much," Raedwulf says, offering me a bowl of clear broth. "But you have to eat, Emeline. I know you are worried, but there is no use in both of you being sick."

"Thank you." I accept the bowl, but when my nauseous stomach turns the moment I smell the food, I set it aside.

This has nothing to do with the broth the monks prepared, but rather the fact that I am sick to my stomach with worry. I can't do anything but keep vigil by Skarth's side. I pray for a miracle because that's what we need.

Raedwulf sighs but doesn't push.

He sits near me, offering me comfort by gently rubbing my arm. "He's strong. This will pass. Skarth the Godless does not die in the house of the Lord. He will wake."

I know he's trying to offer me words of encouragement, but they are words he does not believe as Skarth's condition only worsens. The wound to his side was deep. I believe it may have punctured an organ. Or maybe two. I don't know. I'm no physician. I'm just a princess who can't seem to stay out of trouble.

"Princess—" Raedwulf starts, and I know why he suddenly pauses. "We cannot stay here for much longer. Wessex Guard will be looking for us. We put everyone at risk."

"If you wish to leave, Raedwulf, then please do what you must. But I'm not going anywhere. Until Skarth awakens, I will remain here."

"And what if he does not?"

The fire crackles warmly, filling the empty silence.

"He must," I reply, broken beyond words.

Reaching out with trembling fingers, I gently brush the

long hair from his brow.

Seeing Skarth unguarded is a rare thing, and I take a moment to admire the man who has my heart. Even on his deathbed, he takes my breath away. He isn't sickly. He still radiates strength. His jaw is covered in a thicker beard, but it's soft and groomed as Skarth takes pride in his appearance. He always has.

The ink markings on his skin still mesmerize me even though I've looked at them countless times. I trace my finger along his *Aegishjalmr*, transfixed by everything it represents.

We are so different—worlds apart—but for some reason, destiny had us meet. It can't end this way. This can't have been for nothing. Valhalla will have to wait, for he cannot leave this earth without me telling him, just once…that I love him.

I know he is wed, and no matter my feelings, that doesn't change who we are. I, a Saxon, and he, a Northman. We don't belong together. But regardless, I need him to know that doesn't make a difference, for I will never feel for another as I do for him.

A tear trickles down my cheek, but I quickly wipe it away with the back of my hand. "I hate that he's so still."

Skarth doesn't rest. Seeing him this way just feels so unnatural.

"Princess, please, if you will not eat, then you must rest." Looking up, I see Sister Ethelyn standing close by. I didn't even hear her enter.

"I cannot do either," I confess sadly. "How can I when

Skarth lies wounded?"

"I understand. But he would not want you to sit here, pining for him. He also would not want you to get sick yourself."

She's right.

"I suppose I do need to stretch my legs. But only for a moment."

Coming to a stand, I stretch the fatigue from my bones as my body whines in protest. I dither on my feet, for I have barely eaten or drunk. Raedwulf gently wraps his arm around me, silently offering support.

"I will escort thee, Princess."

I allow him to guide me because I fear if it were up to me, I would just turn back around and return to sitting by Skarth's side.

The monastery is quiet as everyone is asleep.

There is a peace within these walls, and I wish we could stay here forever, but Raedwulf is right. Our time here is running out, and I know the longer we stay, the more danger we put ourselves and the monks in. If they're found to be harboring outlaws, monks or not, they will be punished.

King Egbert won't stop until he finds me. He sees me as his property. However, Aethelwulf won't stop until he gets his revenge for what we did.

I think of Sigrith and how she must suffer for our sins. I also think about how Skarth chose me over her. I know when he wakes, he will never forgive himself for that choice, which is why he must wake and soon so we can rescue Sigrith.

I will not leave her behind.

It's cool out, and I huddle into Raedwulf's side. He will be out of favor with my brother and the king for being here. He will be seen as defying the king's order. I fear that his fate is as dire as mine.

We enter the lush green gardens, and being under the night sky does soothe me. Peering upward, I take a moment to bask in the twinkling of stars. I am a mere speck in the greater scheme of things, and I wish I could just fade away.

But I'll never have that luxury for as long as I live.

I don't know what faces me because I don't belong anywhere. I'm a traitor to both Wessex and Northumbria, so I don't have the protection of either king. Everything is just a mess.

"Thank you, Raedwulf. You have risked your life for me. This isn't the first time, however."

He was the one who came for me when I was locked away in the dungeons. And I thanked him by knocking him out cold.

"You are welcome, Emeline. But wanting to protect you comes instinctively to me."

His candid confession stuns me.

I attempt to gently pull out of our embrace, but he doesn't let me go. He puts me out at arm's length.

"I do not care about your past," he says, his blue eyes twinkling under the starlight. "I wish for your happiness…and I hope you'll consider that happiness to be with me."

I stare at him, mouth agape, unable to speak.

"It is no secret that I have been in love with you"—he clears his throat—"that I love you. And I want you to be my wife."

I still don't know what to say.

I'm flattered and incredibly touched, but I do not think of Raedwulf in that way. "Raedwulf, I—"

But he doesn't let me finish.

He tightens his hold, his desperation showing. "I understand now is not the time to discuss this, but I need you to know why I am here. When Skarth came to me, I did not care about the consequences. You are worth them, Emeline. It's always been you.

"I will fight your brother and father to protect you. I do not care about the cost. I ask for your hand in marriage, and I promise to honor and protect thee for all the days of my life."

This is what every girl wishes for. A good, honorable man proposing marriage. Regardless of my past, regardless that I am no longer pure, Raedwulf does not care.

He is handsome, there is no question about it, and I know many ladies at court would kill for such a proposal, but I will not insult Raedwulf by accepting. He deserves someone who wishes to return the devotion, and that is not me.

He reads my silence as shock.

"Take your time, my dereworthy darling. I do not expect an answer right away." He kisses the back of my hand.

Marrying Raedwulf would be the sensible choice, for my

past makes me spoiled goods. But I would rather remain a single woman than marry for convenience or because it's the practical thing to do.

"I am touched, kind lord." I curtsey in gratitude, unsure what else to say or do.

The freedom I once felt being out here under the night sky has gone.

"Are you cold, Princess?"

Raedwulf rubs my arms, mistaking the tremor racking my body as a chill caused by the cool breeze.

"Yes, a little."

His hands on me feel so wrong as his touch doesn't set me alight. But I don't make a fuss as I do not wish to wound Raedwulf. He has professed his love and his intent to marry me, so I will not hurt him by pushing him away.

Raedwulf draws me into him, wrapping his arm around my shoulders. "Let us go back inside."

I don't argue and allow him to escort me back.

Once I enter the cellarium, the tension eases as it always does when being in proximity to Skarth. I look at Sister Ethelyn with hope, hope that a miracle occurred and Skarth has awakened, but she shakes her head with regret.

I gently unfold myself from Raedwulf's arms and make my way over to Skarth. Dropping to my knees, I stare at my Northman, wishing to see any changes in his condition.

There are none.

He looks to be lost to a deep sleep.

Sister Ethelyn reaches for my hand, squeezing gently. "All we can do is pray."

"How can I pray to a God he does not believe in?" I question, beseeching she give me the answers I so desperately seek. "For is he not a sinner in the eyes of our Lord?"

Sister Ethelyn bows her head in servitude. "The Lord works in mysterious ways, Princess. Trust in Him for you are a devout servant and He is most merciful. He sees the sacrifices you make in the name of the Lord and the king.

"He will offer you His strength when you are depleted. But you must not give up on Him, as He will never give up on you."

Her words offer me some comfort, but it's difficult to believe in Him when all He seems to do is test me every chance He gets. This is just another hardship. However, it's one I'm unsure I will survive.

Sister Ethelyn leaves me alone with Skarth as she retires for the evening. She too has risked so much for me. They all have.

Lord Robert stands guard inside the monastery walls, watching for any threats. He barely sleeps or eats as he risks his life to protect me, just how he always has done. We are all traitors to our kingdom.

"How can He be merciful when all He does is take?" I question aloud, not expecting an answer.

Raedwulf sighs heavily before taking his position near the fire. He lies on the ground, drawing a fur over him for warmth.

He won't leave me unattended.

Skarth's chest rises and falls steadily, confirming that regardless of his motionless state, life flows through his veins. That life force has always sung to mine. I want to feel it.

Raedwulf's back is turned, but even if it wasn't, I would still act this way. I lower myself onto the ground and pull back the furs which cover Skarth. He only wears trousers. The fire licks at his bronzed flesh, almost setting it alight.

Fatigue suddenly cripples me, and I give in to temptation, nestling into Skarth's side. Tucking the furs around us, I place my arm over his chest and curl up beside him, inhaling his earthy scent. Basking in the heat from his soul.

A comfort I've not felt before overwhelms me, and I realize that Skarth and I fit in every sense of the word. A small sigh slips past his lips, and I wonder, wherever he's lost to, if he can feel this too?

This sense of coming home.

I close my eyes, slipping into a slumber as deeply as the man I love.

It's light when I wake, and I am refreshed. It feels like it's the first proper sleep I've had in years.

Raedwulf has arisen, so he would have seen me curled up

beside Skarth. A pang of guilt stabs at me, for I know the sight would have wounded him. But I don't want him to believe in something that is not there.

Yawning, I sit up and stretch overhead. My sore muscles whine in protest. "Hurry and wake," I impishly say to Skarth. "For my body cannot take another night sleeping on this cold floor."

His cheeks appear to have a little more color.

"I'll be back soon. I need to freshen up." And after speaking with Sister Ethelyn yesterday, there is something else I must do.

Rearranging the furs around Skarth, I wrap a cloak around my shoulders and slip into my shoes as I fear snow is coming. The monastery is quiet because at first light, the monks spend their time saying prayer or reading text.

I believe it's too early for morning Mass just yet, which is why I quietly make my way toward the chapel once I have washed and redressed. This is on the north side of the monastery as it does not block the sun from reaching the cloister.

Everything has a place and purpose here. I can't help but wonder what mine is.

When I enter the chapel, I see that although not donned in gold and jewels, its worth is priceless. The large wooden crucifix sitting on the altar is a beacon of hope for us all. I'm alone, which I'm thankful for as I would like some time alone with my God.

Genuflecting before the altar, I slide across the pew and

instantly drop to my knees, interlacing my hands. A stained glass window allows the morning light to send arcs of color across the room, and it gives me hope that not everything is shrouded in shades of blackness.

"Lord God most holy, Lord most mighty, holy and most merciful savior, deliver us from the bitter pains of eternal death," I whisper under my breath. "Banish the demons which plague me, for I am your dutiful servant.

"I promise to forever be in your service if you grant me this kindness. Skarth is not your child, but he is...he is so important to me. I am supercilious for asking such a favor, but please, kind, loving Lord, please let him wake.

"Please guide him toward the light, not the darkness, for I will perish without him. I will do anything you ask. Just tell me what it is. I will sacrifice everything for him for I...love him."

I lower my head as I know the sacrilegious act I've just committed by confessing to loving a Northman. But I wish to confess it all, so He will see just how much I'm willing to sacrifice. I will accept any punishment He deems fit for my subversion.

And when a bell tolls loudly, it seems He believes my punishment should be delivered sooner rather than later.

The commotion outside can mean only one thing.

"Princess, you must hide!" Raedwulf cries, bursting into the church where I pray.

Standing quickly, I meet him down the aisle, where his grip

on my shoulders hints that whatever faces us is dire.

"What faces us?"

"Northmen," Raedwulf replies, his eyes darting around the room, desperate for a place to hide me. "And many of them."

But we both know there is no hiding from the Northmen. They are here for riches, in any form they can find.

Breaking free from Raedwulf's hold, I run from the church as I cannot leave Skarth unguarded. He cannot defend himself, and although he's a Northman, he's seen as a traitor for abandoning his people to side with the Saxon king.

They will take great pleasure in killing him.

Monks flurry in every direction, and my heart breaks, for they mean no one any harm. They only wish to live in peace and follow the word of the Lord. They are simple people, and now their blood will stain this holy ground.

But I cannot allow it.

"Princess! Emeline! Don't thee dare!"

I ignore Raedwulf's pleas and make haste toward the gatehouse where Lord Robert stands on guard. He is the only one protecting this place of worship. I won't allow him to sacrifice his life for me.

"Princess!" he exclaims. "You should not be here."

"Nor should you, Lord Robert," I reply, standing my ground as the army of Northmen approaches us in the distance. "I cannot allow them to harm him. I cannot allow them to harm any of you."

Some are on horseback while others are on foot. Their army stands strong and firm. We don't stand a chance.

"Offer them the heathen. His head is far more valuable than relics which hold no wealth," Raedwulf orders, but that will not be happening.

Lord Robert waits for my command, but I shake my head.

"Emeline! Do not be stupid. We will die. And for what? For a Northman? I cannot allow it."

"You do not allow anything. This decision is mine to make," I reply, my gaze never wavering from the Northman formation. They move with precision and skill—no wonder no army but one led by their own can defeat them.

I'm almost hypnotized by the sight because I've never seen so many Northmen before. They draw closer and closer, and clutching the crucifix around my throat, I take my first step toward the unknown.

Lord Robert and Raedwulf follow, but they stay behind me, for I will not be stopped. The Northmen are close.

"Princess, if you do not retreat, they will slaughter us all."

"Then make peace with your God, Raedwulf, for I will not surrender."

I escort the men into the grassy knolls, where I come to a stop. The Northmen approach, and my attention is riveted on the impressive man who rides a white horse. I take a guess that he is their leader.

Skarth has told me stories of his people and their curious

nature, so I have faith interest will override greed. I have faith this Northman will want to know why a young woman dares to stand in his way.

"They will kill us." Raedwulf's cowardness just confirms I could never marry him. I would rather die on my feet than live on my belly—words I'll die by.

I stand tall, the wind rustling my hair as I do not waver. I dare not breathe as the Northman gets closer and closer. The horses' hooves vibrate all the way to my very core, and the energy I feel at being faced with impending death excites me.

The Northman does not slow down. And I do not tremble in fear as I meet his sharp blue eyes.

Raedwulf flees, his frantic footsteps reverberating in the grass. I don't blame him for being afraid. Lord Robert doesn't leave me, however. He was born for battle, as was I.

The assembly of men and women is vast. Their faces are painted unforgivingly, prepared to scare the enemy into defeat. But I know this is a war tactic the Northmen use, so I continue to stand strong. Their colorful shields are raised as they are ready for battle, but when their leader raises his sword toward the heavens, pulling back his horse, they soon cease-fire—for now.

The man clucks his tongue, his horse obeying and slowing to a trot. He stops when a few feet away.

He does not speak.

Nor do I.

I take a moment to study him.

His long blond hair is cut and styled similarly to Skarth's, but it is lighter in color. His face is sharp. His eyes incredibly blue. His full lips appear quite pink because of the dirt slathered on his skin.

Openly staring at a strange man is quite unladylike, but I won't submit. If this man wants to kill me, then let him look me in the eyes when he does.

"Is there a reason you stand in my way?" he asks with an accent akin to Skarth's.

Swallowing down my nerves, I nod. "I will not allow you to harm anyone inside the monastery's walls."

The man cocks his head to the side before a deep rumble spills from him.

"Allow me?" he challenges with a crooked smirk. "How do you propose to stop me?"

He is trying to intimidate me, but I cannot back down. "By the order of the king, I demand thee leave."

"The king?" he scoffs, turning over his shoulder and laughing joyously with his assembly. "I plan on paying him a visit after we leave here. I will be sure to pass on your well wishes."

"Mock me, Northman," I state, pulling back my shoulders. "But I am the Princess of Northumbria, and you, merely an ignorant heathen. You do not scare me."

"Princess," Lord Robert warns under his breath, for he

knows what I've just done.

"Princess?" the Northman says, his interest instantly piqued as I knew it would be. "You are far from home."

"You are right. I am. I was once the future Queen of Wessex, but now"—I swallow down my disgust for this is the only way to save him—"now…I am the king's whore."

A gasp leaves Lord Robert as he was not aware of my situation, and his surprise is what proves to the Northman that I speak the truth.

"I have escaped the palace. The king's guard hunts me. I am worth far more than any riches you'll find within the monastery walls. Take me in exchange for the lives of the innocent men whose only fault was granting me sanctuary."

The Northman weighs over what I shared.

"Ulf, no," says a warrior woman behind him. She is beyond beautiful, but I don't mistake her beauty for meekness. "Kill her and be done with it."

But with eyes locked on the Northman leader, Ulf, I know he won't kill me—yet.

With grace, he dismounts the horse and closes the distance between us. I remain calm.

He towers over me, not just in height but in physique as well. If not for the fact that my life is in danger being in his presence, I would say he is quite comely, even with the large scar running down his left cheek. But I know better than to let that affect my judgment.

"Indeed, you do not fear me. You have been around my people before?"

*This* is what I fear. I cannot let him know Skarth is the reason I do not cower.

"Northman, you are called monsters, but I have looked into the eyes of evil, and yours do not compare."

"I don't believe you," he challenges, folding his arms across his broad chest. "I think you have learned the way of our world, for I have never met a Saxon who didn't fear us."

I need to think quickly, which is why I remove my cloak. Ulf watches with interest as I lower the top of my dress and turn my back so he can see the scars my brother left.

"Courtesy of my brother who threatened to degrade me in other ways if I did not submit to his cruel ways."

Lord Robert's jaw clenches as this is the first time he's seen the true extent of my brother's malice.

In case Ulf needs more proof, I turn around to face him once again and pull up the hem of my dress to my knees so he can see my shins.

"And these"—I say, showing him the jagged scars on my legs—"are thanks to my husband at the time who broke my legs to stop me from escaping."

I don't want pity, so I drop my hem.

"And there are others scars, ones which you cannot see, for he is buried in an unmarked grave. He was taken before he had a chance to live." I sniff back my tears.

The once turbulent field is now quiet, for my confession has stunned them into silence.

Ulf appears to digest everything I've shared. I hope it's enough because if he decides to storm the monastery, the blood spilled will be on my hands.

But a miracle suddenly occurs…

"All right, Princess. You have a deal."

The woman who objected curls her lip, disgusted with the trade. But Ulf doesn't allow her abhorrence to change his mind.

"I will spare the life of these people and leave their sanctuary intact. But if I find out you are lying…I will come back and torture them in ways that would have them wishing I'd killed them the first time we met. Do you understand?"

"Yes, I do." I will agree to anything to keep them, to keep *him*, safe.

Lord Robert steps forward but knows he's no match for the army of Northmen. "I will find you, Princess. I promise."

The truth is, neither of us knows what I'll face. But at least I leave here without any bloodshed. "Thank you, Lord Robert. Go back to Northumbria. My father will show you clemency, for you were always his favorite, as you are mine."

The brave guard nods with tears in his kind eyes.

I wait for a command, as Ulf is now my master. I promised I'd never submit to any man, but to save the life of the man I love, I'm now, yet again, a prisoner.

A boorish man appears, gripping my arm as he snaps a

metal collar around my neck. I don't fight him. I allow him to shackle me. His touch is cruel, but something else is behind Ulf's inquisitive eyes, something I can't quite place.

The man threads a rope through the hoop on the collar and drags me toward his horse. "Let's go...*Princess*," he mocks, mounting his horse as I remain shackled by his side.

Taking one last look at the monastery, with a beam of light breaking through the thick clouds and shining down onto the cellarium's roof, I walk with pride toward the unknown.

# TEN

*Skarth the Godless*

"Emeline!"

Jolting upright, I frantically search the unfamiliar room for her, but she's nowhere to be found. I have no idea where I am.

The last thing I remember was…

*"Why won't you wake?"*

We made it out alive—just. But the injury I sustained; it was too much. I lost so much blood, which is why I'm here, wherever here is.

Peering down at my side, I see it's wrapped in cloth. Only Emeline would care enough to tend to me this way. I need to find her.

Just as I attempt to stand, Sister Ethelyn enters and rushes over to help.

"I do not need your help," I snarl, but she doesn't listen as she wraps her arm around my waist, offering me support. "Where are we?"

Once I'm on my feet, I gently shrug free.

Sister Ethelyn wrings her hands in front of her. "Clones Monastery."

"We're still in Wessex?"

When she nods, I curse under my breath. "*Skitr*. Where is the princess?"

Sister Ethelyn grips the crucifix around her neck.

"Where is she?" I repeat dangerously low.

"She's gone. Your people took her." It's Raedwulf who replies as he enters these dark, dank chambers.

"If you do not explain yourself, I will rip that useless tongue from your throat," I warn Raedwulf. He is no use to me if he doesn't have the information I seek.

Lord Robert follows Raedwulf, a broken man. "She sacrificed herself for our well-being," he explains, carrying more wood for the fire. "The Northmen were going to raid, but Emeline offered them herself in exchange for our safe passage."

"And you allowed it?"

"I am sure you know we do not allow anything when the princess is involved," he corrects because Emeline cannot be controlled—something I adore about her. But not when her safety is at stake.

"How many days ago?" I ask, long forgetting my injuries as I begin to dress.

"Two," Lord Robert replies. "She wanted us to return to Northumbria."

"I do not care what she wanted," I state, reaching for my sword. "What you decide to do is your choice. But I'm leaving here. Now."

"Wessex Guard will capture you. They have swarmed the countryside." Raedwulf is nothing but a coward.

"They can try," I reply, sheathing my sword onto my back, "but they will fail."

Sister Ethelyn crosses herself as she knows I will spill copious amounts of blood until I find Emeline. And I won't stop until I do. I've already wasted so much time.

I'm furious at myself for succumbing to illness. I won't let Emeline pay for my weakness.

"What did they look like? My people," I add, drawing a distinct line because with Emeline gone, we are no longer on the same side.

"Like you," Raedwulf spits, making his hate for me clear.

Lord Robert ignores him. "The leader was a young man. No older than you. He had a scar down his left cheek. They called him Ulf."

And just like that, the breath is stolen from me, and I'm not sure if it'll ever return.

"You know of him?"

"Yes, Lord Robert, I do." I don't elaborate further because finding Emeline has become even more important.

With that information in hand, I leave this place and make my way down the long, dark hallway in hopes of finding the exit and soon.

"Who is he?" Raedwulf questions, chasing after me. I don't stop.

When I see an archway that leads to a garden area, I quicken my step. "He is someone who should not be in possession of a princess."

"Why not?"

I ignore him because he should not have let Emeline leave here in the first place. I know she is stubborn and strong-willed, but Raedwulf should have done everything in his power to stop her.

He grips my wrist, attempting to stop me, but no one will.

Twisting his arm, I shove him against the wall, lowering my face inches from his. "Do not touch me. Ever," I caution, curling my lip as he pathetically attempts to fight me. "The time to show courage has come and gone. Now, I must do what you could not."

"Do not speak as if you are better than me. It's because of you we are in this position. Emeline would not leave without you. If we had, she'd be safe, and we'd be back in Northumbria, preparing to be wed."

I press my forearm across his throat, my temper rising. "What did you say?"

"Unhand me, heathen." When he attempts to break free, I only press down harder.

"Do not make me repeat myself. You will not like the consequences if I do."

He gasps for air as he replies, "Emeline has accepted my proposal of marriage. I will make an honest woman of her."

"She doesn't need a man for that," I state, eyeing him fiercely. "She is far too good for any man."

He snickers, proving me wrong. "She mustn't agree, for she was overjoyed at the prospect of being my wife."

It takes all my willpower not to choke the life from him, but if what he says is true, then Emeline would never forgive me. So, because of my affection for her, I let Raedwulf go.

He sags forward, clutching at his throat as he gulps in mouthfuls of air. I cannot believe Emeline would agree to marry this weakling.

"You should be ashamed you let the woman you're about to wed be taken."

But men like Raedwulf don't feel shame. They are given second chances in life because of their social standing. It does not matter that they are spineless fools. I'm the heathen, not them, for they are cultured and obey a fake God.

But I'm the one who will save Emeline from the hands of an animal—Ulf the Bloody…my once best friend.

Monks gasp and scurry when they see me, afraid I will exercise my reputation and paint this monastery with their blood. But there is only one whose blood I shall spill.

Ulf and I fought beside one another since I can remember. We were inseparable, as were our fathers. But that changed when King Egbert destroyed my family. I died on the battlefield alongside my father. Ulf wanted to fight together, but I knew we couldn't win.

We lost many men and women during battle, and without my father, the *Hersir,* which is equivalent to a king, I knew the only way to avenge his death and find my family was to surrender. Ulf and the remaining *Drengrs* saw it as weakness, as a warrior never acquiesces, but my father taught me battle comes in all different shapes and sizes.

This was the only way to win, for I would not allow his death to be in vain.

Ulf made clear that if I left, I would be the enemy, and he would hunt me as he would any Saxon. The only reason I still stand is because he could never beat me in battle. But now, that's changed.

Now that he has Emeline, I will do anything he wants.

I can only hope she does not reveal who I am to her, for mentioning me will not do her any favors. But she is smart. And Ulf has always been distracted by a pretty face.

Leaving Raedwulf before I go back on my word and rip out his throat, I quickly walk into the gardens and seek out the gatehouse. Monks stay out of my way, and although I am thankful they offered me sanctuary, I know they only did so because of who I was traveling with.

They will always look at me as a pagan, no matter that I willingly risk my life for one of their own.

"Skarth!" It's Sister Ethelyn who chases after me.

I stop because I know she will do anything to save Emeline.

"Take this," she says, placing her gold crucifix into my palm. "It was a gift from the king. It will help you negotiate for Emeline's return."

She's right. It's pure gold and encrusted with colorful jewels.

But I shake my head, closing my hand over hers. "I have something far more valuable."

"What could be more valuable than gold and that of a king?" Her green eyes widen, and although she's a child of her God, she is extremely pretty. It seems a waste she squanders that beauty on her God.

"Me," I reply with a slanted smirk. "I will trade my life for Emeline's. I am a bastard among my people and yours, Sister."

"Godspeed then, Skarth the Godless. I will pray for thee. Your horse waits for you by the gates."

I appreciate the gesture, but her prayers are wasted on me.

I go to turn, but she reaches out, gripping my arm softly. Her blonde hair, which has been cut short to obey her religion, catches the wind. Emeline told me the absence of a veil is a sign she is not yet fully ordained. And that is the reason she helps me.

She hasn't surrendered completely, for I believe she is rebellious at heart. Her being here, helping a pagan, is a sure sign of it.

"Bring her home," she says, pleading I don't fail. "You are the only one who can."

"I will, Sister Ethelyn."

She doesn't hide her surprise that I've referred to her in this way, acknowledging her position in the church. She watches as I make my way toward the gatehouse, where, as she said, my white horse awaits.

Lord Robert waits for me by the gate, and I know he wishes to come with me. But he cannot. If my people see him, they will kill him on sight. I am the only hope for saving Emeline.

Mounting the horse, I nod at Lord Robert in a silent promise to find Emeline and bring her home.

When I cluck my tongue, the steed doesn't need further command and breaks into a trot. I ride away from the monastery, unsure what faces me. What I am certain of is that come nightfall, I will find Emeline for I will follow the North Star.

# ELEVEN

*Princess Emeline*

"What's the matter, *Princess*, you don't like your new lodgings?"

Curling into a ball, I ignore their jibes because I will not let them break me.

This metal cage is my new home, it appears, for once I was unleashed, I was stripped almost bare, thrown into it, and locked away. It sits in the middle of the large wooden feasting hall on display for all the Viking clansmen and women to do with me what they please.

My chemise is soaked in piss, for the men thought I looked thirsty, and the only drink I was worthy of was from their cocks. The women aren't any better.

The freezing night air chills me to the bone as the fire provides me no warmth. It's so cold my teeth chatter, but I cannot show weakness. This is what they want. This is why they've thrown me into this prison cell.

But I've lived through far worse.

We've ridden for three days and came here, to where I believe is Ulf's kingdom.

Once belonging to Saxon people, Ulf and his men have made it their own. No more are Saxon structure. The farmlands flourish here, which is why I believe they chose this location. But they stole it. They killed whoever once lived here and took the land out from under them.

I now understand why they are feared and hated amongst my people. They *are* nothing but heathens, with no respect for anything holy. But Skarth, he is different. He is not like them. Even before I grew to know him, he was never a brute such as these men and women are.

However, Ulf appears different. He hasn't spoken a word to me since he captured me, but I see the way he watches me. He sits on his throne, observing his people drink and be merry, but he doesn't engage in the drunken, lewd acts.

He simply examines—how a mighty ruler should.

A large man with bright orange hair and a matching beard seems to have taken an interest in me, for he continues to walk past this cage, watching me like a hungry wolf. When I don't answer his many questions, he pokes me with the handle of his ax.

"Maybe she is stupid?" one man says as they stand in front of my cage.

"Or maybe she believes she's above us. Is that what it is, Princess? Do you believe you are better than us?"

When I remain silent, curled into a small ball, it seems the man's patience snaps. I hear the latch unlock and the door whine open. Cruel hands reach inside and brutally yank me out. I am no match for him, so I don't fight.

I allow him to drag me to my feet.

He fists my hair, arching my head back as he lowers his face to mine. "I can make you talk, Princess," he repulsively states, not masking how he intends to do that. "I can make you scream if I want to."

In response, I spit in his face.

The feasting hall suddenly falls quiet as everyone anticipates his next move.

A menacing smirk spreads across his lips before he tightens his hold on my hair and drags me through the hall. Men and women laugh, shouting loudly as they toss food and ale at me. This vulgar spectacle excites them.

As I pass Ulf's chair, I lock eyes with him, begging he do something for this is not how a ruler should behave. His men are animals who show no discipline or control. But he merely leans back, crossing his ankle over the knee as he sips his ale from a horned cup.

At this moment, I promise I will kill him and burn his unholy kingdom to the ground.

The man leads me outside, and only when he guides me toward a barn do I begin to fight. My struggles are only fuel to his depravity, and he laughs hoarsely.

"Let me go!" I scream, slapping at his hand threaded in my hair. "Beshrew thee!"

My insult only encourages the oaf to laugh louder.

Once in the barn, he tosses me onto the straw-covered ground and makes his intentions clear as he unfastens his belt. But there is no way I will allow another man to violate me ever again.

With unpredicted force, I charge at him, knocking him off balance. I desperately try to push past him, but he pulls my long hair and smashes my head into a wooden beam. The blow has my vision blurring.

Staggering on my bare feet, I attempt to fight, but the wind escapes me as I am punched in the stomach. He forces me to the ground, keeping me pinned down with his foot as he frantically undoes his pants.

I fist handfuls of straw, desperate to flee as I flail wildly, but when I feel my chemise being lifted and his rough fingers prod into me, I know it's too late.

"Your cunt is tight, Princess," he whispers into my ear, fingering me brutally. He smells of ale and rotten meat. "That will change once we are finished with you, for the men have needs. They will break you."

"Damn your soul to hell!" I curse hysterically, for that won't happen. I was taught to fight by Skarth, the greatest warrior of all time. I need to stop and think. What would Skarth tell me to do?

"Scream louder. I love it when they scream."

The man mounts me, and I surrender, for I know he will lower his guard…which is what he does. Just as he removes his fingers and positions his disgusting prick at my entrance, I swiftly reach around and seize the knife at his belt.

His pants are around his ankles, so he cannot escape as I drive the blade into his flank. I stab blindly, over and over. I don't know where I'm stabbing him. All I know is the warm, sticky substance coating my hand drives me to continue.

He is still on top of me, fighting to overpower me, but he grows weaker and weaker. The blade slips from my hand where I slice my own flesh, but it only spurs me on, and with a scream, I stab him and drag the knife downward.

A winded wheeze leaves him, and his weight grows heavy, as do his arms as he sluggishly attempts to fight me. When his movements are stilled, I turn around and shove him off me, using my arms and legs. He smashes into the wooden beam and collapses onto his arse.

I don't waste a moment when I dart to where he sits, straddling him as I drive the blade straight through his heart. I am slathered in his blood as I laugh maniacally.

"Scream louder. I love it when they scream," I mock, using his own words as I twist the knife in deep.

His eyes widen as he gasps for breath. But it's too late. I win. He loses.

Only when he stops breathing do I remove the knife, wiping the blood across his chest.

Suddenly, the reality of what I just did hits me, and I crawl off his corpse and begin to vomit violently. I've not eaten anything, so all that I bring up is bile. But regardless, it feels good to purge this sickness within.

Wiping the spittle from my chin with the back of my hand, I remain on my hands and knees as I peer at the feasting hall. The heathens are oblivious to what just happened, which means this is my chance to flee. I do not die here today.

With the knife in hand, I rise but keep low and make a mad run for the woods. The shadows protect me as I flee. My feet are bare, but I ignore the pain and continue running like the wind.

I don't look back and sprint with my heart in my throat as I know the kinsfolk will find their friend soon. I need to be as far away as possible when that happens. The world passes me by in fast-forward because I won't stop running until I am far away from this hell on earth.

Voices echo in the distance, and when they become louder, I know I'm being hunted. There is no way I'm going back, so I push harder, running faster than I've ever run before. The chase animates me, for I killed a heathen who underestimated the rage that runs through my veins.

I may be a princess, but my heart is that of a warrior, and when I peer into the night sky and see the brightest star beaming ahead, it's time I found my North Star. I knew Skarth to be different, but being around his people has enabled me to see just how different, just how special, he truly is.

A clearing is up ahead, and just as I charge for it, someone tackles me to the ground. The knife falls from my hand.

I fight violently, but this man is strong, unlike the weakling whose blood still stains my hands. I attempt to stand, but he rolls me onto my back and pins me with his weight. When I look into his eyes, I realize my time has come.

"You killed Bo," Ulf states, smirking when I spit in his face. "How does a princess know how to fight?"

His question has me treading with caution as I cannot mention Skarth. So, I don't reply.

"He was one of my best warriors, yet a young girl was able to overpower him. I do not understand."

"If he was your best, then I suggest you amass another army."

I'm expecting Ulf to punish me for my insolence. But he does the opposite.

He bursts into husky laughter.

"You are something else entirely, Princess Emeline."

I don't know what that means.

He rises, and before I have a chance to lunge for my fallen

knife, he kicks it away and lifts me up by the wrists. I don't know what it is about him, but I know he won't hurt me. I knew it from the first moment we met.

"Come." He gestures with his head that I'm to follow him when I stand rigid. But I'm not going anywhere with him. "Have it your way then."

He scoops me up before I have a chance to fight and tosses me over his shoulder, laughing huskily as I pound my fists against him.

"Put me down, you big, ugly brute!"

"Oh, you wound me, sweet princess," he mocks, only tightening his hold on me.

He walks through the woods calmly with me slung over his shoulder. I don't stop squirming or demanding he let me down, but Ulf ignores me, whistling happily to drown me out.

He does not act how a leader should.

If this were anyone else, they'd kill me for killing one of their own. But not Ulf. He confuses me, and I do not like it.

When we arrive back at his kingdom, the angered cries of his men and women alert me that they're waiting for us. I can't see them, but that makes their intentions clear as they demand blood.

"Kill her," a woman exclaims.

"Why is she still alive?" another asks.

"You insult Bo by carrying her back here. We demand her blood! You are Ulf the Bloody. Your name is in the shadow of a wolf! Punish her!"

Ulf stops, as do the demands, because his presence commands their attention, reminding them who their leader is.

"It seems you've forgotten who rules," he states evenly. "I am your *Hersir,* and I do what is best for *Skalavik.*"

No one dares to challenge him.

"Now, if you have finished, I am going to bed."

"What about Bo?" I recognize the voice. It is Inga, the woman who expressed her hatred for me the moment we met at the monastery.

I think she and Ulf are together, for she hovers quite close to him, and I believe they share a bed. But I am unsure how Northman relationships work. It is something Skarth never educated me about.

"What about him? His weakness allowed a young girl to defeat him. He deserves to be slumped in that barn, flaccid cock exposed as a reminder to all—never underestimate anyone, no matter how small."

Was this a lesson for them all? Did Ulf know I would fight Bo with my last breath? If he knew that…then he knew he was at risk of dying, and it seems he doesn't care. He was willing to risk one of his greatest warriors to see my worth?

A chill racks my body, and it has nothing to do with being out here in the cold in only my chemise.

Ulf bursts through his men and women, indicating this conversation is over. When he walks past them, I crane my neck to see Inga standing in front of the group, for she is their leader, second after Ulf, it seems. She narrows her eyes at me, and I know I should fear her more than any man here.

For now, however, I fear where Ulf is taking me.

He walks past his chambers to a barrel of water where, without warning, he dunks me inside. The cold water sends my body into shock, but I soon realize Ulf is acting in kindness, allowing me to bathe.

I break the surface, gasping for air as I brush back the wet hair from my face. Ulf stands before me, grinning. The full moon catches his straight white teeth.

"I thought you'd like to bathe before bed."

"Whatever for?" I sarcastically ask, glaring at him. "Only to be thrown into my cell?"

"You will be sleeping with me," he reveals, folding his arms across his broad chest.

"I cry your mercy!" I exclaim, horrified. "I will do nothing of the sort. Throw me back into my cell please, for I would rather that than sleep anywhere near thee."

I stand my ground, not bothered that I'm sopping wet and standing in a barrel of water.

Ulf smirks, and before he can toss me over his shoulder once again, I very ungracefully climb out of the barrel and stomp off, shivering in the cold. He chases after me, laughing deeply.

I know this isn't optional, so with great anger, I enter his small but elaborate wooden house. I know these are his quarters as the other houses are long and larger. I guess that's because the men and women share the lodgings.

But this is Ulf's alone.

There is a large wooden bed draped with animal skins and straw. It does look very comfortable, but I'd rather eat my own tongue than admit that to him.

My curiosity has me marveling at the structure, which is quite advanced. The walls are lined with clay to keep the heat from the roaring fire in. The slanted roof is quite clever to keep the rain falling at a proper angle.

"What's the matter, Princess? You weren't expecting such lodgings from uneducated, ungodly heathens?" Ulf teases, and when I turn to tell him what I think of his uneducated, ungodly self, I almost choke at the sight of him topless before me.

My cheeks instantly redden, and I immediately lower my eyes.

He is even larger without clothes, and I'm ashamed to confess I like what I see. His muscled chest is covered in intricate patterns, inked onto his bronzed skin. His waist is tapered, and he has defined muscles shaped into a V.

A light sprinkle of hair between his pectorals continues down his stomach into his low-slung trousers. I suddenly am no longer cold.

He is flawless, appeared to be carved by God himself.

"Are you going to stand there all night?"

With a measured breath, I meet his piercing blue eyes. "Excuse me?"

He makes his intentions clear when he pulls back the furs on his bed.

And I make mine perfectly clear when I shake my head. "I am not sleeping with you."

"Who said anything about sleeping?"

My cheeks rival the burning fire feet away, and once again, my eyes are downcast.

He strolls to where I stand and lifts my chin with his pointer finger to meet his intense stare. "I will not force myself on you, Princess…for you will want me one day. I promise you that."

His arrogance is the slap to the face I needed, and I recoil from his touch. "You do not know me, Ulf, so I can promise *you* that that day will never come."

"We will see," he replies, rubbing his thumb along my bottom lip.

I resist the urge to bite him—only just.

"Have it your way then," he leans down and whispers into my ear.

Before I can reply, I watch in interest as he reaches for a length of rope.

"Sit," he orders, gesturing with his head toward the corner of the room, by his bedside.

I do as he says as the sooner I get away from him, the better, for I lose myself when he's too close, and it scares me. I sit cross-legged and peer up at him, unable to place the look on his face as he stares down at me.

He winds the rope around his large hand, his broad chest rising and falling steadily as he continues staring at me. "Are you sure you wish to be tied to this post and…not my bed?"

He's making his intentions very clear, for something has shifted between us by me killing Bo. He sees my worth and the blood I spilled, and it excites him. I'm not the pitiable little princess he believed me to be.

I don't bother replying. Instead, I place my arms behind my back and look away.

He doesn't speak as he comes up behind me and commences tying my hands to the wooden post. His fingers work deftly, and when they brush over my wrists, my pulse begins to spike. He chuckles softly as he is aware of my response to him.

"Sleep *tight*, Princess," he whispers into my ear, tightening the rope. I don't struggle, however.

He comes to a stand, his imposing height even more predominate as I sit tied to this post. I'm at his mercy.

It's suddenly impossible to breathe.

I shouldn't trust his word, but I do. But I disturbingly wish he would go back on it and force me to do things I think I'd enjoy. Disgusted with myself, I turn my cheek, ignoring the rustling of furs as he settles into bed.

I do not wish to think of him snuggled amongst that comfort and how he offered me a place beside him, for I need to remember he is the enemy, and the first chance I get at escape, I'm taking it.

"Time to eat."

My brain takes a moment to remember where I am…and that I'm tied to a post, in a Northman's chambers, in only my chemise.

My eyes pop open, and I attempt to scurry back, but thanks to my hands still being bound, I'm not going anywhere.

Ulf is crouched in front of me, holding a bowl of what looks like porridge in his hands. However, it smells quite sweet, and my stomach instantly growls in hunger. But I won't give Ulf the satisfaction of knowing that.

"I am not hungry. I thank thee." My response is far from grateful.

Ulf's nostrils flare, and it gives me great pleasure knowing I've annoyed him. "You will starve yourself just to spite me?"

"You think too highly of yourself, heathen, for I do not think of you at all."

I know what I'm doing, but I can't help myself. If he thought I'd be a docile prisoner, he thought wrong. And besides, I know he likes me more than he should. I can see it in the way he looks at me.

But that doesn't mean he won't be cruel.

"You know, I can make you eat. I can make you do whatever I want," he declares, scooping up a spoonful of porridge.

He shuffles closer, so close that our knees touch.

He runs the spoon along my mouth, leaving a tiny trail of sweetened porridge behind. The honey and buttermilk linger, but I don't give in to temptation and seal my lips shut.

Ulf chuckles, his blue eyes almost eating me alive. "Why do you defy me? Why do you not fear me?"

I interest him, which is the only reason I'm still breathing.

If I told him about Skarth, that he's the reason, I know that interest would only grow, for he and I both know that Skarth will be coming for me. I refuse to believe he's succumbed to his injuries. I would have felt it if he had. I know in my heart of hearts that he will find me.

Up until then, I have to try to stay alive. But that doesn't mean I have to roll over.

"Why should I fear you?" I ask honestly. "What can you do to me that hasn't already been done?"

A look washes over him, a look of pity, but thankfully, it's gone just as quickly as it appeared because I don't want pity.

"I am very creative," he states, gently slipping the spoon into my mouth. "There are many ways to make someone fear you."

The suggestion to his tone warms me from head to toe.

I clench my teeth, but that isn't a deterrent as Ulf continues to work the spoon into my mouth. He won't give up, so I release my teeth and allow him to feed me.

But that doesn't mean I will swallow.

"You stubborn, arrogant little girl," he says, half in anger, half in awe. "Swallow."

I will do nothing of the sort.

Instead, my cheeks billow, stuffed full of the porridge I refuse to consume.

Ulf groans in frustration as he continues to spoon-feed me, and I continue to defy him. Porridge trickles down my chin, but I will not concede. I lock eyes with him, daring him to persevere as I breathe steadily through my nose.

Ulf doesn't like to lose, however, so he pinches my nose. But I don't yield. I can feel my face turning red as I hold my breath, mouth stuffed full.

"Swallow!" he orders, squeezing my nose harder.

My lungs are quickly deprived of oxygen, and I know I will soon pass out, but there is no way I'm eating, being spoon-fed like some incompetent child. So, I decide to do the next best thing.

With a deep breath, I spit out the porridge, projecting it all over Ulf's face.

He appears to be in absolute shock as his mouth hinges open. Porridge is caught in his long beard, sprinkled like speckles of snow. He looks utterly ridiculous with a face full of breakfast.

"Thank you, Ulf, but I simply could not eat another thing,"

I quip, taunting him, for I know he is moments away from exploding.

He grins, but nothing about the gesture is pleasant.

He calmly places the bowl and spoon beside him. I believe he'll wipe his face clean, but he does not. Instead, he grips my throat in his palm and arches my neck backward. He lowers his face to mine.

"Do not test my patience, Princess, for you will not like the consequences if you do," he warns, his blue eyes suddenly engulfed in a darkness that rocks me to the core.

He squeezes harder while I swallow deeply beneath his grip. "What exactly do you plan on doing with me? I thought I was supposed to be a trade. But here I am, tied to a post as you spoon-feed me," I mock because I want to know what he plans on doing with me.

"I plan on doing everything to you," he ambiguously promises.

I don't cower, but I can't deny that being this close to him and inhaling his unique, manly scent does things to me which it should not. He is undeniably handsome, and his arrogance just adds to the appeal.

Something suddenly happens, something which I don't understand. Beneath the thin material of my chemise, my nipples swell, and heat gathers in my belly. Ulf's gaze drops to the front of my gown, where a smug grin spreads across his full mouth.

I am angered at my body's response. I think of Skarth, and how he is the only man who I've ever reacted to in this way. I instantly am ashamed, for Ulf is my captor, while Skarth is my protector.

Ulf appears to want to say something but changes his mind at the last minute as he releases me.

I gulp in mouthfuls of air, but I'm unsure if I'm breathless because of the tight grip on my throat or mayhap something else…

I watch as Ulf stands, wiping the porridge from his face with a cloth. He reaches for his knife, and I hold my breath as he comes up behind me, only to cut the ropes at my wrist.

"Get dressed," he orders, tossing a brown strapless gown into my lap.

It's very beautiful. It is embroidered with intricate, colorful patterns with beads hanging from the front. The hem has the same pattern sewn around it. As it is strapless, I will wear my chemise underneath.

I finger the soft gown, unsure why he's giving me such a lovely garment to wear. But I don't argue.

Coming to a shaky stand, I slip into the gown, never breaking eye contact with Ulf as he watches me dress. I fasten the belt around me, which gives the garment shape and draws attention to my slender waist. The leather belt is long, so it dangles low.

I've never seen a dress such as this before. But I instantly feel like it's a second skin.

Ulf simply stares at me. I don't know what he's thinking, which scares me.

"It's time we discussed our attack, Ulf," Inga says, barging into Ulf's home. She comes to an abrupt stop when she sees me dressed in her people's clothes. "She dresses like one of us now?"

Ulf shakes his head as if clearing whatever was plaguing him. "You'd prefer she freeze to death? What use is she then?"

Inga glowers, and the black strip of paint she's coated across her eyes just seems to emphasize her hatred for me.

Ulf dumps a fur shawl at my feet before following Inga out the door. Once he's gone, I let out three deep breaths I didn't even realize I was holding. I don't know what it is about Ulf, but he is dangerous in every possible way.

With shaking hands, I reach for the shawl and wrap it around my shoulders, thankful for the warmth.

I don't know what I'm supposed to do, so I step outside, the harsh morning light almost blinding me. Shielding my eyes, I take everything in and examine the Northmen in their natural environment. It's an almost surreal experience as I'm not sure how many people would be given the opportunity to be here.

Men and women work the lands, and the flourishing crops reveal what skillful farmers they are. Skarth told me his people left their homelands far away from here in a place called Scandinavia and traveled the seas to better their lives. I can see that here.

Although brutal, the Northmen are like Saxons in the sense they merely wish to establish a home. Maybe we can coexist? Maybe there can be a place where Northmen can settle so the bloodshed can end. But that would mean King Egbert would have to delegate land for the Northmen.

And I don't see that happening anytime soon. It's a nice thought, however. It would put an end to so much war.

A young boy with bright orange hair stops in front of me, openly staring. It seems he's as intrigued by me as I am by him. "Good morrow. How met?"

His hair is cut short on the sides with a long plait down the middle of his head. I am fascinated by Northman fashion. No matter what the occasion is, they are always ready for battle. I admire how they radiate such strength and brutality.

Even Ulf, who appears to be in talks with a group of men and women.

"My mother says your God was killed. My gods live in the sky," he reveals, tonguing the corner of his mouth. "Odin, Thor, and Loki are my favorite."

"They are?" I ask, bending low. "Why?"

"Odin is the god of wisdom and war, and Thor, he is very strong. That's why I wear this." He reaches for a pendant around his neck shaped as a hammer. "He is my favorite. Loki is part god, part devil. My mother says Loki influenced my father, and that's why he's dead."

I gulp, as this story has suddenly taken a morbid turn, especially when he looks at a blackened pile of ash in the distance.

"He is in Helheim, for he did not die in battle. But my mother said we tricked Hel because my father was stabbed through the heart, and Hel would think the injury was inflicted in battle."

A sense of dread overcomes me, for I think I know how his father died—I killed him.

"Your father is not in Valhalla?"

I've heard of this place, and I thought all warriors are destined for here. But when the young boy shakes his head, I fear I've condemned his father to a miserable afterlife.

"No, Valhalla and Folkvangr are for warriors who die in battle. The goddess Freya, she gets first pick of which warriors she chooses. I wish my father was there."

Heathen lore is quite complex. I have much to learn.

"Come, Erik," says a woman, glaring at me. No doubt, this is Bo's widow.

Instantly, I lower my eyes, ashamed for killing her husband, no matter that he was a wretched bastard.

Erik bounces away, oblivious that he was speaking to his father's murderer. I grip the crucifix around my throat, needing to say a prayer. But I cannot do that here.

I don't have a place here. I need to know what Ulf is planning, so I casually stroll to where he conducts a meeting.

They are huddled around a fire underneath a structure that appears to store their wood and food.

"We attack them at Carhampton. The terrain is at our advantage. It's close to the seas. Soil rich," a man states, rubbing his hands over the fire. "King Egbert is an old man with a weak army. We can defeat them. The raid on the place the Saxons call the Isle of Sheppey in Kent proves they can be defeated."

"With what army do you propose we attack?" Ulf questions calmly. "King Egbert may be an old man, but he has the loyalty of hundreds to act on his behalf. Who do we have? We've lost many in battle. And we were deserted by a traitor."

There is bitterness to Ulf's tone, and I believe this traitor was someone close to him.

"We can't just wait for them to attack us," Inga says, and it astounds me that women have a say in talks of war as it is not the case in my world.

"I know, Inga," Ulf declares, annoyed, and I'm suddenly struck with an idea.

"Trade me."

The Northmen fall silent, turning to look at me.

"Now she has a say in the matters of our war?" another man spits, curling his lip at me.

But Ulf ignores him. "If you wish to eavesdrop, then come close and not lurk in the shadows."

I do as he says because, in essence, we want the same thing—the fall of King Egbert.

I don't stand near them, for I know we are not equal. They give me their attention.

"I am not sure what you know of King Egbert," I start, wringing my hands nervously. "But he is Bretwalda, the ruler of all of England. He has conquered Kent, Surrey, Sussex, Wales, and my home, Northumbria.

"He has done this viciously. He tricked my father. He was able to overthrow Mercia. He is unstoppable. And so is his son, Prince Aethelwulf."

"And how will trading you help us?" Inga questions blankly, not seeing my worth.

The men wait for me to reply, clearly annoyed I'm wasting their time. But I'm not.

"Because King Egbert will do anything for my return," I state, sickened. "Send word that you are holding me prisoner and that we are to meet at Carhampton for the trade. You were always going to trade me. But now, we both can win."

The men and women look at one another before bursting into jubilant laughter, all but Ulf, and that's because he knows this will work.

"Why would you want to help us?" he asks, which silences the laughter.

"Because he tricked me, and in turn, he made me Wessex's whore."

The mood soon changes, and no one speaks a word.

"This will work, for I am seen as his property. I defied the king and still live. He cannot let that pass, for that will be seen as his greatest defeat."

"What do you want in return?" Inga asks, the only one who doesn't appear affected by my truth.

"All I ask is for my freedom…in whatever form that may be. If you win, I ask you let me go free where I can live a life I choose. I cannot go back to his kingdom, so if you lose, then I ask you kill me, for I would rather die than go back to being the king's whore."

Ulf hisses, a look of anger surpassing him.

"I do not ask for protection. Just my freedom. You know this will work."

"How will King Egbert know we are telling the truth?" Inga isn't stupid. She knows he will want proof.

With utter grief, I confess, "Allow the messenger to inform the king that our son is buried in the cemetery. A small cross is the only marker that he was once ours."

Although I've told Ulf of my unborn son, he was not aware the father was King Egbert. This changes everything, just how I knew it would, and in a sense, it gives my son a purpose—his death was not in vain.

"I will leave you to discuss my proposal." With a curtsey, I leave them to deliberate on what I just offered.

Suddenly exhausted, I decide to retire to Ulf's chambers, and this time, sleeping in his bed is welcomed, for I will be alone.

"Princess."

With a groan, I open my eyes and see it's dark out. I have slept longer than I thought.

Ulf lays beside me, watching me closely. "We accept your proposal. We will trade you to the king in exchange for Carhampton. We expect a fight. However, we will be ready, and we will win. This plan allows us to at least gather Wessex men in one place, instead of a surprise attack," he says softly and with somewhat regret.

I wonder why.

"We will send word come first light."

"Very good," I reply, shifting away as I suddenly am aware of how close he is to me. But he seizes my chin between his thumb and finger.

I am stunned into submission by his tender touch as he runs his thumb along my lips. "How did you escape? Who taught you how to fight?"

Ulf's interrogations reveal he knows I'm not telling him the whole truth.

"My father's men—"

"Enough with the lies," he demands, cutting me off. "Tell me the truth, and I will protect you."

"I do not need nor want your protection, Lord." But my

words hold no weight when a whimper slips past my parted lips as Ulf slips the tip of his thumb into my mouth.

"I know, but I want to protect you," he confesses, expressing his confusion as neither of us understand it. "Have you ever been kissed without force?"

"What do you mean?" My cheeks redden.

"Have you ever been kissed and welcomed it? Wanted it?" he clarifies while my heart begins to race.

There has only ever been one man whose kisses I've wanted. But he's never wanted mine in return.

"No," I reply honestly because Skarth has never kissed me the way a man who wants a woman does.

"What a shame."

Before I can speak, Ulf closes the distance between us and slams his mouth over mine.

My eyes pop open, as I'm utterly shocked, but that soon turns to something else when Ulf nudges my lips open with his tongue. I do not know what he's doing as I've not kissed with tongue before. But it does not feel unpleasant.

I like it.

"That's it, *ástin mín*."

The moment he speaks in his language, I think of Skarth and am showered in guilt. "No, I cannot."

"Yes, you can," he amends, setting me on fire with his firm command.

I try to pull away, but Ulf doesn't let me.

He wraps his hand around my nape and kisses me deeply, holding me prisoner to him, to his delicious scent, and I am helpless to stop it. I should recoil, but I cannot, and that's because I don't want to.

I lose myself to his touch, to the feel of his lips sliding against mine and his tongue dominating mine.

He rolls on top of me, his weight surprisingly perfect and not squashing me as others have before him. He is everywhere, all over me, and I am lost to this brutal beast who touches me with nothing but yearning.

He dominates my mouth and body, our lips suddenly moving at a frantic pace as I thread my fingers through his wild, long hair. It feels like silk, just how his lips do, and learning from him, I massage my tongue against his.

A pained hiss leaves him as he cups my cheek, pressing us even closer together as he kisses me passionately. A wetness pools between my legs, something which has never happened before. I wonder what is happening.

His hardened chest is pressed to mine, and I can feel the thrashing of his heart. It's in tempo with mine. Nothing else exists but this.

"You will be the death of me, Princess," he whispers against my lips before robbing me of air as he continues to kiss me obscenely.

He doesn't attempt anything more, merely kissing, which has never happened before. This is all so new. But who knew kissing could feel this good.

He touches my face, my hair, unable to get enough of me, it seems, as we kiss for what feels like hours. I can feel his arousal pressed between us, and I shamefully want more. If kissing Ulf can feel this good, I wonder what lying with him would feel like.

His mouth is firm, hot, wet—it's a perfect combination of heaven and hell.

I pull at his hair, a growl leaving him as he grinds his arousal into me. I've long forgotten my God as I am about to ask for more, but when the blowing of a horn sounds loudly from outside, I realize God has not forgotten me.

I pull away, the realization of what I've just done hitting me hard. I quickly scrub at my lips. But the betrayal is scored onto my very soul.

Ulf smirks arrogantly as I did what I said I wouldn't do—I surrendered. "Too late, Princess, I will always be a part of you now. And I know you liked it. I can smell how much so."

Horrified, I slap his cheek and shove at his chest to push him off me. He chuckles as I frantically crawl away from him, my back hitting the wall behind me as I draw my knees toward my chest. I am utterly ashamed and disappointed in myself.

When Inga comes charging in, however, he pretends nothing happened and is quick to arm himself. She looks at me, realizing what she walked into, but doesn't address it because we have far more pressing matters to deal with.

"Wessex Guard ride toward us."

"How many?" Ulf asks, sheathing his large sword.

"A hundred or so."

"*Faen!*"

He tosses a sword onto the bed before marching toward me and gripping my arm firmly. "You are to stay with me." I don't have time to protest when he adds, "I cannot have my most valuable chattel harmed."

He has now wounded me by making me feel like nothing but a whore.

Roughly shrugging from his hold, I grip the blade and stand on my own two feet. I will never allow him to touch me ever again.

Inga laughs, seeing me as nothing but a helpless maid. "You cannot fight on your own."

"We will see," I challenge before I shove past them both and face the danger headfirst.

The Northmen prepare for battle as they stand together, strong in formation in their shield wall. Ulf follows after me, demanding his army stay solid.

"Stay strong! Hold!" he orders, looking ahead at the approaching army of Saxons, a Wessex flag flying high into the night sky. "They have the numbers, but we have heart! If not, we feast in Valhalla!"

The roars erupt into the darkness, and my skin breaks out into tiny prickles, for we face certain death. But these men and women aren't afraid—they embrace it.

Ulf stands beside me, his unique scent slathered all over me. I wish I could wash it away, for if I'm to die, it'll be his touch, his scent, that lingers on my skin as I meet my maker.

"Scared, Princess?" he mocks, his astute gaze never wavering from the approaching guards.

"No, Lord, I am not, for I defeated the king's guards once before, and I plan to do so again."

"So, you did fight them?"

Turning to look at him, I'm now the one who smirks arrogantly. "Of course, I did. And you are right…one of your men did teach me. A warrior far braver than you'll ever be. So, take that to your death, Ulf the Bloody. You allowed a traitor to enter your kingdom and kill one of your men, all because you wanted to wet your cock."

A look of fury overtakes Ulf. "Who?" he snarls between clenched teeth.

"Ulf! They're coming," Inga warns, demanding he get into position behind his warriors. But he doesn't move. "You are arguing now? Seconds away from battle? Have you lost your mind?"

He and I stand in the middle of the field, the war between us far more important than the one mere seconds from erupting.

"Tell me who!"

Our gazes never waver from one another, regardless of what faces us mere yards away.

"It's someone who has had my heart since I was twelve years old! Everyone else, a mere distraction for who I really want."

I've chosen my words with intent because when Ulf flinches, I know I succeeded in hurting him just how he hurt me. There is no time to recant, however, because as Ulf looks behind me, his jaw clenching, it seems things have come full circle.

"Skarth the Godless," he growls, shocking me as I did not mention his name.

I frantically search for words to protect Skarth, but when someone grips my arm and I take to the air, I understand that Ulf meant Skarth is here, now.

I also realize he knows of my Northman, and by the anger stamped on his face, I dare say he knows him well.

"Always getting into trouble, I see," Skarth quips as he positions me onto his horse. "Hold on, Princess."

I do as he commands, looping my arms low around his waist as he clucks his tongue and pulls at the reins, resulting in our horse dashing away from danger, leaving Ulf and his army to defeat the guards on their own.

Turning over my shoulder, I see Ulf stare after me, a look of anguish overtaking him. He doesn't seem to care that Wessex Guard attack his men and women, who stand firm, but there are so many of the king's men.

"Fight!" I mouth to Ulf because even though I am angry with him, I do not wish for him to die.

He shakes his head and lays down his sword as Wessex

Guard swarm him. When one pierces him with their sword, a guttural scream leaves me.

"We have to go back!" I demand, squeezing Skarth's waist.

"Princess?"

"Please," I beg, as I cannot live with myself if anything were to happen to these people. "I killed a little boy's father. I cannot allow myself to be the cause of his mother's death as well. Please, Skarth. We have to help them."

A frustrated sound leaves him. "I am the reason the king's men are there. Now you wish for us to go back?"

Skarth must have given word to where I was, and when I peer into the heavens and see the brightest star above, I know this is how he knew where to find me; just how he promised he always would.

"Please."

If he were to refuse me, then I would understand. But I know he won't.

"*Sorðinn!*" he curses with a roar, but he tugs at the reins. The horse whinnies as Skarth directs him to turn back around.

We race toward the battlefield where I look on, heart in my throat, as the Northmen have broken formation and are scattered across the land, fighting for their lives. We ride like the wind, and the moment we're close, Skarth dismounts and runs toward danger, sword raised.

I cannot allow him to face this alone, and I take the reins, riding toward battle, prepared to kill anyone who stands in my way. The moment I reach the Wessex Guard, I am teemed by men, but I am on horseback, and I carry a mighty sword.

With one hand holding the reins, I swing my sword in the other, cutting down men who wear silver armor and fight in the name of a merciless king. I do as Skarth taught me. I don't lose focus because although outnumbered, we fight for a far greater cause.

Blood coats my face and arms as I fight the king's men. Their armor does nothing to protect them, for I know where to pierce. My horse's white mane is soon stained a bright red, which glistens against the full moon.

A girl's scream has me peering ahead where I see a young Northman being dragged by her long blonde hair toward the feasting hall by three guards. The battle is long forgotten for them. But I will not allow it.

Clucking my tongue, I ride toward her, slashing and slicing anyone who stands in my way. Men's bodies twist and fall as I slice my sword through the air. One man grabs my leg, attempting to pull me off my horse, but I kick him hard, and he stumbles backward onto the end of Skarth's sword.

He uses his foot to pry the corpse off his sword, and the sight of him bloody and breathless and in total control stirs a raucous longing within me. I want him—in every way there is.

I have to ensure I survive this, for I refuse to die without tasting those pert lips.

I gesture where I'm going, and he nods, flipping his sword

and stabbing a man behind him through the gap between his body and arm. He did this without looking, for a warrior uses all senses to fight. Another lesson he taught me.

Leaving my Northman, I ride toward the feasting hall the men and girl disappeared into. I fear I may be too late. I tug at the reins, compelling the horse to ride faster, and when he jumps over three men, I shout in delight.

When I arrive at the feasting hall, I charge in, not bothering to dismount, and when I see a man rutting into the girl who is thrown over the table, her dress lifted high, anger like never before animates me, and with a roar, I slice my sword through the air, taking his head clean off.

The other men reach for their swords, but it's too late. I slice off the hand of one man, taking his hand and cock in one fluid movement, for he was yanking at his disgusting length as he watched his friend defile and plunder the young girl.

She doesn't hesitate and stabs the remaining man straight through the throat. He collapses to the ground, twitching.

"Thank you," she pants, adjusting her dress before grabbing her sword and running into battle.

I follow, and when I smell fire, I see the guards have set Ulf's chambers alight. Fire is the least of our worries as buildings can be rebuilt, but lives can never be revived.

I search the bloody field for Ulf, and when I see him fighting one-armed as the other hangs limply by his side, I sigh in relief. I am glad he is still alive.

Skarth is a beast, and although I've heard tales of him in battle and seen him fight when he taught me, actually seeing him in action is an entirely different thing. He cannot be beaten, and I witness with my own two eyes as he takes on five men at once.

He twists and turns, his movements so fast I almost miss them when I blink. My Northman is merciless, and he is here for me.

Clucking my tongue, I ride fast, cutting down any remaining men. Each man I kill is one step closer to getting my revenge on Wessex. I don't feel a thing. I should. But all I feel is elation at shedding blood.

Ulf stabs one man through the neck, and when another man drops to his knees, begging for mercy, he swings his sword and decapitates him in one stroke. His head rolls along the blood-soaked field, coming to a stop at Skarth's boots.

He uses the head as a rest as he places his foot on it and locks eyes with Ulf.

Ulf roars, pounding his chest, and a string of words I don't understand spew into the night sky. He is daring Skarth to fight him.

"No," I say aloud, for they cannot fight. They are on the same side.

But clearly, they are not, when Skarth stomps on the head beneath his boot, pulverizing it under the pressure. His hollowed cries echo as he runs toward Ulf, and Ulf runs toward him.

What are they doing?

I kill anyone who stands in my way, and when I see the men are dwindling in numbers, I order Inga as I ride past her, "Keep one alive! We need him to deliver a message to the king."

She nods firmly, her face slathered in enemy blood.

"Stop!" I shout, riding toward Ulf and Skarth as they charge toward one another, ready to rip off the other's head.

Their attention never wavers from the other as they circle each other, ready for the other to strike. The way they move is very similar, making it clear they've fought together before. But now, they fight against the other, and I need to know why.

Ulf makes the first move, but Skarth blocks his attack with ease, laughing happily. This enrages Ulf, who goes on the offense, attempting to bring Skarth down with a flurry of blows. Although Ulf is injured and fighting with one arm, so is Skarth as that's all he needs to bring Ulf down.

He punches him in the face, tossing his sword down to the ground. Ulf staggers back, shaking his head, but Skarth doesn't stop. He punches him in the jaw, then the nose.

I'm close enough to hear Ulf speak as he spits out a mouthful of blood. "I am surprised you are here. Did the king grant you permission to leave? Whoever will massage his tiny feet?"

Ulf mocks Skarth, so he knows what Skarth did. Is Skarth the traitor Ulf spoke of? Were they once friends?

The thought of what I did with Ulf moments before Skarth

arrived assaults me, and vomit rises, for I have done a very bad thing. I didn't know who Ulf was, but that doesn't lessen the guilt.

"No one granted me permission. I'm here for the princess… for she is mine."

"Yours?" Ulf questions, chuckling loudly, for he is a privy to a secret Skarth isn't.

I refuse for Skarth to find out that way, so I tap my heels into the horse's side, forcing him to ride faster.

"Stop it!" I scream, thankfully capturing the attention of both men. "Stop squabbling like two old maids."

Both men turn to look at me.

"Princess, I am pleased to see you," Ulf says, smirking smugly, for we share something which Skarth and I do not as I told him I've not been kissed before.

I ignore him and deal with one dilemma at a time. "Inga has a Wessex Guard. The plan still stands."

Skarth arches a brow. "What plan?"

A husky chuckle leaves Ulf. "You have a lot to catch up on, it appears. Lead the way, Princess, for this is *your* plan."

I narrow my eyes at him, and a part of me regrets turning around to save him.

His arrogance isn't needed, but this is who Ulf is. He is hurt that Skarth left him, and now he's going to hurt him by using me. But I will not allow it.

I turn around and ride toward Inga, who has the guard on

his knees in the middle of the bloody field.

Men's bloody bodies lie in grotesque, twisted heaps as far as the eye can see. They're missing arms, legs, heads—war is brutal. The soil is stained red, forever tainted with what occurred here tonight.

"Please spare me," the guard begs, interlacing his muddied hands as I approach him. "You are a good Christian. I can see that by the cross you wear. Do not kill me."

"We are not going to kill you," I reveal, tugging the reins to stop the horse.

He sighs in relief.

"For you serve a far greater purpose."

His relief soon turns to dread.

"You are going to deliver a message to the king," I reveal. Ulf and Skarth stand on either side of my horse. "You are going to tell him you saw me here and that the Northmen want a trade."

Skarth peers up at me, dangerously slow. He doesn't need to utter a word, for his face says it all.

"The trade is to take place at Carhampton in three weeks," Ulf states, for I assume this is how long they need to gather more kinsfolk. "We give him the princess, and in return, he gives us Carhampton. We do not wish to fight. We simply want land in exchange for his beloved."

The guard's eyes widen. "That is the message I am to deliver? The princess does not look to be in despair, however."

He is right, and if he delivers that message, the king will

know this is a trap, which is why when Ulf yanks on my arm and pulls me down from the horse, I don't fight him. I don't fight when he slaps my cheek so hard my teeth rattle in my mouth.

Skarth advances forward, but I discreetly shake my head. This is the only way.

Ulf rips the crucifix from my neck and spits on it before tossing it to the ground. He is about to tear my chemise, but the guard nods hysterically.

"All right! I shall deliver the message to the king. Forgive me, Princess." His brown eyes are filled with regret for doubting me.

Blood trickles from the corner of my mouth, which I don't wipe away. "Go, now. Take a horse and do not stop until you reach the palace."

He rises to his feet, running away in case we have a change of heart. We watch as he mounts a horse and rides as fast as he can. When he's no longer in sight, Skarth tips his face to the heavens and inhales slowly.

"You have no idea what you've just done. This plan *will* fail. The king will see this for the trap that it is and will recruit hundreds more men to defeat you. He will take the princess and kill all of you. You are foolish if you think you will win."

The reality of Skarth's words sends a shiver through me. "That is a risk I am willing to take, but I will not be taken alive."

"*What?*"

Skarth lowers his clenched chin, glaring at me.

"You heard me," I state, bending down to retrieve my necklace. "This is the only chance we have at defeating the king. He will come. You know he will."

"Yes, Princess, he will, but he will be armed well."

"Isn't it fortunate we have a skilled Saxon *and* Viking fighter on hand then?" Ulf says, grinning broadly because things have suddenly fallen in his favor.

With Skarth on his side, he knows he can't lose.

"With news of your return, we can recruit our own army, where you can teach our people the way of the Saxons. We will be at an advantage, for you have taught them how to fight."

"I taught King Eanred's army. I do not know the ways of King Egbert's," Skarth growls, turning to face Ulf.

"They are Saxons; how different can they be? But if you wish to leave the fate of the princess to the gods—"

Skarth clenches his fists while Ulf shrugs as he knows Skarth will agree to anything he proposes to protect me.

"I intend to see our deal through, Princess," Ulf says, looking at me.

"What deal is this?"

Gulping, I know Skarth will regret coming back for me because all I seem to do is cause him trouble. "That if King Egbert does win, I will ensure he does not take the princess alive."

Skarth storms forward and punches Ulf in the jaw. His

head snaps back with a sickening crack, and I know if I don't intervene, they'll kill one another.

"You will not touch her. Ever."

"Enough!" I run between them, separating them at arm's length. "Bickering amongst ourselves will not win this war. We must work together, for we want the same thing. Sigrith relies on us. We must go back for her."

The mention of Skarth's sister has the fire in him simmering, but the same cannot be said for Ulf.

"You *left* her there?" he cries, eyes livid. "How could you?"

His fury reveals Sigrith is someone he holds close.

Before Ulf can say another word, I speak for Skarth as this is my fault. "He did it to save me," I reveal on a quickened breath as I want Skarth to know I appreciate his sacrifice. "He could only save one of us…and he chose me."

Inga and Ulf stare at us, completely dumbfounded.

"He came to Wessex with intent to take me away. And in turn, he left his sister behind and was severely injured in the process. He did all of this for me."

Skarth doesn't say a word, but the hard press of his jaw reveals his anger.

"That is why I made the trade with you," I explain to Ulf. "I knew if you found Skarth on his deathbed, you'd kill him. I could not allow it, so I sacrificed myself, just how he has done for me time and time again."

Our relationship is a complex one, one Ulf can never fully

understand as it's one I don't even understand myself.

"You turned your back on your people," Inga spits in disgust. "You are nothing but a traitor. You owe us this, Skarth the Godless. You will help us defeat King Egbert's army at Carhampton, and then you can go about living your new Saxon life, forgetting who you really are."

Inga doesn't hide her hatred for Skarth's choices. She will never see him as anything but a traitor to his kind.

"If not, your precious princess's life is at risk. And it's evident you will sacrifice everything for her. So let us pack everything up. We cannot stay in one place. We need to move, as the king will seek us out now that he knows we have her."

Inga is right.

Even though I have no doubt he will meet us at Carhampton in three weeks' time, he will still send his guards out to look for me. Meaning we are all fugitives.

She storms off, helping the fallen Northmen. It pleases me that not many fell victim to Wessex as the men mortally injured are mainly the king's men.

Standing between Skarth and Ulf, I can only pray they work together because we want the same thing—to see King Egbert fall from his throne.

"Do we have a deal?" Ulf asks Skarth.

Skarth has been thrown into a war he wanted no part in. "What choice do I have?" he poses, making his feelings clear. "I will help you win your war, Ulf. We gather as many men and women as we can find."

"I will send word as they will not take direction from a traitor."

"Then how do you expect me to teach them the ways of Saxon war?"

Ulf ponders on Skarth's question. "Because when I, their *Hersir*, promise them victory, they will agree. I never abandoned them. I promised them wealth and land, and now is the time to claim what is ours.

"So, here we are, once again fighting on the same side. Just how we once did."

"We are no longer those people," Skarth says, shaking his head. "I only do this because my hands are tied."

What he means is he does this to once again protect me.

"Skarth—"

But he won't look at me.

He turns his back, leaving me to deal with the mess I've made.

# TWELVE

*Skarth the Godless*

I was stupid to think this would be simple.

I believed I would ride away with Emeline and finally be free.

But there is no such thing for us.

I am now, once again, tangled in a war I wanted no part in. All I wanted was to save my family, but I never factored Emeline into the equation. She hit me like a thunderstorm, and I'm still drowning in the rain.

I do this for her as I know with or without me, she will see this through. She will happily end her life for retribution, but I cannot let her do that.

Cecily awaits my return. I fear King Eanred may have taken

his anger out on her once he discovered I was missing. She can look after herself, but so can Emeline, which is why I don't understand; why do I keep coming to her aid?

Why do I continually put her first? Above my sister? My wife?

I want to believe it's because I owe her something for sparing my life. But that would be a lie.

My feelings for her are irrational. They will get me killed, for she is all I see and all I think of. She has always been a part of me, but now, I want her with me always.

I think of Cecily, what a doting, caring wife she is, and I'm ashamed for thinking of another woman the way I do of Emeline. But Emeline has never been another woman to me. She has always been the one.

When a child, I cared for her fondly, but now as a woman, I care for her how a man cares for the woman he…loves. I do not know what this means for us. All I know is that I fight to protect her, even if that means working with Ulf once more.

He made it clear where the power lies, in case I'd forgotten. It's been so long since I've been around my people, but it surprised me how quickly I fell back into the role. It's here where I belong. I never turned my back on them, regardless of what Ulf believes.

I did what was right by my family. I knew of the sacrifice I made.

I am now skilled in both Saxon and Viking warfare, making

me unstoppable. My father taught me to evolve, as it was the only way to survive. Ulf may not see it, but this is the only way to defeat the enemy. The world is so vast, and I want to learn.

But he is so stuck in his ways, and he refuses to accept anything but the way of our people. So much more is out there, and if I learned that by being a traitor, then I accept it.

Stripping out of my clothes, I enter the lake to bathe.

The cool water feels wonderful, and I dip underneath, holding my breath as I allow the water to wash away the world as I know it. The unknown doesn't scare me, but now that I fight for Emeline's freedom, I am frightened of failing her.

Breaking the surface, I gulp in air, but it's not enough as I think of Emeline riding on horseback through battle, killing without pause.

To see her in my people's clothing, fighting like the warrior queen I knew she was, my cock instantly hardens at the thought. I am always aroused after battle, for there is something erotic about taking another man's life.

I am alive on the battlefield, and that energy still thrums through my veins. It won't go away until I find a release.

I am submerged to my chest, so I grip my length and begin to work my shaft firmly. My hand is a poor substitute for who I want, but when I think of Emeline in battle, slathered in the enemy's blood, I pretend it is she who strokes me firmly.

I think of her full pink lips and the curve of her hips. I think of how she defies me because she knows she can. I think of what it would feel like to punish her for such defiance. I think she would like it. I know I would.

Tossing my head back, I increase the tempo, losing myself to the woman I want with every breath I take.

However, when I hear the snapping of a branch, I instantly spring into attack mode and strain my eyes to see in the dark. Who I see isn't the enemy, but she's just as dangerous.

Emeline strips off, leaving her dress near my clothes. Thankfully, she has the good sense to leave on her chemise. She walks into the water, skimming the surface with her palms. I turn my back to her because seeing her wet and willing will not help settle my straining cock.

She continues walking toward me even though I won't look at her. She stops close behind me. "Are you angry with me, Lord?"

"No, Princess, I am angry with myself."

"Why?"

"I seem to make things worse even when I try to make them better," I confess. "Maybe I should stop trying."

"Never say such a thing, for if you stopped, I would succumb as well. We do this to change the wronging done to us. We cannot be faulted for that."

She's right.

"I am sorry for once again involving you in my troubles."

"There is no need for apologies. I am here because I want to be."

Silence.

The rippling of water alerts me that she's coming closer. "Why?"

I can feel her breath on me. That's how close she is.

"Why what, Princess?"

"Why do you continuously save me? I do not expect it from you. You owe me nothing, so please do not feel obligated in any way."

"I don't," I reply, unable to stop myself. We are treading dangerous waters, for my self-control is slipping.

"Then answer me plainly; why are you here? You could have ridden back to Northumbria once you were well. But you did not. You came here."

"Emeline," I warn as she slowly rounds my body so we're face-to-face.

Under the full moon, she appears like a goddess, and in some ways, I believe that she is, for I am under her spell.

The water is deep so all I can see are her shoulders, but when she removes her chemise, regardless of the fact that the water shields her nakedness, my cock hardens further being this close to her when she is bare.

"My skin prickles all over," she confesses, biting her pouty bottom lip.

She reaches out and toys with the relic around my neck. It's Thor's *Mjolnir*, one which I wear with pride.

"It's because of the battle," I explain softly, gently

withdrawing from her touch. "The thrill of it…the blood still pumps intensely in your veins."

"Does it in yours?"

"Yes."

She wades the water, watching me closely. "What do you usually do to make this flutter in your belly go away?"

Her innocence will be the death of me.

"I usually go for a swim."

"And?" she coaxes, knowing there is more.

"And have some ale."

"What else? Tell me," she presses lightly when I hesitate.

"And fuck."

Her cheeks instantly redden as she averts her eyes.

"Have I offended you?"

With her chin downcast, she shakes her head. "What happens when you cannot?"

"Cannot what?" I ask, confused.

"Fuck," she says with a pause, and that word slipping past her virtuous lips doesn't help my predicament.

"I usually do not have that problem."

She lifts her chin, her surprise clear as she understands what this means.

"It's just physical. It does not mean anything. Cecily understands what being away from her for months at a time means. We do not speak about it, but she knows I seek out the comfort of others when I am away from home.

"A kind touch helps appease the wickedness inside me."

"What about now? Will you seek out someone to appease you?"

"I will not."

She paddles closer toward me. "Why not? I am sure many women here would offer themselves to you."

"Because I do not want any of them," I snap, instantly regretting the sharpness of my tone.

She purses her lips, moving them from side to side in contemplation. I know what she's about to say, condemning us both to what she calls hell.

"What about me? Do you feel that way about me?"

"Emeline—"

But she doesn't let me finish. Instead, she boldly slips her hand under the water and gently takes hold of my cock. Instantly, a pleasured hiss escapes me, and I am powerless to move away.

"Because I want to appease you, Skarth," she confesses, moving her hand up and down my length. "For it will appease me as well."

"Please stop," I plead, for I will not be able to help myself, and if I do this with her, unlike the countless women I've been with before, this *will* mean something. That is why I do not seek anyone out, because Emeline will never just be a warm body to fill the void.

"You do not mean that. I can feel it by the hardness in

my hand. You are so well-endowed. The feel of you…it only strengthens my burn," she breathlessly acknowledges. "Touch me…please, Lord. Help me smother this ache, for I fear I will die if you do not."

"Emeline, please do not ask this of me."

"Why?" she asks, increasing the tempo of her strokes as her small hand attempts to cover me from base to tip.

"I do not satisfy you? Tell me what you like."

"You satisfy me," I correct, wishing to soothe her worries. "You satisfy me in ways you cannot imagine."

"Then touch me. I know it will mean nothing, and I accept that." She lowers her chin.

But she does not understand the effect she has on me.

Lifting her chin with my pointer finger, I confess, "That is where you are wrong. This will mean everything, which is why I need to stop."

I try to pull away, but she reaches for my hand and places it on her soft breast. Her nipple is erect, and my mouth waters for a taste.

"Do not stop," she demands, "for if you do not touch me… then I will touch myself."

My cock twitches at the thought.

"That pleases you? To watch?" she asks, always curious.

"Very much so," I huskily respond.

This is where we can meet in the middle to help us put out the fire without crossing a line. I want Emeline more than I need air to breathe, but I am afraid if I do this with her, I will lose myself completely to her.

I am not ready for that. And neither is she. She is animated from the fight, and I fear come morning, she will regret her rash decision. I don't want her to hate me for taking advantage of her in her vulnerable state.

"All right then," she says, droplets of water sticking to her lips. How I wish to chase them with my tongue. "All I ask is you never look away. I want to look into your eyes."

"Whatever you wish."

She removes her hand from me and I from her, and I can't smother my sigh of disappointment. But when she places the hand which was on my cock between her legs, that disappointment turns to appeal. She locks eyes with me, stroking herself slowly.

Her cheeks redden, but she doesn't stop.

"I wish it was your fingers inside me," she professes softly.

"I wish that too. Describe what you feel."

"I am wet," she reveals huskily. "That has nothing to do with the water. My—"

She pauses, struggling for the right word.

"*Kunta*," I offer, and she moans, appearing to approve.

"My…*kunta* is hot. It feels to be on fire in my hand. It burns me deeply. And I like it."

"What else?" I encourage, for hearing Emeline speak such filth has me almost losing control.

"My fingers are touching something swollen. It feels…oh." She gasps, her mouth popping open. "It feels rather delightful."

"That is your sweetness," I reveal deeply, "where, if you touch it in just the right way…it will shatter your world."

"I do not know how."

"You have never experienced it before?"

She shyly shakes her head. "Is there something wrong with me?"

"No, Princess," I assure her, angered she's never been brought to pleasure before. "There is nothing wrong with you. You are perfect."

"Will you teach me how?"

"Yes."

Her breaths become quicker as she maintains eye contact.

"Keep touching yourself. How many fingers do you have inside you?"

"One," she replies, her lower lip quivering.

"I want you to add another," I instruct, watching for the moment when she does.

"Gramercy!" she cries, her mouth forming an O shape.

"Feel good?"

"Yes. What else?"

Emeline enjoys taking some orders, it seems, and that only makes my cock grow even harder.

"Move your hips."

She does as the water splashes around her.

"Now, I want you to touch your breasts. I want you to feel what I did."

She continues working her fingers into her and moves the other hand to cup her full breasts. I'm envious of those fingers touching those soft mounds of perfection.

"Faster," I order, unable to look away from Emeline pleasuring herself.

Not being able to see entirely is what gets me even harder because it's so wicked. My mind fills in the blanks, and a throaty groan escapes me.

"Do you…do you like what you see, Lord?" she breathlessly asks, arching that beautiful body.

"Yes, very much."

"I like what I see too," she bashfully confesses. "The moonlight reflects the water clinging to your bronzed skin, and it really is enchanting. I also like your hair when you wear it down."

"It satisfies me to know I please you, Princess."

"Oh, God have mercy on my soul," she pants, her rhythm increasing. "Something is happening. I do not understand it."

"Tell me what."

"I-I…my body is a bundle of nerves, spinning out of control. I am afraid."

"Don't be," I assure her, never breaking eye contact. "Let it overtake you. I promise…just let go."

"Please continue to s-speak," she begs, her body writhing,

her mouth parted.

"You are a vision," I confess, wading closer to her so I can catch her when she falls. "Your body is utter sin. But so is your heart. I want…I ache for you. I *munuth* you."

"Please speak to me in your native tongue. I love it when you do."

She is moments away from experiencing her first *la petite mort*. And I will do anything she wishes to make it an experience she never forgets.

"*Du er vakker, hjartað mitt.*"

"What does it mean?"

Usually, I would not confess what I said, but I cannot deny her. "You are beautiful…my heart."

Her eyes flutter, but she doesn't look away. She works herself hungrily, and when I swim closer, closing the space between us and placing my mouth over hers, she does as I commanded and lets go.

I swallow her pleasured screams, kissing her deeply as I want to consume her—every part of her.

Her small body writhes violently, allowing me to dominate her as she surrenders to my touch. Her cries are long, guttural, and I like that she was able to experience this because of me. She tastes sweet, and I am addicted to the taste—to her.

Her raspy breaths tangle with mine, and for this moment in time, we are one.

With a gasp, she collapses against my chest, attempting to

catch her breath. I wrap an arm around her, running my fingers up and down her back.

"Thank you," she pants, snuggling close, and although we're both naked, there is something more to this moment than just a physical connection…and I know that will be our downfall.

But for now, I enjoy the feel of my woman in my arms. Because come tomorrow, I know things won't be as simple as this.

I've stayed away from Ulf because I can't control my temper around him. We may be forced to work together, but that doesn't mean I have to talk to him.

We have gathered everything and are on the move, leaving Ulf's kingdom, *Skalavik,* behind. I know it pains him, for the soil was rich and his kinsmen had built a home for themselves there.

But knowing Carhampton will be his new home softens the loss.

We are on the move to another village where our people have settled. I expect my arrival won't be welcomed, but I'm not here to rekindle what once was as I have bigger plans.

While Ulf and others have their sights set on Carhampton, I'm thinking somewhere bigger.

Being in service to King Eanred has taught me many things. It's taught me that Eoforwic in Northumbria has far greater value than most lands combined. And beyond England, Frankia.

These are two places I wish to conquer, but all in good time. For I know to invade Eoforwic, I will have to overthrow Emeline's father and brother.

We've not discussed what happened last night.

She timidly unfurled herself from my arms and walked to the bank, dressing in my shirt as her chemise was lost. I didn't go back to *Skalavik*. Instead, I slept outside under the stars.

She has kept her distance since then, which I assumed she would.

What we did last night changes things, and I think she needs time to process. For me, it only strengthened my desire for her. I hunger for her, and it's only getting worse.

But I cannot act on impulse. I need to be smart. The best thing for Emeline is for me to fight with a clear head, for her life depends on it.

And that is why I do not acknowledge her, for what can I offer her? I'm married and have a life with Cecily in Northumbria. I would not do that to Emeline or Cecily.

But when I look at Emeline, all I can see is her bountiful body twisting in pleasure, and all I hear are her breathless cries.

"Straggling behind everyone else? The battle got the better of you, *vinr*?" Ulf says, his voice ruining whatever happiness I felt.

"I am not your friend," I state, refusing to look at him as we trudge through the mud. "And I think you are the one who was beaten and by Wessex Guard, no less. What would the gods think?"

I don't mask my ridicule, which infuriates him.

He's lucky the stab wound he received wasn't fatal. I'm surprised he got injured in the first place because even though I would never admit this to anyone, especially Ulf, he is as good a warrior as I am. Which is why we were unstoppable when we fought side by side.

I wonder where his father, Sten, is. His father and mine were good friends, as Ulf and I once were.

"And what would the gods think that you chose a Saxon over your sister?"

Ulf and Sigrith were once in love. This is what she tells me, for Ulf never admitted his feelings. But his bitter response to her being left at the palace is all the answer I need.

With a menacing growl, I turn toward him.

He smirks in response. "I understand the interest, however. She tastes as sweet as she looks."

Time suddenly stands still.

"What did you say?"

"You heard me," he replies smugly, supporting his wounded arm, which is bandaged. "It was my bed she lay in before you came to rescue what is *yours*."

"You lie."

"I do not. Ask her if you doubt me."

I suddenly feel like I cannot breathe for the thought of Emeline and Ulf together…it makes me beyond murderous.

"Ah, we are here," Ulf says, knowing what his revelation has done to me.

I clench my fists, for now is not the time as we have arrived at *Kleifar*, a village settled by my people. It was plundered from Saxon folk, which means the king's men can attack at any moment, especially once word reaches the palace about Emeline's capture.

We cannot stay here for long.

"Ulf!" Gorm happily says, running toward him.

Gorm is Ulf's uncle. He was also a friend of my father's, so when he sees me, he doesn't hide his distaste that I'm here.

"Why is the traitor here?" he asks Ulf, refusing to acknowledge me.

"He has finally decided to do the right thing."

Gorm curls his lip. "It is too late, for he has already pissed on his father's, Gunder Bloodaxe's, memory by becoming King Eanred's dog."

"I am no one's dog, Gorm," I grimly state.

"No?" he questions, his orange eyebrows rising in contempt. "Have you avenged your family like you said you would? Are your mother and sister no longer slaves to the Saxon *eldhúsfífls*? And what of your brother, Knud? Does he see through his eyes because of your *sacrifice*?"

I do not know where Knud is as he left on a ship one night and has never been heard from since. I was told he returned to our homeland, but I cannot know for certain. He wanted to forget this place and those who remained here.

"A man who waits will eat the ripened fruit," I say because I knew this quest would take patience and resilience.

I don't expect Gorm or Ulf to understand it because it wasn't their family who was destroyed. It wasn't their lives or names they ruined all in the name of revenge.

"I can see what ripened fruit you bring," Gorm says, peering at Emeline, who helps a child down from a horse.

It surprises me when Ulf responds before I can. "She is not to be harmed."

His stance is quite firm but soon relaxes when he notices me looking at him inquisitively. Why does he feel the need to jump to her defense? Could it be true? Did Emeline share his bed, after all?

The rage I feel intensifies, and I leave Gorm and Ulf alone before I go back on my word.

Gorm's village is vast, and the faces are ones I recognize. They were ones who once belonged to my father's clan. With his death, our people separated and formed smaller colonies, it seems. But they remember, regardless of the new families established.

As I walk past them, they spit at my feet or mutter under

their breaths how I am not welcome here. If it weren't for Emeline, I would not have come. But I fear I've misread her feelings.

When we lock eyes, she smiles timidly. The first sign of acknowledgment all day.

In response, I turn my back and commence unpacking the weapons from the cart.

Ulf now beds Inga, which is why she has taken a dislike toward Emeline. This is further confirmation of Ulf's claims.

I need to hit something and hit it hard.

"Look, it's Skarth the Cowardly," says Orm, Gorm's son, to his friend.

He was just a boy when I left. Although grown, he's still a pup as he has no idea what he just started.

It appears the gods smile down on me.

"And it's Orm the Smelly," I counter as I remember quite well when he shit himself when he came face-to-face with a bear.

His cheeks redden as his friend, whose name I cannot recall, snickers under his breath. But this has merely shown me his weakness as well, for what friend wouldn't defend his friend's honor?

With shield and sword in hand, I toss one to Orm and his friend. They fumble but catch them. They look on, confused, while an amused chuckle leaves me.

"Are these your bravest warriors, Gorm?" I question,

thumbing my bottom lip in scrutiny. "I fear we are doomed if this is true."

Gorm storms forward, angered. Ulf smirks at my boldness.

Orm doesn't appreciate me laughing at his expense and charges for me with a roar. I stand solid, and when he swings his sword, I punch him square in the nose. The sword drops from his hand as he cups his broken nose, where I then punch him in the stomach.

His friend now finds his *bellir* and comes rushing toward me, shield raised, but I strike out and kick him in the knee. He topples over, howling in pain, while I yawn, bored by this spectacle.

"Get up!" Gorm orders, standing close by and watching in disgust as his son squirms on his back like a bug.

"It may be better if he stays down there," I tease. "I would not want him to fall over his feet trying to get back up."

The village erupts into laughter, but that soon dies when I address the issue of why I'm here.

"No matter what you think of me, I am your best hope at getting what you want," I state, eyeing everyone closely. "We left our homelands to better our lives, but is this enough?"

I spread my arms out wide.

"We plunder these lands, but we are always at risk of an attack from the Saxons, wanting to claim back what is theirs. I wish for that to change, and we have the opportunity to do that."

No one dares speak.

"We will take Carhampton in three weeks' time, which will show the Saxons who we really are. We are not going anywhere. We are here to stay! They can either come to an agreement with us, or…we kill them."

The kinsfolk erupt into loud clapping and howls of approval.

"The gods tell us to be brave, to fight for what we want, and what I want is to make Wessex suffer! To see her bleed!

"Northumbria is weak, as are the other kingdoms. Wessex is who we fight against. But to win, we need men and women who are willing to fight for our future. Warriors who are willing to die for our cause. I cannot do this alone. But I am willing to teach you how to defeat a Saxon army, for I am a traitor, after all," I say, wanting everyone to know that if they do this, they'll be obeying an absconder, something which will displease them every single day.

"But being a traitor has allowed me to gain knowledge and power, and it's because of this…we will win. King Egbert does not know of our fighting style, but King Eanred does. King Egbert will combine forces with Northumbria, for we have something both kings want."

I meet Emeline's eyes.

She stands alone, the fear etched on her beautiful face, the face which will haunt me to the end of days, for she knows what this means. She will not only have Wessex fighting for her return but Northumbria as well.

"We have Princess Emeline, who is King Eanred's daughter. But…she is also in favor with King Egbert. She was once the future Queen of Wessex. Both kings will do anything for her return."

I don't want to put her in harm's way, but the men and women need to know what they're fighting for.

This was the reason I wanted no part in this war because whichever way we approach this, Emeline loses. My people will look at her as payment, as will the kings of this realm. She is wanted by all, which puts her life at risk.

She can be used as collateral by everyone as she holds value to all. Therefore, I have no other choice but to guard her with my life. There may be no freedom for her, which means the only mercy I can grant her would be death by my sword.

My heart shatters at the thought, but the decision was made before she was born when her father struck a deal for his own selfish gain.

Her price is far greater than any riches this nation has ever seen, and men and women will exploit that. I can't trust anyone with her safety, which means I need to protect the woman who torments me in ways I cannot explain.

It aches to be near her, for she is a temptation I cannot have, but I cannot leave her side. I am forced to smother these feelings I have for her because her safety is all that matters. I cannot ensure that if my feelings are involved. I will not fight with a clear head if I do.

Emotions make a man weak, they cloud one's mind, and I will not endanger Emeline in that way. I am the only person who will fight for her because of…love. And it's because of that that I must push her away. I cannot allow another incident like last night to occur as this will give Emeline mixed signals. I am here to ensure no harm comes to her and nothing more.

I need to remind her I am nothing more than a depraved heathen and not the man who loves her with every beat of his heart.

"The princess is willing to help us as she has offered herself as a trade," I reveal, breaking eye contact with her because I fear I will go back on my word otherwise. "Which means…she is not to be harmed. We need her to succeed."

I hate referring to her as nothing but an object, but this is the only way to make them understand.

"Without her, King Egbert will win. Without me, he will win. So, here, now, I ask that you pledge your loyalty to me, Skarth Gundersen…son of Gunder Bloodaxe. I know you do not like me, and that is all right…for I do not like you either.

"But we need one another. The choice is yours, for once you make it, it will be sworn before the gods and will be punished if you disobey them. Make the right choice as our gods are not forgiving…and neither am I."

It's a warning—their first and only one.

If they betray me, if they hurt Emeline, I will kill them and kill them brutally.

Ulf is the first man to step forward and clasp my lower arm—our custom that he agrees to my terms. Of course, he does, as once this deal is done, he will be a very powerful man.

As for me, I merely wish to be left alone.

The men and women soon follow Ulf's lead, clasping my forearm as a sign of respect and promise. Although they pledge alliance with reluctance, they know I am their best hope at winning.

Emeline is last in line, and although she is not a Viking, she wants to show her respect. All eyes are on us as she stands before me. I expect her to extend the same acceptance as others, but instead, she curtseys.

"I am your humble servant, Lord."

Hearing her submission just adds to the longing inside my chest, but I nod firmly. "Good because, for once, you are going to do what you're told."

Her emerald eyes snap up, livid that I would speak to her this way. But this is how every exchange will occur from now on. In order to survive, she has to fear me and the consequences she faces if she doesn't obey me. I see now that I must rule with cruelness to curb her rebellion.

If she thinks I have a weakness for her, she'll believe I will be lenient and that she can do whatever she pleases. But I cannot allow it. She will hate me come the battle of Carhampton. It's the only way to keep her alive.

Ulf smirks as he knows how it pains me to treat her this

way. I have no doubt he'll offer her comfort—again. Just the thought has me dismissing her with a wave of my hand.

It's time for the princess to see why they call me Skarth the Godless.

# THIRTEEN

*Princess Emeline*

He's cruel.

I don't understand why.

He is angry with me for something, but what did I do? Is it because I avoided him after last night—the best night of my life?

I thought it was what he wanted, and I was reserved for my forward behavior. But I clearly know nothing at all.

I help the Northman women cook a feast for their tribe as we have cause for celebration. I didn't think my proposal through, but Skarth did. He knew I would be wanted by both kingdoms, which is why I believe he is outraged.

He is angry I would put my life at risk this way. But doesn't he understand I would rather die free than live a life shackled with invisible manacles?

I need to speak with him, but he's not acknowledged me since he crudely dismissed me as nothing but a puerile child. He speaks with the Northmen, talks of battle, no doubt, as I've overheard talks of sending for over thirty ships of men to arrive for the battle at Carhampton.

Wessex will be outnumbered, but King Egbert will send for reinforcements. All kingdoms will fight this war, for they wish to please Wessex. This is far bigger than I thought.

Focusing on the large iron pot over the fire, I stir the stew as I need to do something with my hands. I fear the silence otherwise.

I've learned the Northmen drink an alcoholic concoction similar to ale. It is called mead. A woman offers me a cup crafted from a cattle horn. I accept, with no intention of drinking it, but when I see Skarth appear with two women on his arm, laughing shamelessly, I take a long swallow.

It doesn't taste bad, just very strong. It is also sweet, I think from the honey it's been brewed with.

They are such resilient farmers. The Saxon people could learn from them instead of fighting. But I don't think a treaty will be had anytime soon.

The woman laughs when I pull a face once I've swallowed down half the mead.

Most are accommodating, but I know they merely tolerate

me, for I serve a greater purpose to them all.

The men gather, a sign it's time to eat. There are many of them, and I do not know how their hierarchy works, so I step aside and allow the women to dish up the meal. I nurse my mead, discreetly watching Skarth as he openly flirts.

I thought after last night, things would have changed, but all it's done is make me feel a fool.

I help myself to more mead as my appetite has long gone. This is the only thing that quenches my appetite—well, the second thing, for the thing I want won't even look at me. I swallow the entire cup of mead, wiping the fallen liquid with the back of my hand.

"Careful, Princess, any more and it will be an early night for you." It's Ulf who stands by me, the arrogant bastard who seems to be enjoying my discomfort.

"Do not tell me what to do," I say, reaching for the jug of mead.

"I wouldn't dare," he mocks, grinning. "I know you do not do anything you don't wish to."

His comment has nothing to do with my drinking and everything to do with our kiss. The kiss I should regret, but don't.

I don't tell him that, however.

"You do not have anyone else to annoy?" I smugly state, sipping my drink.

"There is no one else I would rather annoy than you. Skol!"

he says, banging our cups together.

I assume skol is the phrase they use to applaud something, not that there is anything for me to celebrate. I hate that Skarth is ignoring me, and I hate it even more when Inga offers him a bowl of stew and sits beside him so they can eat together.

"Not hungry?" Ulf says, following my line of vision.

"I seemed to have lost my appetite," I reply, turning my back and sitting on a stool.

I expect Ulf to leave me be, but to my surprise, he sits by me and places a bowl of stew in my lap. "Eat."

"Fancy another face full of food, Lord?" I tease, smirking as I happily recall the image of Ulf covered in porridge.

"For a princess, you are impossibly disobedient."

I arch a brow and mock, "What a shrewd observation."

His full lips pull into an amused line. "Are you sure you are not part Viking?"

"I do not know what I am," I confess, finishing my mead in one long gulp. "I do know, however, that all I am to you is your opportunity to become infamous in Wessex and beyond."

I expect him to agree or respond with sarcasm, but he does neither.

"You insult me, Princess." He leans in close, taking my breath away when he whispers, "I kissed you before this opportunity arose, before Skarth hatched his ingenious plan."

"I was always a trade." I dare not move, too afraid of the consequences if I do.

"This is true, but now, things have changed. You cannot deny that."

He's right.

When he kissed me, our plan was in its infancy. Does this mean he kissed me out of free will?

"You turn the loveliest of pinks when you are uncomfortable," he says, so close to my ear, his lips brush it. "I wonder where else you flush."

"I cry your mercy!" I exclaim, pulling away to face him.

We are a hairbreadth away, and I hate that he stirs something in me. He is infuriating, arrogant, and will exploit me to get what he wants, yet I can't seem to push him away.

My gaze drops to his lips and I remember how they felt pressed to mine. How *he* felt. He felt good. But so did Skarth.

"Whatever you are thinking, I'd very much like to know."

"And I'd like to leave now."

Jolting upright, I quickly walk away, needing to put space between Ulf and me. I don't know what it is about him, but he annoys and entices me all in the same breath.

As I stomp through the mud, I realize the world has tilted slightly, and I think the reason for that is because I am drunk. The mead was stronger than I thought.

I stop near the barn and pat my faithful horse on the nose.

I don't know how I ended up in this position, where even though I am out of the palace walls, I am still very much a prisoner to my duty of being the Princess of Northumbria.

I am suddenly exhausted.

But there is no rest for the wicked, it seems, when I hear someone come to a stop behind me. I know who it is before he speaks. I've been bound to him since I was twelve years old.

"I believe you are drunk, Princess."

"And I believe your female companions are missing your company, Lord."

I turn around to face Skarth, folding my arms. I'm cold, as I am in borrowed clothes two sizes too big, but I'd rather freeze to death than tell Skarth that.

"Stop being such a spoiled little monster," he has the audacity to say. "We are here because of the deal *you* made."

"Spoiled?" I spit, narrowing my eyes. "Everything I have ever done was for the sake of others! And now that I refuse to be mistreated, refuse to be treated as nothing but property, I am spoiled? Fuck you…*Northman*."

This word is one I've heard the Northmen use quite often. I am not sure what it means, but it sure as…fuck feels liberating to speak it.

"You mock the company I keep," he says, his blue eyes pinning me to the spot I stand. "But it's obvious the people you chose to interact with have turned you into a foul-mouthed brat."

He is referring to one person in particular.

"At least they talk to me," I counter quickly, for I won't allow him to belittle me for the language I choose to use. "And you are not my father. I can speak however I wish."

"No, I am not your father, thank the gods for that."

This conversation is going nowhere as the more he speaks, the angrier I become. "Leave me be. I came here to be alone."

He appears wounded. I asked him to leave, but he started this war between us.

"You have not acknowledged me all day. Last night, I—"

But when a snicker leaves him, I regret opening my mouth. "What were you expecting, Princess? To awake in my arms where I whispered sweet longings into your ear?"

"I did not expect anything." The truth is, however, I did.

I expected it to mean something to him because it meant something to me. I've never been that way with a man before—vulnerable and trusting—and this is how he responds. Treating me no better than the men before him.

His steps are measured as he strolls toward me. The shiver that racks my body has nothing to do with the cold wind.

"I understand it was the effect of the battle and nothing more," I quickly project. "Let's not speak of it again."

But that doesn't stop him from coming.

My heart threatens to rip from its cage as he reaches out, clasping my wrist. He pulls me toward him, pressing us chest to chest. He towers over me, but I don't cower. I look up at him, daring him to do his worst.

What he does, however, is ruin me forevermore.

"Do not lie to me, Emeline. You forget I know you better

than you know yourself," he declares, brushing a strand of hair from my cheek. He doesn't remove his fingers, and I lean into his touch. "I know you have been aching for my touch.

"You've practically begged for it since I can remember."

I suddenly don't like his tone or accusations and attempt to pull away, but he doesn't let me go, for he isn't done.

"My needy little princess…always wanting more. Did you think your inexperience was a temptation for me?" he mocks, chuckling arrogantly. "You forget, it may have been the first time for you, but it wasn't for me.

"It may have been special for you, everything your amorous heart desired, but it's not like I haven't done it before. And I have done a lot before…and I plan on doing a lot more come morning. Sorry to disappoint you, Princess, but your cunt is nothing but a distant memory."

"How dare you!" I shove him away and slap his cheek so hard, I fear I've broken my hand. But the pain is worth it. "You are nothing but a filthy heathen!"

Cupping his cheek, he smirks. "And you are nothing but an inexperienced little girl."

He knows how to wound me because that is the worst thing he could possibly say. Or so I thought.

"But maybe you are not so inexperienced, after all?"

"Now you more than insult me," I cry, narrowing my eyes.

"So you did not lie in Ulf's bed?"

My mouth hinges open, revealing my guilt.

"Did he force himself on you? Were his advances unwanted?"

All I can do is wonder when my Northman turned into the cruelest man I know.

"Answer me, Princess. You are quick to judge me, while it seems I do not know you at all."

Refusing to allow another man to belittle me ever again, I pull back my shoulders and stand proud. "No, to both your questions."

He stands strong, but I can see I wound him with my response, and I don't intend on telling him all we shared was one kiss. It's no business of his.

"What I do and who I do it with is none of your business," I state with conviction. "And the same applies with you. Bed whomever you like. It makes no difference to me. Last night was merely something for me to learn from because you are right, I *am* an inexperienced little girl, and there is only one way to change that."

He insulted me, so now I insult him. He believes me to be nothing but a whore, so I will behave like one.

"I attained what I wanted from you, so thank you, kind lord. But I am not interested in being yet another mistress to a self-absorbed, stupid arse. I will cherish our time together and think back on it fondly. Or maybe as a comparison for future conquests. I am not sure yet."

A feral growl leaves him, but he can go back to the hole he

crawled from.

Shoving past him with intent, I bump my arm into his. "I bid thee farewell. I hope you are not too exhausted come morning. I would not want you to slip and fall on your sword."

A not-so-subtle warning that we are no longer friends, and he best sleep with one eye open.

I walk away, unable to wipe my smile clean because no longer will I stand for a man treating me like dirt. Last night didn't go as I expected it would—it was better.

Excitement swells in my belly, and I take off into the darkness, my feet unable to keep up with my exhilaration as I run freely with no destination in mind. But it's not about the destination, rather the journey, and for the first time ever, I'm excited for what's ahead.

My loose hair whips in the wind, and an animated scream leaves me as I roar into the night sky.

I don't understand why Skarth is behaving in such a manner. Is he angry with me because of Sigrith? I would usually be beside myself with apprehension, but I realize it's time I worried about myself.

No longer will I be used and abused by anyone.

I continue running into the wilderness until I can run no more, then I take my time exploring this foreign land like a smart predator does. It's quiet when I arrive back. Most are asleep inside their homes. Others by the fire.

I've not planned on where to sleep, so I head for the barn

as my loyal horse is the only man I trust. However, when I pass a longhouse and see a fire burning brightly inside and hear impassioned moans, it seems not everyone has retired for the night.

I should walk away—that's what any God-fearing Christian would do—which is why I mask my footsteps and skulk toward the doorway to get a better look.

The door is ajar, allowing me to see inside. At first, however, I don't understand what I'm seeing. It's a coupling of arms and legs and lots of bare flesh. I grip the doorway and take a closer look inside, and that's when a gasp escapes me, for I now know what I see.

Two women and one man lost to the throes of passion.

I am utterly fascinated because I never knew this was possible, but it clearly is when I witness a man's bronzed, muscled arse pumping back and forth at a hypnotizing speed. He sinks into the lax woman who lays on her back.

Her moans are smothered because her mouth is draped by the woman who rocks against her mouth. She rides her face how one would ride a horse and when the man lowers himself, taking her nipple into his mouth as he viciously humps the other Northman, I see the woman is Inga.

Vomit rises, and I cover my mouth to stop it from expelling and mute my anguished screams, for I know who this man is.

Skarth stuck true to his word of occupying his time till morning.

He is brutal. There is no kindness to his touches. But I suppose there never was. This is who he is.

Inga arches backward, moaning as Skarth pleasures her. Her long blonde hair cascades around them, encasing the three of them in a world made solely for them. The woman Skarth plows is merely an object as it's clear the real attraction is between him and Inga. But she and Ulf were together, I thought.

That doesn't seem to make a difference to the Northmen.

They take whatever they want, and it seems Skarth wants it all when he pushes Inga away, only coaxing her onto her hands and knees. He pulls out of the woman, who cries out in pleasured pain.

"On your hands and knees as well," he orders, his deep, husky voice touching me low even though I don't want it to.

She quickly does as he orders.

Both of the women's arses are on show, and now is the moment I should turn around. But I cannot.

Skarth's long hair is out loose, falling delicately across his broad back. The thin plait held together with beads catches the light from the fire and under the glow, even though I hate him, he is the most beautiful thing I have ever seen.

He radiates raw, carnal passion, and I am envious of the women, for they have what I will never have again.

Skarth cups their round, firm arses before slapping each one hard, so hard both women jar up the bed from the force. They don't whine, however. They come back for more.

Anchoring Inga's hips, Skarth enters her slowly.

Her moans reveal her approval, but when the other woman cups her cheek, drawing Inga's mouth to hers, it seems everyone approves. Skarth commences pumping into her violently, the noises leaving his parted lips animalistic. He likes it.

Just as he slams into Inga, he retreats just as quickly before entering the other woman.

My eyes widen as I cannot believe what I'm seeing as Skarth humps both women brutally. But the sated moans that spill past their locked lips expose their pleasure. He doesn't stop. He viciously plows them both—in, out, in, and out before it's just a flurry of bodies and a collection of moans.

My cheeks are hot, and just like last night, I'm wet between the legs. But hunger aside, I want to murder each woman for touching what is mine.

I hate Skarth the Godless with every breath I take because I am certain he hoped my curiosity would get the better of me, and I would look inside. Why else would he leave the door open?

This is his way of showing me that I may have won the battle, but he will always, *always*, win the war.

Inga's body trembles before a wild cry leaves her.

Skarth pulls his member out of her before falling onto his back, his chest rising and falling evenly. Although the world is upside down, he tips his head backward slowly so he can see me clearly as I stand by his doorway, tears in my eyes.

We stare at one another, and what I see reflected back at me scares me, for I see nothing at all.

Inga straddles his lap, taking his enormous length into her as she rides him hard. With sunken eyes still locked to mine, he allows the other woman to mount his face, where she mimics Inga. Both women come together, kissing passionately over the man I love.

I've seen enough and quietly escape into the night, but no sleep will be had tonight.

I was awake before dawn, and that's because I've not slept. Every time I closed my eyes, all I could see was Skarth and the two women lost to the throes of passion.

Deciding to get an early start on the day, I collected some rocks, twigs, and anything else I could find because I can't get the battle of Carhampton out of my mind. The landscape is to the Northmen's advantage. With the coast close by, this allows their men to arrive via ships with ease.

But they need to remain undetected so this will be a surprise attack.

Sitting on the floor with the rocks and twigs spread out before me, I use each object as a marker for the terrain at Carhampton. It's easier for me to envision the battlefield this way.

Northmen gather around me, watching on in curiosity as I mumble strategies under my breath.

I rode through Carhampton with King Egbert, so I know the land well.

"The coast from here," I say to myself, shifting a twig to sit alongside a large rock, "is more accessible from the sea. If the Northmen's ships sail in from this point, they can use the coverage from the mountains and large rocks."

Sitting back on my heels, I close my eyes and touch each rock and twig, envisioning the landmark they represent. I can see it clearly in my mind.

"King Egbert's men will attack from land, not the seas. They'll have the advantage on land, while the Northmen on water. But what if, what if the Northmen ambushed them? The terrain is vast. What if the Northmen tricked them?"

"And how do you suggest we do that?"

Ulf's interested voice has me opening my eyes, seeing the crowd of Northmen has doubled in size.

He stands before me, arms folded as he looks at the grid I've created.

Licking my lips, I push a pile of rocks into the middle of the imaginary battlefield I created. "These are the king's men," I reveal, staring at the rocks and picturing my plan.

"And these the Northmen." I point at the three twigs aligned like soldiers.

"If your men are concealed here"—I gesture toward a pile of leaves which denotes a wooded embankment—"you can wait in hiding. The king's men will be too focused on the Northmen coming in from the seas and also attacking on land that they won't see this ambush.

"Once all of the king's men are in the middle of the battlefield, you attack from the other side, boxing them in. They will be fending off men from behind, each side, and also advancing forward. It'll be a massacre."

"How do you know there is an embankment there?" Ulf asks, thumbing his lip in deliberation.

"Because I have passed through there on horseback. I know the terrain well. The men and women can easily be concealed with vegetation."

"And we are supposed to just take your word for it?" It's Inga who speaks, and when I meet her eyes, I can't help but scowl.

"Take my advice, or do not. But when you are defeated and have lost more than half of your men, do not complain as it will be too late."

"How many wars have you fought, Princess?" She snickers, attempting to belittle me.

"Do not underestimate me," I warn, which excites the onlookers as they smell what's brewing.

"Why not show us then?" Inga suggests, throwing her arms out wide. "Fight me and let us see who the better warrior is. If you beat me, I will no longer question your word. What you say, I will do."

"And if you beat me?"

She grins, a sure sign she believes there are no ifs about it. "If I beat you, then you must fight for your own freedom. You are on your own on the battlefield."

"Inga!" Ulf scolds, angered.

But I wave him off. "All right. It's a deal."

Inga laughs, confident she's already won this war. "She is a big girl, Ulf. She does not need you to fight her battles. She's made that very clear."

Ulf clenches his jaw, clearly not happy with Inga, but like I affirmed last night, I don't need a man to protect me. I can win my own war.

Coming to a stand, I accept the sword and shield Ulf offers me. He doesn't hide his worry that I've accepted Inga's challenge because I know there is no going back now. Inga arms herself, a confident smile hinting she thinks this will be an easy fight.

I wonder if she wore that same smile when Skarth was plowing into her relentlessly. The thought provokes my anger, and I get into position, ready to take this witch down.

The Northmen gather in a circle with Inga and me in the middle. They watch on with interest, howling at the prospect of seeing blood spilled. I never take my eyes off Inga because even though I can fight, I know she can too.

She waits for me to make a move, but she has no idea who

my teacher was. Skarth taught me that all good things come to those who wait, and when Inga grows impatient, it appears my waiting has paid off.

She attacks me, and I defend, but when she smirks arrogantly, already believing this war is won, I decide to taunt her as that will make this victory all the more sweet.

She strikes out, and even though I can block her attack, I don't. I allow her to knock the sword from my hand. It crashes to the ground.

The Northmen cry out loudly, encouraging Inga to finish the job.

She charges for me again, and I defend with my shield. She swings her sword, it smashing into my shield, and when I sidestep her attack, she strikes me in the ribs. I'm winded, but I've sustained much worse. However, when I drop my shield, gasping in air, Inga thinks she's won.

"Finish her!" the Northmen scream, revealing where their loyalty lies.

I fold in half, hands on my knees as I stage breathlessness. "Please do not harm me," I pathetically cry, pretending to be afraid.

Inga shouts something in her language, and when I raise my eyes, I see Skarth watching on closely.

His arms are folded across his broad chest, a slanted smile spread across his full lips, for he knows like a cat, I'm merely playing with my meal. He's taught me better than to surrender, so when I reach for my fallen sword, he nods in approval.

But I don't need his approval. I don't need anything at all.

With a roar, I stand and swing, slapping the sword against the back of Inga's legs. It catches her unawares, and she falls onto her knees. Before she has a chance to fight back, I stand in front of her and place the tip of my blade to her throat.

She clenches her jaw, glaring at her sword only a step away. "Never turn your back on your enemy," I calmly state. "But you like being on your knees, mayhap?"

I arch a brow, wanting her to know I saw her last night with Skarth, offering her arse to him, conceding to her carnal lust.

With a snarl, she turns her cheek, admitting defeat.

"I win," I smugly state, offering her my hand.

She slaps it away, rising on her own, and pushes past the shocked Northmen. They underestimated me, all but one.

Skarth continues staring at me. And I at him.

Ulf follows my line of sight, appearing to realize just who taught me everything I know.

Skarth turns his back, soiling my victory, but this isn't about him. It's about me and how I've just proven myself to the Northmen. They no longer look at me with animosity but rather with curiosity as I am nothing like the Saxons they've met before.

"Come take a walk with me, Princess." Ulf gestures with his head that I'm to follow. He doesn't look behind as he knows my curiosity will get the better of me.

I give my sword to Erik, who smiles a toothless grin. His mother still despises me, and that's okay as I did kill her husband. Even though he was a filthy rat, he was her filthy rat. I seem to understand her stance well when I look for Skarth, but he's nowhere to be found.

I follow with my head held high, wondering what Ulf wants. I wonder if he's mad at me for embarrassing Inga. But she embarrassed herself by underestimating me.

Ulf walks into the forest and stops when we're covered by thick foliage. I stop a few steps away.

He doesn't turn around to face me right away. He simply tips his head toward the sky and inhales deeply. "Skarth taught you well."

"He did." I'm not sure why he needed privacy to divulge that, so I guess he has something else to say.

"You are not like anyone I have ever met before." He lowers his chin and turns slowly to look at me.

"Thank you. I think?"

He smiles, which is a rare sight as it appears genuine. "We will follow your plan," he states with conviction. "It's smart, and it will work."

"Of course it will," I affirm with confidence. "The king's army will be too occupied with trying to survive that they will not see the ambush. We lie waiting until the perfect time to strike. Not a moment before."

"And you're okay with your people being crushed this way?"

"Yes," I reply without pause, "for they were okay crushing me. Wessex and Northumbria both deserve to pay for their sins."

"Whatever will your God say?" Ulf teases with a grin.

"I fear He has already passed judgment on me."

"And what does He say?"

Ulf walks toward me slowly, his piercing eyes burning a hole straight through me.

"That I am a sinner. And even if I repented for the rest of my days, it would never be enough."

"Your God sounds very boring."

He stops mere inches away, towering over me in not only stature but presence as well. He looks at me with nothing but interest, like I am a mystery he wishes to solve.

"Perhaps I was never meant to bow before anyone?" I pose, suddenly feeling warm.

"I think given the right circumstances, you would enjoy being on your knees."

Now, I know we are no longer speaking of religion.

He reaches out and thumbs my bottom lip softly. I want to push him away, but I welcome the tenderness of another.

"Would you consider it with me?"

"Consider what?" I ask from around his thumb.

"Consider being with me."

He slips his thumb into my mouth when it parts in surprise. What is he saying?

"The thought of any harm coming to you…it makes me want to kill whoever wronged you, Inga included," he confesses. "When you made that deal with her, I would have fought her to the death to protect you."

I don't know what to say.

"I thought you and she—" I leave my sentence unfinished as he can work out the rest.

"Just something to pass the time."

"And what of Sigrith?" The way he reacted when he discovered her fate led me to believe he has feelings for her.

"Sigrith and I," he commences, removing his thumb with regret. "She was someone I cared for very deeply."

"Then I assume you are angry with me for the position she's now in?"

"No, Princess, I am not angry with you. It was Skarth's job to protect her. That's why he left us. Did he tell you that?"

I nod.

"Did he tell you we were once the best of friends? That we would have died for the other? Just how our fathers would have? But now, we fight like enemies because his arrogance would not let anyone help him. What was done to his family, he saw to be his fault.

"No one could have stopped it. Not even the gods themselves. But Skarth will never forgive himself for it."

I didn't know of their past, but it explains their rivalry. It pains me to know Skarth suffers this way. It also reveals how much he cared for me to leave Sigrith behind.

But I don't understand his behavior. He treats me like dirt, but is there a reason for it?

"He has an evilness inside that will destroy him and everything he touches."

"I do not believe that," I argue as I know Skarth. "He is wedded to a brave, beautiful woman named Cecily. She would have never married him if that were true."

"He married a Saxon?"

I bite my lip, fearful I've revealed too much.

"He is more lost than I thought."

"Cecily is a good woman," I say, defending both Skarth's and her honor.

"If that were true, why is he here? Why is he risking his life for you? Why is he in Inga's bed?"

I lower my eyes as I don't have the answers.

"Did you like it when I kissed you?"

I'm not sure what this has to do with our conversation, so I keep my eyes downcast.

"Because I liked it."

"I am not fooled by you, Lord," I say, shaking my head. "I merely serve a purpose, and once that is met, you will discard me. I interest you, for I am something you wish to understand. But I do not mistake this for something it is not."

I know Ulf's interest in me is pure curiosity. I'm something rare in his world, but once he tires of me, once the novelty wears thin, I will just be a means to an end. And I know without a doubt he would trade my life to get what he wants.

"You misjudge me," he says, lifting my chin with his finger. "You interest me as you are something I want. I will never understand you, how can I? You are a Saxon. But that doesn't make a difference to me."

He leans down while I hold my breath.

"Your strength sings to mine," he confesses, his lips a hairbreadth away. "I do not understand it. But I want to."

Our breaths soon become one, but he doesn't close the space between us. And neither do I.

I can't deny the attraction I feel for him, regardless of knowing the truth. His disgust at Skarth marrying Cecily is a sure sign that our differences could never be put aside. He will always choose his people, and me? I'm not sure who I would choose—in more ways than one.

"My bed is always warm for you, Princess," he declares, heating my cheeks. "And I know, no matter how hard you try to resist, it's my bed you will end up in. Maybe not tomorrow or the day after, but you and I, we are connected…whether you like it or not."

"Or not, Lord," I reply, but there is no bite to my tone. "I will not be enslaved to any man ever again."

"Who said anything about being enslaved? We are equal. But I will dominate you, and you me, where it matters."

"And where would that be?" I'm almost afraid to ask.

"Wherever you want it to be, Princess. On the battlefield. In the kingdoms. Or in my bed," he adds, grinning as I whimper. "Although, I would not need a bed, for I am ready for you—always."

With eyes locked to mine, he closes the small distance between us, and just when I think he's going to kiss me again, he turns his cheek.

I stop myself from falling forward, hiding my disappointment—not that he pulled away, but that I continue allowing myself to fall under his spell.

"I will tell the men and women of our plans. We will decide who will sail out tonight to gather our people."

"All right. That seems wise. I am unsure how long it takes to sail to Scandinavia?"

He arches a brow. "You know of my people?"

"I know a lot of things, Ulf the Bloody."

"It seems so."

I need to put some distance between us, so I push past him even though I have no idea where I'm going. But the freedom is what entices me to continue.

I don't know what it is about Ulf, but sometimes, he has me forgetting the world exists beyond us. It terrifies me.

I don't know if what he says is true. If he, in fact, feels what he says he does. I don't know anything at all, it seems. The one thing I thought I did know was that Skarth would always be with me. But I was wrong.

Tears fill my eyes, and I don't even know why I'm crying. I weep for so many things. For the girl I no longer am. And for my broken heart, broken by the man who I can't seem to stop loving, regardless of everything he's done.

Tears blur my vision, and I don't think they'll ever stop, but I hear it a second too late…before my world is thrown into darkness—thanks to a king's guard who steps out from behind a tree.

# FOURTEEN

*Skarth the Godless*

As the twentieth Viking falls to his arse, I shake my head because we are doomed.

They're barely fit enough to fight me—and I am not even fighting at my full capacity—let alone an army of men. They've become lazy, and I don't know if that's because of arrogance or lack of leadership.

My father would have never allowed his men to fight this way. They embarrass us. We don't stand a chance against the Saxons.

Ulf watches on, reading my thoughts as he too is surely disgusted with the efforts of these men and women who are supposed to be his finest warriors. I have no idea how they've survived this long.

Turning away as Gunn gets off the ground, I subtly search for Emeline. She's been gone for over an hour, and although I'm trying to keep her at arm's length, not a second goes by when I don't think of her.

She hates me, which is what I wanted. I thought it would help keep her safe because if she hates and fears me, she'll do what she's told. But now I'm worried I've gone too far. I knew she was watching last night. I knew what it would do to her seeing me with women who weren't her.

I pushed her away for her own good, but I feel like a rotten bastard for doing so. She looks at me with hurt and confusion, and it kills me inside.

And now I fear by trying to keep her safe, I've done the complete opposite.

"Where is the princess?" I casually ask Ulf as he sharpens our swords.

"How would I know?"

"You are the one who chases after her like a lost lamb," I taunt, as I don't want to rouse any suspicion.

I don't fail to notice the way he watches her closely. He's interested in her, and that interest has nothing to do with her being his opportunity to triple his wealth. But I don't know if he's intrigued by her because she is a Saxon.

Or if he's fallen under her spell too.

Both possibilities have me wanting to rip out his eyeballs

and feed them to him.

The men laugh at my comment as they, too, no doubt, have noticed him chasing after Emeline. But when I glare at them, they quickly get back to practicing their swordsmanship before I toss their arses to the ground again.

Storming away, I decide to look for her.

This is the problem that plagues me. I can't stay away from Emeline even though I know I should. And when she isn't in sight, I want to kill everyone in my way.

Inga steps into my path, but I can't deal with her at the moment. After what she did to Emeline this morning, she's lucky I haven't tossed her arse into the river. She believes after last night, she has some say over what I do, but it meant nothing.

We were both using the other, as I know she did it to make Ulf jealous and hurt Emeline.

She doesn't follow, knowing better than to annoy me when I'm in a mood like this.

Emeline followed Ulf into the forest, and I didn't see her return. So I walk toward it, unable to shake this feeling that something bad looms. It could just be my temper souring everything, but she's been gone for a long time.

We aren't safe here, even if we have the numbers. Wessex Guard are looking for us, which means the king will have eyes everywhere. I quicken my step, agitatedly pushing tree branches out of my way. The farther I walk, the more frantic I become because it's too quiet.

This has me softening my footsteps, allowing me to be invisible as I search for Emeline. I use all my senses because it's not only sight which allows one to see. Closing my eyes, I take in my surroundings and try to retrace her steps.

Her sweet scent no longer lingers. Nor does the echo of her spirit. She's been gone for a while.

Reopening my eyes, I drop to a squat and gather some disturbed dirt between my fingers. Peering ahead, I see tracks. There are three sets.

Rising slowly, I unsheathe my sword and creep through the forest on high alert.

When I get closer to the footprints, I see the smaller ones are flanked by two larger sets. The sudden drag marks indicate my fears—whoever these belonged to didn't leave here on their own accord.

They continue for a while, and when there are no horses' hoofprints, it's safe to assume they traveled on foot. Just as they take a left, I see something which has me gripping the handle of my sword.

A gold crucifix necklace lays hidden amongst the orange leaves. As I get closer to it, I see it belongs to Emeline.

Bending to pick it up, I rub my thumb over the relic. "You will protect her," I demand. She has served her God her entire life, and it's time He served her.

Placing the necklace into my pocket, I continue following the tracks, and that's when I see a white ribbon that was fastened in Emeline's hair dangling from a low-hanging branch.

My clever Saxon—she is leaving me a trail to find her.

The trunk of a tree is darker in color, which means someone stopped here for a piss. A man. To the left, I see some disturbance in the dirt as if someone was scrambling to get away. Whoever it was, was pushed onto their stomach and left behind claw marks in the soil.

They were then dragged away as the footprints are now long drag marks in the mud.

With my heart in my throat, I look for any other clues, and I see it when a splash of crimson on a green leaf catches my eye. Running my thumb over the splatter, it comes away red, meaning the blood is fresh.

Finding Emeline becomes all the more imperative because this scene is a violent one.

The splashes of red are my trail to follow, hinting whoever's blood this is, they are still bleeding. I come to a steep hill and only see two sets of footprints, but the trail of blood continues. Emeline must have been carried up this hill because she was knocked out cold.

Taking a calming breath, I continue my trek, and when I reach the top, I see two sets of horse hooves dug deeply into the earth.

This was my worst fear.

They'd be easy to follow on foot, but on horseback—almost impossible as the farther I journey, the more probable it'll be that I encounter many hoofprints.

"Fuck!" I curse under my breath, kicking at the dirt in anger.

How could I let this happen?

I can wallow in self-pity later because now, I need to find Emeline. By the pattern of their boots, I am certain two of the king's guards have her.

I need my horse as I am useless on foot, so I take flight down the hill and through the forest, but before I get to the village, I see Erik, the young boy whose father Emeline killed, playing in the trees. He holds a sword, and it is not Viking.

"Erik!" I call out, demanding he come down.

But his mother suddenly appears from the edge of the forest, her guilt reflected all over her traitorous face.

She doesn't have a chance to explain before I am on her, gripping her by the throat and shoving her back against a tree.

"Where is she?" I snarl, inches from her face.

"She killed Bo!" she cries, slapping at my hand to release her.

"If you do not answer my question, I swear on the gods your son will lose his mother as well! Answer me! Where is she?"

She whimpers, tears streaming down her face. "I did what any wife would."

I squeeze harder, her reasons meaning nothing to me.

Small footsteps sound behind me.

I release the woman whose name I do not know and spin, kicking the boy to the ground as he charges for me with his sword. His blade falls feet away, so he is unarmed as I place my sword to his throat.

"Tell me where she is!" I scream at the woman, who shrieks for me to let her son go.

He tries to fight, but I press my blade deeper into his skin, and when a trickle of red seeps from the cut I made, I grin, for I will spill endless blood to find Emeline and beg for her forgiveness. Nothing else matters.

The woman drops to her knees beside her son, begging I spare his life. "The king's guards have her. I saw them yesterday when I was picking herbs, and I made a d-deal with them. They lay waiting for the pe-perfect moment to strike. She is on her way to King Egbert. It is too late…just how it was for my Bo."

"What deal did you make?" I question, untouched as she sobs hysterically.

"They gave Erik a sword and promised to leave without any harm coming to us. They have no interest in us. Just that whore. I did it for us. We—"

She doesn't have a chance to finish her sentence because I drive my sword into her shoulder, wounding her. "Insult her again, and this blade will end your son's life. I promise you."

She whimpers, cupping her bleeding shoulder as her eyes plead with me that I show mercy.

"Have you gone mad?" Ulf exclaims from behind me as he

runs to where I stand.

He tries to disarm me, but I elbow him in the face. He staggers backward, his shock clear.

"Touch me again, and you will join them," I warn him, my gaze never wavering from the woman and her son. "Where did they take her?"

Ulf's anger is replaced with alarm. "The princess?"

I nod once.

"Dova, what have you done?" he cries, coming to stand near me. "We need her. Without her, we do not have anything to offer the Saxons! How could you be so foolish?"

"She killed Bo!" she sobs, standing before us. "You saw what she did to him! She embarrassed him. He did not die an honorable death."

"He embarrassed himself," Ulf corrects, disgusted. "And he did not deserve an honorable death."

"How could you say such a thing? Bo was your friend! You have all lost your minds over that Saxon whore. I hope they do to her what was done to Bo."

Ulf's cries for me to stop come too late, not that I would have, regardless of his orders. I swing my sword, taking Dova's head off with one clean stroke. It rolls along the ground, coming to a stop at her son's feet.

He peers down at it, his face splattered with his mother's blood and his eyes widen as her headless corpse crumples to the ground with a thud.

I'm untouched by it all.

"Skarth!" Ulf exclaims, his shock clear. "You cannot cut the heads off our men and women!"

"Why not?" I question, looking at the little boy who doesn't cower and cry. He will be a great warrior.

"Because we need them," Ulf explains, but his argument is weak.

"We do not need traitors like her."

"And what are you? You too are a traitor, siding with the Saxons to get your revenge. You are not so different from Dova."

"Ulf, if you do not wish to join your beloved Dova, then I suggest you stop talking. Now, get out of my way. I have to find Emeline."

The young boy reaches for his mother's head and cradles it. The sight touches me, which is why I state, "When you are older and wish to avenge her death, I will be waiting. However, you will only have one chance."

The boy nods once, his innocence shattered by a ruthless beast like me.

I push past Ulf as I've already wasted so much time. Dova was no help as she refused to divulge the whereabouts of the guards, so I will have to trace their tracks by relying on the hoofprints. I *will* find Emeline. Failing isn't an option. I just fear what state I'll find her in.

The thought has me charging through the thick clearing and making my way toward my horse.

"I am coming with you," Ulf says, arming himself. But he isn't going anywhere.

"No, you are not," I state firmly, mounting my horse. "We stick to the plan. Your men will sail home and bring back as many men and women who will fight with us at Carhampton. And you will continue to move and remain undetected by the king's men.

"Isn't that why we are here?"

I dare him to argue because he will have to confess to me what other reason there may be. And if that reason has to do with his feelings for Emeline, I will cut out his tongue.

"I will bring back your beloved treasure," I affirm with disgust.

"She is more to me than just that," he acknowledges. "You know it."

Without thought, I unsheathe my sword, the sword still stained with Dova's blood, and place it to Ulf's throat. "Your true feelings became clear when you expressed them to Dova!"

*"We need her. Without her, we do not have anything to offer the Saxons!"*

That's what he said, so regardless of what he thinks he feels, this is one thing that will always differentiate our feelings for her—I would never use her for my personal gain. Ever.

"So, the only thing I know is that she interests you because you do not understand her, but I know if the choice was given between your wealth and her safety, you will always choose your fortune. Now, get out of my way before I send you to Valhalla myself."

"You do not own her," he angrily spits, but that's where he is wrong.

"Yes, Ulf, I do. And she…she owns me."

Clucking my tongue, my horse gallops away, but no matter how fast he runs, it'll never be fast enough.

# FIFTEEN

*Princess Emeline*

These ropes burn my wrists, but I won't stop trying to break them until I am free.

The two guards who captured me sit feet away, hacking into the hare they killed. They've not offered me any, knowing I would spit it in their faces as I would rather starve to death than be returned to King Egbert.

I can't believe I was apprehended. How did they know where to find me? And why did they leave without leaving a massacre of Northmen behind? It makes no sense.

I have no idea where we are because after I bit one of the guard's noses almost clean off and tried to flee, they forced me to move. When I fought, I was knocked out cold.

I woke a few minutes ago, tied to this large tree.

The men are cruel bastards. One, in particular, watches me like I am prey.

"We will take turns to watch her," says the man whose nose I bit, nasally. "Seeing as I almost lost my nose to that bitch, I retire first."

I smirk happily in response.

The other man—whose name is Arthur, I believe—nods, which wipes my smirk clean. Freeing myself from these ropes becomes all the more imperative.

The guard leaves us, setting himself down under a tree far away, which leaves me alone with this vile creature. He tears into the flesh of the hare, never taking his eyes off me. Or rather, never taking his eyes off my chest.

He is just another man who thinks he can control me just because of the prick he wields between his legs. But he has no idea what men I've been up against.

"I can see why King Egbert has torn his kingdom apart to find you," he says, licking his fingers clean.

The fire is the only light we have as the moon has gone into hiding. I wish I could too. But when Arthur stands, I know that's not an option.

I need to think fast because this man will take what he wants. It's what all men, but Skarth, want from me.

Just the thought of him has me struggling against the rope at my wrists, determined to break free.

"The queen is the only one who isn't distressed by your absence," he reveals, which turns my blood as I suddenly realize he has no intention of returning me to the king.

"Queen Redburh paid you to kill me?" I question even though I know the answer.

"Yes, Princess, but not before I delivered a message."

"And what message is that?" My throat dips as I swallow nervously.

"To fuck you how you fucked her husband."

Tears sting my eyes, but I refuse to let them fall.

I never chose this life. I never chose to be the king's mistress. But Queen Redburh doesn't care as she sees her husband's infidelity as my fault. And now, I will pay with not only my life but my dignity as well.

"Don't worry, Princess," he says, walking toward me with a grin. "You can scream all you want. No one will hear you. There isn't a soul for miles."

I desperately tug at the ropes, but they won't budge.

Arthur thrives on my dread and snickers as he lifts his chain mail vest and undoes his trousers. When his disgusting cock slithers free, bile rises because it looks like a curled-up sausage. He expects fear, so I give him the complete opposite.

I laugh. Loudly.

Arthur pauses, watching me like I've gone mad, which makes me laugh even louder. "I'm sorry," I say, trying to catch my breath. "But that's the smallest cock I have ever seen. I understand it is cold—"

He rushes forward, clutching my throat in his cupped palm. "This cock is going to destroy you."

"I doubt that."

He squeezes harder, and I hope he will just do what Queen Redburh ordered and kill me right now. I would rather that than feel his body pressed to mine.

I gasp, on the cusp of passing out, but he lets go, chuckling, and I know why that is when he grips the back of my head and jerks me toward his crotch. I frantically fight, but he holds me tight, and I'm bound to this tree, so it's futile.

He pries my mouth open with his fingers, and before I can bite down, he shoves his cock down my throat.

Instantly, I gag, and tears leak from my eyes as I fear I'm about to choke. A sated moan leaves him when I taste his salty member pulsating against my tongue.

My first instinct is to bite it off, but he still has a hold of my jaw and works it up and down crudely. He moves my head back and forth, and before long, all I am is his puppet to do with what he pleases.

He rams his cock in and out of my mouth, groaning each time he hits the back of my throat. "What do you think of this small cock now?" he taunts, punishing me brutally as he forces me to take him deeper.

Spittle dribbles from the corners of my mouth because I can't swallow, but it just provides Arthur with the lubrication he needs to glide in and out with ease.

Glaring at him, I promise myself he won't get away with this. There is only one way I'm going to escape this, so I relax my throat and stop fighting. I allow this man to violate my mouth because the moment he relaxes his grip…I'm going to gnaw off his cock.

He grunts and thrusts while I think of all the ways I am going to make those who hurt me pay. I detach myself from this assault because it won't break me. I've lived through worse, and it's because of them that the moment Arthur's grip slackens and I can move my jaw, I bite down so hard, I almost shatter my teeth.

A strangled gasp leaves him before the realization of what I've just done hits hard.

He pushes my forehead, desperate for me to let go as he tries to pull back out, but he was so eager to stick this disgusting slug into my mouth, no way am I letting go.

"Plea—" his cries for help die in a wet gurgle when I savagely shake my head from side to side, like a dog and her bone. I taste blood…and fear.

Gnawing harder, I hack through flesh and muscle, and when hot, sticky blood squirts down my throat, I know I've won.

With a strangulated cry, Arthur drops to his knees, but not with his cock, for that is in my mouth. I spit it out, it bouncing off the center of his forehead and tumbling to the ground.

Where his cock once was is now a gaping, bloody wound.

"You whore!" he wheezes, and with the last shred of strength he possesses, he reaches for his sword, prepared to take my life in exchange for me biting off his cock.

I brace for death, but it never comes as I feel him before I see him, but when I do lay eyes on him, I sag in relief because I do not wish to meet my God drenched in blood.

Skarth runs for us but stops when he sees Arthur on his knees, bleeding profusely from the crotch. When he sees the curled-up sausage that once belonged to Arthur feet away, he bursts into husky laughter.

"Is that all of it?"

"Help me," Arthur pleads, his sword falling from his hand.

"All right, my lord. Let me help you." I watch in exhilaration as he picks Arthur up by the throat before driving his sword straight through his belly.

He hangs off the end, gasping for air.

"I will help you into the place you call hell."

He uses his foot to pry Arthur off the end of his sword, who collapses to the ground with a hollowed thump.

My mouth is agape, blood and spittle running down my chin, but I can neither speak nor move because Skarth found me. He's here. He didn't abandon me.

His chest rises and falls quickly, a sign of his excitement over what just unfolded. The pulsating energy befalls us once again because bloodshed seems to titillate us both.

He silently walks over to where I am and walks behind me. I feel the sharp sting of his bloody blade as he cuts through the rope at my wrists with precision.

With a sigh, I shake out my hands.

"The other one?" he asks, and I gesture with my head toward where the other guard is. He knew there were two as he tracked me down, no doubt.

Skarth nods and mutes his footsteps, disappearing into the dark.

I come to a shaky stand, wiping the blood off my chin with the back of my hand. I strain my eyes to see in the dark, but when I hear a throttled gasp, I know the guard is dead. Skarth returns moments later, his sword covered in blood.

We look at one another, neither appearing to know what to say.

I'm shocked he's here. I thought he didn't care. Unless…he's here because he doesn't go back on his word. He made a deal with Ulf, and he plans on seeing it through.

"We cannot stay here," he says. "We need to be as far away from here as possible."

As I nod, a shiver overtakes me when I realize what I just did. But as always, Skarth reads my thoughts.

"You did not kill anyone, Princess. You merely bit off his pathetic excuse of a cock." This conversation would be comical if not for the fact I was force-fed that cock. "Are you all right?" he asks, gripping the handle of his sword.

"Fine. I just want to go."

He appears to want to say something but changes his mind at the last minute. "My horse is this way."

I follow as he leads me away from what would have served as my resting place if not for Skarth. I'm confused by his chivalrous behavior, so I remain silent as we walk through the forest. He mounts his horse and offers me his hand.

A fire begins to burn within, but I ignore it and slip my hand into his. Once settled behind him, I wrap my arms around his broad back and hold on tight as we gallop into the night.

Being with Skarth this way, under the stars, just us, feels right. It feels like home. Regardless of what happened, I feel comforted being pressed this closely to him.

The smooth stride of the horse and the warmth of Skarth's body have my eyes drooping shut. Soon, I slip into a comfortable lull and press my cheek into Skarth's back. His earthy scent sings to my soul, and all I want to do is bask in it and never return.

We ride for what feels like hours, and I wonder if we're going back to the village.

I am embarrassed he had to ride out to save me. I can't seem to stop getting into trouble, no matter how hard I try.

A flowing stream up ahead catches the twinkling of stars, and the thought of washing Arthur from my mouth has me gently tugging on Skarth's vest.

"May we stop here?"

Skarth clucks his tongue and gently tugs the reins. His

horse slows down.

Once he stops, I jump down and make haste toward the water. Dropping to my knees, I cup it into my hands and take long mouthfuls. The moment it hits my throat, I think of Arthur's length slipping in and out of my mouth, and instantly, I gag.

Unable to stop myself, I dry retch, wishing to expel his taste, his memory, from me, but nothing comes up. Tears leak from my eyes, and I know it's merely a psychological response to what happened. But I suddenly can't stop shaking.

I am sick of men taking from me. When will it stop?

I measure my shaky breaths to stop the hysteria from overcoming me.

"Do you wish to bathe?"

Skarth's smooth voice calms me, and I nod. "I would."

"Take your time, Princess. I will wait for you by the horse."

I don't turn around, but the rustling of downy grass alerts me to his departure.

Coming to a stand, I slip off my clothes and slowly enter the stream. The water is glacial, but I barely notice the cold once I begin to wash Arthur from my flesh. I bob up and down, wetting my hair and enjoying the feeling of being reborn as the filth is washed away.

I peer into the heavens, still wondering if the Lord will present me with a sign. I've asked for many throughout my life, but I still don't know why He made me disobedient. It would have been easier if I weren't.

But out here in the darkness, out of the palace walls and away from reign and duty, I know that this was who I was always meant to be. I was never meant to serve another. I cannot submit to rule, for I want to lead, not follow.

I'm not sure what my future holds, but I will die fighting for my freedom. Of that, I'm sure.

The cool wind picks up speed, and I decide to get out before I catch a chill. Wet and completely naked, I peer down at the clothes I once wore. Putting them back on sickens me, especially as they are stained with Arthur's blood.

Peering into the darkness where I know Skarth stands, I gather the garments into my hands and use them to cover my nakedness as I walk toward him. My front is covered, but my back isn't. However, I'm not bashful, for I was standing naked with Skarth a few nights ago when he did more than just look upon my bare form.

The moment we lock eyes, he appears confused as to why I'm not dressed.

"I did not wish to wear clothes that were soiled," I explain.

He doesn't say a word as he removes the animal fur cloak he wears and steps forward. I hold my breath as he wraps it around my shoulders. It's large enough to cover my entire front and stops below my knees.

"Thank you," I whisper, peering up at him.

He removes the clothes from my hands without a word.

Being swathed in his clothes and engulfed in his smell has me swaying on my feet as I am suddenly exhausted.

"There is a cave up ahead. We can rest for the night."

Nodding, I follow as he leads me through the dense forest.

I know we can't stay for long, but under the cloak of darkness, I can't help but feel safe. Come dawn, it will change, but I'm thankful for a place to lay my head for a few hours.

The cave is small, and I suddenly am aware that I'll be sharing this small space with a very large Northman.

"I will fetch some wood for a fire. Are you hungry?"

I shake my head.

"I will not be long. I will water my horse and be back very soon."

It's unlike him to talk so much.

"Here." He slips off his leather vest, exposing his blue tunic beneath. When he reaches overhead and removes it, I almost forget to breathe.

He stands before me, chest bare, and all I can do is marvel at the beauty that is Skarth the Godless. His body is that of a warrior; muscled yet slender, which enables me to appreciate the swell of his abdominals.

The light dusting of hair on his chest and arms only adds to his manliness. I like it.

He is covered in scars, and his traditional ink highlights his rocky planes.

His long hair is tied back, but the shaved sides only draw

attention to his full pink lips and those piercing blue eyes.

I know I'm staring, but he takes my breath away.

"You can lie on this," he says, revealing why he took his tunic off.

In this small space, his scent is amplified, and I bite the inside of my cheek to smother my moan.

"Thank you." I accept and turn my back before I do and say something I will regret.

He exits the cave, leaving me to deal with my racing heart and heaving chest.

I need to remember I was angry with him. I can't allow my obsession with him to cloud my judgment because he was in the arms of two other women to spite me.

With that as the motivation I need, I lay his tunic on the ground and arrange it so I can lie down comfortably. The moment I'm engulfed in his comforting smell, my eyes droop shut.

I vaguely hear Skarth enter some time later, but I'm too comfortable to move. The roar of the fire thaws the chill from my bones, and I let out a contented sigh. When I hear Skarth setting something down by the fire, I slowly open my eyes.

He is arranging my clothes on a rocky ledge. "I washed your things. They'll be dry come morning."

"Thank you," I sleepily say. If I was thinking properly, it's what I would have done. But the past few...years have been taxing.

"I am certain you'll want your clothes back," I tease, snuggling into them with no intention of ever returning them.

When he clenches his jaw, I wonder what I said to offend him. "Yes, that would be best."

Suddenly, my fatigue is replaced with annoyance, and I shoot up, enraged. "If you are going to be so sullen, then here, take your clothes!"

I'm about to take off the shawl, but he thrusts his arm out over the fire, seizing my wrist. He is barely in control. "Do not."

"Do not what?" I spit at him. "I thought you wanted your precious clothes. Take them!"

"I said don't," he warns, his low tone menacing. "Why do you not listen?"

"Why do you not leave me be?" I counter angrily. "You clearly can't bear to be near me. Or your clothes, for that matter."

When his gaze drops to my chest, I realize by thrashing about, the cloak has slipped down, revealing the tops of my breasts.

"Please cover yourself," he snarls, turning his cheek, which merely infuriates me further.

"My nakedness offends you? You did not seem to have that problem when you were fucking two women!"

I want him to know I am aware of his capers.

"Don't use such vulgar language."

"Now my language offends you?" I mock. "Mayhap it's best I sleep outside in case my breathing will disturb your peace."

I attempt to stand, but he thrusts me back down. "Sit."

"You have no right to tell me what to do!"

"I have every right. For if it were not for you, I would not be here. I would be with my wife instead of a spoiled child."

He knows this insult hurts, and I glare at him over the fire.

I don't have anything to say because he's right. He's here because of me. But I never asked him to.

"You speak with jealousy, Princess. Do you wish it was you I was fucking? You believe a little girl like you can compare to two women? You amuse me," he taunts with an arrogant smirk.

Now he merely wishes to hurt me.

Yanking my wrist free, I don't reply, but that doesn't mean this argument is finished.

Settling onto the ground, I turn my back and wait, just like this bastard taught me to do.

I fake sleep, but I am wide awake and ready to attack once the moment is right.

I've listened to Skarth's breathing, and it's become shallow. It's been this way for a while. I must strike now because there is no way I'm spending another moment alone with this brute.

Coming to my feet silently, I never take my eyes off him as I reach for my clothes. They're still damp, but I'm not waiting for them to dry. With my heart in my throat, I commence a slow, quiet backward walk toward the cave's exit.

Skarth doesn't stir. He looks so peaceful. But I know better, for this rotten bastard is the devil himself.

I use my hands as guidance, touching the rocky walls as I creep toward freedom. The cool air on my back alerts me that I'm almost there, but when I stand on a rock, and it rolls along the ground, I freeze, eyes wide.

I expect him to wake, to punish me for intending to leave him here.

But he doesn't.

He sighs before his shallow breathing continues.

Holding my breath, I continue my escape, and when my feet step onto the grass, I almost cry out in relief. But I don't have time for that. Now, I must run.

Spinning, I run as though my life depends on it, ignoring the rough terrain digging into my bare feet as I make my way down the hill to where Skarth's horse is tied to a tree.

I am still naked beneath the cloak, but I will dress later.

My fingers fumble as I desperately try to untie the rope. I've done this a thousand times before, but I can't get it undone. I need to calm down.

Taking a deep breath, I focus on the rope and my fingers, and instantly, the rope comes undone. I will celebrate later when I am away from the man who continues to break my heart because I let him.

Tossing my clothes onto the horse, I mount him—freedom awaits.

Or so I thought.

Before I can fight, warm arms wrap around my middle and drag me to the ground, where I fall face-first onto my stomach. A heavy weight presses into my back.

"Let me go!"

But I'm not going anywhere.

"You were going to leave without saying goodbye?" Skarth quips into my ear as he seizes my arms and yanks them above my head to stop me from flailing. "I am wounded, Princess."

"Good. It was my intention to hurt you in every possible way."

He laughs in response, and my heart leaps at the sound.

His chest is pressed to my back, and I'm not going anywhere unless I lie, cheat, and steal. "Please, get o-off. I cannot b-breathe."

When he doesn't budge, I grow lithe and cry staged tears. "Why do you wish to hurt me? What did I ever do to you?"

After a pregnant pause, his hold on me relaxes, which is the opportunity I need to buck him off and scamper away on hands and knees. The leaves beneath give me no purchase, and as I slip and slide, Skarth viciously flips me onto my back.

Before he can seize my hands, I slap his cheek—hard. "How dare you! I hate you!"

"Good," he snarls, moving his jaw from side to side.

But there is no way I'm surrendering, so I do as he taught me and draw up my knee, connecting with his plums.

His eyes grow wide, and he rolls off me, gasping for breath.

The sound should please me, but it doesn't. However, it's now or never, and I rise to my feet, desperate to flee. Just as I take a step, Skarth grips the cloak, seizing me in my tracks. Without thought, I shrug free from it and am suddenly very naked.

With cloak in hand, still catching his breath, he realizes it too, and instead of running away, I'm held prisoner to the spot by his heated gaze as he examines me from head to toe.

This is the first time he's seen me bare. Although we were stripped once before, the water concealed our nakedness, but now, nothing separates us.

Rising to full height, he doesn't offer the cloak. And I don't conceal my body from his animated eyes.

"Are you going to ride away from here, naked, for all to see?"

"I will do anything to get away from you," I reply, but it's weak.

"Go then," he says, his entire being making me grow weak at the knees. "I offer you this one chance, but you better not fail because if I catch you…I shall never let you go."

There is a promise behind his words, and it excites me, for I never want him to let me go. He owns me; he always has. But the chase…it excites me more.

Without hesitation, I turn, my heels kicking up the dirt as I run as if my life depends on it, and in some ways, it does.

A husky chuckle leaves Skarth as he will give me a head start, but when I hear him take flight after me, I know I'm going to lose.

I run naked through the forest with the man I love biting at my heels. The wind whips through my hair, and my heart leaps from my chest as I've never felt freer—in every sense of the word. I let go of everything and just feel.

"Got you."

I don't know who lunges for who first, but Skarth is suddenly on me, like a wild animal capturing its prey. He wraps his arms around my middle, lifting me off the ground as he slams my front into the trunk of a tree.

He's at my back, kissing the side of my throat as I bend into him, wanting more.

He isn't gentle, but I don't want him to be. He bites over my thrashing pulse before licking away the sting with his wicked tongue. I want more, so I arch my neck backward and slam my mouth to his, kissing him with ferocity over my shoulder.

This kiss isn't chaste or guarded, for this is our first proper kiss. And it wreaks havoc on my very soul, just how I knew it would.

He grips my chin and coaxes me to bend further as he controls the kiss with his fierce domination. His tongue circles mine, groaning when I match his speed. We are untamed and zealous, and when I feel his length press into me from behind, I know the time has come to give in to the inevitable.

It's what was always destined—no matter how hard we tried to fight it.

Spinning around, I press my bare chest to his. His trouncing heart is in sync with mine. I stand on tippy-toes and kiss him once again.

He fists my hair, angling my mouth for his pleasure as well as mine. The smooth glide of his lips and the flick of his tongue have me whimpering as my center throbs for more.

Breaking apart a mere fraction, I whisper against his lips, "Please…I want you to—"

However, I don't say the word the Northmen use to describe the intimate act between man and woman as he lost his temper when I used it last.

But he surprises me when he demands, "Say the word."

"The last time I did, you called me vulgar."

"I could not stand to hear you say it because I knew I would not be able to control myself around you. Those filthy words passing these sinful lips—" He thumbs my bottom lip, his eyes on fire. "But now, I want you to say it. Tell me what you want me to do to you."

When I hesitate, he dips a hand between us and fondles my mound. I thought it pleasing when I touched myself, but that pales compared to Skarth's large hand stroking me intimately. Our gazes are locked, and I open my legs wider, granting him permission to touch me any way he likes.

A gasp leaves me as he caresses my flesh back and forth. I don't have much hair on my womanhood, so every glide of his fingers is felt all the way to my toes.

He lowers his mouth to my right breast and suckles it ardently. I am consumed, but it's not enough. So, I seal our fates forevermore.

"I want you to fuck me."

A hiss vibrates from around my breast, and Skarth lifts his head, eyes locked with mine as he sweeps his tongue around my areola. I'm going to explode.

"All right, Princess," he says in defeat, giving in to me— finally.

I expect him to throw me onto the ground, but he does nothing of the sort.

He lifts me, coaxing me to wrap my legs around his middle as he walks us uphill. He smashes his mouth to mine, robbing me of breath, but who needs air when Skarth is my life force. We enter the cave, and the warmth from the fire as well as from Skarth's body have me heating in all the right ways.

He lowers my feet to the floor and severs our kiss.

I miss him instantly, but when he steps back and those blue eyes hungrily rake over my body, I suddenly feel empowered in ways I've never felt before.

Bedding a man has never been a pleasant experience for me. I thought that was normal. But as Skarth stands before me, besotted with what he sees, I realize I've never experienced pleasure because it was with the wrong men.

I already feel light-headed from Skarth merely looking at me.

"Has anyone ever kissed you there?" he hoarsely asks, and when he points at the junction between my legs, my cheeks turn crimson.

"No."

"Would you like me to?"

"Yes, very much so," I whisper, rubbing my thighs together to lessen the burn.

He comes closer, cupping the back of my neck and pressing our foreheads together. This is a moment of promise between us and trust.

He kisses the side of my neck while I bow backward, closing my eyes and losing myself to bliss. When Skarth gently coaxes me to lie down on his tunic, I surrender, pushing my fears aside. He kisses my lips deeply, then he detours to my chin.

I lie back, watching him as he works his way down my body. His broad, muscled back covers my entire form, and although his hands have killed many, they deliver nothing but kindness when they touch me now. I lose myself to his touch, to his lips, and open my legs wider for him to settle between.

He kisses my breasts, taking each one into his mouth and suckling them softly. His tongue laps over my nipples. I think I'm going to perish.

He kisses between the valley of my breasts before spreading kisses down my abdomen. When he twirls his tongue in my navel, I arch my hips, a whimper escaping me.

No one has touched me like this before. I didn't know pleasure like this existed. But now that I do, I never want it to end.

Skarth's lips descend lower, his eyes never leaving mine as he kisses above my quivering mound. "You smell like sweetened honey," he says, and before I can utter a single word, he licks my opening in one long sweep.

"And you taste like it as well."

My cheeks redden.

He places his mouth over me and commences licking, nibbling, and all I can do is stare at the sight of Skarth the Godless between my legs. He grips my hip and clenches tight as he breaches me with his tongue.

"God have mercy on my soul," I gasp, arching my back.

I am lost to his tongue, his mouth, his hands as he uses each one to pleasure me. He buries himself deeper, coaxing me to spread my legs out wider so he can destroy me further. His mouth and tongue work in unison, and I feel like a feast as he eats me wildly.

His beard adds to the heightened sensation, a perfect combination of pleasure and pain as he moves his face from side to side. He gorges himself, his tongue flicking over the swollen part of me he called my sweetness.

The familiar coil in my belly begins to wind tighter, but I don't give in. Not yet.

Gripping his long hair, I use it as reins as I need something to hold. The noises coming from him are pure carnality and reverberate throughout me. He encourages me to arch my hips, and when I do, he comes up on his hands and devours me madly.

I cradle the top of his head, pushing him deeper into me as I shamelessly thrust my hips into his face. He inserts two fingers alongside his tongue, cramming me full. Before long, I am riding his face, bucking and holding him prisoner.

But he doesn't seem to mind.

He sucks over my mound, creating a pressure that steals the air from my lungs. I am lost to him and grow lax as he devours me like I'm his last meal. He moves his face from side to side, and when he bites over my ripened bud, I lock eyes with him, pleading he ends this ache within.

He tosses my leg over his shoulder, opening me up wider, and when he sucks my center while flicking his tongue deeply inside me, I release the building pressure and explode with a guttural scream.

I'm certain I'm about to die because my heart and body are convulsing uncontrollably, but when Skarth tenderly caresses my quivering stomach, I focus on his touch and the way his mouth never leaves my throbbing flesh.

Tears escape from the corners of my eyes, but they are tears of joy. I ride this wave of pleasure with Skarth, and when he kisses over the lips of my womanhood, I collapse in a heap, breathless and consumed.

He crawls up my body, leaving kisses in his path, and when he reaches my mouth, he kisses me deeply. I can taste myself on him. I should shy away, but I don't. I deepen the kiss, relishing that my scent is slathered all over him.

"Thank you," I whisper, my voice hoarse. "I never imagined it could feel that way."

"We've only just begun." And with that promise, I watch as he sits back on his heels and commences to remove his trousers.

When he lowers them and his manhood springs free, I swallow because I knew he was well-endowed, but he is considerably larger in the flesh. I take in the length and the girth, and suddenly, I am doubtful he will fit.

A light dusting of hair shelters the base, and when I admire his muscles which are shaped into a V, I see where the hair from his navel leads to. It has my mouth watering.

Once he is naked, he lowers himself back down onto me, kissing me savagely. I thread my fingers through his hair, loving the way it encloses us into our own private kingdom.

With our lips still entwined, he walks his hand between us, and when he inserts two fingers into me, my eyes widen.

"Shh, Princess," he coos, working his fingers in and out, in and out. "Trust me."

I've not had this before. When a man was ready, he would

ram his manhood into me, not fingers, but as I do as Skarth says, I feel my muscles relaxing as I begin to grow wet between the legs.

"There you go."

I don't know what he means, but his approval only has me becoming wetter.

His necklace hangs low. I reach up, fingering the swinging silver relic. "What is this?"

"It's a *Mjolnir*," he explains, never breaking eye contact or touch.

"What does it mean?"

"It is the weapon of my god, Thor," he explains, and his smooth voice merely stokes the fire burning within me.

"What does your god do?" I ask, bending to his touches as I rock my hips.

"Thor is the god of thunder. The protector of all the gods. The *Mjolnir* is a symbol of power and protection because it controls the power of lightning."

The more he speaks, the further I lose myself to him, to this moment in time.

"He sounds like a very worthy god."

He smirks, and I know it pleases him to hear me speak of one of his gods this way.

He removes his fingers, only to align his manhood at my entrance. I'm suddenly nervous and seize up. But Skarth kisses my lips.

"The *Mjolnir* is so powerful; it cannot be lifted by anyone who is not worthy."

His smooth voice thaws out my worries.

"It's our symbol for safety and protection," he continues, never taking his lips off me as he kisses my mouth, my cheeks.

Instantly, I relax, lost to his voice, detailing a tale that makes Skarth who he is. "Well, you are my *Mjolnir* then. You are my safety. And you are my protection."

His eyes soften before a look of possession overtakes him. "And you are my *hugrekki*."

The moment he says that word, I open up to him as it reminds me of how far we've come.

"Always"—he gently nudges into me while I open my mouth, breathless at the delicious intrusion—"and forever."

He slowly enters me, and the farther he sinks, the more lost I am. The connection brings tears to my eyes.

Skarth pauses, a look of worry plaguing him. "Have I hurt you?"

Shaking my head, I reach up and cup his cheek. "No, these tears are ones of joy. I have wanted this for so long."

"Me too," he confesses and steals my breath when he thrusts his hips, burying himself to the hilt.

He doesn't move; I dare not breathe as I need a moment to compose myself and allow my muscles time to adjust to his size. The corded veins in his neck have me fearful he's in pain.

"Can I move?"

I nod, welcoming him to take what has always been his.

A low hum passes his lips as he commences to sink in and out of me, stretching me wide. At first, it burns, and I am fearful that I am ruined, for there is no pleasure felt. But when Skarth bends and takes my nipple into his mouth, the pain is soon replaced with pleasure.

His strokes are slow at first, and I think this is done for my benefit. I don't know what to do with my hands as I was told by others to keep them by my sides. But when Skarth intertwines our fingers and coaxes me to wrap a hand around his nape, I realize I may as well be untouched because this act of passion and love is one I've never experienced before.

He grips my hips while I grasp his nape. We anchor to the other, intent on never letting go.

The rhythm of his strokes begins to grow faster, harder, and the slamming of our flesh is coupled with our raspy breaths. I love being under him as he sinks into me without restraint. I love that I am the one responsible for him losing control.

"Harder," I whimper because I want more.

With a slanted grin, he gives in to my demands and pulls out before slamming back into me so hard I shift upward from the force.

He kisses me brutally, cupping my chin to dominate me all over. This is the one time I surrender without complaint. His manhood feels like taut fire stabbing me deeply, and I open my legs wider, wanting more. I have no control over my body and am his loyal subject to do with what he pleases, for Skarth the Godless is my god.

The animalistic noises spilling from his parted lips stoke my passion, and that rumble of excitement swells. He drives his hips wildly, for Skarth fucks as he fights—brutally and with passion. He was made for both.

I run my fingers down his back, marveling at the warmth of his skin and the stretch of his muscles. Just touching him has me whimpering in need.

Staring up at him as he sinks into me over and over, I brush the hair from his cheek, wishing to look into his eyes as I experience a sensation that takes me to another world.

"These eyes are ones I have lo—"

But he doesn't let me finish as he seals his mouth over mine.

"Don't," he gently says.

I don't have time to question why because he suddenly changes position. He gets onto his knees while coaxing me to lift my legs upward to my chest. I cry out because he continues driving into me, and at this angle, it hits me hard.

He cups my outer thighs and leans over me to lift my hips and meet him stroke for stroke.

"Put your feet up against my chest," he says, and I do.

I feel like I am being bent in half as Skarth batters into me. This position still allows me to look into his eyes, but the angle, the penetration, is so much deeper, and I cry out when Skarth rocks me against his straining length.

"Feel good, *hugrekki*?"

Biting my lip, I nod quickly as I can't speak.

I grip Skarth's hips, holding on tightly as he brutalizes me in ways I enjoy.

"Do you want a release?"

"A release? I do not—" My words die in my throat as Skarth begins to play with my swollen bud.

My sensitive flesh begs for a reprieve as I'm not accustomed to this act lasting this long. It's usually a few pathetic thrusts, and then I am discarded. Never have I been asked what I wanted nor have I been given pleasure this way.

I am saddened for this to end, as I wish for it to never stop, but when Skarth sinks into me so deeply, I gasp for air, and I nod.

"Yes…please."

"I like it when you beg me, Princess."

His cool arrogance, coupled with the way he touches me, has me rocking against him, and when he anchors my hips, encouraging me to ride him in a way that strokes me at just the right angle, I release—loudly.

He doesn't stop driving his hips as I scream in bursts of pleasure. I erupt, squeezing my eyes shut as I'm certain I'm moments from death as my heart thumps uncontrollably and a tremor racks my body. I chase the decadence, and when I fall, I gasp in mouthfuls of air.

Words spill from Skarth, words I don't understand, but

they appear to be filled with his pleasure too.

I open my eyes and peer at our connection, surprised to see that Skarth is still hard.

"Have I done something wrong?" I ask, my fears exposed.

"You did not believe we were done, did you?"

"I—"

His smirk destroys me as he grips my legs and tosses them over each of his broad shoulders. He seizes my thighs and holds me tightly, thrusting into me brutally. I'm convinced he is a sorcerer, for how does he maneuver these positions with such skill?

He watches my swaying breasts with hunger, the way they bounce with the force of his strokes. He groans when his eyes fixate on his manhood and how it sinks in and out of me. I like the way he looks at me, for he is just as captivated as I am.

I want him to find his release too, so I clench my muscles around his length.

"*Faen*," he hisses, throwing his head back.

I do it again as it pleases me to hear him cry out in pleasure.

He pumps his hips, slamming into me, and I move with him, bending and bowing as we are one. As the tempo increases, I lose myself to this feeling and give everything I am to Skarth.

"You were mine from the moment we met," he says, eyes locked with mine. "I never wanted to be owned…but I belong to you, *hugrekki*."

I don't know what that means for us, but at this moment, I

embrace it and lock it away.

"And I belong to you."

A hiss escapes him, and with two hard, deep thrusts, he tosses his head back and roars. I watch as he shatters before my eyes, exploding because of me.

I feel powerful.

I feel loved.

Skarth collapses, untangling himself from our union. He lays a kiss on my mouth before settling down beside me on his back. We are both breathless, but when I feel a warmth on my belly, I peer down, confused by the white ribbons streaking my skin.

Curious, I run my finger through the sticky substance. I know this is what is needed to be with child, but I've never seen it before. It has a bitter taste and made me sick when forced to swallow it before, but I think Skarth's would be different.

Skarth turns his cheek, watching as I bring my finger to my mouth and run the fluid along my lips. My tongue darts out to taste it. It tastes like Skarth.

"Oh, Princess," he moans, drawing me into his arms. "You have no idea what you do to me."

Hugging afterward is something I've not experienced before, and instantly, fatigue overcomes me, and I yawn.

"Go to sleep, *hugrekki*."

"I am afraid of what happens when I wake."

"Why?"

Nestling closer into him, I whisper, "I do not know what this means for us, but I never want this feeling to end."

A sigh leaves Skarth, but he doesn't reply.

Eventually, I fall asleep in the arms of the man I love, unsure of what tomorrow holds.

# SIXTEEN

*Skarth the Godless*

I left Emeline sleeping soundly by the fire as I went to hunt. I hate to admit that leaving her was harder than I thought. After last night, I know things between us have changed.

Whether for the good or bad—I still do not know.

I thought my heart was about to burst from my chest when she was about to confess her love for me. I stopped her because those words cannot ever be taken back, and I fear if she said them, I would be lost forever.

But this ache in my chest reveals I already am.

I don't know what will happen at Carhampton. If I survive, I don't know if I will return to Northumbria. Or if I will venture on my quest to explore England and beyond.

But what I do know is that I will protect Emeline with my life.

I think of my wife and how I have wronged her, for I cannot return to her as her husband. She will despise me for what I've done, which is why I have to set her free.

Life has been thrown into chaos, but the only thing that makes sense in this turmoil has given herself over to me willingly. I have been with many women before, but with Emeline, I was ruined from the very first touch.

The way her body fits with mine—it seems almost as if she were made for me. I like that thought.

With my catch of fish and berries in hand, I make my way toward the cave, wondering how Emeline will feel after last night. I know confusion will plague her because she will want to know what this means for us.

I enter and find her standing by the fire, dressed.

It's a shame to cover such perfection even though I know she doesn't see herself that way. The scars on her back have faded with time, but my vengeance has not. Aethelred will pay for what he did to Emeline with his life.

I know he and King Eanred will be at Carhampton, as everyone will be fighting to win Emeline back, and this is why I need to keep her far away from the battle. She will want to fight, but she cannot.

She will hate me for suggesting she needs to be as far away

from the battle as possible, but if she is captured, they won't allow her to escape the next time around. She will forever be imprisoned in Wessex or Northumbria, and I fear I won't be able to save her.

The moment she meets my eyes, her cheeks flush. The sight stirs my longing, but I need to focus on what's important, and that's feeding my princess and then leaving this place. We have already been here for far too long.

"Good morning, Princess."

She smiles, brushing a piece of hair behind her ear. "Good morrow."

I want to kiss her, but instead, I busy myself preparing the fish I caught. After I skewer them onto a branch, I place them over the fire to cook. Emeline stands across me, watching me with those curious eyes.

"Once we eat, we have to leave," I inform her, turning the fish over.

"Yes, of course. Will we meet Ulf at Carhampton?"

This would be the logical thing to do, but I have no intention of her stepping foot there.

"Skarth?" she questions when I don't reply.

"Eat," I instead say, offering her a fish and some berries over the fire.

"I will eat once you answer me," she stubbornly rebukes. "Backtracking to *Kleifar* does not make sense. We should proceed forward, not backward. A larger group is more likely to be seen. But if it's just us—"

Her voice trails off when she realizes why I have not addressed her.

"Unless, unless you have no intention of me going to Carhampton. Is that so?"

I simply stare at her.

"You arrogant charlatan!" she cries, angered. "You will allow Northman women to fight, but not me? Am I not fitting enough to fight in your army?"

"You cannot be anywhere near Carhampton," I state, removing the fish from the fire. "It is too dangerous."

"I am well aware of what it is. I was the one who formulated this plan, remember? I know of the consequences, and I accept them. I *will* be fighting alongside you, whether you like it or not."

I'm not surprised she's reacted this way. Taking this right away from her is wrong, as she deserves her vengeance, but I can't fight and win if I am constantly looking over my shoulder for her.

This battle is one she has never seen before. It will be larger than any battle I have ever fought in. Of that, I'm sure.

"You cannot stop me, Skarth," she says, knowing that regardless of her wishes, I will ensure she is far away from Carhampton.

"Yes, Princess," I calmly refute, "I can."

Her eyes narrow into slits.

"Now, eat." I make clear this isn't optional when I toss a fish at her.

She catches it and angrily picks at the flesh before placing some meat into her mouth. She chews distractedly as I know her shrewd mind is formulating a plan.

She doesn't speak further, and we eat in silence. The air is so thick, I fear what happened last night is now shadowed by Emeline's anger. She will come to realize why I'm doing this— eventually.

Once we have eaten, I prepare for our departure.

Emeline isn't reckless. She won't run. She will, however, fight me until I concede, which will be never. When we return to Ulf, I will tell him that the only way to keep Emeline safe is to put her on a ship.

King Egbert will never suspect she's hiding at sea, as I believe he will search the lands high and low for her. If trouble faces her, then at least she has a fighting chance at survival being at sea. She can sail away to uncharted water by the Saxons, but not to my men.

If her life is at risk, then I will command the men to take her to my home country, where she will be safe under my protection. I will then meet her there.

Ulf will agree because as much as it angers me, I know he cares for Emeline more than he should. He will want to keep her safe, but he will also want victory at Carhampton. Which is why we need to devise a plan on how we intend to do that and keep Emeline safe.

King Egbert needs to believe we want no war, and for that to happen, he will need to see Emeline on the battlefield. But she will be far away from him.

Emeline continues to ignore me as she mounts the horse and grips my waist. There is no tenderness to her touch. She merely holds on so she doesn't fall off.

Clucking my tongue, we ride toward where Ulf and the kinsfolk will be. They're on the move, but I know Ulf and this landscape. We will reach him in a day's time. Until then, all that surrounds us is the galloping of my horse's hooves and the uncomfortable silence.

We keep to the secret tracks, shrouded by the thick foliage and towering trees. Wessex Guard can be anywhere, and after last night's encounter with two of them, it's evident they are out for blood.

Emeline can look after herself—her chewing off a man's cock proves this—but what happens if her luck runs out? I'm having these thoughts because I do feel guilty for denying her this fight. Only with her. If this were anyone else, I wouldn't be questioning my decision.

But Emeline has me questioning my very existence.

"Over there," she whispers, disturbing my thoughts with her panicked voice.

I follow her finger as she points above the hill. In the distance, Wessex Guard awaits.

Tugging the reins on my horse, I coax him to stop and silence our presence. There's nowhere to hide on horseback. Quickly jumping down, I offer her my hand, which she accepts, and we crouch low, using the horse as a shield.

"What are they doing this far away from the palace? King Egbert's men never venture this way," she whispers as we peer around the horse and at the men.

"Nowhere is too far while you are still out here," I reply, examining how many men lie in wait. "He is sending out smaller groups of men instead of a large army."

"Why?"

"To cover more ground this way," I disclose, frustrated. "Every corner we turn, there will be men waiting. It makes it harder for us to remain hidden this way."

She senses my annoyance. "So, we are doomed?"

Turning to look at her, I give in to instinct and gently skim my thumb across the apple of her cheek. A small whimper escapes her.

"This is merely a challenge, Princess. One we will overcome."

"How?"

"We give them what they want."

Her breaths are measured when she asks, "And what is that?"

Thumbing over her bottom lip, I whisper, "You."

Her eyes widen, but she doesn't have time to speak as I call out, "I have Princess Emeline!"

The guards instantly spring into action, searching where the voice has come from.

I grip Emeline by the back of the neck. "Down here!"

"What are you doing?" she cries, slapping my hand and attempting to break free. "Skarth! Let me go!"

Her yelps draw the guards' attention, who instantly rush down the hill, swords raised, prepared for battle. But when they see a terrified Emeline, their hostility simmers. They come to a stop a few feet away. There are six of them.

They watch me with untrustworthy eyes while I raise my free hand in surrender. "I just want a trade. Fifty pieces of silver for the princess."

"You insufferable bastard!" Emeline exclaims, squirming madly.

The guards laugh, their fight dwindling as they no longer sense a threat.

"Is this all of you? No other men fight with you up on that hill?"

One guard shakes his head with a snicker. "It is just us, and we don't have any silver to trade."

"Well, I will settle for your sword instead."

They look back and forth at each other, unsure if this is a trick or not.

"A sword?" Emeline scoffs. "Is that all I'm worth to you? Filthy heathen!"

"At least the sword does what it is told," I quip, chuckling as she stomps her foot in anger.

"All right. Give me the princess, and I will give you my sword," the guard says.

But I shake my head.

"We exchange together. I hand over the princess, and you toss over the sword."

"I cannot believe you are doing this. I will find you and kill you myself. I swear it," Emeline snarls while I raise my eyes to the heavens.

Even in the face of danger, she wishes for my death. How her spirit rouses me.

With sword in hand, the guard nods and waits for my command, but I know he has no intention of letting me leave here with his sword or my life. Once the exchange is made, they will attack, as they believe they have the numbers.

But they have no idea who they're fighting against. And I don't merely mean me.

With a sharp nod, I release Emeline, who turns around, ready to slap my cheek, but when the guard tosses his sword, and it lands by her feet, I duck low and reach for it.

"I'd at least ask for one hundred pieces of silver, Princess," I quickly quip, pressing the handle of the sword into her hand to stop her from striking me.

"You cunning bastard," she exclaims, but thankfully her scorn can wait until *after* we kill these *fifls*.

Withdrawing my sword from its sheath, I advance, catching

the guard unawares as I slice off his head in one swift stroke. It rolls along the ground, coming to a stop as it crashes into the boot of one of his friends.

They realize they've been tricked and spring into action, but what they don't expect is Emeline's wrath. With an animalistic roar, she charges for them, stabbing one right through the stomach. She withdraws her bloody sword, the body of the man she just killed not even dropping to the ground before attacking the next.

Watching her fight is a carnal sight, stirring lewd cravings which I cannot control. I'll welcome her fury once these guards are dead, as I know she will be one wrathful princess with a lot of pent-up anger she'll need to expel.

Emeline and I work together, two guards each. I don't dare steal her revenge. We focus on the men who fight for their lives. But they're no match for us.

I stab one through the heart. Emeline cuts off one man's head. The remaining two decide to attack Emeline, but I spin and slice one of them across the back. He falls to his knees where I swing, and with my razor-sharp sword, I slice him in two.

The last man attacks Emeline, who fends him off with ease, and I stand back, watching the princess play with him. She dodges his attacks with laughter, her loose hair catching the wind. She is simply beautiful.

When we lock eyes, I know what is about to transpire, and

I will happily accept my punishment. The guard charges at her with a snarl, but she spins, her sword raised, and delivers a fatal blow across his back.

The gurgling of blood catches the wind, followed by his pained oof as he collapses onto his front. The bloody corpses of the men we slaughtered surround us, but it doesn't make a difference to Emeline as she tramples over their bodies.

I stand motionless, slathered in the enemy's blood as she rushes for me and slams her mouth over mine. Her body is trembling, but it has nothing to do with fear. The battle has aroused her, and she wants to unwind by using me in the most carnal of ways.

I allow her to dominate me.

She stands on her toes, wrapping a hand around my nape to hold me prisoner as she devours me wildly. She uses her anger to punish me with her brutal kisses, and when she threads her fingers through my hair, she yanks my head back.

Her dominance has my cock instantly hardening, and when she rubs herself against me, I know kissing is not enough. She severs our union and then slaps my cheek with a snarl.

"That is for tricking me."

A feral grin is my response, which infuriates Emeline further.

She shoves me onto my back before diving on top of me and straddling me. She frantically works at my trousers, her impatience only making me harder. When my cock springs free and she grips my length, a moan slips past my lips because she isn't gentle.

Her small hand grasps me tightly as she moves up and down.

I am her prisoner and watch with hunger as she lifts her hips and raises the hem of her dress. She positions her cunt over me and doesn't need any encouragement as she lowers herself onto my length. She takes me whole while I arch my neck, watching her use me in the most wicked of ways.

When I'm buried to the hilt, she begins to move wildly.

She uses my chest as reins as she holds on tight, milking her pleasure from me as she rides me hard. She finds her rhythm, bouncing, rocking, never apologizing for taking what she wants. I grip her thighs, coaxing her to move faster.

She bows her back, fucking me hard, and when she lifts her hips, only to slam back down so I hit her deeply, I realize she's eager for a quick release.

I tear at the laces on the front of her dress, causing her heavy breasts to spill free. They bounce with her untamed movements, and I run my thumb over her erect nipple before cupping her breast in my palm. I know she likes it when I touch her breasts, so I fondle them with passion.

Her milky flesh is perfect, and it kills me to simply lie here when I want her on all fours as I fuck her from behind. But this is Emeline's chance to display dominance. Her chance for retribution for not being privy to my plans.

"You will not," she pants, rocking on me roguishly. "You will not do that to me ever again."

Before I can reply, she rummages for a dead guard's knife and presses it to my throat as she continues to fuck me hungrily.

"Say it," she commands, digging the blade in deeper, so deep, I feel a trickle of blood spill from the wound.

"I will not trick you ever again, Princess," I state slowly, allowing her to abuse me brutally, because I like it.

"You will never lie to me again." Her body is quivering around me.

"I will never lie to you again."

"And I *will* be fighting at Carhampton. Say it."

Her words are as heavy with craving as her movements as she increases the tempo.

"Say it!"

Arching my neck, she gasps, eyes wide because her blade digs deeper into my neck, cutting me.

"Skarth!"

But I don't stop, and when I feel the blade sink in farther, I grip her hand, holding her prisoner as she tries to yank free in fear that she's hurting me.

"I promised not to lie to you, Princess. Therefore, I will not say it."

Her skin turns a sweet pink, and I know she is close to chasing her release. "You stubborn h-heathen," she pants as I thrust my hips, meeting her strokes brutally.

She bounces on my lap, and when her body grows lax, I pry the blade from her hand and toss it aside. "I will protect you with my life, Emeline. I protect what is mine."

"I am yours?" she questions, her body writhing.

"Yes, you always have been. Even when we were stupid to believe otherwise. We are joined as one—in all the ways that there are."

She rocks against me, a sated cry leaving her as she releases long and hard. She is so beautiful when she lets go, for her vulnerability reveals her true strength.

The moment her trembles cease, I lift her and position her onto all fours. With her plump arse in my face, I reenter her viciously and chase my release, condemning us both to the place she calls hell.

It's nightfall, which gives me some sense of peace.

We made it through another day.

Today confirmed we will be hunted until the battle at Carhampton. King Egbert will do anything to find Emeline, which means he wishes to avoid a war. He hopes that Emeline will be found beforehand so innocent men won't be slain over a war which I'm certain hasn't pleased the Witan.

They would rather let Northumbria deal with her.

But King Egbert's obsession with Emeline won't allow it. He wants her back, lost to the notion that she is in love with him. As for Prince Aethelwulf, he merely seeks revenge. If Emeline is captured, no matter that she will have the king's protection, she won't live to see her nineteenth year.

Emeline is in danger in Wessex and Northumbria. She has nowhere to go, which is why I must protect her.

We've both been silent, lost to our thoughts. No doubt, Emeline is conspiring ways to change my mind. But I will not be swayed. The more thought I give to it, the more it makes sense that Emeline is to leave this country and make a life for herself in Scandinavia until we can figure out a plan where it's safe for her to return.

She is still the Princess of Northumbria, and I'm certain she will want to claim that birthright. She will happily fight her brother for governance. But a woman challenging a man...I don't know if it can be done.

What I do know is that nowhere is safe for her at the moment.

"How do you know where Ulf will be?" Emeline asks, breaking the silence.

She wraps her arms tighter around my waist, nestling into my back.

Peering overhead, I look at the bright star which has guided my people over turbulent seas and when lost in a foreign land.

"North of the stars," she softly says. "Just like us."

"What do you mean?"

"You've been called many names by the Saxons: heathens, Danes, The Ungodly, Sea Wolves, and Northmen. Your home is north of here, I assume?" she wisely says. "Seems we're both connected to the north then.

"Both of our homes are north of the stars."

"My home…it's with you, Emeline," I confess, needing her to understand why I wish for her to go to Scandinavia.

"But what about Cecily?"

"That is something I am yet to figure out."

"We were fated from the moment we met," she whispers.

"Yes, Princess, we were, and that is why I cannot allow anything to happen to you. I know you want to fight at Carhampton, but I ask that you do as you are told. Please."

A small sigh leaves her. "And what am I to be told?"

"It's safer for you at sea than it is for you on land. I ask that you sail to my motherland, Scandinavia, until we can work out a plan where you can return here safely.

"Northumbria is your home, but you cannot go back there, not now. Your brother will have you killed. Or your father will just send you back here. You are a fugitive wherever you stay."

"What of the other kingdoms? The realm is rich. I could start anew in East Anglia or Mercia."

"What do you think will happen when word spreads that a princess inhabits their land?" I pose. "You are valuable to so many."

"That is all I seem to be," she sadly replies, pressing her cheek between my shoulder blades. "Just someone's collateral to better their life, not caring that they are ruining mine."

Rubbing over her hand tucked around my waist, I confess, "You are so much more to me than that."

She doesn't speak, and I hope that's because I've given her something to think about.

We ride in silence until I hear faint voices in the distance. Ulf is here.

I'm not sure how I'm going to contain myself from cutting out his eyeballs if he looks at Emeline the wrong way. I already want to rip out his tongue for kissing her.

It does bother me that she returned his kisses.

But I can't be mad at her. I am married, after all.

We ride toward the temporary camp and are welcomed with a riotous cheer. The men and women are only happy because as Emeline said, they see her as their collateral. She huddles closer to me as she too understands the risks of her being back here.

"How did the guards find me?" she asks, as all she remembers is being knocked out cold.

"Dova, the wife of the husband you killed," I plainly reply. "She told the guards where to find you. It was her retribution for what you did to Bo."

"What did you do to her?"

Emeline knows what, but she wishes for me to say it aloud.

"I killed her."

"And Erik?"

"He lives for now."

She doesn't ask any more questions.

I make eye contact with Inga, who smiles. Not the response I was anticipating. Something is wrong. I jump down from the horse and offer Emeline my hand.

Until I find Ulf, I'm not letting her out of my sight.

She places her hand in mine, and the moment her feet hit the ground, she gasps, eyes wide as she stares behind me.

On instinct, I spin around and protect her with my body as I gauge what the threat is. But this isn't a threat. This is my karma.

"Skarth," Ulf says with a smirk, arms out wide, walking toward us. "I am so happy you are back. We were worried."

But I can't look at him because if I do, I will kill him.

"What are you doing here?"

She flinches, and I realize my tone is sharp.

"She missed you," Ulf replies for her. "And she also wanted to tell you the good news."

"What good news?"

Emeline grips the back of my vest, sensing everything is about to change once again.

She steps forward and pulls back her long black cloak, exposing her swollen stomach—swollen with my child.

"You are going to be a father," Cecily says, her half smile revealing she senses this reunion is far from a happy one. "I am with child."

Emeline loosens her grip and takes a step back while I stare at my wife and unborn child, speechless.

How things have now changed…

# SEVENTEEN

*Princess Emeline*

ecily runs over to Skarth, throwing her arms around him
while I take one step back.

And then another.

Ulf watches me closely with a smug smirk, for he knows
what this is doing to me. Was he the one who sought Cecily
out? I feel sick to my stomach.

With shame riddling me, I fold my arms across my chest.
The laces on my dress are crudely tied together to conceal what
Skarth and I did with one another earlier. But that's a thing of
the past because everything has now changed.

He is going to be a father.

And me? I am a mistress...something I promised to never

be again.

"Princess," Cecily gushes, letting Skarth go and bending into a curtsey before me. "It's so good to see you."

All I can focus on is her rounded belly.

"And you," I reply, quashing down my need to scream into the heavens. "If you'll excuse me, the journey has exhausted me."

I don't wait for her to reply and quickly make my way toward a tent and disappear inside. The moment I'm alone, I bend in half, place my hands on my knees and take three calming breaths. It does nothing to calm my nerves.

Even though I've always factored Cecily into my relationship with Skarth, her being with child was something I never foresaw. How can I ask him to choose me when there is a child involved?

I can't.

"Everything all right, Princess?"

Ulf's smooth voice has me taking a final calming breath before coming to a stand.

"Yes, I am fine. Just tired. May I retire in here?"

"Of course. You are always welcome in my bed."

I'm too tired to fight him, so I make my way over to the furs spread out before the fire on the ground and lie down. Turning on my side, I use my hands as a pillow and stare into the flames.

Every inch of me is numb.

With Skarth by my side, I felt that there was hope, but now, there is none. Tonight, his wife and unborn child will sleep in his bed while I sleep beside a man who I don't particularly like but can't seem to stay away from.

Ulf comes to rest beside me, but my back is turned to him because I cannot face him as I'm certain he is aware of what happened between Skarth and me.

"What bothers you?"

"Everything," I reply softly. "Did you seek Cecily out?"

I need to know if she found Ulf or if he sought her out.

"She was not hard to find," he confesses. "As it was, she was looking for Skarth."

"Of course. To tell him the good news," I assume, although my tone sounds far from jubilant.

"Yes, but to also inform him of your father."

"What of him?"

I turn around to face him.

He doesn't shift away, so we are lying very close together. "Cecily said he has assembled a very large army to fight with King Egbert and that anyone associated with any Northman is in danger. That's why she fled."

I gasp, horrified. "What of her family?"

I have fond memories of them, of Osanna and Cuthbert as they welcomed me into their home.

If my father has done anything to hurt them, I'll never forgive him.

"She did not say, but for her to flee, it seems no one is safe."

"I cannot believe I am his kin," I whisper to myself. "All that matters to him is his wealth and his title of king. It makes me sick."

Cecily, like me, it seems, is a fugitive too. No wonder she came looking for Skarth.

"It does not bother you that your father fights with Wessex for your return?" he poses in interest.

"I've learned long ago that I am merely a trading pawn for my father," I reply. "He does not care for my happiness. Only his."

"Is that why you are here? With the heathens instead of the Saxons?"

"You think I do this to defy my father? To thumb my nose at him like a spoiled little brat?"

His silence is the answer I need.

"I can assure you, that is not the reason."

"Then what is?"

I know what he is doing. He wants me to confess my feelings for Skarth, because what would that mean now that Cecily is here?

"It is the reason for my very existence," I admit, unable to stop my feelings from spilling free. "But things change, and sometimes, you are forced to change with them."

He nods. "So what happens now?"

"Skarth does not want me to fight. He wishes for me to go hide on a ship while you battle against the men who destroyed my life," I share, not omitting my bitterness. "He wants me to go to Scandinavia until we can work out a plan where I can return back here safely."

"And what do you want?"

"I do not wish to hide like a frightened little mouse," I declare firmly. "This is my fight as well. Against Wessex *and* Northumbria."

"Then fight," he states with conviction.

And that is the difference between Ulf and Skarth—Skarth would sacrifice everything for my safety, knowing I will hate him for denying me, while Ulf would simply say anything in hopes I will submit to his advances.

"That's all I've done my entire life," I confess, closing my eyes.

With a gentle touch, Ulf strokes my cheek. I would usually shy away, but I am so tired, tired of everything.

"Sleep, little mouse," he says. "Things may seem simpler in the morning."

But I know that's not true because come dawn, I will have to face a reality I wish I could escape.

I jolt upright, my heart almost exploding from my chest.

Brushing the matted hair from my brow, I peer around at

my surroundings because, for a split moment in time, I had the luxury of forgetting where I am. But as the truth comes crashing into me, it's evident sleep hasn't helped numb this pain in my chest.

The fire is still burning, thanks to Ulf. I wonder where he is.

I don't wish to rise, but I can't stay hidden forever, so I stand, stretching the sleep from my bones. I assume that the Northmen will eat before we move on. We can't stay in one place for too long, which has me wondering what that means for Cecily.

The journeys will be long and treacherous. I can't imagine Skarth would want her accompanying us in her…condition.

I can't even bring myself to say it, and I know how selfish that is.

Putting on a brave face, I step outside, clutching the fur around my shoulders. It's not mine, and I'm fairly certain it's Ulf's. He has been kind to me, but I'm still unsure if he's doing this because he cares or because I am valuable to him.

"Good morning, Princess."

Ulf appears, offering me a cup of ale.

My queasy stomach gurgles. "Thank you, but it's a little early."

"It is never too early for ale," he teases but doesn't push.

I keep my eyes on him because I'm afraid of what I'll see. "Are we leaving soon?"

"Yes. The king's guard will be looking for us."

"Okay. I just need to freshen up."

Ulf nods, and I quickly head for the woods where I can have some privacy. I keep my head down the entire time because I don't want to see Skarth.

Once I have relieved myself, I pick some mint and chew on it to freshen my breath and ease my stomach. There is a small stream that runs through the woods, so I cup the cool water to wash my face and freshen up.

Cleanliness is next to godliness, our priest would say. If he knew of the sins I committed, I am fairly certain he would agree there aren't enough prayers to save my soul.

The rustle of the leaves hints I am no longer alone.

Coming to a stand, I turn and am disappointed Ulf stands before me and not Skarth. But I don't let it show.

"We are to make our move," he says, but what he reveals next has me almost inhaling my tongue. "We all agree that it is safer and wiser to travel in smaller groups. You will come with me, Inga, Gorm, Orm, Bodil, Skarth, and Cecily."

"Why must we travel with them?" I ask when I can speak.

"With who?" he questions with an arrogant grin.

I don't give him the satisfaction of replying because he knows whom I speak of.

Putting on a brave face, I march past him, and when I push into the clearing in the forest, I come face-to-face with the man who can render me speechless with a look alone.

Skarth and I lock eyes, and it's the first time I've seen

him since I all but fled into the night like the coward that I am. Someone speaks to him, but he isn't listening because, as it's always been between us, the world simply fades into the background when we stare in each other's eyes.

I can see his confusion, his pain, which dances with mine. I almost wish we never left the safety of the cave because it was there we could finally let down our walls and give in to temptation.

But as Cecily appears, reality comes crashing down around us, and I instantly avert my gaze.

"Princess," she gushes, bowing.

"Please, Cecily, there is no need to bow," I instruct. "Not in your condition."

Skarth clenches his jaw while Cecily smiles, none the wiser. "Your kindness knows no bounds. I believe we will be traveling together?"

"Yes, I believe so," I reply, quickly peering at Skarth.

"I am glad. Time has passed us by, and I am saddened we have been unable to talk."

I try my best to smile because she doesn't want to hear what I want to say. "Then let us talk until our hearts are content. I wish to know all about your family. How is Cuthbert? Osanna?"

However, when she casts her gaze downward, it seems there is much to discuss.

Ulf towers behind me, and I don't fail to notice Skarth's eyes narrow into slits. He doesn't like Ulf standing so close. He has no right to me, not when his pregnant wife stands by his side.

"You are riding with me, Princess." Ulf doesn't give me an opportunity to decline.

With one last look at Skarth, I follow Ulf as he walks toward his horse. He mounts him before offering me his hand.

"I won't bite…unless you want me to," he adds with a sultry tenor.

Raising my eyes to the heavens, I place my hand in his, ignoring the heat which washes over me. Although he annoys me to no end, I cannot deny this attraction I feel for him. Though it borders between love and hate.

I sit behind him, but he reaches around and moves me closer so we are pressed flesh to flesh. The heat soon revolves into an inferno, but the flames douse when Skarth and Cecily ride up beside us.

Skarth's eyes focus on my arms around Ulf's waist. When I attempt to retreat, Ulf simply holds my hands prisoner in one of his. He is challenging Skarth to react.

He doesn't, which selfishly disappoints me.

"Never let your guard down," he warns Ulf. "We keep off the tracks. We ride until nightfall."

"*Hvat segir þú?*" Ulf says lightly.

A low growl escapes Skarth, which has me guessing that whatever Ulf just said is, yet again, another challenge. "You heard me. Protect Emeline with your life."

The mood soon turns serious as Ulf nods.

Skarth clucks his tongue, commanding his horse to make haste. Ulf follows, and we commence our journey toward the unknown.

We've ridden all day, and I know this landscape well. We will arrive in Carhampton on schedule. As long as we continue to avoid the king's guard, that is.

Today, we were fortunate. But I know every day won't be as lucky.

Ulf said his men should have reached his homeland by now and that his people will be preparing for the journey to England. I don't know how many are coming, but I expect a lot.

I know this battle will be bloody, and many lives will be lost. But losing isn't an option. We must win.

Skarth slows down when we reach a thickly wooded area. There is coverage and a stream close by. I assume we will rest here for the night.

Ulf directs his horse toward the stream.

He dismounts and offers me his hand. I accept, but he surprises me when he drags me toward him and wraps his arms around my waist to lift me off the horse.

I am suspended in his arms. Our faces are inches apart. My breathing hitches. My heart begins to race. This is awfully close, but I can't seem to pull away.

"Do you want me to carry you, Princess?" he quips, which is what I needed to remind me of the arrogant bastard which lies beneath this handsome face.

"No, I do not." There is no conviction to my tone, but Ulf does as I request.

My shaky legs take a moment to adjust, and I assure myself that's because of riding all day and has nothing to do with Ulf.

I leave him to tend to his horse and decide to seek out Cecily. I cannot avoid her. I see her sitting on a fallen tree branch. She looks pale.

"Cecily!" I call out, quickening my step. "Is everything all right?"

"I am fine. Just a little nauseous. It will pass. Please, sit with me."

I sit beside her, and the dots of perspiration lining her brow confirm she is far from being all right.

"Are you able to keep anything down?"

She shakes her head. "I have been told this is normal, but I worry."

"It is normal," I assure her gently. "I experienced it too."

Her eyes widen. "You were with child?"

My heart still aches at the fact. "Yes, I was. He was not meant for this world, though. God had other plans for him."

This is what my priest told me, but I can't help but feel this is merely an excuse, for what merciful God would take an unborn child? What God would take his life before he had a chance to live?

"Oh, Emeline," Cecily coos, tears in her eyes. "I am so sorry."

"What is done is done," I reply, not wanting sympathy. "Now, we must ensure your child is fed."

I stand, but Cecily reaches for my hand. "Thank you, Princess. You have always been so kind to me. I thank God for the day we met."

All I can do is smile because I don't think she would feel that way if she knew what I have done.

I decide to hunt for herbs as I know of some which helped ease my nausea. Cecily will be able to stomach something after this.

"Where are you off to?" Ulf asks, walking beside me.

"I am going to find something to help settle Cecily's stomach."

"She shouldn't be here," he says, surprising me.

"Then why did you seek her out?"

He grips my arm and gently ushers me away from prying eyes. "I've been thinking about Carhampton."

"What of it?"

"Will you fight?"

"Of course I will," I state, not interested in yet another man telling me what to do.

His hair is interwoven into three braids where it comes together in one long plait that runs down his back. This hairstyle flaunts his face, and I hate that his face is undeniably handsome. He is rugged and commands control with those piercing eyes.

I should look away. But I can't.

"I know Skarth will do everything in his power to ensure that does not happen," he says, revealing he has insight into Skarth's thoughts. "But I want to assure you, I will do what you want me to. I will not take your choices away.

"This war is yours as well as mine. I vow to protect you on the battlefield…and off it if you wish."

This isn't the first time Ulf has said this to me. At first, I believed it was because he needed me to succeed in his plans. But now, I'm not so sure.

"Would you like that, Princess?"

"I do not need your protection. On *or* off the battlefield," I counter, but my argument is weak.

Ulf lowers his face to mine. "Do you fear me? Is that why you continue to refuse me?"

"No, I do not. I have faced far worse things in my life than a coquettish Northman," I spit, refusing to cower.

Ulf shakes his head, however, revealing I have misunderstood. "You fear me because of what I make you feel," he states hoarsely, inches from my lips. "You do not want to like the monster of this story because what would that say about you?"

He is so close; I can feel his breath against my heated cheeks.

He is aware of the effect he has on me, which is why I stand on tippy-toes and reply, "It would say keep your friends close, but your enemies even closer."

A slanted smirk spreads across his face. "You can keep me as close as you want, Princess."

He always has an answer for everything.

With a snicker, I decide to leave this conversation, afraid of what I will say because I seem to lose good sense when Ulf is involved.

Pushing past him, I make my way through the thickets, thankful the thick shrubbery conceals me because I need time alone. I venture deep into the woods, needing to get away from everyone. The person I need to escape from the most, however, is me.

I don't know why I allow Ulf to get under my skin. I shouldn't allow him to affect me, but he does. He has from the first moment we met.

I always envisioned a future with Skarth, even when I was a wife and a mistress, but everything is different now. I didn't anticipate Cecily being with child nor did I predict I'd meet someone like Ulf the Bloody.

His vow to protect me has left me feeling unsettled.

I decide to search for some peppermint and chamomile as this concoction helped me when I was with child. On instinct, I place my hands on my flat belly, thinking of the son who never saw the light of day. I wonder if I will experience that again.

Sniffing back my tears, I venture deeper into the woods,

enjoying the silence. I find chamomile growing robustly and bend to pick some, but before I have a chance, someone is at my back, shoving my front against the trunk of a towering tree.

I don't fight because I know who it is.

"I taught you better than that," Skarth says into my ear.

"Why fight the inevitable?" I reply, my heart beginning to race.

Skarth's chest is pressed to my back, and even though I can scarcely breathe, he's not close enough. This is the first time he's spoken to me since our lives were turned upside down.

"Because you fight. Always," he states with conviction, and I sense there is a hidden meaning behind his words.

"Just how you are fighting for your wife?" I counter with bite. "Fighting for her and your child's safety?"

"I didn't know, Emeline."

"It matters not now, for you are going to be a father. Do not worry, I will not tell her what happened between us."

"I am not worried. I am…" But he pauses.

"You are what?" My breaths escape me in a rush of winded chaos.

"I am murderous…and I have no right to be because my wife is here, but all I can think about is…you. About your taste and your desperate moans as I buried myself inside you.

"All I can think about is how, for the first time in my life, I felt peace. I did not care about the mayhem because when I am with you, Emeline, nothing else matters but us. But now…with

Cecily…and…Ulf."

His snarl before mentioning Ulf has a bubble of hope rising. If he is jealous, that is because he cares.

"It's no longer just us, and Ulf knows it. What did he whisper into your ear?"

"What time?" I'm goading him because I like his envy.

"Do not provoke me," he warns, his lips caressing the shell of my ear.

"And if I do?"

With a growl, he reaches for my wrists and slams my palms against the tree, holding me prisoner. The feel of his hard body pressed to me has me growing wet between the legs.

"Tell me what Ulf said."

The more he speaks, the angrier he becomes. I like it when he's angry. I like when he loses control.

"He vowed to protect me on the battlefield…and off it if I wished," I reply, recounting Ulf's words.

A rumble permeates the air. "And what was your response?"

"What business is that of yours? You are a married man with responsibilities that no longer involve me."

"Emeline," Skarth warns dangerously low.

He tightens his hold on my wrists so hard that it begins to hurt. But I like the pain. It's the first time since Skarth left me that I feel alive.

So I continue to goad him.

"He believes I fear him because of the feelings he rouses in me."

"And is he right?"

"He is not right…nor is he wrong." This neither confirms nor denies my feelings, and that drives Skarth mad.

"Why do you fucking insist on defying me over and over?" he furiously declares. "I should punish you in ways you cannot imagine!"

With a victorious grin, I reply, "And that is the reason."

Skarth spins me around and slams his mouth over mine, robbing me of air as he kisses me frantically. He threads his fingers through my loose hair and angles my head to bend to his command. He is in complete control.

His kisses are punishing. My lips are bruised, but I welcome it because this shows me that he cares. That he is just as conflicted as I am. We know what we should do—what the right thing to do is—but sinning has never felt this good.

He severs the kiss, only to bite me on the side of the throat. He is like an animal, weakening its prey. He trails down and kisses over the tops of my heaving breasts. He slides his tongue between the valley, flicking from side to side.

"I can smell him on your skin," he snarls, and of course, he can because I was pressed to Ulf all day. "I am going to mark what is mine so you will never forget who you belong to."

I wildly tear at Skarth's trousers, and he lifts me, positioning me over his straining manhood. I wrap my legs around him, and without preparation, he slams me onto his length. A pained cry leaves me because he is not gentle, but I don't want him to be.

To feel him inside me again…it is pure ecstasy.

He holds me tightly, encouraging me to bounce on his manhood. And I do.

Each time he sinks into me, I feel him so deeply, it brings tears to my eyes. I rock against him, relishing in the way we fit. With one hand wrapped around my waist, he snakes the other around the back of my nape and holds me prisoner as he pumps his hips.

I am bound to him because I can't move, and I wish to never separate again.

"Tell me who you belong to," he demands, his face twisting in euphoria as I rotate my hips.

"I belong to no one, Lord," I taunt, biting my bottom lip as he increases the tempo of his brutal strokes.

I grow lax, merely his puppet to defile over and over again.

He is a beast, uncontrolled and dominant, as he erases the scent of another man from my skin. He pulls out of me, only to rub his manhood on my nether lips. He truly is marking me, it seems.

I try to take him back into me, but he holds his length, stubbornly depriving me of what I want. What I need.

"Tell me," he orders, cupping my chin between his fingers. "Emeline, no more raillery. Tell me."

His desperate eyes search my face for answers, and I see

that he is afraid; afraid that Ulf is right. My heart hurts, for how could he believe I would want anyone but him?

My tongue darts out, licking his finger leisurely. A sated moan escapes his plump lips.

"Give me what I want, and I will tell you."

We lock eyes as he surrenders and reenters me, painfully slow.

His strength is conveyed as he holds me with ease, bouncing me up and down on his manhood. I lose myself to the rhythm, to the carnality of being with a man who is the ultimate sin.

Skarth owns me—mind, body, and soul.

Under the moonlight, a princess and her Northman relinquish what is right and wrong and seal their union with a fated kiss.

"I belong to you, Skarth the Godless. I always have. I always will," I confess, pressing my lips to his. "My heart is eternally yours. As is my body. I dream of the day when we can roam freely, unashamed of the…love we share."

I want to tell him that I love him, that I have loved him since I was a little girl, but he knows. Just how I know he feels the same way about me.

"You are in my heart. Forever."

I know what this is. It's goodbye, for a world where Cecily and Skarth's child exists is a world where we cannot be together. And I knew that from the moment he pressed his lips to mine.

I hold back my tears as he defiles me hard because I do

not know when we can be together like this again. I wish it was different, but I know Skarth won't abandon his family, and that's one of the reasons I love him so.

With a low groan, he releases his seed into me, knowing what this could mean.

I don't have a chance to ask him why he would do that because he drops to his knees before me and lifts my dress to bury himself between my legs. He licks and suckles at my throbbing mound while I thread my fingers through his long hair, holding him prisoner as he pleasures me with his mouth and tongue.

Skarth is a generous lover, ensuring I'm never left unsatisfied. I never knew this act even existed before Skarth. He has taught me so much. And I am going to miss him immensely.

He twirls his tongue inside me, rubbing his face from side to side. His beard adds to the sensation, and my legs grow weak, for it won't be long until I explode. I ride his face, unashamed, peering down and watching my lover pleasure me passionately.

"Do you enjoy my taste?" I boldly ask.

He pulls away, only to lick my nether lips from bottom to top. He continues lapping at them, ensuring to maintain eye contact with me. He flicks his tongue in and out, in and out, before sucking over my sensitive nub.

"All the saints above," I curse, arching into him as he spreads my legs wider.

I don't know how I'll survive without this, for I know I will never experience this passion with another man ever again.

Skarth bites over me, and with a sharp slap of the underside of his tongue against my swollen center, a wave tackles me from the inside out, and I cry out my release, undulating in song with my screams. The world is shrouded in promise, but once the last tremor racks me, I am brought down to earth.

I sag against Skarth, toying with his hair as he remains on his knees before me. I lower my dress, but neither of us is in any hurry to leave.

"I *am* fighting at Carhampton," I say, continuing to stroke his hair.

"I knew you would not give up," he replies, fatigue overtaking him as he closes his eyes.

"And you cannot stop me."

"I will continue to try," he counters, a sure sign this isn't over.

I don't press further because it is nice to bask in the silence. But that is soon shattered when we hear a guttural scream catch the night air.

It's that of a female.

Skarth springs to his feet, running through the woods.

I follow him but am not as fast as he is, and when I finally arrive where the Northmen have set up camp to see Skarth cradle a bleeding Cecily who is lying on the ground, I know this is our punishment for giving in to temptation.

"Let me through!" I demand, rushing over to Cecily.

"Help m-me, Emeline," she sobs, tears running down her cheeks. "I fear my baby is dying."

The front of her dress is stained a bright red.

"Your baby is going to be fine. I promise you. Get her inside," I command Skarth.

He nods, gently picking her up and taking her toward a tent. His love for her is evident, which just hurts all the more.

Retrieving a bucket of fresh water, I seek out Ulf in the crowd. "I need you to find me wormwood and mint."

He folds his arms across his broad chest. "And what do I get in return? If I bend to *your* demands, Princess?"

The world is on my shoulders, and I surrender because I am so tired of it all. I do not have time for games. Without those herbs, Cecily and her baby are at risk. "I accept your offer. I request your protection…on and off the battlefield. I yield to you, Ulf the Bloody. I am yours."

He closes his eyes, inhaling deeply as if savoring the moment of victory. "Then I will go find your herbs," he finally says, opening his eyes.

We stare at one another because although I surrendered, it wasn't all forced…and I hate myself for it. I agreed to Ulf's terms because a part of me wanted to, and he knows it.

He turns his back and does as I asked, but I know he will expect the same of me.

With a bucket in hand, I make my way into the tent, ensuring I don't let my emotions show. Skarth is sitting beside

Cecily, who is lying on her back. He is riddled with worry, which is why he needs to leave.

"Please, will you give us some privacy?"

He looks at me like I've gone mad, as I am asking he abandon his bleeding wife when she needs him more than ever.

"Please, Skarth," I press, coming to kneel beside Cecily, facing him. "I promise, I will try to save your baby, but I cannot do that with you breathing down my neck."

Cecily whimpers, holding Skarth's hand tightly. "It's okay, my love. I trust Emeline. She would never hurt us."

I lower my eyes because I already have.

With reluctance, he agrees, pressing a kiss to Cecily's forehead. Those lips were pressed to me moments ago.

"I will just be outside," he promises her before looking at me.

The silence is heavy with unspoken words. All I can do is nod.

He stands, looking at his wife and unborn baby with love and concern, and at this moment, I know I have to let him go.

Once he's gone, I focus on what's important, and that's Cecily.

"Is my baby dying?" she cries, peering down at her bloody gown.

"Pray to the Lord, Cecily," I say, gently pulling back her dress.

Her inner thighs are stained a bright red.

Memories suddenly assault me because I was once Cecily, but I refuse to let another baby die. Regardless that she and this baby are the reason I cannot be with the man I love, I will not allow any harm to come to them.

Cecily commences prayer while I use a cloth and water to wipe away the blood.

The bleeding has stopped to just a trickle, which is a good sign. However, I need to examine her more thoroughly.

"Cecily, tell me about your wedding day," I say with a small smile as I wring out the cloth.

Her damp hair sticks to her perspiring forehead, and she breathes through the pain. "It was a warm summer's day," she commences, staring off into the distance, lost in thought. "Skarth looked so becoming."

I ignore the pang in my heart and instead focus on gently prodding Cecily. She flinches as I insert two fingers inside her but continues.

"We got married in the village. It was a small affair. But it was everything I could ever wish for."

I turn my fingers, hoping to feel something. This is what was done to me when I was with child. I knew from the face of the doctor what my prognosis was.

"Skarth wore my favorite leather tunic even though I knew he hated it." She chuckles, lost to the memories and not what I am doing to her.

This is why I asked her to recall a happy memory to distract her. Sadly, there wasn't one for me to remember.

"I love him so much," she says, her voice quivering. "I would do anything to make him happy. I cannot lose his baby, Emeline."

"And you have not," I reveal, my fingers brushing over her baby. I exhale a sigh of relief.

She didn't even realize I was examining her until I remove my bloody fingers. "My baby is okay?"

"Yes, your baby is healthy. He is strong. Just like his father," I say, unable to help but feel bittersweet.

Cecily bursts into tears.

Lowering her dress, I wash my hands in the bucket and dry them on my dress. "You must be careful from now on. You must not eat certain foods. Or allow stress to affect you."

"That is all I have been doing," she confesses. "I rode out here to find Skarth, knowing the consequences. But—"

"But love stops for no one," I fill in the blanks because I can relate.

She nods, sniffing back her tears. "Thank you, Emeline. You are righteous. And honorable."

I don't deserve her kind words, so I stand. "Skarth, you may enter."

I know he is just outside, so he rushes in, worry etched all over his handsome face. "Your baby is fine. I have told Cecily she needs to rest. She cannot be out here, exposed to these harsh elements."

Ulf enters, hands filled with herbs. "Is this enough?"

I can't help but smile at his naivety. "More than enough."

He offers them to me, ensuring to brush his fingers against mine, something Skarth sees. But there is nothing we can do, as this proves he will always choose his family over me—which is what he should do.

"Boil this into a liquid and have Cecily sip it. It will help soothe her cramps," I instruct Skarth as I offer him the herbs.

He accepts with a nod.

Ulf doesn't leave, and when Skarth looks at me, he senses that's because Ulf is waiting for me. He doesn't know of the promise I made to Ulf to save his wife and child, and he never will, for I do not want him to feel guilty for the choice I made.

I go to leave, but Skarth reaches out and gently grips my wrist. His touch sets me on fire. It always will.

"Thank you."

He knows if I let any harm come to Cecily and his baby, we could be together, but I couldn't do that. In good faith, I could not live with myself if I stole Skarth that way.

"You are welcome." I look into the eyes of the man I love because this is our final goodbye.

Holding back my tears, I exit the tent and gulp in mouthfuls of fresh air because I'm certain I'm moments away from suffocating.

Ulf simply wraps his arm around my shoulders and leads me toward his tent. When inside, I stand numbly, unsure what happens next.

I then remember my promise.

Mechanically, I lift my dress over my head and stand before Ulf, naked. This is what he wanted, was it not? For me to submit to him.

He stands across from me, his eyes hungrily eating over scraps of flesh. I don't conceal my nudity. What would be the point?

He doesn't say a word as he merely examines me.

I thought he would be on me the moment we were alone, but he does something which changes the course of everything.

Removing his fur shawl, he steps forward, and with eyes still locked on me, he wraps it around my shoulders.

"I-I don't understand," I say, unsure why he is covering me up when he's been desperate to see me disrobe since we met.

He lifts my chin with his finger. "I will not force myself on you. Nor do I want you to force yourself on me. When we fuck…it is going to be because you want me as much as I want you."

My lips part because he has stolen the breath and words from my mouth.

"Nor will you be slathered in the scent of another man."

My cheeks heat because he knows what Skarth and I did.

"And you still want me?" I question, unable to hold back my tears. "When you know what I did? When you know that my heart belongs to another?"

Ulf rubs his thumb across my mouth. "Yes, Princess, because one day, that heart will belong to me. I promise you that."

Once again, I am caught speechless, for a part of me believes his vow.

"I know you want to fight…but with Cecily…it makes sense for both of you to be on water, not land. She will need someone strong to protect her.

"But I made a promise to you. If you wish to fight, then I will protect you with my life."

My heart, which I believed to be shattered beyond repair, beats soundly once again. I don't know what I feel for Ulf, but what I do know is that I misjudged him.

"How do we do that, though?" I ask, wrapping the fur around me snugly. "If King Egbert does not see me, he will not relinquish."

Ulf nods. "As long as we present someone who looks like you, it'll buy us enough time to enforce your plan of attack."

He's right.

Suddenly, another plan surfaces.

Ulf grins, and the sight stirs something inside me. "Princess, your deviancy stirs the longing in my—"

But I cut him off as his vulgarity is not appropriate in a time such as this. "What if I *am* on the battlefield…but we trick King Egbert at the last minute? He will not expect an ambush, especially one where I find haven on the seas.

"He will have his men guarding the lands, but what if we tunnel *underneath*, which will give access to the lands by the Northmen as well as the waters, and also an escape route for Cecily and me?"

Ulf shakes his head, and I mistake his response for a negative one.

"You do not think it can be done?"

"No, I think it is a brilliant idea," he says in awe. "But what it means is that we need to get to Carhampton days ahead of King Egbert and his men."

"Can it be done?"

Ulf steals my breath as he leans forward and whispers inches from my lips, "How fast can you dig?"

We've found common ground, and just like that, the enemy has turned into an ally and also a betrothed.

# EIGHTEEN

*Skarth the Godless*

As I stand back and look at what we've achieved, I know that come sunrise, we will win this battle.

Thanks to Emeline's ingenious plan of tunneling under the land, we will defeat Wessex and claim Carhampton as Northman land. We've ridden for endless days to be here before King Egbert, and once again, Emeline's knowledge of the terrain has given us an advantage.

We were able to implement our plan without detection, and as I stand before the concealed entrance of the tunnel, I can't deny that all of this is possible because of Emeline.

I agreed to do this because of her, but in the end, she didn't need any of us. She did this for revenge, but her vengeance will be had from afar because once she presents herself to King Egbert, we will attack while she navigates through this tunnel to the safety of the waiting ship, the ship Cecily will be on.

Emeline agreed to this plan because of me. She knew if anything happened to Cecily or my child, I would never forgive myself for it. She put her retribution aside for me. Her love for me is more important than her own needs, and I thank her by asking she protect my wife and child.

I am a fucking bastard. I know that.

But it doesn't matter because she and Ulf have grown close.

Since the night when she saved my child, she has stayed by his side. She also shares his bed. I am certain Ulf holds something over her. I refuse to believe she goes to him of her own free will. My heart couldn't take it.

But even if she did, I have no right to stand in her way of happiness because I have hurt her enough. I have asked her to sacrifice so much for me. I am robbing her of her revenge by sending her away.

The only way I can make amends is to ensure every last man and woman who hurt her dies by my sword. This is the only thing I can do to show her how much I…love her, for love her, I do.

More than anything, anyone.

"Talking to the gods?" Ulf stands beside me.

"There is no need, for we will win this," I reply, turning to look at the fifteen longships.

My people are here, waiting to win this battle or to feast in the halls of Valhalla.

Their ships are created for war. The figureheads are carved in the shapes of fierce, powerful animals like dragons and snakes. These are to stir fear in the Saxons as this is something they do not understand. The dragon's head is to also protect my people along the long voyage.

"Yes, you are right." Ulf looks into the distance, where we know an army of Saxons awaits us.

We are simply biding our time until dawn. But what King Egbert doesn't know is that another twenty ships are on the way. He has seen our army, and no doubt, he and his men are strategizing ways to defeat a legion of our size.

He is not expecting any more Vikings to arrive, which is why we will win.

He will be fooled in every possible way, all because he would do anything to get Emeline back. We will win on sea and on land, and I will finally get my vengeance for what he did to my family. It seems unfair, however, because this fight is Emeline's as well.

"Don't worry, *félagi*, I will do what you cannot."

"And what is that?" I ask with a snicker.

"I will keep the princess safe."

I keep my temper under control because I cannot lose focus before the battle.

"She is the one who keeps us safe," I correct, not interested in this petty talk. "She is the one who will grant you your land."

I want to remind Ulf that that is the reason he began this journey.

"That was the reason, but things have changed."

Turning over my shoulder to look at him, I dare him to say it.

"The *princess* has changed things, and I intend to build a life with her here. I have lands to offer and wealth. She will never be harmed again."

"And this is what the princess wants?" I ask, torturing myself.

Ulf nods. "It was when she vowed that she belonged to me."

I measure my breaths—in through my nose, out through my mouth. But it doesn't lessen the need to kill Ulf with my bare hands.

He reminds me that I can offer her nothing, that he is the better man for her when he says, "She no longer belongs to you. That choice was made when you allowed her to be sold like nothing but a slave."

I want to argue, to break his nose, but I cannot, and that's because he is right. I have failed Emeline time and time again.

"If that is what she wants, then *gipta* to you both." I don't mean it, but I won't have her as my mistress. She wouldn't want that either.

Ulf smiles, a victorious sight as we have always fought over everything our entire lives. This time, however, he won the greatest treasure of all.

"Once this is over, I am going to get back Sigrith. And I am going to find my mother."

Ulf nods as it's expected he would travel back to Scandinavia with Emeline. Only when it's safe will I come for Cecily. Emeline is the only person I trust to keep her and my child safe. I know what I am asking her to do is unfair, but I have no other choice.

Ulf would trade Cecily and my child without thought if an offer presented itself, which is why I asked Emeline to protect my family.

All I can offer her in return are the heads of those who betrayed her.

When we hear rushed footsteps behind us, Ulf and I spin in unison, swords drawn. It's Inga, Sten, and Toke, who are to protect Cecily on the ship, with Emeline.

"They advance early," Inga says, half her face stained blue in color. Her war paint is victorious. "It's the king."

Instantly, I look at Emeline, who nervously chews the corner of her mouth.

We didn't know when the king would advance. We have been watching him for days, but it seems he's grown impatient.

"Finally," Ulf exclaims, his excitement vibrant. "He finally found his cock. Let's go."

He's right. There is no time to waste.

I make my way over to Cecily, who shivers in terror. "It will be okay," I assure her, cupping her cheek. "You and my son will be safe. Go with Sten and Toke and wait for Emeline on the ship. Ulf will come when it is over."

"And what about you?"

"You know what I must do," I reply gently because she knows of the plan. "I cannot leave my sister to rot. And I need to find my mother. I cannot abandon my family."

"What about us?" she whispers, her tender eyes filling with tears as she rests her hands on her swollen belly. "We are your family too."

"And it is because you are my family that I am doing this. Northumbria is no longer our home. We need to stay safe and find a new home."

She told me she left our home in the dead of night after King Eanred's men were seen riding toward our village. She left her family behind to warn us of the dangers which face us. She is brave and selfless, and I don't deserve her.

"Please, *sváss*, please go. I promise to return as soon as I can."

Tears stream down her cheeks, and I wipe them away.

"I love you," she sobs, throwing her arms around me.

Peering at Emeline over her head and seeing the pain in her eyes, I don't reply. I cannot tell her I love her, because I do not. She is the mother of my child, and for that, I love her. But in love with her, I am not. I never was.

She was always a surrogate for who I wanted.

I gesture for Sten and Toke to take Cecily away.

She doesn't let me go, holding me tightly. But I gently unwrap her arms from around my neck and kiss her on the forehead.

"Skarth!" she cries, attempting to fight the men. But it's in vain. They have been given orders to protect her with their lives. "Please do not do this! Please choose me. Choose *us*."

Her cries echo in the emptiness as I unearth the entrance to the tunnel so the men can lead her to the safety of the awaiting ship. This is where Emeline will come once the battle commences, and that's all I care about as I re-cover the entrance with branches and rocks so it blends into the scenery as Cecily disappears into the darkness.

Slamming my fist against the bluff edge, I hang my head low, feeling utterly powerless. I have failed my wife. And I have failed the woman I love.

"I will protect her. I promise you." Emeline's sweet voice is the salve I need to cure this complete hopelessness within.

When I turn to look at her over my shoulder, my body demands that *I* protect *her,* for Emeline has misunderstood my anguish. She believes I am dismayed that Cecily leaves, but the truth is I don't want to let Emeline go. I don't want her to belong to another.

And if the gods decide today is the day I die, then I need her to know that.

Before she can protest, I cup the back of her neck and draw her toward me so we are pressed brow to brow. I inhale her scent, her essence, into me because she completes me.

"Skarth?" she whispers, afraid.

"Please, just listen," I say, needing to express this before I change my mind. "I knew from the day we met that we were fated. It should not make sense, a princess and a Northman, but it does. I have never known anyone like you, and I know I will never meet anyone like you ever again.

"You hold my heart, Emeline. You always have. And I want you to know that. I want you to know that I will never…that I will never crave or…worship anyone as I do you. I will go into battle fighting for your honor as well as mine.

"And I fight to survive not for Cecily…but for you. It's *you* who gives me strength."

A sob leaves her, and I capture it when I press my lips to hers. A salty kiss is our legacy. It's one which I will revere when I kill every last arsehole who hurt her.

She kisses me back with passion, which confirms she will always be mine. Regardless of our circumstances, we will always belong to one another.

She tugs at my hair, whimpering when I devour her without regret because I don't know when I will see her again. This memory will keep me going when I want to surrender.

I break our kiss, nudging her nose with mine. "Be safe."

"I will."

Without thought, I remove my silver arm ring and place it into Emeline's palm. "This was given to me by my chieftain when

I was twelve. It is a link between a Viking and his gods," I explain, stroking over her hand. "But my people, before a long voyage, we would give the arm rings to our beloveds as a symbol of our love."

A gasp leaves Emeline as I didn't give this to Cecily, but to her.

"I will cherish it forever," she whispers, closing her hand around it.

She then gently removes her necklace and wraps it around my wrist. "This is a sign of devotion to my God…but you, you are the only one I wish to bow before."

The crucifix dangles off the end, and it seems fitting I go into battle with her God wielding my sword.

Ulf stands by, his face twisted in rage but also pain. He really does care for Emeline, which means he will ensure nothing happens to her. He quickly pulls back his shoulders because now we go to war.

We make our way toward the open field, where our men and women wait. More remain in hiding, ready for the ambush.

"Word has been sent to the remaining ships," Inga informs us.

King Egbert has no idea what faces him and his army. We attack from land and sea with forces seen and unseen.

The air is filled with a palpable excitement because we are warriors. We live to fight. And to win.

Our men's and women's faces are stained with color; their

war masks give them the strength to survive this battle. They look fierce and fearless, and when we see three Saxons ride toward us in the distance, that ferocity turns lethal.

They get into position, just how I taught them, shields raised, ready for war.

Ulf does as we discussed—he binds Emeline's hands together with rope since she is supposed to be our prisoner.

Once bound, she stands in front of us, awaiting her fate.

Ulf and I stand behind her, as we have an army at our back. No harm will come to her.

It's still dark, but dawn approaches soon. The stage is set for a bloody battle to take place between darkness and light. Mist rolls in, settling around us like invisible fingers ready to draw us into the ground if we fall.

Ulf keeps his eyes on Emeline as do I.

This plan will work as we have the numbers, but I still can't shake the feeling that something is amiss. It was almost too… easy.

The closer the Saxons ride, the more animated things become. Our men and women commence banging their wooden shields with their swords in a melody of warfare. The song King Egbert will take to his grave.

Emeline stands strong, and it takes all my willpower not to go to her.

"*Argr*," Ulf spits under his breath when King Egbert rides toward us, bearing the flag of Wessex.

"Do not react," I firmly warn. "We let him believe he has won."

Ulf has always been more quick-tempered than me, so I need to remind him what's at stake.

"I want to shove that flag up his royal arse."

"He is mine," I remind him.

Ulf grunts.

King Egbert rides toward Emeline and tugs the reins to stop his horse a few feet away. This time, Ulf is the one to remind me to keep calm when he grips my arm to stop me from advancing and gouging out the king's eyes.

He looks at Emeline with such possession. I cannot bear it.

"Are you all right, my lambkin?"

"Yes, Lord," she replies, bowing accordingly.

King Egbert looks over her head, eyes locked with mine. "Skarth the Godless," he says, attempting to remain civil. "The last time we met, you were fighting to free the princess, but now you give her back? I do not understand."

With a casual shrug, I reply, "She was always to be traded. In one way or another. I knew her worth and was waiting for the best offer."

Emeline stands tall.

King Egbert's attention shifts to Ulf. "You are the one who wishes to trade the princess for Carhampton?"

King Egbert assumes Ulf is the one who ordered me to kidnap the princess and blackmail the king into giving in to his demands.

"That would be me," Ulf says, his disgust clear that he is talking to the king. "Seems a fair trade. Your property for mine."

King Egbert's nostrils flare as he doesn't like anyone speaking about Emeline as their property because he believes she is his. "How do I know this is not a trap?"

"You don't," Ulf replies blankly. "But you see my army. What is one princess compared to all this?"

He spreads his arms out wide.

"Her trade will safeguard our settlement here as I want this to be official. I want this to be Daneland. Once you forfeit your right, this will be ours lawfully. *That* is how you know this is not a trap."

To speak of Emeline so flippantly angers me, but we will say anything to have King Egbert agree because it will make the victory, the deception, all the more satisfying.

"Please, Lord," Emeline pleads, knowing how King Egbert loves when someone begs. "I want to come home. With you."

She chooses her words wisely, as she knows how to play a king.

He softens, and again, it takes all my willpower not to spear him with my sword.

"All right, Princess. I will give all of this up for you." He, too, chooses his words wisely, ensuring Emeline knows what he is willing to sacrifice for her. But he also wants her to know she will be indebted, enslaved, to him for the rest of her life.

He gestures for his guard to give him the parchment I assume is the deed to these lands. He scribbles something on it before the guard rides toward us and tosses the parchment at Ulf. We read over it and see that King Egbert has signed his name, renaming Carhampton as Daneland.

The guard offers the feathered writing tool to Ulf, but Ulf has his own ideas when he reaches for his blade and slices the tip of his finger, signing his name in blood.

It's done. We got what we came here for.

"Princess," he says, offering his hand. "Let us go and wash the filth from your skin."

He means that in every sense that there is.

With a nod, she walks toward him, keeping to the plan. It's dangerous as she will need to escape his clutches once we engage in battle. But Ulf and I will ensure she flees.

We both watch as she allows the guard to search her for weapons, which is why she needed to be unarmed. Once he assures the king she is weaponless, she accepts his hand and gets onto the back of his horse. She keeps her eyes down. To see her holding King Egbert has the rage inside me almost burning me alive.

King Egbert grins, and we know the time is now. He was never prepared to make a deal. And neither were we. "We could have been great allies, Skarth," he commences. "My dear friend, King Eanred, told me of your greatness.

"You single-handedly taught his men to be the greatest

army England has ever seen."

I wait for him to continue because, on my command, the time for talk will be over when the horn sounds.

"And it's because of you, because of your training, that you will single-handedly lose here. Today. For those men are here, the ones you trained, and they are to kill every last heathen on my command. Your blood will stain this land forevermore."

I don't speak, and King Egbert mistakes my silence for surprise.

"You did not think I would come alone?" he poses with an arrogant laugh. "Wessex and Northumbria fight for the princess's return. She will be brought back to where she always belonged, and you will pay with your lives for daring to take what belongs to Wessex."

"The princess belongs to no one," I state, folding my arms across my chest.

"That is where you are wrong. A dowry was paid. She was promised to Wessex before she was born. Promised to my son."

"Yet it is you who is here?"

King Egbert clucks his tongue. "Do not fret. He is here too. As is King Eanred and his son, Aethelred. You are surrounded, and you will die today. We have no deal, for I do not make deals with heathens."

Emeline lifts her chin. She isn't afraid. She is enraged.

"I am going to rip that little crown from your head," I state calmly. "And then…I will detach that head from your shoulders."

"You can try," he smugly says. "But the army you trained will destroy you because they know how you fight."

"We will see."

Ulf shoves the parchment down his pants and wipes his arse with it. He then tosses it at King Egbert. "This is what I think of your treaty."

He then gives the signal when he raises his fist high in the air. The horn sounds, and the battle begins.

King Egbert circles his finger, and a swarm of men come running from the north.

"Hold!" I cry, ensuring the men and women hold their stances. We can't go early.

King Egbert's men continue to come while Ulf and I join the line of warriors as we form a shield wall. Peering down the procession, I see that we are strong. Ulf keeps his eyes on King Egbert because the moment we attack, he will go for Emeline.

The men get closer and closer while we stand firm. "Hold!" I order again.

King Egbert will stay, as he wishes to see his army destroy us. The moment he senses he's in danger, however, he will flee. We can't let that happen.

The war cries become deafening, and they fuel us. We are here to fight and kill.

The men get closer and closer, their swords raised as they prepare to slay. I can smell their excitement, their fear, and when they are within reach, I raise my sword.

"Stay in formation!"

Wessex Guard soon charges with a roar, but we stand strong as they attempt to break our line. They stab between our shields blindly, but they are no match for my warriors. We take one step backward together, holding our position as more men ram into us.

"Skarth!" Ulf cries, gesturing with his chin over his shoulder.

I follow his line of sight to see Northumbria's flag flying proudly behind us.

King Egbert wasn't lying, it seems, for King Eanred's army attacks from behind. They intend to box us in, which is what I suspected they would do.

Locking eyes with King Egbert across the battlefield, I smirk. "You are right, King Egbert," I scream to be heard above the screams. "I did train King Eanred's army. Therefore, I know how *they* fight too."

His arrogance soon fades as he understands what this means.

I taught these men everything they know, which means they are my puppets. I am not theirs.

I raise my sword high in the air, and the horn sounds for a second time, which alerts our men and women it's time to come out of hiding.

They rush the terrain where they were hiding low to the ground. They were concealed with any foliage we could find. If

King Egbert looked hard enough, they would have been seen. But his arrogance has made him complacent.

He thought he could outsmart us by using the same plan and ambushing us with Northumbria's support. But our army outnumbers his and King Eanred's, which he sees when Wessex Guard are attacked from all sides.

"Now!" I scream, bringing my sword down. "Victory or Valhalla!"

My army howls in exhilaration because they can finally break formation and fight.

Men and women battle head-to-head, the clanging of swords setting the darkness on fire. The sight is macabre, a vision from the bowels of *Hel* as I charge forward, killing any Saxon who stands in my way.

Ulf fights by my side because, together, we have always been an unstoppable force. We move in sync—where one defends, the other attacks—which allows us to plow through the enemy with unrelenting speed.

Ulf stabs a man on a horse, shoving him off it as he mounts the steed quickly.

"Do not have all the fun," he quips with a slanted grin before riding off to get Emeline to safety.

I would have gone, but this is my army, and they obey me.

We fight without restraint or mercy, but the Saxons continue to come. The battle is bloody. There are many casualties from both sides. As I take down a Saxon, a flash of white catches my eye.

It's Aethelwulf.

He is riding a large white horse, slicing his sharp sword through the air and killing anyone who doesn't believe in his God. The black patch conceals what I did to his eye. I relished in his screams and long to hear them again.

Charging for him, I easily slay any Saxon who has the gall to hinder my revenge. I think of what he did to Emeline when she was just a young lady. How he used and humiliated her for his personal gain. Nothing will stand in my way.

The field is littered with twisted corpses, and soon, Aethelwulf will be joining them.

With a roar, I leap forward and tackle him off his horse. We tumble to the ground with a thud. He reaches for his fallen sword, but I punch him in the face, breaking his nose. His blood showers my face, fueling the madness within.

Gripping him by his chain mail until he is sitting up, I continue punching him, each strike feeding the need for more and more bloodshed. He attempts to fight me, but I reach out and snap his wrist. The crack reveals I broke it, and I intend to break more than just his wrist.

I elbow him in the mouth.

His head snaps back with a crack, but there is no way his death will be merciful. I intend to torture him until he begs for death.

Coming to a stand, I grip his hair and commence dragging

him through the battlefield. I fight with one arm, never letting Aethelwulf go. He writhes desperately, trying to reach for a weapon, but his broken wrist doesn't allow him to grip anything.

Once I get to where my horse is, I quickly yank Aethelwulf's arms above his head and tie them to the horse's back legs. I cluck my tongue, and Ulf's horse soon appears. I then do the same, tying Aethelwulf's legs to the back of Ulf's horse's legs.

He is suspended between the horses with no place to go.

"You will regret this!" he spits, peering at the restraints overhead.

"No, I do not think I will," I smugly state. "On my command, these horses run…and they take you with them. Well, they'll take parts of you because you will be ripped in half…just how you ripped Princess Emeline to pieces with your cruelty."

What he says next changes the course of everything, however. "We do what we must to survive…just ask your mother."

Placing my blade against his throat, I snarl, "What do you know of my mother?"

"I know that she keeps the bed warm for many Saxon kings. I believe King Eanred is her favorite."

"You speak lies!" I exclaim, barely holding back the urge to drive my sword through his neck.

"I do not. It seems to be quite the scandalous affair. Your mother fucking Emeline's father. It seems your mother and whore are both mistresses to kings."

"Skarth!" Ulf's anxious screams in the distance are the only reason I don't end this *bacraut's* life. Besides, I now need him alive.

I speak to the horses in my tongue, telling them to stay—and they obey, for now.

Searching the battlefield, I see the Wessex flag in the distance. It's time I delivered on my promise.

Spearing a man off his horse, I mount it and ride toward King Egbert. This is the moment I've been waiting for. It's time to avenge my family by cutting off the king's head, just as he did to my father.

Dawn breaks, and the sun peeks out from behind the knolls, revealing the true massacre left behind. Saxons still fight, and I look at where Ulf is, fighting three guards with ease. Whistling, he turns to me and nods.

Emeline is safe.

And that is when I give the third and final signal.

Flipping my sword, I raise it high into the air. The red jewel on the end catches the daylight, setting the battlefield on fire. Emeline's crucifix around my wrist casts a shadow on the trenches, a morbid sight that gratifies my heathen heart.

"*Vega!*" I scream, and the horn sounds, alerting the final warriors, the ones waiting in the tunnel, that it's time to attack.

King Egbert continues to fight, but when he hears the riotous roars of the warriors, he realizes he's been tricked—again.

The fight is no longer even; we outnumber the Saxons—five-to-one.

Men and women kill without mercy, and the bodies are piled so high, my horse cannot navigate through the field without jumping over the fallen corpses. My heart begins to beat faster, and it's the first time this has happened in battle as I am usually calm, but I've never wanted anything more than killing King Egbert.

King Egbert fights desperately, but he soon sees he's lost. He cannot beat us. This victory is ours.

Jumping from my horse, I run for King Egbert because I will not kill him on horseback. I want him to be on his knees. Ulf is beside me, covering me as Saxons try to protect their king.

"Where are King Eanred and Aethelred?" Ulf screams to be heard over the anguished cries of the dying.

One man grabs my leg, begging for mercy. I show him some as I stab him through the heart.

"I thought you killed them when you took Emeline?"

He shakes his head. "I did not see them. I thought you did the same."

With King Egbert fighting here, I assumed King Eanred and Aethelred were fighting at the other end of the field. That is what would usually happen as kings do not fight side by side.

Suddenly, the noise circles to silence when two ravens with feathers as black as night hover above Ulf and me, changing everything forever.

"No," I cry, peering into the sky. "It cannot be. It is Huginn and Muninn? They are here as Odin's ears and eyes?"

Ulf shoves me out of the way, but it's too late, and a sword penetrates through my shoulder. But I do not care. If Huginn and Muninn are here, Odin sees all. He sees we have failed.

Two Saxons attack Ulf, and usually, he would fend them off with ease, but one stabs him in the thigh.

"Skarth!" he shouts, leaning into me for support. "Have we upset the gods?"

"I do not know."

King Egbert soon appears a few feet away, smiling in victory. Although we have won the battle of Carhampton, he has prevailed in something far more precious.

"Retreat! Retreat!" he screams, turning and galloping away.

The cowardly Saxons retreat with their lives intact.

I don't understand what is happening.

The ravens swoop low, their eyes relaying to Odin what they see. Both Ulf and I drop to our knees, paralyzed, helpless to the ravens who are a manifestation of Odin himself.

"Have the gods accepted our gift of sacrifice?" Ulf asks, clutching at the blood-soaked earth.

"I do not think so, for we have failed."

"Failed? But how? We are victorious. Look." Ulf sweeps his arm toward the carnage, but no matter how many Saxons we kill…it'll never bring her back.

"Skarth!"

As I peer into the distance, I see that the seas are on fire. The waters are burning red, just how my need for revenge burns brighter than it ever has before.

"Sten and Toke?" Ulf exhales on a pained breath.

Our injuries are minor, so I know this is our punishment from the gods.

The two men who vowed to protect Cecily and Emeline are here, so where are the women they swore to protect with their lives?

"She's gone," Sten pants, clutching his bleeding side. "The king took her. They were waiting for us."

"How?" It's all I can say.

"They knew about the tunnel. They knew about the ships in waiting."

"How?" I ask once again even though I know.

Sten and Toke lower their eyes, as they know they failed me. They failed the gods.

"There is only one person who knew. One person who could easily communicate with the Saxons to inform them of our plans. There is only one person who could have made us believe we had a clear path to Carhampton, but the truth was, this person gave us blind faith."

"Who?"

The ravens caw loudly, swooping and circling, wishing to see how this ends.

"It was…Cecily. She betrayed us. She was the one who gave

Princess Emeline to her brother and father. She was the one who said the princess would never have you. That she sacrificed everything for you."

Ulf growls, punching the ground. "*Sorðinn*! *Sorðinn*! This is your fault!"

And he is right.

This is my fault.

I asked Emeline to protect Cecily, but the truth is, Emeline was the one who needed protection against my wife, who sided with Northumbria. For she knew a world where Emeline lived is a world where she would never have my love.

The ravens suddenly disappear.

I exhale loudly, my strength returning as I come to my feet. Ulf does the same.

We turn to face one another, slathered in blood, and make a promise here and now.

We won. We won a battle, but the war, the war has just begun.

"We go find her, and I swear to the gods, I will kill your wife for what she's done."

Nodding, I accept his challenge as his anger has shown me the truth.

Two Vikings.

One princess.

Who will win?

All's fair in love and war.

Two best friends, fighting for the one girl.
Let the better man win…

*Man må hyle med de ulve man er i blandt*—One must howl
with the wolves one is among.

***BOOK TWO COMING EARLY 2022!***

**Subscribe to my Newsletter:**

https://landing.mailerlite.com/webforms/landing/b4j1v6

**North of the Stars Playlist:**

https://tinyurl.com/an26e3kh

# ACKNOWLEDGEMENTS

My author family: Elle and Vi—I love you both very much.

My husband, Daniel. Love you. Always. Forever. Thanks for putting up with my craziness.

My ever-supporting parents. You guys are the best. I am who I am because of you. I love you. RIP Papa. Gone but never forgotten. You're in my heart. Always.

My agent, Kimberly Brower from Brower Literary & Management. Thank you for your patience and thank you for being an amazing human being.

My editor, Jenny Sims. What can I say other than I LOVE YOU! Thank you for everything. You go above and beyond for me.

My proofreaders—My Brother's Editor and Rumi Khan, you are amazing!

Michelle Lancaster—You are my soulmate. This cover is because of you.

Christopher Jensen—You are amazing! I'll never forget what you did for me.

Sommer Stein, you NAILED this cover! Thank you for being so patient and making the process so fun. I'm sorry for annoying you constantly.

My publicist—Danielle Sanchez from Wildfire Marketing Solutions. Thank you for all your help.

To the endless blogs that have supported me since day one—You guys rock my world.

My bookstagrammers—Your creativity astounds me. The effort you go to is just amazing. Thank you for the posts, the teasers, the support, the messages, the love, the EVERYTHING! I see what you do, and I am so, so thankful.

My ARC TEAM—You guys are THE BEST! Thanks for all the support.

My reader group—sending you all a big kiss.

Samantha and Amelia—I love you both so very much.

To my family in Holland and Italy, and abroad. Sending you guys much love and kisses.

Papa, Zio Nello, Zio Frank, Zia Rosetta, and Zia Giuseppina—you are in our hearts. Always.

My fur babies—mamma loves you so much! Dacca, I know you're hanging with Jaggy, Dina, Ninja, and Papa.

To anyone I have missed, I'm sorry. It wasn't intentional!

Last but certainly not least, I want to thank YOU! Thank you for welcoming me into your hearts and homes. My readers are the BEST readers in this entire universe! Love you all!

# ABOUT THE AUTHOR

Monica James spent her youth devouring the works of Anne Rice, William Shakespeare, and Emily Dickinson.

When she is not writing, Monica is busy running her own business, but she always finds a balance between the two. She enjoys writing honest, heartfelt, and turbulent stories, hoping to leave an imprint on her readers. She draws her inspiration from life.

She is a bestselling author in the U.S.A., Australia, Canada, France, Germany, Israel, and The U.K.

Monica James resides in Melbourne, Australia, with her wonderful family, and menagerie of animals. She is slightly obsessed with cats, chucks, and lip gloss, and secretly wishes she was a ninja on the weekends.

# CONNECT WITH
## MONICA JAMES

**Facebook:** facebook.com/authormonicajames

**Twitter:** twitter.com/monicajames81

**Goodreads:** goodreads.com/MonicaJames

**Instagram:** instagram.com/authormonicajames

**Website:** authormonicajames.com

**Pinterest:** pinterest.com/monicajames81

**BookBub:** bookbub.com/authors/monica-james

**Amazon:** https://amzn.to/2EWZSyS

**Join my Reader Group:** http://bit.ly/2nUaRyi

CPSIA information can be obtained
at www.ICGtesting.com
Printed in the USA
BVHW060303200122
626629BV00010B/811